The Silent Neighbours

The Silent Neighbours

Watchers Book 2

S T Boston

Copyright (C) 2015 S T Boston
Layout design and Copyright (C) 2021 by Next Chapter
Published 2021 by Next Chapter
Cover art by Robin Ludwig (www.gobookcoverdesign.com)
Back cover texture by David M. Schrader, used under license from Shutter-
stock.com
Edited by D.S. Williams

In memory of both my Dad and Nan, both of whom were with us when I began this project but sadly taken before its completion.

Science fiction writers and Hollywood film producers have always shown us that if we ever faced a threat from a hostile alien race, we would be locked into a bitter fight to evade extinction at the hands of a race who bear no resemblance to life as we know it. They were wrong. When it came, the threat from space was much closer to home than any of us could ever have imagined, and they were already here. They lived among us, worked among us, and all the while they schemed against us. They were our silent neighbours.

-Adam Fisher-, Watchers
The Story Behind the Reaper

Chapter 1

The stars hung brightly in the sky, a thousand fairy lights connected by an invisible mess of tangled wires. Sam Becker hunched his shoulders down in his Berghaus jacket and pulled the collar up an extra few inches to try and keep out the biting cold sea breeze, which felt like a frozen blade against his skin. Steadying the tiller on the small, four-horsepower Honda engine, he gunned the twist-grip throttle until it reached the stop. As the small Honda maxed out, he whipped his wrist away from the engine, instantly killing the motor by activating the emergency cut off.

Eyes fixed firmly on the approaching shore, Sam focused on the rhythmic sound of the water lapping at the aluminium hull, and the continuous distant whistle of the biting wind. He tried his best to relax. Just as he began to think he'd killed the engine too soon, a breaker picked up the rear of the boat and fired him toward the shore, faster than the feeble outboard could manage at full revs.

As the bow hit the shingle beach with a satisfying *crunch*, Sam was on his feet and jumping ashore, a spiked tie-off rope clenched in his cold, gloved hand. Driving the spike down hard into the shingle, he heaved the front of the tender onto the beach, leaving the rear end bobbing in the shallow water, resembling a cork in a bath tub. Satisfied the small boat was secure, he hiked his kit bag onto his back and scurried up the shingle bank, making more noise than he would have liked.

The large chateau that was Sam's folly, lay in a blanket of ominous darkness at the edge of the beach, surrounded by long grass scrubland to either side. The chilled breeze stirred the unkempt plants and they swooshed softly and invisibly in the night, a multitude of whispering voices announcing his arrival.

Reaching the edge of the shingle beach, Sam hunkered down by the wire perimeter fence and slid the backpack off his tensed shoulders. Removing the damp thermal gloves, he dove an icy hand into the bag and removed a pair of latex ones. They offered nowhere near the same amount of warmth, and the cold sea air blowing in off the English Channel felt as if it were slicing right into his flesh. Satisfied that they were fitted correctly, he closed the bag and removed a small pair of wire cutters from a pocket on the side. Starting at the base of the fence, he began snipping at the thick wire, one section at a time. Each time a thick strand of plastic-coated wire gave way, it sent a shockwave of pain through his icy fingers.

Satisfied that he'd created a hole big enough to gain access, he pushed his backpack through and lay down on the coarse grass springing up through the fringes of the beach. With small wriggling movements, he squeezed his way through the breach and emerged on the other side. He was in.

Bending the wire back and disguising the hole as best he could, Sam collected up his bag, dusted himself down and ran in a half-hunched position across the grounds toward the building, his soft-soled shoes almost silent on the well maintained grass. An impressive fountain lay to his right, the water switched off; it seemed as if the concrete gargoyle perched proudly at the top had his stone-cold eyes on Sam the whole way.

As he reached the back wall of the magnificent beachfront property, Sam breathed for the first time in what felt like an age, feeling exposed despite the cover of night. Back pressed to the masonry, he silently slipped along the building line until he reached the door. It was precisely where he'd estimated it to be when he studied the satellite image of the house. Utilising the kit in his pack once again, he removed a small screwdriver from the same pouch and proceeded to pop out the beading from around the bottom UPVC panel. Timing the removal of each bead with a strong gust of sea air, he snapped all four panel-retaining beads out of place. Despite the wind helping to disguise the noise, each time one popped out it seemed alarmingly loud.

Pausing for a second to slip the screwdriver back into the pack, Sam removed a small electronic pass-card reader from his bag and gripped it in his teeth. With hands too numb and cold to be performing such a delicate operation, he tapped the loosened panel with his fingers, right at the base, causing it to fall in. With a swift and surprisingly accurate movement he caught the top before it could clatter to the tiled floor on the other side. Allowing himself another deep breath, he climbed headfirst through the gaping hole he'd made.

The warmth of the chateau hit him like a deliciously snug blanket, but there was no time to enjoy it. The alarm panel immediately began beeping angrily, as if annoyed by the intrusion. Quickly scanning the kitchen, Sam located the box from its flashing red light. He had precisely twenty seconds to deactivate it. The soft black plimsolls made almost no sound as he padded briskly across the darkened kitchen, which looked big enough to host a TV cooking competition – camera crew, celebrity chefs and all. Such shows were a thing of the old world, however; the world before The Reaper.

Reaching the panel, he removed the pass-card reader from between his teeth and slid the credit card-sized section into a slot at the base of the panel. Holding the LED number pad in his shaking hand, Sam watched as the small electronic device worked its magic. *Ten seconds*, he thought to himself. The seconds ticked by like long, drawn out minutes as the each of the six-digit deactivation code numbers appeared on the screen in bright red. With no time to spare, the full code blinked up at him. Sam hit the enter key on the control box and instantly relaxed a little, when the main alarm control box stopped its low-pitched rhythmic beep and the light pinged to a welcome green.

Awash with a mixture of relief and elation, for the first time he noticed the smell of freshly-ground coffee, mixed with the scent of bread that had no doubt been baked the previous evening. It made him yearn for a mug of the hot liquid and something to eat –one, to help him get some heat back into his cold bones, and two, to take away the salty taste of the spray which had continually assaulted him on his trip from the cruiser to the shore. But there was no time.

Removing the card reader, he crossed the vast kitchen and hooked his hand through the hole in the door, scooping up his bag. Putting away the reader, he removed two syringes from a netted pouch at the top of the bag and slid them into his jacket pocket. Making his way toward the reception hall, a large clock, big enough to display the time in a Victorian railway station, told him it was fast approaching midnight. In less than five minutes the job would be done and with luck, he'd be back in that god-forsaken launch and on his way to the cruiser, which would be at full throttle and pointed firmly toward the English coast within minutes of his return.

Sam knew the layout of the chateau well from the plans he'd studied the previous day, and without pausing for thought, he reached the right-hand side staircase which led to the first floor. Tiles gave way to plush cream carpet which looked almost grey in the gloom. He was in no doubt that all welcomed visitors would be asked to remove any footwear before even going near it. He had no time for such etiquette. Taking the stairs two at a time, he was soon on the landing and looking at a line of white painted, Georgian-style doors. A mirror image of the layout was just visible on the opposite wing of the entrance lobby. For a split-second, Sam wondered if he'd picked the correct side, but he brushed the thought away in an instant, certain he was exactly where he needed to be. Stopping at the third door he carefully depressed the handle, the coolness of the brass seeping through the thin latex glove. The large child's bedroom was empty. Bright moonlight streamed in through a grand window on the far wall, casting strange shadows and highlighting the neatly-made and empty replica race car bed. The Lighting McQueen duvet cover seemed somewhat out of place in this grand and overly lavish home, but the image of the bright red, grinning race car smiled enthusiastically at him all the same. The intelligence

had been right, much to his relief; the family were away for the weekend. Despite Sam holding no compassion for his target, the thought of
carrying out his task with a child in the house made his blood run cold.

Leaving the door slightly ajar, he continued down the landing, arriving at an identical door which brought the passage to an end. With
the same level of stealth, Sam unlatched the door and slid inside.

The cream carpet gave way to an impressive wooden floor, which
still seemed to shine ever so slightly in the dim light. At the far end
of the room was the king-sized bed, where Sam expected, and hoped,
his target would be.

He drew closer one tentative footstep at a time, his breath almost
clogged in his dry, parched throat. This was the tenth such target he'd
taken out, then tenth time he'd been in this situation. It never got any
easier.

The rhythmic rise and fall of the mounded bed covers told him his
target was exactly where he wanted him to be – in bed and fast asleep.
Removing one of the syringes from his jacket, Sam bit the end cap
off with his teeth and tucked it away in his trousers. He was close
now, he could hear the guy breathing; that slightly laboured sound
of someone slightly overweight or not in the best physical condition.
The guy's leather Armani wallet was on the bedside table, Sam carefully placed the syringe on the ornate looking table, collected it up and
thumbed through the cards. The target's French driver's licence was
there; pulling it halfway out Sam looked at the name and the photo,
confirming this was his man. Just before he closed the wallet something else caught his eye – tugging the three strips of white card free
from the section where you'd usually keep your bank notes, Sam removed a single airline ticket. The destination listed was Lima, Peru,
the flight due to leave the following morning. Not a cheap purchase
in this recovering world, but he reminded himself his target was a
wealthy man. No matter what the cost of the ticket, it was one flight
that this sleeping guy would certainly be missing. Sam slid the ticket
back, replaced the wallet carefully onto the night stand and collected
up the syringe.

Standing over the sleeping body, Sam whipped one hand down over the target's mouth, and in the same instant he slid the needle into the man's exposed neck and depressed the plunger. Instantly the target's eyes flew open, wide and panicked, a muffled cry of fear reverberating from the underside of Sam's hand; at the same instant, he felt warm saliva through the thin latex.

"Shush!" Sam said, in a soothing and sympathetic tone, "shush." But the sympathy was only evident in his voice; his eyes told a different story.

The Pancuronium took seconds to work, the dose just enough to send Sam's target into a state of complete muscular paralysis. Beneath his gloved hand, the man's tense jawline relaxed, confirming that the injection had worked its magic. Holding one hand to his lips to gesture for the target to stay quiet, Sam gingerly removed his hand. A long trail of saliva formed a strand between the target's bottom lip and Sam's thumb, stretching out for a good six inches before finally breaking and falling back onto the target's stubbled chin.

"Mathis Laurett?" Sam questioned in a low voice. "Is your name Mathis Laurett?" Sam knew he had the right man; he'd studied his target's picture more than once and seen his somewhat chubby face on the driver's licence. Despite his dishevelled appearance, the man before him was undoubtedly who he was after. Despite this certainty, some small part of Sam still liked them to confirm it verbally.

"Ye-yes," the man croaked, struggling to speak when he had virtually no control over his throat muscles.

"Do you know who I am?" Sam asked calmly.

"Ye— yes," Laurett repeated, as if it were the only word he could manage.

"Good. Then you know why I'm here?"

"Ye— yes," Laurett replied, his eyes wide and full of fear. More drool had joined the web-like strand on his chin, giving him the appearance of someone who'd just suffered a grand mal seizure.

"Mathis Laurett," began Sam. "Under order of the Arkkadian Council you have been sentenced to death for your part in The Reaper Virus, which twenty-nine months ago, led to the deaths of almost one billion people. It has been identified that you are an Earth-Breed. Investigations have shown that you were employed in the staff of Jacques Guillard, an Arkkadian Watcher. During that time, you were responsible for helping to identify him and ultimately, that identification led to his death." Sam paused; he'd read out charges like this on ten previous occasions, however the man before him was without doubt, the biggest player he'd executed since shooting Robert Finch back in the bowels of the Pyramid, over two years ago. Laurett offered up no comment other than a choked attempt to swallow. "Further to this, we have information to suggest that you were travelling out of Heathrow Airport on the day that The Reaper Virus was released into the population, and we believe you were responsible for releasing one of the four vials of pathogen."

"Please," croaked Laurett. "Please, I ha— have a f— family."

"And what of the millions and millions that virus killed – didn't they have families?" spat Sam. "Do your family know who you really are?" A deep rage burned in Sam's chest; if he had his way, he would have beaten Laurett to death then and there with his bare hands. But that wasn't how things were done.

"No," Laurett croaked, swallowing deeply to regain control of his voice. "P— please, I have useful information, if you s— spare my life."

"I'm listening," Sam replied. Laurett's words had taken him off-guard, none of his previous targets had begged for their lives, or offered up anything in trade.

"The one— the one you seek. he is here, and he has plans."

An icy cold hand ran its spidery fingers down the length of his spine. For a second, he saw a wicked smile flicker in Laurett's eyes before he continued.

"Your silent neighbours are many in number, and they are coming for you!" Despite the Pancuronium coursing through his body, Laurett managed to spit the last word out with considerable venom. Beads of sweat were forming on his wrinkled forehead, and they ran down into his eyes and backwards, into his messy grey hair.

"Bullshit," Sam replied, his voice sounding higher than he felt comfortable with. They were alone in the house, but he still felt as if the walls were listening.

"Believe wh— what you want, Mr. Becker. Y— you will see." Laurett's gaze darted around wildly, as if he were searching for something – or someone – and it made Sam uneasy. Sam had only administered a miniscule amount of the drug, diluted down in a saline solution, and the effects were fast wearing off. This time Sam did see him smile, an unmistakable hint of it on the bastard's chubby face. His lips drew back, exposing his yellowing teeth, "E-n-o-l-a," he gurgled.

"Who the hell is Enola?" Sam demanded, biting the protective end cap off the second syringe.

"You – will see," Laurett croaked, grinning like a loon.

Sam refused to listen to anymore craziness and plunged the needle deep into Laurett's neck. The smile disappeared from Laurett's mouth. The second syringe contained a second, larger, much stronger dose of Pancuronium – a deadly one. This dosage would be enough to paralyse every muscle in Laurett's body, including his heart. A cry of fear spewed out of Laurett's drool-covered mouth when the needle plunged deeply into his fatty neck. Five seconds after the plunger hit the stopper, his body convulsed violently before falling back against the sweat-drenched covers, dead.

Stuffing the empty syringes into his pack, Sam headed out of the room and ran swiftly down the lavish stairway. Laurett's final words rang through his head remorselessly. *He is here, he has plans and he is coming for you!* And *Enola*. What the fuck was all that about? He didn't like it, not one bit.

In the kitchen, he threw his bag out through the missing door panel and hastily followed. Not bothering to carry out any repairs to hide the evidence of his visit, he hurried to the fence. Sam was always keen to flee the scene of an execution, but on this occasion, the desire was greater than ever before. It seemed as if he were running from some invisible pursuer, someone who would charge out of the night and grab him just when he reached safety. He knew one thing – he wanted to get as far away from the Laurett Chateau as possible. He was even looking forward to the five-minute ride in the freezing cold launch, certain every inch he put between himself and the French coast was a good inch. Thinking of the warm coffee he would make once back on the cruiser – with a hit of something a little stronger in it for good measure – and the phone call he would make to Lucie, Sam was relieved when his feet touched the loose shingle of the beach. He almost slid down the bank to the shoreline, stones avalanching around his feet. In the next instant he froze – the small tender was gone. Frantically he scanned left and right, certain he'd secured it right here, in front of the chateau. "Where the fuck are you?" Sam questioned, his whispered words igniting the cold night air with vapour.

A dazzling spotlight forced back the night abruptly, lighting the beach up like a stage. "Monsieur, restezoùvousêtes et placezvos mains survotre tête!" Someone called.

Sam whirled around, trying to focus on where the amplified words were coming from, his mind racing, *"English!"* he shouted, his heart pounding in his chest and echoing through his ears. *"I'm English!"*

"Monsieur, remain where you are and place your hands on your head," the voice responded in a heavy French accent. "Police," the man added, as if he'd forgotten to include that important piece of information.

"Shit," Sam cursed, adrenalin rushing through his veins. He heard footsteps crashing across the stones, heading his way. The bright light made it impossible to see what direction they were coming from. Deciding that any course of action was better than none, Sam dropped his hands and ran, but he was too late. As he took flight, a heavy hand grabbed the back of his jacket, almost lifting him off his feet. A fist connected with his kidneys, and his legs gave way. Sam went down hard, face first onto the cold hard shingle; he tasted blood on his lips, mixed with salt. Struggling to focus and ignore the foul smell of the air-dried seaweed, he saw a shiny pair of black shoes crunch to a stop before his eyes. Hands yanked him up onto his feet, way before his legs were ready to take his weight.

"Monsieur," the man with the very clean shoes began. "You are under arrest, on suspicion of burglary."

"Burglary?" Sam croaked trying to focus on the guy's face. A mere arrest for burglary would have been fine with him at this point in time – hell, he'd have pleaded to it right then and there if the deal were offered. However, Sam knew that the pending burglary charge would soon change – once they looked inside the chateau.

Chapter 2

In a layby on Chemin des Terrois, on the outskirts of Le Havre, France, a hulk of a man stood wearing a long dark overcoat. His black hair was thick and slicked back against his skull, making it almost invisible in the darkness. Shivering in the unusually chilly September air, his flat grey eyes watched in fury as blue lights flashed crazily off the Laurett Chateau, as if there were some manic party going on at the end of the road. This was no party, however. A second male, who appeared almost identical to the first alighted from the X5 BMW, stood by his brother and spoke. "I can't get used to how clean the air smells here." To any other person, his accent would have sounded like an exotic mixture of several regional dialects. "Do we have a problem?"

"Yes," the first male replied. "It would appear we were too late." His voice was virtually indistinguishable from that of his brother. "It would seem that Mathis Laurett is already dead."

"Nothing but a casualty of a war that we are on the brink of winning; it matters not," the second male commented in an emotionless tone. "And Becker?"

"Likely in custody. This will delay our plan somewhat, and time is very short." The first male shrugged his shoulders into his coat and popped the collar.

"A minor problem that we can overcome, brother," replied the second male, as he sat himself back into the 4x4.

"You're right."

"About what?"

"The air here is very clean, it's the cold I just can't get used to!" The first male started the engine and crept the vehicle forward, watching the blue lights fade into the night through the rear-view mirror. With a sly smile that revealed his dazzling white teeth, he slowly began to form a plan – a plan that would have Samuel Becker in his hands before first light.

Chapter 3

"Do you not find it all a little bit morbid?" The first question came from a slightly nerdy, spectacle-wearing student in the second row, whose hair looked like it hadn't seen a comb in a few days.

"How can the truth be morbid?" Adam retaliated, clutching the lectern tightly with both hands. He could just about see the question poser under the glare of the bright stage lights, which were focused mercilessly on him, highlighting the nervous sheen of sweat covering his forehead. His white cotton polo shirt was damp with sweat where the fabric ran down his back. Despite only having showered a few hours ago, he felt dirty and far too hot.

"But it isn't the truth, is it?" the young man fired back insistently.

For fuck's sake, thought Adam. *What is this a trade-off of one question for another?* He smiled falsely and tried to swallow, but his throat was dry. "If you go around your whole life with your eyes closed, you will never see anything," Adam replied, trying to stay calm and sound professional.

"Your book, Watchers," began the student, waving a copy in the air as if to highlight the fact. "Whilst there is no doubt that it's a very clever story based around the tragic events that happened almost two and a half years ago, a story is all that it is – fiction!" Despite the impediment of the stage lighting, Adam could see him glancing around the half-filled conference room triumphantly, searching for someone to back him up.

Adam had known he was in for a rough time at his first book launch talk; however, Mike Warren, his publicist, had insisted he get out there and, *Promote, promote, promote!* He could still hear his annoying and slightly high-pitched cockney accent, the words ringing round his head like a bell. "This book could have legs, I don't care if any of that shit is true, this is going to be controversial, and you know what controversy makes, Adam? Money, a fuck load of money, and if there is one thing we all need right now it's *money!*"

Six months after returning home, Adam had finally finished writing his account of the nightmare that he and Sam had gotten tangled up in. The world they'd returned to, however, was a very different one than they'd known. With one seventh of the population dead from The Reaper Virus (so nicknamed due to the aggressive and unforgiving way it had swept through whole nations, killing millions, like a deadly scythe), and the entire planet without electricity, society was hinging on outright anarchy. The first year was the toughest by far. While the British Government, which was nearing collapse itself, did their best to get the power back, trouble had brewed in the streets. Food rationing had been resurrected for the first time since the Second World War, a situation a wasteful modern society didn't take kindly to. The army were drafted in to help maintain order and in many places, martial law had been invoked. The past few months had started to see the military-governed areas being handed back over to local law enforcement. It was a slow process and the army still had primary control in a few of the rougher areas of the country, but a full handover was only months away. With one in seven dead, even more in urban areas, the British Government had held a recruitment drive, looking to replace the police officers lost to the virus.

Reports were saying that around eighty percent of the globe now had power, albeit on a limited basis for many people. Oil-run power stations struggled to operate for more than a few hours a day, which didn't help matters. Six months ago, the terrestrial and mobile phone networks had started to reappear. Those who were lucky enough to have such luxuries were paying a heavy price for them. In fact, any electrical consumer was paying top dollar for the privilege. Someone had to cover the cost of the vast amounts of work involved to get the pulse of the planet pumping once again. In those first few months of relative normality, as the countries of the world raced to restore the electrical grids, it became clear that new tensions were rising between the East and West. While companies and contractors worked tirelessly to repair the damaged power networks, and smiling politicians gave empty promises that things would soon be back to normal, oil prices began to rocket. Russia controlled the Siberian fields – which before the Reaper had provided around eighty percent of the planet's dwindling oil supplies – and began to put a stranglehold on the precious commodity. Despite what front a government uses to justify war; at the end of the day, oil is always a good reason. While no one had yet fired a shot in anger, there was a new and deadly race developing. The race to repair and prepare the nuclear weapons which had been rendered un-launchable by the EMP. News reports were informing the public that over the next few days, those defence systems would be back online and it was highly likely the planet would find itself locked into a second Cold War. Oriyanna's hopeful prediction, that the global tragedy would help to unite humanity on Earth once and for all, had been drastically wrong. The EU had all but broken down in the wake of the disaster. Although Britain still held on to the euro, many were calling for the beloved pound to be brought back into circulation. With every nation on Earth facing economic ruin and food shortages, it had turned into a case of every man for himself. Small amounts of mutual aid had been seen between the USA and Europe, but it was rare and on a minimal, 'you scratch my back and I'll scratch yours' basis.

With the reintroduction of the phone system, the internet had finally made a re-appearance, albeit on a very limited basis and with download speeds that hadn't been seen since the demise of dialup. With the web starting to grow once again, Adam saw his chance. He released Watchers into the public domain as an online publication. Within certain circles the book went viral –as viral as it could get on an internet service which was a shadow of its former self. Unfortunately for Adam, the readers who believed his account were the kind of people the rest of society didn't take too seriously, the kind who walk around with tin foil on their heads to stop aliens reading their minds. The clear majority of readers saw it as no more than a fictional story, one that cleverly used the most tragic event in human history as its plot line. It was fair to say the book was controversial; this of course led to Adam getting offered a deal from a newly-formed publishing company, who promised to get three thousand physical copies of his book into circulation, with more to follow if it took off. To try and fend off some of the criticism and flak the book was attracting, Adam agreed to split the profits from his sales between the many charities who tried to help the less developed parts of the world, the areas that were still suffering and didn't have the luxury of food, let alone power. For some of these countries, the end of The Reaper was only the start of the suffering. Following the rains that had cleansed Earth of the rabid alien virus, Earth-born ones took hold. Ebola swept through parts of Africa, on a scale not seen since the 2014-2016 outbreak. With aid virtually non-existent in those early days, and many of the doctors as dead as the patients they'd so desperately tried to help, Ebola ran wild, decimating already ravaged communities. It was like an aftershock to the worst humanitarian disaster since the Black Death.

He pulled his attention back to the young man in the audience. "And you prefer to believe the odd, disjointed accounts given by the governments of the world, do you?" Adam asked, hoping that no one else would join the attack.

"It certainly seems more plausible than some elaborate plan by a highly-developed human species to wipe us out, so they could claim the planet as their own," the student smiled. "Do you also believe that the world's governments know the truth and are deliberately trying to cover it up?"

"No," Adam replied, leaning toward the small microphone. It was a good question and the first sensible thing that this bespectacled, spotty student had asked. "I believe they have no idea about how things really happened. They've looked at the events of those tragic few days and tried to explain them as best they could. I don't think there's any cover up." Adam scanned the rest of the audience. Much to his despair, he spotted two rather odd-looking middle aged men, sporting tee-shirts that read in big bold letters '**JESUS WAS AN ARKKADIAN & HE'S COMING BACK!**'

"So then," the student began, obviously not willing to let his point go, "you think they believe that a breakaway section of Al-Qaeda were responsible for the virus?"

"I do, yes. But do you?"

"Why should I question it?"

"Because there had been a six-month period of peace in the time before The Reaper, because all reports suggested that Al-Qaeda had dissolved and was all but at an end," Adam defended. It almost made his blood boil, knowing how closed-minded some people could be. "That virus was indiscriminate, it killed in every corner of the globe, some of their own men would have died. It makes no sense. Not to mention the veracity of it – I fully believe that a virus that aggressive, able to spread and kill so swiftly, was beyond anything even the most talented scientist on Earth could develop."

"It wouldn't be the first time terrorist activities were continued by a breakaway faction during a period of supposed peace. Look at what happened with the IRA." The student was grinning, looking rather pleased with himself. He'd obviously chosen to ignore Adam's rather accurate reasoning.

"A few shootings and car bombings are in a slightly different league to a virus which wiped out close to a billion people," snapped Adam. "Sure, some fanatical breakaway group claimed responsibility. I have no doubt that's true, but really? They would never have the technology or the means to do it, as I said before."

"I guess we'll have to agree to disagree," the student replied smugly.

Adam took a deep breath. "Thanks for your question; shall we let someone else have a turn?" Adam scanned the audience again, ignoring one of the tee-shirt sporting nut jobs, who was waving his hand frantically. "Yes, you madam," he said, pointing to a smartly-dressed woman two rows from the front. She looked like a reporter; coming from that background, he was good at spotting his own.

"Does that mean you also dismiss the claim that the EMP was caused by a period of unusual solar activity, even though this *has* been confirmed by NASA?"

"Look," Adam said, releasing his grip on the pine-trimmed lectern and rubbing his clammy hands together. "As it details in the book, the EMP was caused by a major disruption in the Earth's magnetic field, a side effect of turning on The Tabut."

"You mean The Ark." She grinned. "Lest we not forget that not only did you save the world, but you also managed to find the Ark of the Covenant. You're a regular little Indiana Jones, aren't you, Mr. Fisher?"

"Okay," Adam sighed, letting his eyes fall to the floor and away from the burning stage lights. "I knew I would be open to all sorts of criticism for my work. Hell, if I read it I probably wouldn't believe it myself, so I don't blame you. It seems pointless that we keep going over the official account of what happened during those few days. I know that a terrorist group claimed responsibility for the virus. I know that NASA believe a solar storm caused the EMP. I'm no astrophysicist; for all I know the effect of the Tabut powering up could have all the right characteristics to replicate a solar flare. But surely you find it hard to believe that the weeklong storm which followed was a natural, freak weather occurrence, caused by the EMP? And that after the storm that covered the entire globe, the Reaper virus magically disappeared?"

"Harder to believe than what?" questioned the woman, flicking a long strand of auburn hair back from her face. "That space aliens cured the planet with a storm? No, Mr. Fisher, I don't find the official account hard to believe at all. I'm almost surprised that they didn't tell you to build an Ark and place all the animals inside, to protect them from the flood!"

"God on high saved humanity after washing the lands clean," cried the frenzied voice of a scruffy, grey-haired elderly man at the back. Adam rolled his eyes. The old guy might be as mad as a hatter, but he wasn't too far wrong.

"Look, it's getting late," Adam replied, squinting at the clock. It was just past ten thirty. "Thanks for attending, if you'd like a signed copy of the book, I'll be in the foyer in ten minutes." The announcement was met with a murmur of dissatisfaction from the eclectic mix of people in the small audience, before the first few attendees stood up and made their way toward the exit. Although later than he would have liked, it was the cheapest time available to hire the room for a few hours and the most his cheapskate publicist was willing to pay for the first promotional talk that he deemed so important. With everything so expensive, price was more important than convenience. Satisfied that his non-adoring public had gotten the message, Adam stepped away from the lectern and began to pack his notes into a small plastic storage box which also contained a few copies of his book. He didn't expect anyone to be waiting in the foyer, eager to purchase a copy. He had no doubt the tee-shirt-wearing guys at the back would be waiting, hungry to barrage him with a volley of questions. The type of mad talk that he didn't want to air in front of an already doubtful audience.

"I believe you," came a slightly accented, yet soft female voice from somewhere in the now-empty conference room.

"Thanks," Adam replied, placing the last of his things into the plastic container. "As I said, if you want to purchase a signed copy I'll be in the foyer shortly, or if you want your copy signed I'd be happy to oblige." He clicked the handles down over the lid and collected the box from the floor.

"Just how many Earth-Breeds has Samuel Becker killed now? Ten?" the voice replied, an air of nervous tension in its softness. Adam felt the hackles rise on the back of his neck, as if someone had just stomped carelessly over his grave. Clutching the box, he whipped around and tried to glare through the lights that stung his eyes. Three rows from the back he could just make out the figure of a dark haired young woman, still in her seat.

"I never wrote anything about that in the book," he said warily, a nervous octave higher than he would have liked. Naturally, there had been several things he'd left out. Their home town and the details about the Gift being another. If people took it seriously, he didn't want some whack-job to try and find them, eager to test out either of their healing abilities. "Just who are you, exactly?" His voice echoed through the empty room, amplified by the PA system.

"Maya Tomenko," she replied. Adam side-stepped the stage lighting and hopped down from the temporary platform. He saw that Maya was a young woman in her mid to late twenties, her dark brown, almost alabaster coloured hair fell over her shoulders, deepening her tanned complexion and highlighting her granite grey eyes. She was smartly dressed in a three-quarter length black coat; beneath it Adam could just make out a white blouse. Her black trousers disappeared into the top of a pair of boots that came half way up her calves. "It's imperative that you listen to what I have to say, the survival of both you and your sister depend on it!"

For a split second, it seemed as if someone had vacuumed all the air out of the room; Adam's breath caught in his throat. The young woman remained seated, eyes fixed on him pensively.

"How do d—do y—you know th—this?" he finally managed to stammer, relieved when his chest relaxed enough to let some much-needed air in.

"Let's just say I'm someone who isn't keen to end up on Sam Becker's kill list," she announced bluntly, her wide and somehow familiar grey eyes fixed intently on Adam. He remained three rows away from her, the plastic box tucked firmly under his arm.

"You're Earth-Breed?" he spat, gripping the plastic container tightly.

"Was. I mean yes, but I'm no threat to you, I'm here to help."

"Why the hell should I trust you?" he growled, the fear gradually settling into anger.

"Because if I was here to kill you, I'd have been waiting silently outside your aunt and uncle's old house. I'm guessing that's where you're staying tonight," she said calmly. "Being in Brighton, I'm guessing you don't plan to drive back to London at this hour." The mention of his aunt and uncle's took him off guard – the last surviving members of his and Lucie's immediate family had been claimed like so many by the Reaper.

"How do you know about that?"

"There were a good few of them – us – left after the events at the Pyramid," she began, her eyes growing distant. "Your names were known to the Earth-Breed who didn't die that night. It wasn't hard for them to find you."

"If that's the case, why didn't they come for us before? Why did they let Sam kill ten of their— I mean *your* kind?"

"The first few were inevitable, the rest were casualties of war," she said coolly, as if she were discussing the weather. "We were also leaderless and directionless; laying low you might say. The few who remain have direction now, a leader. I don't have time to go into the finer details, either trust me and survive tonight, saving Lucie's life in the process, or take your chances on your own and be dead or captured by first light."

"What about Sam?" Adam snapped.

"They know he's taking a target in France tonight. It may already be too late – they plan to take you all at once." She stood up and swept her dark hair back behind her shoulders. "Please, Adam," she continued, a hint of panic in her voice. "You're not the only one being hunted. I risked a lot to do this, I was on the team sent to capture you, only I had other plans. I'll explain everything once we're moving. Time is short."

"What's in it for you?" he asked, his brain working at warp speed to try and reason the fast-developing events. His first concern was his sister – he hoped Sam could handle whatever was coming his way. "And what the hell has Lucie got to do with it? She wasn't even involved."

"She's your sister, and six months ago, she married Sam. They want to make you pay for what you've both done – anyone in your family is fair game. There are much bigger things in play here than you, but you three are his first concern," Maya fired back, eyes looking hungrily towards the exit. "You need to call Lucie," she added, "I just pray the mobile phone network is functioning near her bar. If we stall any longer, it will be too late." Maya gave Adam a last, fleeting look before she headed towards the door, long black coat tails trailing behind her.

"*Wait!*" Adam cried, discarding the box full of notes and books on an empty chair. "They know she runs a bar now?"

"They know everything." Maya reached the door and flung it open, bathing herself in light from the hotel foyer. "Where's your car?"

"Parked across the street." Adam ran to catch up with her, brushing past the two men in the Jesus tee-shirts.

"Good. Give me the keys, I'll drive – you need to call Lucie." She shook her wrist, revealing an expensive watch. "Shit!" she exclaimed. "You need to get her out of that bar, Adam. You need to do it *now!*"

Chapter 4

Lucie Becker tugged the receptacle free from the coffee machine and knocked the spent, ground beans into a small waste bin at the side of the counter. Satisfied that it was empty, she stole another quick glance at her mobile phone, the tenth such check in under a minute, and willed it to ring. *He'll call any minute, any minute now,* she kept telling herself over and over in her head. Sam always called when he was away on a job – once the deed was done and he was back to safety, he always called. Clipping the container back into the espresso machine, she picked up her annoyingly silent phone and hit the menu button, bringing it to life. The somewhat unreliable phone network was working; she even had five bars of reception, something of a miracle in these uncertain times. Hitting the volume button, she double-checked that it wasn't set to silent. It wasn't, but she'd known that already. *Just ring,* she thought again, as if the mere power of thought would magically force the call through.

In the days following Adam and Sam's return home, Adam had spent his time penning the events that had changed the modern world forever while Sam had practically moved into their family home in Eltham. It was no surprise to either Adam or Lucie, as he'd never spent much time at his own place anyway. Dark days had followed, days of uncertainty, days when it wasn't safe to wander the streets of London in the day, let alone at night. Over those first few months, when the three of them had literally been barricaded like prisoners in the family home, only venturing out in the daytime to collect food that was being strictly rationed out by the military, she and Sam developed a closeness which blossomed into a relationship. Despite the fact she had known Sam her whole life, it didn't feel odd – more like a natural progression. He'd turned out to be the missing piece of a puzzle, the piece that had made everything fit and as time past and their situation improved, they'd grown to rely on one another more and more. Then one warm and sunny day in July, while they'd been picnicking under the canopy of two ancient oaks in Oxleas Meadows, enjoying the summer sun on their faces, Sam had proposed. A full-blown, down on one knee affair, not the kind of romantic gesture she would ever have imagined him making. She agreed then and there. With most of the UK still under strict martial law and things far from normal, they knew they had a wait before any kind of service could even be planned.

Over a year had passed since the virus claimed so many lives; and conversation about the events of those fateful days had petered out, even between her brother and Sam. There were times when they were almost able to fool themselves into pretending that nothing had ever happened, times when they were together at the house and chatting about childhood memories and people now lost. Then on one oppressively muggy August day, which rumbled with thunder and threatened rain, a package had arrived.

That was how it all began. Contained within the package was a gun. Accompanying the gun was a sheet of paper, detailing the name and address of the target, and two syringes with instructions on how to use them. Lucie had made herself scarce that night while the boys had talked about the strange parcel.

It was how the hidden war, the war against those responsible for all the death and suffering had begun. It was also the first sign that the Arkkadians were once again a presence on Earth, albeit a very elusive one. At first, Adam had insisted on being involved in the justice that they'd been chosen to mete out. Sam had refused Adam's request outright, saying that despite the baptism of fire he'd endured during their time in the States and Egypt, he was not a trained solider. Eventually, Adam had listened and agreed to let Sam do the job.

Lucie's pleas for Sam not to go had fallen on deaf ears. "Hey, don't worry," he'd said before leaving that first time, "I was always a difficult bastard to kill; now I'm practically the Terminator."

The first job had been close to home, on the other side of the city. It was a stark reminder that the Earth-Breeds left behind could be anyone you'd pass in the street, without being able to distinguish any difference between them and humans. Much to both Lucie and Adam's relief, Sam had returned home within five hours, rumbling noisily up the dark street on his Triumph risking arrest for being out past the government curfew. As time went on, and overseas travel began to get up and running, the targets had become wider spread. The introduction of the first transatlantic flights had seen Sam gone for three weeks. With no domestic telecommunications working, the first Lucie knew he was safe was when he walked through the door, clutching his Deuter backpack, a stupidly smug grin on his face.

Those tasking the targets never made themselves known; merely ensuring Sam had the tools needed to do the job. One of the benefits was the ludicrously large sums of money which started appearing in his account. Lucie would have gladly given it all back however, if those unwelcome intelligence packages would stop. Six months ago, once law and order, and a general standard of living had returned, they were married. Nothing posh, just a small service with Lucie's best friend Claire and Adam. Most her other friends were either dead or had fled the city and couldn't be contacted.

On their wedding night, she'd finally managed to ask Sam the question which had been eating away at her ever since his proposal. Both slightly drunk, and laying in each other's arms, she'd turned to him. "You do know that I'm going to grow old? You'll have to watch it happen while you remain unchanged. Do you think you'll still love me?"

Sam had chuckled. "Oh, I fully intend on chopping you in for a younger model once you hit forty – being eternally youthful has its perks." It was Sam's way of putting her mind at rest, in a way that only

Sam could. He followed up by swearing that if he ever saw Oriyanna or any Arkkadian Elder again, he'd ask for the process to be reversed. While the Gift was undoubtedly handy for healing minor wounds and preventing those annoying bouts of summer and winter flu, eternal life wasn't an idea he relished.

Placing the phone back on the counter, Lucie glanced at the one customer still in the bar. When she looked up, the lone male quickly averted his eyes and retuned his attention to the latte he'd been nursing for the past twenty minutes. It was growing late and she badly wanted to lock up and head home; she didn't normally close until half an hour before curfew, but the stress of the day had taken its toll. Despite the growing sense of law and order in the city, it was still best to be back in the safety of your home when the power went off at one. Thankfully the small bar-come-coffee shop was minutes from the house, allowing Lucie to make the most of the last minute trade, no matter how sparse custom was. The government were promising the daily interruptions to service would soon end. Essential maintenance work was the official line offered as an explanation. Many suspected it was to help enforce the curfew, which conveniently began at the same time the power shut down. Those like Lucie, who ran businesses that opened late were issued a permit, granting them an extra half an hour to travel home, but thankfully she'd never needed it. Tonight would be no different; it was only just gone half past ten, but she'd had enough.

Sensing that she'd caught him staring the guy looked up briefly from his coffee and offered her an unsettling smile. The smile didn't reach his eyes, which were cold and devoid of any emotion. A chill ran through Lucie's body. Looking away from her again, the man lifted his mug and drank from it, although Lucie was sure that by now the coffee inside must be stone cold.

The loud ring of her phone snatched her away from the unsettling hold the customer had on her and her stressed body filled with a sense of relief. *Finally, Sam, thank god,* she thought turning her back to the creepy guy and reaching for her phone. The relief was only temporary however, when she saw Adam's number displayed on the screen. Although she was always happy to speak to her brother, the thought of him tying up the line at a time like this was annoying. Snatching the phone off the counter, she hit the answer button. "Adam," she began, instantly feeling guilty when she heard the annoyed tone in her voice. "What is it?"

"Are you still at work?" The line was unusually clear; she heard a hint of panic in his words that caught her off guard.

"Ye— yeah, why?" she replied, turning to face the shop floor. Her lone customer was once again watching her with more interest than she was comfortable with.

"Is anyone with you? Just answer yes or no."

"Yes," she replied anxiously.

"How many?"

"Just one," she muttered in a low voice.

"Male or female?"

"The first option," she replied, thinking on her feet. Her earlobe had begun to sting, the smart phone pressed to her ear far more tightly than was needed. She fiddled with her long, brown ponytail, twisting the locks through her fingers.

"I think you're in danger, but I can't explain now," Adam said hurriedly. "You need to get out of the shop, and you need to go now!"

"I don't un— under— underst— stand," Lucie stammered, her pulse quickening.

"Please, trust me, just act natural and head to the rear of the building," her brother fired down the line. "Go straight out the back door and get into your car. Don't bother stopping to lock up and don't approach that customer and ask him to leave, do you understand? Make it seem like you're just going out the back to grab something."

"No problem, I can sort that out for you," she said, trying to make it sound like a normal call.

"Once you're in the car, drive to the place where we used to spend summer holidays with Mum and Dad."

Lucie knew exactly where her brother meant. The family had inherited a small thatched cottage from her mum's parents, it lay in the sleepy village of Alton Barnes in Wiltshire. The place held many fond memories for Lucie; the small, modest cottage would have been laying empty for the last few years, and no one had been there since the world had changed. While she knew exactly how to get there, the idea of driving well over a hundred and twenty miles wasn't a tempting thought. And why the hell was he even asking her to make the trip? Her hands begin to shake, and she instantly tried to quell it by moving her hand from her hair to her apron, clutching at the front pocket and pressing the phone even harder against her burning ear, so hard her earlobe throbbed.

"O– okay," she managed. "I can do that, I'm off tomorrow so I'll meet you then." She offered her lone customer a faint smile. He gave no reaction, other than to continue watching her with interest.

"Good thinking, sis." Adam's voice came down the line, and in the background Lucie could hear the sound of a revving engine; wherever her brother was, he was in a car and on the move. "Call me when you're clear, before you get out of London and lose the mobile phone signal."

"Okay."

"Oh, and sis?"

"Yeah?"

"Be careful!" The line went dead.

Removing the phone from her ear, Lucie dropped her hand to her side and collected up a rather grubby-looking cloth from the counter, before making her way to the small kitchen area at the back of the shop, letting the swinging door shut behind her. In the artificial light, she took a deep, steadying breath and grabbed her bag from the top of the microwave. Opening it, she made a cursory check for her car keys. Snatching them out, a cold hand wrapped itself around her mouth and pull her backwards, and the keys and the phone clattered onto the tiled floor. She gave a small, muffled cry of surprise and fear and her already shaky legs turn to pure jelly.

"Shushhh," came a surprisingly soft voice from behind her. "Do not scream, I am here to help." The voice was unmistakably female. Lucie's head swam with questions; every part of her had expected the attacker's voice to be male. As suddenly as the hand had grabbed her it was gone, and Lucie whipped her body around defensively, to try and protect herself from an attack she felt sure was imminent. Readying her fists to punch out, she froze. The woman standing in front of her had the bluest eyes she'd ever seen, and her long blonde hair flowed down over her shoulders where it met with a black, tight fitting long sleeve top. Her trousers matched, giving her an almost assassin-like appearance. Before Lucie's spinning mind had time to question it any further the swinging, saloon-style door to the kitchen burst open.

The coffee-nursing customer came rushing in, a gun clenched firmly in his hand. At that exact instant, everything seemed to slow down. The woman's hands pulled Lucie out of the way; her shaky legs could offer no resistance so she just went with the motion. The deafening sound of gunfire erupted through the small, confined kitchen and somewhere, far off in a world where time was operating at the correct speed, Lucie heard crockery smashing. Her back hit the wall, sending a selection of stainless steel ladles and spatulas crashing to the floor, and Lucie watched as the woman ducked low and removed a pistol from a belt around her waist. She moved far quicker than what seemed possible, her brilliant blonde hair whipping around her like a shawl. With deadly accuracy, she discharged a round. Through wide, frightened eyes Lucie watched blood spray from the customer's neck and splatter over a bunch of aprons that were hanging up just behind the door, giving them an odd, abstract art effect.

Time suddenly caught up. With an unearthly cry of pain, the man went down hard. His head split open on the corner of a stainless-steel workbench as he fell, and his upper cheekbone making a sickening *crunch* when it made contact. He was dead before he hit the tiled floor.

The woman's wide, blue eyes darted about the small kitchen, ready to take on any new threat. Seeming satisfied that they were alone, she grabbed Lucie by the wrist and pulled her toward the back door which was slightly ajar and resting on its latch.

"We need to go, now!" she said urgently, stress laced through her voice as she spoke. Lucie didn't argue as the woman scooped up her phone and keys, which were in danger of getting soaked by the ever-increasing pool of sticky red blood that was creeping across the floor like an incoming tide. Turning, she flung the door open, the unusually chilly late September night air hitting Lucie's chest and making the breath catch in her throat. "Which one is your car?" the woman asked, scanning the few vehicles that occupied the small parking lot.

"Th— the Mini," Lucie gasped, pointing to the slightly grubby red Mini Cooper which sat directly in front of them. The woman let go of Lucie's wrist and passed her the keys, before rushing around to the passenger door. Lucie hit the key fob and the indicators bathed the darkened car park in a flash of orange light. Jumping into the driver's seat, she turned the key in the ignition and gunned the engine.

"Who the hell are you?" she asked, settling her nerves slightly. She suspected she already knew the answer, but her brain refused to accept it.

"Oriyanna," the woman replied, smiling. "Lucie?"

"Y— yeah," she stammered, her mind reeling.

"It's nice to finally meet you. Now, can you please drive, I don't think that man was alone."

Chapter 5

Sam Becker adjusted his position on the unforgiving wooden slats and pushed the heels of his hands into his eyes, trying to rub away some of the stress and gritty sleepiness. Blinking his stinging eyes, he watched the small clock's second hand ticking away tediously behind the anti-vandal grating which protected the cheap plastic timepiece. It was almost three AM, and the last few hours in custody had been tedious. As the minutes ticked slowly by, he grew increasingly anxious about the phone call to Lucie. It seemed that the almost universal right to a phone call after arrest had been flushed down the pan with the rest of society. Not surprisingly, Sam hadn't been asked if he wanted a solicitor, and he hadn't bothered bringing the subject up. It was more likely to end in a beating than any helpful legal advice.

Laurett's final words continued to spin in his head. *He is here, and he is coming for you! – E-N-O-L-A.* Silently reciting it gave Sam the chills, producing small goose bumps over his arms and making the fine blonde hairs stand to attention. He was in desperate need of both food and water, or better yet, a nice hot, sweet cup of tea. Sam almost chuckled, thinking how easily prisoners and detainees used to get it; he would have been the first to say they had it too easy. Now however, he wasn't so sure. Being on the wrong side of the law, especially the law in this fragile new world, wasn't a good place to be. He'd only been arrested once before, when some guy in a nightclub back in the old world, had singled Sam out as being the one responsible for hitting on his girlfriend. One shove from the lager-fuelled oaf had been enough to make the punter wish he'd never picked on the wrong guy. Sam had busted his nose with one punch and well and truly broken his pride. Thankfully, after a night locked up in one of London's many cell blocks, Sam was interviewed and released. The case never went any further; the guy had dropped the charges the following day, once the beer had worn off and he'd seen sense. That night in a cell had been like staying in a five-star hotel compared to this.

Following his arrest, the man with the shiny shoes and two armed and uniformed gendarmes had escorted him roughly off the beach and into the back of a waiting cell van. The man with the shiny shoes had proceeded to slam the door shut with such force, it had reverberated through Sam's whole body, doing nothing to alleviate the swiftly developing headache that was threatening to ruin his night further. A few minutes later the shiny shoed man, who Sam quickly discovered was Inspector Ackhart, returned with a very grim expression on his face. Sam didn't need it spelled out; they'd searched the property and found the lifeless body of Mathis Laurett. The Inspector proceeded to inform Sam of what he already knew. The pending burglary charge was gone, replaced instead with a far more serious charge of murder. Inspector Ackhart proceeded to slam the van's door a second time, with even more vigour, as if to hammer home the point that Sam was well and truly fucked.

The Laurett Chateau was located on the northern French coast, around fifteen miles from Le Havre. Sam wasn't sure which police station he'd been taken to. The journey time seemed about right for the fifteen-mile drive, so he guessed he was in Le Havre, which meant he could easily find travel to Portsmouth, or at the very least the Channel Islands, if only he could escape. Forcing his eyes away from the clock, he examined the small window for what seemed like the hundredth time, running his tongue over the lip that had been cut when he hit the stones at the beach. Of course, there was no trace that the wound had ever been there, it had healed even before they'd arrived at the cell block. Even after more than two years, his magical healing abilities still mystified him. He grimaced, playing out a scene in his mind where he was in court, the French judge handing down a life sentence – and these days, life would really mean life. He wondered how long they would keep him for, once hey realised he wasn't aging. It was fair to say that life for Sam could mean a very, very long time behind bars. Pushing the thought from his mind he got back to the task in hand; ensuring that day in court never happened.

Breaking out of the cell was going to be impossible; he had about as much chance of tunnelling through the thick stone wall as he had of getting through the cat-flap sized window. He would need to bide his time. At some point, they would collect him for interviewing. He just hoped there would be a moment of weakness that he could exploit, but somehow, he doubted it. His mind wandered once again to Lucie, who had no doubt informed Adam by now that something was wrong. Sam forced the thoughts from his brain; he needed to stay sharp and focused if he stood any chance of getting out of this.

Leaning back on the bench, the cold stone wall bit through his Tom Wolf fleece. Sam heard a key being placed into the heavy lock and instantly sat bolt upright, watching as the cumbersome door swung open. The smartly dressed figure of Inspector Ackhart filled the door frame, silhouetted by the brighter lights of the corridor outside.

"Monsieur Becker," he began in heavily accented English. "It is time for us to have a chat." He gestured for Sam to stand, moving to one side to let a very large, uniformed guard into the room. The guard, who obviously couldn't, or wouldn't speak English, motioned for Sam to place his hands in front of him.

Great, thought Sam. *There goes my chance of an easy escape.* The guard secured a new set of cuffs to Sam's wrists. They should have been sore and bruised from his earlier manhandling, but naturally, they weren't. The guard, who had just one long, almost jet black monobrow which spanned the width of his forehead, shoved Sam toward the cell door and the waiting inspector.

"This way, please," the inspector said flatly, leading Sam down a drab corridor, painted in ugly magnolia and lined with a host of battleship-grey cell doors. All the doors were open, confirming that tonight, Sam was their sole resident. Here and there, black scuff marks streaked the tired paint job, reminders of past struggles with people who hadn't been keen on being hauled up in a cold stone box for hours.

"Don't have power rationing here?" Sam questioned, noticing the place was awash with electrical lighting.

"This is an emergency services building, Monsieur Becker," Ackhart replied, not looking back. "Unfortunately, the French Government also sees fit to turn the power off at one AM, and we have been provided with a backup generator for when this happens. It would be impossible for us to function effectively without it." Sam felt like cursing himself for asking the stupid question. He suspected the same happened back home; but he wasn't in the habit of spending his spare time locked up in custody.

The inspector reached the end of the corridor and turned left and Sam followed, the uniformed, monobrowed guard right behind; so close that Sam could smell his fusty, coffee-laced breath. Halfway down this second corridor the inspector swung a door open and waved Sam inside. The room was about the same size as the cell; Sam was sure at some point in its life this room had been another cell. Now, however, it housed three chairs and a table, all bolted securely to the floor to prevent unruly prisoners from smashing the place up. A black recording device sat on top of the table. The uniformed guard beckoned Sam around and pushed him forcefully into one of the chairs, before kneeling and securing Sam's ankles to the chair legs with a pair of manacles.

These guys aren't taking any chances, Sam thought, as the all-too-familiar sensation of cold metal restraints settled against his skin. The guard stood up and backed off, and Ackhart spoke to him in a flurry of French which Sam had no chance of understanding. Sam watched as the guard nodded reluctantly and left the room, closing the door with a heavy clunk. Sam could just make him out, peering in through the door, keeping a watchful eye on his superior – presumably in case Sam turned out to be a famous English escape artist, as well as a suspected murderer. The inspector crossed the room and slid a thick manila folder from his chair before sitting down. He placed the folder onto the desk and began thumbing idly through its contents.

"This is a peculiar situation," he announced, stopping at a random page and staring at it blankly. "Why would an Englishman be here on French soil, in the middle of the night, carrying out an execution-style murder on a former member of the French and European Government?" Ackhart stopped speaking and glanced up from the folder, catching the uneasy look in Sam's eye. "We Europeans are all supposed to be on the same side, are we not?"

"It's a long story," answered Sam wearily.

"What I find even more puzzling," the inspector continued, returning his attention to the folder and thumbing over to a fresh page, "is why I have found reports of four killings, one in your home country and three in the United States, with exactly the same modus operandi." An icy hand clenched at Sam's stomach. "It took some digging," Ackhart continued. "Sadly, the internet and intelligence sharing between forces is not the machine it used to be. But I had to investigate; random murders or bungled robberies do not generally end in a victim being poisoned. We are yet to identify the substance in the syringes we found on your person, but I suspect, as in these reports, we will find it to be Pancuronium. Am I correct?"

"I'll talk to you, inspector," replied Sam, unsure of what he would tell him, "but first, I'd like a glass of water and to make a phone call."

"As you may have noticed, monsieur, the way we do things now is somewhat different to how it used to be. I will not permit you a phone call, on the grounds that you are being investigated for a serious offence and I suspect allowing you to call your wife could lead to vital evidence being lost. This rule has never changed." Sam nodded slowly. Although he didn't like it, he could see things from the inspector's point of view. He'd begged him for just one phone call to Lucie whilst in transit to the station as he knew how frantic she'd be if he didn't check in with her. "I am willing, though," he continued, "to offer you a drink, if you promise to tell me what this is all about. I suspect that in a few hours' time, this case will be taken from me by Interpol or one of the serious crime investigation teams. It's likely, though, that you will be in court for a plea to be entered in the morning, the next day at the latest. Help me to help you, monsieur."

Sam nodded again, not sure whether to tell the inspector the truth, but he didn't know if he could come up with a feasible cover story in the next few minutes, hell he'd been trying since his arrest and as yet his mind wouldn't play ball. He suspected, the truth would land him in the nearest nuthouse.

"Do we have a deal?" The inspector raised his salt and pepper eyebrows, which matched his neatly cropped hair.

Sam studied him for a moment, trying not to stare at the man's bulbous red nose. He looked like a heavy drinker. "We— we have a deal," he replied reluctantly. "Although I don't think you'll believe me," Sam added with a wan smile.

"Intriguing," muttered Ackhart, pushing a small red button positioned on the wall next to him. The monobrowed guard instantly burst into the room looking almost disappointed to see Sam still sitting securely fastened to his chair. "Can we get Monsieur Becker a glass of water please, Claude?" he asked in English, obviously for the benefit of Sam. Claude nodded and slipped out of the room, still seeming dejected. Sam noticed Claude left the door ajar; had he not been manacled to the seat he might have taken a chance and tried to escape. After all, once you're facing a murder charge there isn't much you can do to make the situation worse. In less than a minute Claude was back, a plastic cup brimming with water clenched in his hand. He set it down in front of Sam, and some of the liquid slopped onto the scarred wooden table. Clasping the cup between both hands, Sam drained the contents in two long swallows. The water was far from cold and had a nasty metallic aftertaste. *Beggars can't be choosers*, he thought, as he set the cup down and wiped his mouth with his hand.

"So – monsieur," Ackhart began, "I held up my end of the deal; now it's time for you to hold up yours."

"Like I said, I'll tell you, but I don't think you'll believe it."

"Stop messing around," the inspector spat, his voice agitated. "I have been in the police force for twenty years, the last fifteen of those spent dealing with all manner of serious crimes. I have had the unfortunate pleasure of witnessing some of the darkest depths of human depravity. I'm more than sure that whatever it is you have to say won't shock me in the least!"

"Are you a religious man?" Sam asked, his heart rate increasing.

"What does that have to do with anything?"

"Because if you are, it will make what I'm about to tell you even harder for you to believe. So I'll ask again. Are you a religious man?" Sam resisted the urge to start chewing anxiously at the skin below his bottom lip.

"Not that I see it as relevant, but yes... well, I was. Events of late have made me..." he paused and ran a hand through his greying hair, "question my faith, you could say. But I still hold some hope that there is someone looking out for us. I still don't see how this relates, however?"

Behind the stern and frustrated expression, Sam could see something else on Ackhart's face. Intrigue.

"God and the devil are real," Sam said seriously. "Although they're far more tangible than you could ever imagine."

The inspector's tanned, worn complexion creased in a mixture of frustration and anger. "This is horseshit," he snapped, slamming his fist down on the table and the empty cup toppled and rolled off onto the floor. "Apart from the information I found on the other killings – and I have no doubt you were involved in, or had some knowledge of them – I also managed to pull your file." He opened the folder once again and scanned through pages until he found what he was looking for. "You were a former sergeant in the British Army. You carried out several tours in some of the world's worst hell-holes before getting pensioned out after being shot, an injury you obtained during the rescue of a reporter. An injury that saw you awarded with the George Cross." He scanned the page, running his finger over the paper. "It all gets a little hazy then. After a period of rehabilitation, you went back to the Middle East as a private contractor – is that correct?"

"It is," Sam replied, not sure what the inspector was angling at. He was shocked that Ackhart had managed to pool so much information about him in just a few short hours. There was obviously a far less clunky online community for the security services.

"What I'm getting at is— you're not the kind of person we usually have under investigation for murder. In fact, I have no doubt you're a person of the highest integrity. I too, have a military background. Air Force. This killing, along with the others, reeks of an assassination, a contract killing. Just who are you involved with?"

"What – I'm – involved – with," said Sam slowly, "is a battle between good and evil on a scale that you could never imagine." There was no point trying to cover it up. Sam decided to go for broke and come clean. At least if they sectioned him as crazy, he'd have a better chance of escape than if he was thrown in jail.

"And what side of that fence are you on exactly, monsieur?"

"Like you said, inspector, I'm a person of the highest integrity, so the good side, obviously." Sam offered Ackhart a confident smile. "What if I told you that Mr. Laurett was not who you thought he was? What if I told you that he was partly responsible for some of the horrors we've witnessed over the last few years?"

"Impossible," spat Ackhart, as if he'd just tasted something bitter. "He was a member of the French Government. He worked with Jacques Guillard on plans that held the Euro Zone together. A breakaway group of Al-Qaeda were responsible for that virus." Sadness flushed across the inspector's face, and Sam was sure he must have lost someone close because of the virus. It made the ground Sam was treading even more dangerous.

"Do you really believe that?" Sam asked cautiously. "For one, do you think they would have been capable of engineering such a thing? And secondly, even if they could produce such a virus, why would they release it at a time when we'd virtually seen the end of all terrorist attacks? Not to mention the fact that many of their own people would have been killed. That virus was indiscriminate; there wasn't a nation on the planet that didn't become infected. Every living person knows someone who died."

"But they claimed responsibility," Ackhart defended, suddenly sounding uncertain of what he was saying.

"Smoke and mirrors," Sam cut in with a wry smile. "Although I'm certain that no one, apart from a handful of people – myself included, know what really happened. If some small breakaway extremist group wanted the so-called honour of those atrocities, then it was an easy explanation for the governments of the world to run with. Far more feasible than what really happened."

* * *

Inspector Ackhart sat back in his plastic chair and exhaled a long, over-exaggerated breath, feeling the backrest sag under his weight. This was certainly not the direction he'd anticipated his interview with Samuel Becker would go. He'd lost count of how many prisoners he'd interviewed over the years, and liked to think he could easily spot the tell-tale signs of a liar. Becker was displaying none of them. Either there was truth in what he was saying, or he was a pathological liar and a dangerous psychopath. Unfortunately, Ackhart didn't believe the second option for an instant.

"You believe Monsieur Laurett was involved?" he asked, unable to believe he'd even asked the question.

* * *

"I don't believe, I know," Sam replied with conviction.

"Is this some kind of domestic terrorism?"

"No!" said Sam firmly. "If only it were that simple. The group he was involved with were far more dangerous than any threat we've ever known." Sam saw the inspector turn his gaze to the recording device. "Just look at the events in the few weeks before the virus, and the few weeks after. During that World Summit, three of the delegates disappeared. Euri Peterson, Tillard, and the chap you mentioned who worked with Laurett – Jacques Guillard. Then the next day, John Remy – the U.S. President – turns up dead. Suspected assassination by one of his own Secret Service Team, Robert Finch." Mentioning his name made Sam pause, as he recalled how he'd shot Finch at point blank range in the head, back in the Pyramid. "Then two weeks later, this virus appears. Look hard enough and you'll also see that on the day the virus first made an appearance, there was a major seismic event reported in Egypt, near the Plateau, that caused substantial damage to the Great Pyramid of Khufu. The story was, not surprisingly, dwarfed by the EMP that fried the globe and left us in the shithouse situation we're in now. Another smoke and mirrors event which the scientists of the world put down to a massive solar flare they never saw coming. Fast-forward another eight days, and we see a major storm hitting the planet that lasts for seven days, causing widespread flooding. Following that the virus is gone, leaving one in seven people dead. As you well know, that unusual storm was once again put down to solar activity disrupting Earth's weather patterns on an unprecedented scale. Because all of our technology was useless by then, scientists were never able to quantify the claim. I figure they were just too embarrassed to admit they had no clue how it all happened and had to offer some feasible explanation to a very demanding public. If they could have, they would have found that none of those events were linked to a cosmic occurrence at all."

Inspector Ackhart massaged his temples with his fingers. "What exactly is it that you think you know, Monsieur Becker?"

"Like I said, inspector, I'll tell you everything. The question is, how far down the rabbit hole do you want to go?" Sam smiled at the phrase, recalling how Laurence Fishburne had asked Keanu Reeves the exact same thing at the start of the first Matrix film. It was a cheesy line, but it somehow fit the situation.

"I think maybe I should start recording this, it might be evidence of your insanity when this whole mess comes to trial."

"No recording devices," Sam fired. "If you want to know, this is between you and me. I have reason to suspect that I might be in danger."

"How so? You're in police custody – apart from facing a long prison sentence, and possibly the death penalty if the Americans choose to extradite you for the crimes committed on their soil – you are, for the time being, quite safe and secure."

"Something Laurett said before I killed him," Sam replied uneasily. "And the fact I'm locked up offers no protection from these people – they have a very long reach. If things start going bad, as I suspect they will, it will pay to have someone of authority who knows the truth, whether you believe it or not. I fear that in a short time, you might have no other option than to accept what I'm about to tell you. It's going to be hard for you to accept and it will make you question everything you thought you knew."

"Very well," said Ackhart reluctantly, "I always liked a good story. So, how did you become involved in this?"

"Well, it all started with a road trip," Sam began, remembering how Oriyanna had been so reluctant to try and explain it all to them. He now had a little empathy for how she must have felt. "At the time, my friend, Adam, and I could never have known what we were about to become involved in. It's fair to say it has changed our lives – forever."

Chapter 6

"That's your car?" asked Maya, sounding a little surprised by the old, slightly tatty-looking Mazda RX7 as Adam reached the door and unlocked it.

"What can I say? It was cheap, and the parts to fix it were readily available. After the EMP, many of the newer cars needed a lot of work to get them running again. Older stuff, like this, was much easier to fix. Sam sorted it out for me, I was never that mechanically-minded." Maya slid into the driver's seat and gunned the engine as Adam climbed in beside her and fastened his seat belt. "Go easy on her, she's practically a classic!" Before the car started moving, he'd located Lucie's number and hit the call button.

"Get her to meet you somewhere that only the two of you will know about," Maya said, as she hastily reversed the Mazda out of the parking bay and engaged first gear. "Somewhere that they won't know about!" Adam knew in an instant that his grandparents' old cottage near the small village of Alton Barnes was going to be a reasonably safe bet. Not only was it in the middle of nowhere, it had been sitting empty for the past couple of years. Unless they dug very deep, which would be nearly impossible now, nobody would never know about it.

The property had belonged to Adam's maternal grandparents, and the couple had been married for sixty years. Adam had little memory of them, other than some vague recollections from visits to the small thatched cottage with his parents.. Sadly, they'd both died when he was seven years old. His grandfather had passed away very suddenly; collecting timber from the local sawmill one Saturday afternoon, he'd collapsed in the yard while loading his old Ford with kindling. Grandma, so Adam's mum told him, had died of a broken heart just four weeks later. Tragically it seemed they'd been unable to live without each other. The cottage was inherited by Adam's mother and aunt, who chose to keep the quaint little house, renovate it and rent it out to people for holidays. He and Sam had spent many a drunken weekend at the cottage during times when Sam was home on leave, both of them stumbling back from the local pub, The Barge Inn, after sampling a glass or three too many of the vast array of ales and ciders on offer. The walk back always took them past the sawmill where his grandfather had died, along the canal towpath, and across the road to the house. Lucie loved the place – as Adam's junior she'd had no memories of her grandparents –but she recalled long summer weeks spent there as a child with Adam and their parents, and later on with their aunt and uncle.

"There's a place in Wiltshire," Adam told Maya, still not sure if he could trust his new ally with the exact address. If things went sour and he had to make an escape from her, Maya would need to scour the whole county to find him. The call to Lucie, as usual, was taking an eternity to connect. "You are – were – a part of it all. Do they know about the house in Wiltshire?"

"I don't think so," Maya responded as she reached the bottom of a steep hill leading to the sea. She took a right and screamed the pokey engine through the gear box. Brighton Pier sat in darkness, standing out against the clear, cold September sky. She navigated a small roundabout and kept the Mazda heading west, the cold waters of the English Channel to their left. White breakers broiled angrily as they hit the shingle beach, foaming and bubbling for a second before they were drawn back into the dark, icy water.

"Keep heading this way," Adam said, listening impatiently to the rhythmic clicks on the line as the call tried to connect. "In a few miles, you'll see signs for the A27; follow those toward Portsmouth." Finally, the welcome sound of Lucie's phone rang in his ear. Maya nodded her understanding and swung the car around a slow-moving council vehicle which had a flashing orange light affixed to its roof.

"Adam. What is it?" Lucie's voice sounded annoyed, an unusual occurrence and his bowels churned with anxiety. He hated the thought that his sister was about to be drawn into whatever mess was developing. He took a deep, steadying breath and told her all he knew.

"Is she safe?" Maya asked when he ended the call and tucked the phone into his trouser pocket.

"I'm not sure."

"What do you mean?"

"I think one of your kind was with her in the bar, a lone male customer," replied Adam, making no attempt to hide the bitterness in his voice. "She's leaving now, I asked her to call again once she got clear. If anything happens to—"

"I'm sure she will be fine," Maya cut in, although she didn't sound certain of the truth in her statement. She took one hand off the wheel and brushed thick dark hair away from her face, securing it behind her ear.

"I suggest that now would be the time to start talking. I don't think I trust you yet."

"I don't blame you," Maya sighed . "Thank you for giving me a chance. I know I can never put right what we've done, I just hope I can stop what is about to happen."

Adam's stomach tightened. "This isn't just about killing us, then?" he asked reluctantly.

"No. You form just one small part of the plan. There are bigger things in play here, something far worse. It will be easier if I start at the beginning; that way it will make more sense."

A strangely familiar sensation of intrigue and dread washed over Adam. Not for the first time, he was racing through the night with a strange woman who had a story to tell. For the briefest of moments, he experienced a pang of longing for Oriyanna, recalling their time together in the RV on that strange night back in the States. What he wouldn't have given, for her to be here with him now. He gazed out the passenger window momentarily and watched the beach give way to a darkened marina, which housed numerous small yachts and motor boats. Many looked as if they hadn't been used in a long time. He suspected that many would never be used again, their once proud owners long dead. Somewhere out there, across the dark expanse of the English Channel was Sam. He just hoped that whatever was happening hadn't reached him yet – it was a shallow hope, but it was better than none. Shivering a little, he reached forward and cranked up the heater. Thankfully, Maya's driving had quickly warmed the rotary engine and hot air poured out of the vent. "Back before the virus," Maya began, not taking her eyes off the road, "I worked in the Russian office of Integra Investments. I take it you know who they are?"

"No, sorry," he answered. Realizing he wasn't concentrating, he forced his eyes away from the darkened marina and turned to face her.

"They were the official face of – Buer's operation here," she paused before she mentioned his name, almost as if it were difficult to say. "I'm surprised you didn't know that."

"I have very little knowledge of events before the virus."

"Around eighty-four years ago, when the first of the Elders came to Earth, they set up an investment firm in order to accrue assets and money. It was necessary to cement themselves firmly into Earth society for the plan to work, essential that they had decades before the virus, to build up the wealth and assets they would need. Shortly after their arrival, they began the Earth-Breed program." Maya paused, glancing at Adam. "We were engineered in a lab," she admitted sadly. "They wanted a race who had been born here on Earth, and who knew nothing of life on Sheol; it was believed this would be the best way to integrate the Earth-Breeds into society. The likes of those you had dealings with – as well as me – are known as second generation Earth-Breed. Our mission was to infiltrate world governments and businesses, seek out and identify the Arkkadian Watchers. Some had more involvement than others. We were engineered with differing intellects, I guess you could say we were created to be role specific. While I was created with a higher intellect, I never got involved in the hunt for the Watchers. I worked solely in the investment firm, alongside many Earth-Humans who had no idea of what we really were."

"Take a right here," Adam instructed as they sped toward a small roundabout which displayed a sign for the A27 and Portsmouth. Maya swung the small car to the right, the tyres squealing on the tarmac. Adam dug his phone from his pocket and eyed it uneasily. *Lucie should have called back by now*, he thought.

"Around a week before the virus hit and things went wrong, the Earth-Breeds working in various offices around the world – the ones not employed in the important roles – were called to the States. The official line was that we were being given an opportunity to visit the company's head office. A benefit that was promised to everyone; even the Earth-Humans working for us. The truth behind the announcement was far more sinister. We knew, of course, that the plan was nearing its end game. We were going to the American Headquarters in Allentown, about two hours from the company's office in New York. The Earth-Humans who worked for us would never get to the States; they were being left to die like cattle with everyone else." Her voice hinted at sadness and regret. "You need to understand that from birth I was educated to hate Earth-Humans; we were brain washed from an early age. I knew nothing else. I didn't create or release that plague – I can't be held responsible for what they did."

"Do you really think you can shirk your guilt so easily?" Adam laughed bitterly. "You're all accountable in my book! So, tell me? What led to you being here now? Why switch sides suddenly?"

"During my time working with the Earth-Humans I made many friends." Her voice grew distant, as if she were recalling the time before the plague with some fondness, something that she didn't deserve, as far as Adam was concerned. "I even had a boyfriend," she laughed.

That wasn't hard for him to believe, despite his dislike for her and what she had stood for, there was no denying she was beautiful, reminding him of Oriyanna and many other Arkkadian females he'd met during his brief stay on the idyllic planet. It was easy to see how earlier

Earth-Humans had mistaken them for angels. Maya, however, was not Arkkadian, she was Earth-Breed, but Adam was sure she had a hint of that alien gene in her, something that made him uneasy.

"I began to doubt their cause," Maya continued. "By the time I reached the US I was wracked with so much guilt, I considered taking my own life." She took her eyes from the road momentarily and eyed him, her expression sincere.. "I could never bring myself to do it, though."

"And were there others like you who felt the same?"

"I don't know. No one would ever dare voice such an opinion, it would have led to immediate execution, no questions asked." Maya sped through the small coastal town of Shoreham-by-Sea and guided the Mazda onto the A27. "What are the curfew laws around here?" she asked,.

"Major cities are still maintaining a one AM rule," Adam replied, making no attempt to hide the contempt in his voice. "We'll be clear of Portsmouth and Southampton before it comes into play. Once we hit more rural areas, we should be fine. They tend to let people in less-populated districts go about their business as usual. Unless we have any real issues, we'll be in Wiltshire way before it comes into effect."

"This is good," said Maya, trying to sound upbeat. "Your sister should be calling soon."

"Let's hope so," he sighed, feeling a little sick. "So how did things play out for you – during and after that week?"

"Soon after the virus had been released, things started to go wrong; very wrong. I never got told the whole story to begin with, but I was aware that an Arkkadian vessel had reached Earth and a hunt had commenced to locate an Elder who survived the crash." She turned away from the road once again and regarded Adam intently. "I have read your account of events, I know about your involvement with her – Oriyanna."

The mention of her name caused another pang of longing in Adam's chest.

"Just before the EMP, we received information that our team had reached the pyramid, shortly after that all the electrical systems went down. For over twenty-four hours we had no way of knowing if we'd been successful or not. It was then when we received information from a craft we had in orbit around Earth. Some of our more sophisticated technologies still worked, because they weren't susceptible to the pulse that fried the planet. It soon became clear that they could pick up no trace of Buer, or anyone else in Egypt. The craft had detected a sizeable explosion beneath the plateau. The more senior Earth-Breeds feared that we – *they* – had failed. A transmission was sent to Sheol from the orbital craft; Sheol, however, is another one hundred and fifty light years further away than Arkkadia, and the signal never reached them in time. It was soon after that when we lost all contact with the vessel, and then the rains began and we knew. Fearing some kind of backlash from Arkkadia, or even Sheol for our failure, we scattered."

"Just as the Arkkadian people thought you would," Adam cut in. "They had no idea how many of you were here, but they were determined to try and track down as many as possible."

"I know," Maya replied, just as Adam's phone lit up with an incoming text message. "With the ones who died during the incident in the lead up to The Reaper, and the ones Sam has killed, there aren't many higher intellect, senior Earth-Breed left." She watched him anxiously as he scanned the phone's screen before he let out a long, relieved breath. "Is that your sister?"

"Yes. She can't get a connection to call, but she says, 'I'm safe, have things to tell you, see you soon.' Thank God." Adam checked his watch. "How are we for fuel?" He craned his neck to read the small gauge.

"We should be fine," replied Maya, flicking her dark eyes down to the dimly lit dash. They passed the hulk of a crashed passenger jet, abandoned in a field to their right, its bulbous front end silhouetted against the sky like a man-made mountain. Every time Adam saw these things, it reminded him how lucky they'd been to escape from the Egypt Air flight with barely a scratch. There were many grim reminders like this one, scattered all over the globe. There just weren't enough resources left to clean up all the wreckage. One day, hopefully soon, macabre monuments such as the wrecked 747 they'd just passed would be gone. "After we fled I was on my own for many months, living as best I could, like many of the remaining Earth-Humans. As society slowly got back on its feet, I was contacted by another Earth-Breed – Benjamin Hawker – he was a former US Government employee." Maya looked a little forlorn. "He was directly involved in the hunt for you and Sam when you were— on the run. He informed me that one of our kind had been killed in an execution-style murder here in England. He feared the Arkkadians were once again here on Earth, intending to track us all down. At the time, we had no idea it was Sam Becker. We now know that the Arkkadians are the ones selecting the targets, they're just using Sam Becker to carry out their work."

"How the hell have you managed to learn so much?" Adam asked, adjusting the heater. It was becoming more than a little stuffy in the small cab of the Mazda.

"That's not important right now," Maya replied curtly.

"I think it's very important, if I'm going to trust you. How do I know you're not still working for them? How do I know that this isn't some clever ploy to take me easily?" Maya fired him a look which revealed she was hurt by his last statement. "You've got to admit it would be a very easy way to do things cleanly."

"I see your point," she conceded, sounding glum. "Do you know anything of what the Arkkadian people have done after your return to Earth?"

"Nothing." Adam had often wondered how things had played out in the months after he and Sam had been sent home. Almost every fibre of his body had wanted to stay on that peaceful planet; had it not been for Lucie, he wouldn't have returned home. Oriyanna had told him she would likely be sent to Sheol to oversee the war effort, and it had crossed his mind more than once that something might have happened to her. It was fair to say that returning home was a gamble, a gamble which had paid off. Without the benefit of the Tabut, or Ark as he preferred to think of it, it had taken them a full seven days to get back aboard one of the Arkkadian scout vessels. Despite his never ending wonder at the technological marvel they'd travelled in, the seven-day trip had seemed to take an age. Not a waking minute of the trip had gone by, without him thinking of his sister and whether he'd find her alive. His brain sent him back to that day for a minute. He and Sam had returned to London in the early hours of a Sunday morning. The rains which had washed the virus from the planet had stopped. That day, the sun was just starting to peek over the tops of the terrace houses, and the air had been pleasantly warm with the promise of an unusually hot May day. Despite the pleasant warmth, there had been something far more sinister in the air. The smell of decay. His back garden, which had once been his father's pride and joy, now resembled nothing more than a muddy quagmire. Small mist trails of swiftly-evaporating water reached up from the ground resembling long, spindly snakes being charmed from the sodden grass as they reached for a sun which worked feverishly to take the vast amounts of water from the ground. At first, Adam had been relieved to see that every window of the house was covered with opaque plastic sheeting. *Thank god, she listened and took my advice*, had been his first thought. Finding the back door locked, he'd spent a good few minutes banging on it inanely with Sam, hoping to see Lucie making her way through the kitchen to discover what all the fuss was about. After getting no reply, he'd gone to the shed and found a pickaxe that hadn't been used since his parents were alive. His father, who'd been a stickler for maintaining his tools, had sharpened the blade on a regular basis. The handle, now a mixture of flaking red paint and clear lacquer, would lead most to believe the tool was useless, but the axe was still as sharp as the day it had left the store. With Sam's help he'd used it to hack away at the door until the lock had been smashed to pieces, and with a metallic clang, fell to the floor. Part of him hadn't wanted the door to give, sure that once inside he'd be faced with the grim task of searching from room to room, wondering with the opening of each door if he'd find his sister lying there, dead. Stepping into the kitchen he'd called her name, but gotten no reply. Shaking uncontrollably, Sam by his side they'd cautiously made their way through to the lounge. Huddled behind the large brown leather sofa Sam had slept on the night before they'd left, clutching a baseball bat in one hand and Jinx the cat in the other, was his sister. For a few long seconds, she'd remained there, staring at him through wide, frightened eyes, seemingly unable to believe her eyes. A tearful reunion had ensued, followed by the long and protracted job of explaining everything that had happened. As painful as it had been for him to leave Oriyanna and her promise of a life together, he knew the moment he saw Lucie behind the sofa that he'd made the right choice.

"In the months after the virus," Maya began, snapping him back from the memory, "the Arkkadians hit Sheol, and the attack was far greater than the one after the Great War. This time, they didn't just want to destroy their craft and maroon them on that remote rock, they wanted to take control. After multiple air attacks they sent ground troops in. Sheol was a mining planet; long before the Great War it was a hive of activity – it has a vast series of nine underground levels, and each has separate structures and caverns. Air strikes were not enough to flush out those responsible, and the Arkkadian troops knew they would have to take the fight deep into the planet itself, to the lowest levels of the old mines. Their mission was to capture the Elders who remained there, wanting to ensure something like this could never happen again. Whilst they wanted to take as many of their leaders as possible, their primary mission was to capture *him*."

"Asmodeous? Adam questioned, and he heard the foreboding in his own voice.

"Yes," Maya replied. "All of the non-Elders on Sheol had been born there; like me, they could not help what they were a part of. They are currently being held on Sheol under Arkkadian rule. Those who are not willing to be repatriated are facing execution. I fear that many of them will die; their hatred for the Arkkadians has built up over many generations."

"Just how many are there living there?" Adam was creating a picture in his head of the hellish place, imagining the Elders and civilian population living within the planet like a massive, evil army of ants.

"Due to the size of the planet and its inability to sustain crops and fresh water without the use of technology, just a few hundred million. They have very strict birth control laws, to stop the planet becoming over-populated."

"They deserve whatever's coming," said Adam bitterly, hatred burning hot in his gut. "I take it the Elders will face execution?"

"The ones they captured, yes."

He turned sharply to stare at her. "What do you mean, the ones they captured?"

"Before the first attack, a single craft – Arkus 2 – made its escape from the planet. She used to be an Arkkadian vessel, hijacked by Asmodeous and stolen during the Great War. Aboard were three Elders and Asmodeous himself."

"Do you know where they went?" asked Adam, although he wasn't sure he wanted to know the answer. There was only one way Maya could know so much about the events of the last few years.

"Where else did they have to go? Here. Earth. They spent many months on the craft, and they didn't come here directly. Only when they had no food or supplies left, did they risk it."

"How long ago?" Adam snapped.

"Six months."

"And you know where he is?" Adam rubbed at his tired eyes and wondered just how much more there was that he didn't know.

"Yes, it's where I travelled from, to reach you today. He is in a place where he once ruled during the ancient times on Earth, before the Great War. Thousands of years ago, there was a city there. There is no trace of it now, however, other than some massive etchings on the ground which Earth-Humans have been puzzling about since their discovery.

"Please tell me I'm won't have to head back to Egypt," Adam groaned. "I'd always wanted to visit the pyramids, but last time, I got a little more of the ancient Egyptian experience than your average holidaymaker."

Maya laughed nervously. "No, the empires held by the Arkkadian people in the old days were vast and spread across the globe. He's in an area known as Nazca, in Peru, and he isn't just hiding there, he wants revenge. The craft he's in, although ancient, is still far more advanced than any Earth technology. He's planning to use it, and a select number of Earth-Breed, against you."

"Impossible," said Adam defiantly, although even he didn't believe his own statement. "If there is a massive spacecraft out in the Nazca desert, I'm sure someone would have seen it."

"Adam, you've been to Arkkadia, you know the technology that's at hand. Even when his craft was built, many years ago, what you would call a cloaking device was considered old tech. I promise you that his craft is out there, in the desert. Those impressive lines on the ground, those were created for him by slaves he bred to create massive monuments in his honour. He truly believed he was a god among the men he and his people had created. His vanity wouldn't have taken him anywhere else on this planet. Despite the city which once lay there being long gone, the ground monuments remained. The Nazca people called him *Viracocha*; they saw him as a creator, but he was far from being that. He's held many names among Earth's various religions but I think you know only too well what name you would know him by."

Adam didn't need to speak it, the very thought of it made his hairs stand on end.

Maya continued. "His hatred for humanity is incredibly powerful. Sheol is lost, and Earth is lost to him and his people. If he can't have it, he'd decided no one can. He's planning a last stand that will leave this planet as dead as Mars!"

Chapter 7

Rico Farez was sure he'd seen that particular lampshade before, and lying there in the grainy darkness, the suspicion turned to certainty. Swallowing back the phlegm which seemed stuck in his otherwise parched throat, his confused, pounding brain tried to deduce where he'd seen it. The answer finally came to him – Ikea. Whoever that lampshade belonged to, must once have shopped at the furniture giant. Rico wasn't sure why his head had been tackling such a pointless and inane question since he came around a few minutes ago, but he felt some satisfaction in knowing he'd managed to solve the issue. The next problem was, what the hell was he doing here staring at a lampshade in the first place? Rolling his head slightly to the right, he felt hard tiles beneath his shaved head. Straining to see in the dimly lit room, he could just make out a tangled mess which was a pair of legs, sticking out at odd angles from behind a breakfast bar in the middle of the modestly-sized kitchen. There appeared to be a thin rug under the legs, breaking the expanse of neatly-tiled floor. As his brain worked on who the hell the legs might belong to, he realised that the owner of the legs wasn't laying on a rug at all. Further inspection confirmed they were laying in a pool of blood which appeared black in the darkness. The thick, viscous liquid had spread out a good few feet from the body, marooning it on its own little island.

With more than a little trepidation, Rico slid his hand from his stomach and touched the floor to his left, searching for his own island of blood. His fears were confirmed when his hand dropped into the thick, sticky liquid that had cooled on the tiled floor. In a moment of blind panic he tried to sit up, the attempt futile when he realised with mounting horror that he couldn't feel his legs. Not only that, but his whole body felt numb, like a piece of old rubber. Turning his head to the left, he could just make out a light, shining brightly in a hallway on the other side of the adjoining lounge. The sound of a gull cawing, outside the house, brought the events leading up to his unusual situation flooding back, "Fisher," he croaked, his dry throat protesting. Rico swallowed, wincing at the pain which flared up like fire in his gut. "Adam Fisher?" The name left his lips posed as a question – he knew it was important, and more than likely the reason he was in this predicament.

Like an unanchored boat on rough seas, his mind bobbed and pitched from one thought to the next, quickly and erratically. He began cursing the Elders, for not granting the front-line agents the Gift, which rendered situations like this avoidable. The Gift had to be earned; the only trouble was, you often died trying to earn it. The irony of the fact wasn't lost on Rico, even in his painfully bleak situation. A wave of thought washed over his brain and that name pushed to the forefront again – Adam Fisher – however this time, the name of a town also slipped in beside it – *Brighton*.

Rico cranked his neck to the side. It felt as if it needed a good oiling, and his bones creaked under his skin, as if they were a set of rusty old hinges on an unkempt garden gate. His eyes focused on the legs still sticking out bizarrely from behind the breakfast bar. He was sure he must know the owner of those legs – not that it would do him much good. He suspected the legs were attached to a body which was well and truly dead. In that moment, a tidal wave of memories overwhelmed him, flooding his mind with the night's events – but it brought him no comfort.

Rico was a dead man – if he didn't die here, he couldn't help thinking that he'd regret it. He closed his eyes and replayed the night's events, hoping to remember a single scrap of information which might spare him, should he ever manage to extricate himself from this small island of sticky, cold blood.

* * *

Rico glanced up at the darkened windows of the bungalow on Wilson Avenue, noting how the road sloped gently downhill toward the sea. In daylight, the majority of these modest homes would have stunning, yet expensive views over the coast.

"His book talk begins in twenty-five minutes," a soft female voice said from the rear seat.

"You're certain he will return here tonight?" Chris Grogan asked, craning his trunk-like neck around from the driver's seat to look at her.

"We tailed him from here to the hotel half an hour ago," Maya snapped. "He won't risk driving back to London tonight – even if he makes it before curfew, the streets are not a good place to be."

Rico cracked open the door of the BMW 3 Series, allowing cool, coastal air to flood the stuffy cab, the smell of the sea instantly wafting around them. In the distance, the sound of waves breaking on the stony beach filtered into the brisk night. "We go in through the rear door, just as we planned," Rico croaked, his Eastern European accent harsh. "As soon as he comes in, Chris will hit him with the tranq-gun, then it's a swift run to the airport, and a short flight to France where he will be reunited with his friend and sister, before…" Rico smiled, relishing the thought of turning both Fisher and Becker over to *him* – the great one. "Let's hope they packed some sun lotion, it's a bit warmer where they're going."

"Enough chat," cut in Maya. "Let's get inside, it's freezing out here." They jumped out of the car and hurried down the brick paved drive; the wind was bitingly cold, late September was promising a hard winter. Since the seven-day storm, the seasons had shifted, earlier summers and earlier winters becoming the new norm. Keeping their bodies up against the half brick, half-timber clad wall, they rounded the back of the bungalow one-by-one. Chris rushed in from the right, his massive hulk of a body powering through the flimsy larch lap gate as if it was made of soggy paper. The gate swung open with a *crack* when the latch broke and it swung back, hitting the fence hard.

Rico watched Maya wince at the loud noise, but it was likely that a good proportion of these houses were empty, and besides, in these uncertain times, people kept themselves to themselves. With a last, tentative glance for prying eyes, they slipped into the back garden.

At the rear door, Rico dug a small cloth roll from his jacket pocket. He uncoiled it on the concrete step at the rear door and fished out a pair of long, thin needle-like pliers. He slipped the implement into the lock and expertly began to feel his way around inside the barrel, feeling for how the key to this lock would work the mechanism. In less than ten seconds the latch clicked, and pressing a little weight onto the door it swung inward, bathing his chilled skin in warmer, slightly stale air. Rico leaned to one side and let Maya and Chris slip past him. He placed the lock-picking tool neatly into the kit roll and secured it in his jacket, making his way in, just a few seconds behind the others, only pausing to shut the door quietly behind him.

The kitchen was a decent size, with a modest breakfast bar standing like an island in the centre of the room. The breakfast bar had a built-in coffee machine, and it looked as if it hadn't been used in a good few years. Despite the tidy appearance, the surfaces were covered with dust. "I'm guessing he doesn't holiday here much!" mused Rico, running a finger through the dust on the espresso machine and rubbing it between his thumb and forefinger. "It's not bad around here," he continued, surveying the kitchen and squinting through the gloom into the lounge, which was visible through a large, open arch. "Pity this will all be wasteland in a few days' time – I could see myself retiring here." He grinned smugly at Maya, but she rounded the arch and disappeared into the lounge.

Rico was scanning the kitchen, hoping to find some food when he saw Maya rushing back into the kitchen. The sound of gunfire followed; whipping around in confusion, he saw a flash of light before

Chris frantically grabbed at his chest. A second muzzle flash lit the room like a burst of summer lightning, before Rico watched in horror as a slug tore into Chris's neck. In an instant, he'd disappeared behind the breakfast bar as if a hole had opened in the floor and swallowed him. Not wanting to suffer the same fate, Rico broke left, trying to reach the lounge.

Maya was faster, and he felt the weight of the gun as she aimed the muzzle squarely at his chest with deadly accuracy. He froze, threw his hands up and turned back to stare at her, her pretty face grim, the expression in her eyes deadly. "Why?" he spat.

"I'm sorry, Rico," she replied, and for a second he almost believed her, because there was a hint of regret in her voice. Then the muzzle flashed again and fire exploded through his body, darkness engulfing him before his body hit the floor.

* * *

Grimacing, Rico pushed himself up onto his elbows, fighting against the inertia of his body which seemed determined to slip in the blood and plant him painfully onto his back. *Why did she cross us?* he thought, as he finally managed to get into a sitting position.

"Chris? Chris! You alive over there?" he called, but there was no reply. His mind raced through the circumstances that could possibly have led to this bizarre situation – though no matter how hard he tried, he couldn't think of a single reason why Maya had done this.

In a panic, he surveyed the blood spreading around him like a wet, red carpet. He'd already lost a lot of blood, and the crimson, life-giving liquid still oozed from the wound in his chest, his heart working to both keep him alive and killing him at the same time. Rico's head began to swim uncontrollably, the room pirouette before his eyes in some insane death dance. Losing the battle to stay upright, he crashed painfully onto the tiled floor, clawing frantically at the hole in his body. His mind still working at a hundred miles an hour, death's warm blanket slid over his body and there was nothing he could do to stop it.

* * *

With a little regret and a touch of sadness, Maya eyed the dead bodies of her fallen comrades, slain by her own hand. Slowly, Maya unscrewed the still-warm silencer from the pistol and cast it aside, even before she'd nailed Rico, the device had started to deteriorate. She had genuinely liked both guys; Rico had been a little flirtatious, but he trod carefully, and respected who she was, never pushing the boundaries too far. Tucking the gun into her coat pocket, Maya slid her phone out and snapped a couple of pictures, making sure to get enough of the room in the shot for Adam Fisher to distinguish where they'd been taken. She thumbed through the shots, nodding approval before she fished the car keys out of Chris's pocket. Reaching the back door, she slipped out of the property and silently paced down the drive to the awaiting car. After the short drive to the hotel, she would dump the BMW – it was easily traceable and she needed to be well and truly off the radar. The dashboard clock told her Adam was due to start his book talk in twenty minutes, and with a little luck she'd get there in time to hear it all. She was very interested in what he had to say.

Chapter 8

Sam took a long swig from a second plastic beaker of the warm, metallic-tasting water, eyeing the inspector over the rim. His seemingly tall-tale had taken over an hour to tell, but to his surprise the inspector hadn't interrupted once, just sat there, silently; not seeming judgmental but in an unsettling manner which made it impossible to read just how he was taking it all. If this guy could remain as stony faced during a game of cards, he wasn't the kind of opponent Sam would want to face. The only words to pass his lips during the whole story had been the occasional 'I see', and 'Huhhm'.

"That's quite a story, Monsieur Becker." Inspector Ackhart finally announced, with more than a hint of doubt in his voice. Sam wasn't sure what he'd expected; he wouldn't have been surprised if the inspector had howled with laughter and packed him straight off to the crazy house. "I have heard some strange accounts, and what people believe to be reasonable excuses for their crimes, but this has to top the list!" Much to Sam's dismay, Ackhart's last words were doled out with a hint of anger. His heavily accented, yet perfect English seemed to only highlight his contempt.

"Believe what you want," Sam sighed, placing the beaker back onto the table. "I never expected you to believe it. I *lived* it, and even I'm not sure I believe it all." He chuckled nervously. "I'm at the stage now where I call shit or bust. I've got nothing left to lose, no sorry or sordid excuses for why I was at the chateau, or why I killed Monsieur

Laurett while he lay in bed, or why I killed the others listed in that file. And let me tell you, Inspector – there are more cases than you have recorded there." Ackhart leaned back in his chair, the faded orange plastic protesting. Running a hand through his greasy hair, he scrubbed his palm across his well-weathered face and rubbed his eyes.

"I will have Claude escort you back to your cell. I will come to interview you officially in a couple of hours, so we can get you into court in the morning. I would encourage you to tell me the truth, unless you plan to plead insanity. I can see no other outcome, other than you being remanded in custody until the trial. After your court appearance, it is likely you'll be permitted to make that call you so desperately want. I see no point in continuing this discussion any further. I don't know of any man of sound mind who would find a shred of truth in your story – and that's what it is, Monsieur Becker, a story! Nothing more!"

"As I said, Inspector, Laurett told me something that might mean you have no choice than to believe what I've said in the very near future. I pray I'm wrong but…" Sam paused and gazed longingly out of the small, barred window, "…I doubt it!" Before Sam could offer anything further, an urgent rapping came from outside the door.

"Enter," Ackhart called, sounding put out by the intrusion. Right on cue the door swung open, and a guy wearing an untucked shirt and loose tie entered the room. Sam was good with faces, and this one was new in the equation. The guy scouted the room quickly, ignoring Sam, who was taking in his every detail. He spoke to the inspector in a flurry of French, which once again left Sam with no chance of understanding with his less than average grade in the language, which he'd earned more than half his life ago. He watched the inspector scowl. "Fucking Americans," he spat, before firing a torrent of French at the visitor, who appeared to shrink from the outburst. Coming from a rank-and-file structured background, Sam knew immediately that Ackhart was this guy's superior officer. He acknowledged Sam with a curt nod before sloping out of the room, leaving the door open.

The inspector stood up, regarding Sam for the briefest of moments. "It would seem," his voice still brewed with frustration, "that the FBI is pushing for your immediate extradition." Dread welled up in the pit of Sam's stomach. "They are arguing that they have the most cases against you and as they seem to have gone far above my pay grade to get their own way, the extradition paperwork is on its way now. It's likely you will be taken to their embassy for initial questioning."

"Wait!" cried Sam. "Don't those things take an age to get authorised?"

"In the old world, yes. Things operate a little differently now, I don't know whose strings have been pulled to get this one through, but I am less than happy about it." He turned his back to Sam and went to leave the room, the fury almost palpable in his movements.

"Inspector!" Sam called. Ackhart stopped and spun around but remained silent. "If you turn me over to them, I'm dead."

"It's likely you will be given the death penalty, yes. But not before they ship you back here and let me have my, how do you English put it? My pound of flesh!"

"No, you don't understand," Sam spoke urgently, "this isn't the FBI, this is *them*!"

"Spare me," scoffed Ackhart.

"It's the truth! Do some digging, please! If you hand me over to them, you might as well put a bullet in my head now. I promise you that once I leave with them, I'll disappear of the map – forever." Sam studied the inspector's face, and for the briefest of moments, he thought he had him, a hint of doubt appeared on his face which was undeniable. "I can prove what I said is true," Sam persisted, and the inspector looking at him doubtfully. "When I was on Arkkadia they changed me, I never mentioned it before, but it's true."

"Please, monsieur, spare me the drama," Ackhart snapped. "I have wasted enough time on your fantasy already."

"It's true, look! Look at my lip." Sam pulled his bottom lip down with his finger. "When I was there they gave me the Gift," Sam had left that little detail out of the account, sure the story was hard enough to swallow without claiming he was immortal. "It's nanobot technology; there are millions of them in my blood stream, and they heal any wounds I get, almost instantly." The inspector eyed Sam's bottom lip with a disinterested expression. "When you arrested me, my face hit the stones on the beach; my lip got cut up, do you remember?"

"As it happens, monsieur, I do not."

"Then let me prove it to you! Cut me with a knife – fuck it, shoot me in the leg! Once you see it heal, you'll have to believe me." Sam nodded encouragement, aware that he sounded nuttier than a rat stuck in a tin shithouse with every word.

"All you are doing, monsieur, is making your case for insanity stronger. If that is your goal, you are doing very well."

Sam sensed uncertainty in the police officer's voice, was sure he'd planted a seed of doubt in his experienced brain – he just hoped he'd fed it enough to grow. "Just double check the papers, please. These people have a very long reach, they had an operative in the presidential protection team, for fuck's sake! This – this *extradition* is nothing for them to arrange, not that I believe it's even genuine. I told you before, they're pretty fucking shit hot at influencing people into seeing whatever they want them to see! All I ask is that you check it out."

"I plan to, Mr. Becker; however, they have a field team on their way to us now, and you are being collected in an hour. From here, you will either be flown to the United States, or taken to their embassy in Paris." Leaving no room for debate, Ackhart crossed the small room in two lengthy strides, leaving Claude to take the prisoner back to his cell.

In the hallway outside, however, Ackhart paused. Becker's panic at the news had taken him off-guard, and while he couldn't bring himself to believe what the man had told him, a small worm of doubt was at work, squirming away in his stomach. Something was not right. Ackhart had done this job long enough to trust his gut and his gut didn't like this case, not at all. He checked his watch, confirming he had just under an hour to get to the bottom of it.

Chapter 9

As night raced in to claim its hold over the Peruvian desert, a brilliant, fiery red sunset cast the eastern sky ablaze, the light tendrils of high-level cloud coloured orange by the sun as it slipped over the horizon.

With his hands clamped together behind his back, military-style, he raised his face to the sky and enjoyed the last of the sun's warmth on his skin. Despite the warm desert air, a shiver of coldness ran through his ancient body. A light breeze tousled his angelic blonde hair; a sensation he hadn't experienced for many years, for in the bowels of Sheol there was no breeze, only an unnatural stillness. Closing his unearthly amber eyes, he remembered a time when this place had looked very different; when a mighty city had stood on this spot – his city. He mused over the way the Earth-Humans had worshipped him, and how at his command, they had worked tirelessly, creating the massive land drawings which had been the only thing to survive the long millennia, ancient monuments carved into the very Earth itself. Following the Great War, the Arkkadians had seen to it that every trace of the magnificent buildings that once stood here had been wiped from the Earth's surface, just as every one of his territories had been; many now nothing more than fabled accounts in various religious texts.

Trying to soak up the last of the warmth, enjoying the wonderfully clean and non-purified air, he remembered the day it had all changed – the day that should have seen the end of the Earth-Humans – the day that should have seen Earth pass into Arkkadian hands. At one time in his life, he *had* been Arkkadian, and had loved his planet and its people. Anger began to broil inside him, a fierce sea of emotion hitting a rocky shoreline. He managed to quell it by recalling that glorious day when the massacre had begun, a massacre which should have spread planet-wide and seen the death of every last Earth-Human. They should all have been wiped from the face of a planet that was never theirs, because they were not a native species to this rare pearl in the never-ending void of space. Had they been the true natives, he would never have sanctioned the killing of the planet's population. – No–evolved and natural life needed to be preserved, and that was just what he intended to do; secure the future of the Arkkadian race against another extinction-level event, similar to the one which had almost seen the end of his kind. Why should a race of people, biologically engineered to work and serve, be given such a gift? For a brief moment, he mused over his own genetic tampering with the human DNA strain in the days before the war. Disgusted that an inferior race had ever been created in the image of his people, he'd set about changing that, elongating the shape of the human skull, deforming it so there was no doubt who was Earth-Human and who was Arkkadian. It was a trend that spread throughout his territories. When Buer first returned to Earth with the handful of Elders from Sheol, he'd sent back some of the studies that Earth-Humans had done over the years following their banishment to that bleak, sun-scorched planet. Remnants of those cone-headed creatures still echoed through the modern world, relics that took pride of place in museums and the personal collections of rich enthusiasts. The Earth-Humans had never learned the truth behind that mutated strain of human DNA however. They didn't know the painful reality of the origins of their kind, and many still foolishly looked toward the glut of religions which had developed as a result of his and his ancestors' intervention. A new surge of anger rose like bile in his ancient, yet perfectly-preserved and youthful body, for they should have known better. Many were now turning to science for answers, some suspecting the awful truth behind who they really were, but these were not the type of people mainstream science took seriously. Some of the developments he'd learned of astounded him; how they'd anticipated harnessing interplanetary travel within a hundred years. He'd read details of the Hundred Year Star Ship program, which had been gleaned from NASA by some well-placed Earth-Breeds, with interest. Amazingly, Earth-Humans had managed to theoretically design an engine very similar to the ones used in Arkkadian craft. Of course, they were still many years from putting theory into practise, but time ticks by relentlessly, and the day would come when that theory became reality. It angered him to think that this imposter race could be so close to unlocking such powerful knowledge, and there was no doubt that the Arkkadian people would welcome them with open arms the moment they perfected the technology.

The morning he'd first tried to wash the Earth's surface clean of the parasites was one of his fondest, and he recalled how he'd given the command to his faithful followers. At first light in the cities under his rule, they'd gone door-to-door, massacring entire families, people who had quite rightly both feared and worshipped his superiority. Killed with weapons that were far beyond their understanding. Having rid his own territories of vermin, they had moved on to civilisations that the foolish, Earth-Human-loving Arkkadians had studied, his craft hitting them by surprise, crushing them to the ground. The sight of his own kind, running and dying with the rats they'd nurtured had given him no joy, but it was the bigger picture that counted, and a few deaths were a necessary evil to achieving his goal. Two planets for his kind to thrive on, thus halving the chance of them being wiped out as they so nearly were, many thousands of years before.

The war and extermination had not progressed as swiftly as he'd planned, and the fighting had spread from the Earth's surface to his home world, with those faithful to him bearing arms against the foolish ones who wanted to protect the abominations which only thrived as a result of their own near extinction.

The great city that had once stood proudly in the Nazca Desert was one of the first to fall; his men outnumbered by the troops sent to protect the Earth-Humans, but they had been too late. Arkkadian had turned on Arkkadian among the stone walls instead;, a fight he'd painfully lost.

Two of his cities, Sodom and Gomorrah, had been the last to fall. When ground and air attempts had failed and the Earth-Human protectors had realised that every one of their children had been slaughtered, they'd opted for the most powerful form of retribution to wipe his kind from the Earth. It was a power that the Earth-Humans had discovered and since used in their own wars – nuclear power. He had fled the Earth long before, preserving himself for a future attempt at seizing the planet he longed to control. His escape had not stopped him from weeping with sorrow, when he'd learned that nuclear fire had wiped out the last two strongholds from the land. Earth had been lost to him – for now.

Over long years, holed up on the barren planet they'd escaped to, he and his ousted followers had rebuilt and waited patiently, knowing their time would come again. He'd been close, so close to his goal, but was thwarted in what Earth-Humans would call the eleventh hour, by Oriyanna and the two who'd followed her. There was no describing the fury which ate at him like a parasite over his plans being quashed. Now though, in these final days, he'd put events into play which would deliver those responsible into his hands. They could watch as he laid waste to the Earth, wiping the Earth-Humans from the land with their own weapons of destruction. Seizing the Earth and preserving it for his kind was beyond his reach; no matter how he lusted for it, things had changed. This was about revenge, and it would be sweet. If he couldn't control the Earth, no one would. He'd rather see it destroyed than in the hands of those who should never have been.

Over the long years, since his first appearance on Earth, history had remembered him by many names. The people of Nazca had called him Viracocha; the Greeks had called him Mammon. Others had called him by his birth name, Asmodeous, but history had most famously remembered him by a name that still struck fear into the hearts of foolish Earth-Humans.

Satan.

Chapter 10

The small and agile RX7 cut its way through the night. The lack of traffic on the road had allowed them to set a reasonable pace; traffic jams and rush hours were a blight of the old world. Many vehicles still sat in driveways and by the roadside, lifeless and rusting, their owners unable to source or afford the parts to fix them. The other more macabre option was that their owners were dead. Adam kept a tense eye on the speedometer, cringing at the way Maya seemed unable to drive in any other way than having her foot mashing the accelerator into the foot well. At the breakneck pace she was setting, he could see them covering the one-hundred and twenty mile journey in just over an hour and a half. Maya was certainly not one to hang around. Although his car had been relatively cheap to buy and fix, it wasn't the most economical of vehicles on the road. Certainly, not ideal in these times of ludicrous oil prices, but he rarely used it normally. With the boy-racer style of driving Maya had, they'd be lucky to reach Wiltshire on a tank. He could understand her wanting to put some distance between them and the major towns and cities on their route, negating the possibility of being stopped by the police or military, or running into the various ne'er-do-wells who roamed the roads at night, robbing and thieving what they could.

From Brighton, they had sped west, cutting past Portsmouth and Southampton. Just past Southampton they had swung north, through Salisbury and out into the open countryside. Around ten miles outside of Salisbury the ancient monument, Stonehenge, had loomed out of the night, silhouetted against the bright moonlit sky. The ancient stones seemed like giants, all meeting in the field where they'd stood for thousands of years. His face pressed against the glass, Adam watched as they slipped past. He wondered what their true purpose was, sure they must have some link to the Arkkadian people who'd had such a huge influence over history, and yet had mysteriously managed to slip into obscurity, leaving very little evidence of their existence apart from a wealth of misinterpreted religions.

The journey had been mainly silent since passing Portsmouth. For every minute that ticked by, Adam found himself trusting Maya more. The longer he spent in her company without her making some attempt on his life, the better he felt. Still, he didn't allow himself to relax fully – knowledge of who and what she was had firmly cemented itself in his mind. When they'd left Brighton in the rear-view mirror, Maya had told him how she and her accomplices had planned to capture him at his aunt and uncle's house following his book talk. He shuddered as she recounted the events which had unfolded in the modest bungalow with its serene sea view. To prove the story, Maya had shown him photographs on her phone, showing two men he didn't recognise, laying in pools of blood, sprawled out on his aunt's kitchen floor. He did know the room they were in, only too well. One guy – Maya had said his name was Chris, still had an expression of surprise on his face which gave him an almost life-like look, but the gaping hole in the side of his neck told a different story. It surprised Adam how easily he could consume such images; death, unfortunately, had become a regular event in this damaged world.

Maya had told Adam about how once taken, he was to be flown to Peru, to *him*. Adam had listened in mute horror, not quite able to believe he was being thrown headlong into this ancient battle once again. He knew only too well that it was nothing short of a miracle to have survived the first ordeal, and he was sure he was fast running out of lives, even with the Gift coursing through his veins. There was one topic he felt reluctant to press Maya for information on; the exact details of what evil was now planned for Earth. The need to ask her burned at him, grew with an unstoppable anxiousness until he could bear it no longer. As the small car twisted through the Wiltshire countryside, fast approaching their destination, he turned his face away from the window and looked at Maya, her delicate face masked with concentration as she navigated through the dark and twisty country lanes that snaked across the rural countryside. On more than one occasion, she'd had to jam the brakes on to avoid hitting the various wildlife which dashed in front of the speeding car, as if they were suicidal. It appeared the Reaper had been exclusively a human virus; there were no cases of the native animal species getting sick in any country. The developers on Sheol who had engineered the killer had been very good at their work.

"What are we facing here?" he finally asked. "You said he plans to leave this planet as dead as Mars. Just what kind of weapon does he have?"

"No weapon," replied Maya, not taking her clear blue eyes off the road, "The ship he is in was once an Arkkadian exploration vessel, it's very ancient, not a craft built for war." Maya guided them through the small town of Pewsey, Adam pointing out the left turn she needed. Hardly slowing down, she threw the Mazda into the corner, making Adam grab what Sam always called the *Fuck Me Handle* above the door, and the tyres squeal in protest against the tarmac. She powered the Mazda down a very narrow road, hitting a railway bridge faster than Adam would have liked and making his stomach lurch as if he was on a roller coaster.

"Just how is he planning to do it then?" Adam watched a small housing estate fly past; a few houses had lights on, but many remained in darkness.

"If he was in possession of such a weapon, do you really think he'd be sitting out in that desert, waiting? No, he would have struck out at Earth as soon as his craft came into orbit, six months ago. He's relying on you Earth-Humans to be the architects of your own downfall." The small housing estate vanished into the night, giving way to a tree-lined road, the old ragged oaks creating their own natural tunnel over the thin strip of unkempt tarmac. "Over the last few months," she continued, as they hit a pothole which shook the car and had her wrestling the steering wheel, "all of the world's superpowers have been locked in a race to repair and bring back online their nuclear launch capabilities." She shook her head sadly. "The race has been on since Russia started to get a little choosy about who, and at what price, they sell their precious Siberian oil to."

"Another mess we're in, thanks to your kind," jeered Adam. "I'm sure you know that one of the Watchers – Euri Peterson, as he was known on Earth – had pioneered hydro-run engines."

"I know."

"Yeah, well after his death, and during the week of the Reaper, Zeon Developments suffered a massive fire, burning the place to the ground. So much of the research and patented information was lost, it set the development of the technology back by years. The members of his development team who are still alive, are back-engineering a few of the jets they had in service, but the set-back from his death and fire has been disastrous."

"You follow the news, then?" Maya asked.

"Of course, every day. You might say I'm a little paranoid now."

"You know then, that there's a naval stand-off about to take place in the Pacific between the USA and Russia over the Siberian oil supplies?" Adam nodded. "Those subs are nuclear ready, and not only that, but the old nuclear launch bunkers and silos are also nuclear ready. You see, the EMP never rendered the payloads useless; the weapons just needed fixing, and new launch and defence programs had to be written. They're just waiting for the launch systems to go live and make every nuke viable once again. It's been a race which will see all the former nuclear powers reach the finish line within a few hours of each other. Or so my sources say."

"So what? He's hoping someone will push the button? I know they're fully expecting another Cold War, but even during the first one, no one had the balls to do it. They used to say nuclear weapons made the world a safer place. Bullshit, if you ask me."

"No, he has a program, one that can assume control of any country's defence systems. Once those nuclear launch systems are back online, they'll be fair game to him," Maya answered gravely.

The tree-like tunnel ended abruptly and the road opened out into fields. Large, rolling hills rose to their right, watching over the fields like a massive, natural amphitheatre.

"We're nearly there," said Adam, it's a left in about a mile." His mind was spinning, it seemed almost impossible that the insecurity and mistrust between the world's leaders was going to give Asmodeous a second chance. The one positive to come out of the EMP was how it had put everyone on a level playing field, weapons wise. It should have been a fresh start, a more peaceful existence without warships and missiles, fighter planes and tanks. If he hadn't seen such a life on Arkkadia, he never would have thought it possible, but it was a fresh start that Earth-Humans seemed incapable of taking. Maybe it was better for everyone if Asmodeous just ended the whole thing – hell right, at that moment, he felt like going directly out to that desert and pushing the button for him. Then he remembered the way local communities had pulled together in the early days, the days when at night all you had was a candle to see by and you kept a knife or a cricket bat by your side when you slept, in case looters decided tonight was your lucky night. He remembered how in his street, they'd pooled their food supply and rationed it out, an informal agreement until the government set things back in motion. Human nature was essentially good, and that deserved preserving, didn't it?

"I've seen how this program will work, Adam." She eyed him with wide eyes. The car reached the junction, the wheels skidding to a stop on a small layer of gravel that had built up on the road. Spinning the wheels, she went left. "The program has a name. Enola. And Enola is very clever. Once those systems are live, it will assess Earth's weather patterns and run predictions for wind and rain patterns over the coming weeks, then target each weapon according to how best the radiation will spread, factored in with initial casualty numbers by the blast of each payload."

"And you think that I, or we, can stop this from happening?"

"I don't know," she said bleakly. "I had to do something."

"Just the other side of the bridge," Adam instructed as they approached the cottage. He felt nauseous, both from Maya's driving and the thought that in less than two days, those systems would be making the planet Asmodeous' own private shooting gallery. "It's a small, thatched cottage on your left."

Maya took this bridge a little slower, and Adam glanced out of the window and got a look at the canal where he and Lucie had swum and kayaked as children. It was hard to tell, but was sure there was a half-sunken narrowboat sticking out at his side of the stone arch.

"Just here," he indicated with his hand. Maya jammed the brakes on, testing the inertia mechanism on Adam's belt. With one final over-exaggerated turn, she fired the car into the driveway and cut the engine. Adam unclipped his belt, eager to escape the stuffy cab. Stretching out he enjoyed the chilled air on his skin. "There should be a key under the large pot in the greenhouse," he called back, heading up the narrow drive, his shoes crunching on the pea-shingle.

Here and there, weeds sprung from the small stones, fighting for their own bit of space. Swinging the back gate open, he activated the torch function on his phone. The garden looked like a miniature rain-forest, nature had taken control over the modest sized plot of land. The grass, although slightly the worse for wear from the recent early cold spell reached up to his waist, and he pushed it aside with his free hand. "Wait there," he called, glancing over his shoulder and pointing the light toward Maya, who shielded her eyes from the glare. He was about to tell her he didn't want her falling over when his foot found a divot of grass, or one of his grandfather's gnomes, which had once taken pride of place on the immaculate lawn. Before he had time to speak he went down hard, his phone spilling from his hand. When pain flared in his ankle he cursed his stupidity, got to his feet and shook the wounded joint, knowing full well that in a few seconds the sharp pain would subside and no evidence would remain that he'd ever taken a tumble. Sure enough, in under a minute he was on the move, phone in hand and sliding the greenhouse door open. Cobwebs hung from the whitewashed glass roof, swirling and stirring gently as the open door let fresh air in to flood the small outbuilding. The large terracotta planter was exactly where Adam expected it to be, and briefly, he tried to recall the last time he'd been at the cottage. It was before the world changed, meaning the place had been standing empty for the best part of three years. Lifting the heavy tub he located the key, where he'd placed it after a weekend's heavy drinking with Sam – it seemed like a lifetime ago. The brass was dull but the metal felt reassuringly cool to the touch. Leaving the greenhouse he followed the path he'd created back to the gate, where Maya was waiting. He stopped briefly at the spot where he'd fallen, crouched down and fished around, rummaging in the overgrown greenery. Finding what he was after Adam tugged it free – just as he'd suspected, the culprit was one of the gnomes. He looked a little worse for wear after being lost in the jungle-like garden, his jolly red hat faded and the paint flaking. Taking the ornament with him, Adam reached the gate and set the sorry-looking gnome on the gravel, facing away from the gate like a tiny watchman standing on post. It was a completely inane attempt to restore some order to the property, but it made him feel a little better.

Reaching the front door, he slid the key into the lock. It offered some resistance, but with a little more pressure the lock slid back. Glancing over his shoulder, Adam swung the creaking door open and went inside. Musty air assaulted his nostrils, dust motes dancing chaotically in the small yet powerful beam of light the phone emitted. Swinging it around the lounge, the furniture cast hectic shadows against the cold walls. Adam flinched when the hat and coat stand briefly took on the appearance of a shadowy man, skulking in the corner. He was on edge, certain a thousand eyes were on him, studying his every move. He wanted to be ready, in case someone was hiding in that empty darkness. He half-expected someone to be sitting on the blackened, musty-smelling lounge, awaiting their arrival, but of course, no one was. The place was empty, and as silent as a crypt.

Chapter 11

"Seatbelt!" Lucie prompted urgently as Oriyanna slammed the Mini's passenger door shut behind her. Before she could grab the buckle, Lucie had the Mini in reverse, gunning the engine the small car jolted backward, and Oriyanna planted her palms against the glove-box to avoid being thrown through the windscreen. When Lucie selected first gear and planted her foot hard on the accelerator, Oriyanna was thrown back into the seat, and with the belt gripped in her hand she finally managed to click it into the receiver. With her spare hand, Lucie tore her apron over her head and threw it into the backseat as they sped away.

Lucie slammed the Mini Cooper down the small concrete ramp leading out of the car park. The front of the car hit the tarmac with a loud scrape which made her grit her teeth. She was a little precious about her beloved car, lovingly named Mavis the Mini. Sam always ripped her about that one but she didn't care; the car was one of the few new vehicles on the road. It had cost a small fortune, but the cash packages which arrived with the seemingly never-ending list of targets for Sam were more than generous and had seen them through some rough times a lot more comfortably than the average person. Now, with a stranglehold on oil supplies and the increasingly regular sight of petrol pumps out of service, Lucie wasn't sure how much longer she'd be able to drive her most prized possession. Although it was a hybrid, it still needed a certain amount of fuel to work. Despite her love for little luxuries, it was a luxury she'd gladly give up to have her husband out of harm's way. Tough as it was, she'd accepted being married to a guy like Sam would mean the odd sleepless night filled with worry; he was who he was, and she loved him for it.

Glancing in the rear-view mirror, Lucie's stomach plunged when she discovered a pair of headlights bearing down on them. Ramming the gearshift from second to third, she flicked her attention between the mirror and the tachometer, and when it redlined she knocked it into fourth. "We're being followed," she said urgently.

Oriyanna spun around and watched anxiously as the lights continued to draw closer. "I feared there would be more than one of them," she said, placing a hand on Lucie's shoulder. An instant wave of relief wash over Lucie. Sam and Adam had both told her how Oriyanna could influence people, but she'd found it hard to believe – hell, the whole story was hard to believe – but here she was living it. There was no doubt Oriyanna could ease a worried mind, faster and better than any bottle of wine.

Lucie powered the bright red Mini down Eltham Hill, and in her panic, instead of keeping left and taking the A20 out of town she went right, toward London. There was no time to turn around, the car on her tail was getting closer. Her little Mini wasn't slow by any means, but there were plenty of faster vehicles out there.

They flew past the burnt-out shell of Blackheath Sports Club, which had gone up in flames one night, shortly after Adam and Sam returned home. Although a good few miles from the house, they'd seen the black plume of smoke rising into the night sky with an eerie orange glow at its base. Speeding toward the Thames, London's financial district rose from the opposite bank, the looming structures dark, silent and broody. The days of leaving lavish lighting on to highlight a building's beauty were long gone, only red aircraft warning lights blinked solemnly to themselves at each building's peak, and even these would be turned off soon, as no aircraft were permitted to arrive or depart any UK airport after one AM.

As the pursuing car drew closer, the driver turned the full beams on, highlighting the fact he was closing in on his prey. The blinding light made Oriyanna and Lucie shield their eyes from the glare which bounced off the vehicle's mirrors. Lucie took one hand off the wheel and pushed the rear-view mirror up toward the roof; it helped, but not by much. Before she could grasp the steering wheel again, the car behind slammed into their rear bumper, and only the seatbelt saved her from reeling face first into the steering wheel. With a shriek of terror Lucie wrestled with the car, as it mounted the kerb and the passenger side hit the railings of a pelican crossing, sending a hail of sparks into the air. Heart hammering she finally got the vehicle under control, "Do something!" she yelled at Oriyanna, "Can't you make them stop?" Lucie knew it was a silly thing to say, as soon as the words left her mouth.

Oriyanna remained silent, glancing back at the other car while she ran options through her head. Sliding the Glock from her waistband, she unclipped her seatbelt and twisted around in the seat. The dazzling lights made it difficult to see, but they did give her a point of reference to shoot at. Oriyanna raised the weapon and fired two shots at the aggressing car, level with where she guessed the windscreen would be. Before her finger hit the trigger guard on the first shot, the rear windscreen shattered with a deafening crash, and the bullet powered through the glass, relentlessly seeking its target. She fired again. It was hard to tell with the beam of the vehicle's dazzling headlights but Oriyanna was sure the second shot found its target and punctured clean through the windscreen. Even so, the pursuing car powered on, relentless and seemingly unstoppable.

Lucie heard both shots, even with the silencer, the usually soft-sounding *Pffft* of the gun going off seemed much louder in real life than it did in the movies. The sound of the silenced gun however was dwarfed by the splintering crack as the bullets slammed through her rear windscreen. Watching in the wingmirror she saw the pursuing car veer violently to the left before collecting up an unfortunate rider on a battered old Vespa scooter, who happened to be in the wrong place at the wrong time. The rider landed square on the bonnet before rolling up over the top of the car and disappearing behind it, no doubt hitting the unforgiving ground hard . Lucie swerved, her full attention not focused on the road ahead, but the grim scene behind. The tardy old 125cc bike, the kind that Sam often scoffed at as being a *Chicken Chaser*, went spinning and tumbling down the road in a hail of sparks as the metal of the small engine found the tarmac, "My god," she shrieked, "That was my fault!"

Their pursuer was almost level with the rear driver's side window. With both engines screaming, the two vehicles careered down a short slope and into the Blackwall Tunnel, disappearing under the Thames.

"Slow down a little," instructed Oriyanna, climbing into the rear seat. Thankfully, the tunnel's lights were on, bathing the car in an artificial orange glow. Lucie did as Oriyanna instructed; there was no time for questions,.

The car drew closer, the front passenger window drawing level with the rear seat of Lucie's Mini. Before Oriyanna could put her plan into play, the pursuing driver twisted the steering wheel to the left, colliding with the rear quarter panel of the Mini. Oriyanna heard Lucie shrieking, over the sickening sound of metal hitting metal and the Mini begin to swerve uncontrollably down the road. The rear tyre hit the high kerb, sending them in the other direction, and the car lost purchase on the road. Lucie frantically threw the wheel towards the left, then right, in a futile attempt to gain control. Oriyanna glanced out the shattered rear window, saw the pursuing car brake suddenly and it ducked in behind them, narrowly avoiding a collision with the rear of a 4x4. It was now or never. Trying to account for the weaving of the Mini, Oriyanna got into position, rested her arms on the parcel shelf and fired, squeezing off round after round until the clip ran dry. The bullets left the gun and slammed through the front windscreen of the chasing car, which she could now recognize was a BMW. There was no time to tell if the shots had found their target, because the mini slid sideways, past the point of recovery. She twisted into the rear seat and rammed her feet against the opposite side of the car, jamming herself in. Over the sound of the chirping tyres, which echoed and bounced off the tunnel walls, she heard Lucie scream. The mini smashed up over the kerb, hit the tunnel wall and flipped. The wall prevented them from slipping into an unforgiving tumble, instead the car slid down the road on its side, metal screaming against the tarmac. As the car lost speed, it eventually tipped onto its roof, where it stopped, rocking back and forth for a few seconds, steam pouring from the tortured engine. Releasing her legs, Oriyanna fell onto the roof.

Lucie was in the driver's seat, held upside down by her belt, her long brown ponytail swinging like a rope over her face. Reaching over, Oriyanna touched her on the head and instantly knew she was alive. There was no need to feel for a pulse, she could feel her life force. There was no blood on her pale blue sweater, or on her legs beneath the line of her pencil skirt.

Leaving her wedged where she was, Oriyanna wriggled out of the rear window, splinters of glass biting at her legs and catching in her hair. The pursuing car had also crashed, though not as spectacularly as they had; it had front ended the tunnel wall and pirouetted a few times, leaving a series of rubber, snake-like marks dancing along the road. Small splinters of the tunnel's wall tiles were embedded in the grill, the BMW badge hung precariously from the bonnet, cracked and broken. Studying the car briefly, Oriyanna noticed there was a nice, head-shaped bulge protruding from the anti-shatter windscreen – it seemed whoever was behind the wheel had failed to secure their seat-belt. Very close to the mound of head-shaped glass were bullet holes, sporadically peppering the spider-webbed windscreen. Oriyanna covered the fifty yards fast, surveying the immediate area she saw the 4x4, which had skidded and stopped a hundred yards or so back down the tunnel. The occupants, a young man and a woman, were both out of the car and gawping down the tunnel toward them, taking in the scene of utter chaos. Sensibly, they had chosen not to approach. Reaching the BMW, Oriyanna wrenched the driver's door open. The guy behind the wheel looked to be in his late thirties, blood was gushing from his head, but small wheezing groans escaped from his lips. His colleague had been on the receiving end of two bullets. He was dead; one shot had obliterated his left cheek, his eye socket collapsed and a gooey white mess leaking down onto his blue shirt. The second round hit his chest. She could see the exit wound, the bullet had passed cleanly through his body and the seat, before disappearing into the rear backrest. Oriyanna unclipped the driver and pulled him free of the seat, placing her hand on his head, she found it sticky with blood.

She closed her eyes and concentrated; once inside his head she poked about in his mind for a few seconds before releasing him. "Earth-Breed," she muttered to herself. There was no time to learn more, or find out if these men were part of the team she'd already encountered tonight. She positioned her hands in a cross position on either side of his face, and twisting her arms quickly she snapped his neck in one swift movement. From somewhere down the tunnel she heard a horrified shriek – the couple in the 4x4 had obviously seen her kill the guy. Leaving the body, she ran toward them, only too aware that she still had Lucie to deal with. "He was dying," she called out as she approached them. "I had no choice, he was in a lot of pain!"

The male was well built, and as she approached he must have decided Oriyanna posed no threat due to her small stature – a major underestimation on his part. He stood his ground, glowering at Oriyanna as she rushed toward him. "I think you—"

He never got a chance to finish the sentence. Oriyanna drew her Glock on him, reached up and grabbed him by the throat with far more strength than should have been possible for a girl of her size. The man let out a surprised cry of fear as she slammed him against the side of his car. This wasn't her usual style, but time was short and they needed some new wheels.

"Don't move!" she shouted, pinning him against the driver's door and fixing the gun to his forehead. The woman had already clambered inside the 4x4 and she started screaming; thankfully the door was closed, muffling her cries. With her hand on his neck and the gun pointed in the general direction of his brains, Oriyanna stared directly into his eyes. The moment she had him, she let the gun fall to her side. She hated showing aggression to innocents like this, but she was in a pinch and needed to get things resolved, swiftly. Fixed on her deep blue eyes, the male was lost. Oriyanna filtered through his thoughts, his fear, and she hated herself for it. *I am not going to hurt you,* she spoke inside his head. *Just walk away, leave the car, it's okay to leave me the car, just give me the keys and walk away.* She released her grip.

The guy snapped back into full consciousness, opened the car door, took the keys from the ignition and handed them over.

"Mike! What the fuck are you doing?" screamed the woman, a red-headed girl in her late twenties, with freckles bridging her nose. Oriyanna captured her attention and smiled, and the woman fell to her gaze as easily as the guy had. A second later, she opened the car door and got out, silently making her way to the back of the car to join her boyfriend. The pair held hands and walked away as if they were out for a Sunday stroll.

It seemed she'd left Lucie alone in the car for ages; in reality, it had been no more than a couple of minutes. Time was short and any moment the authorities would be here, and they needed to be far away before that happened. Firing the engine, she sighed with relief to discover the 4x4 was automatic; she'd driven manual Earth vehicles before, but felt much more at home with what she liked to think of as a 'push and go'. Once back at the stricken Mini she parked the white 4x4 next to it, jumped out and forced Lucie's door open. Adam's sister was still out for the count, her breathing deeper, more rhythmic. Oriyanna unclipped the belt and slid her out of the car, lifting Lucie's slight frame easily into the other vehicle and laying her on the back seat. Checking the clock on the dash she knew they'd have plenty of time to make Wiltshire before curfew. Ignoring the fact she was driving the wrong way through the tunnel, Oriyanna spun the 4x4 around, and sped away from the scene. Not far down the tunnel they passed the couple she'd just carjacked. Amazingly, they offered her a polite wave as she drove by, which made her smile. Earth-Humans were easily influenced; she suspected they really needed to evolve and unlock the rest of their brain power.

As she drove the Nissan Juke out of the tunnel and into the night, next to what had once been known as the Millennium Dome and more recently the O2, Oriyanna bounced the large tyres over the kerb and onto the correct side of the road. She didn't know exactly how to get to the meeting place, but she knew the general direction and that was good enough for now. Reaching the A2, she saw blue lights heading for the tunnel; no doubt on their way to deal with the mess left behind by the brief battle that had taken place under the Thames – the second mess she'd left in her wake in under an hour.

Ten minutes later, with Lucie still out for the count on the back seat, Oriyanna swung the 4x4 into a petrol station, jumped out and looked at the array of different fuels on offer in confusion. Many of the pumps had 'Out of Use' signs on them. In frustration, she took a cursory glance at the back seat, willing Lucie back into consciousness. Not sure which fuel to choose, she popped the filler cap, relieved to discover a small red sticker on the back of the cover which said 'Diesel' . Two of the pumps displayed the same word on an identical red background. Not stopping to consider further, she jammed the nozzle into the opening and began to brim the tank, thankful that this station actually had a couple of working pumps. Tapping her foot impatiently, she watched the litres roll by, painfully slowly. The six euro a litre price tag didn't bother her in the least, she had no means to pay and as soon as the pump clicked off she fitted the filler cap, jumped into the driver's seat and sped off the forecourt, the wheels spinning. A few minutes later she reached the motorway, and being completely unfamiliar with the layout of the multitude of roads which criss-crossed every country on Earth, she relied on her sense of direction and turned right, heading west. Racing across the darkened countryside, London slipped further away in the distance. She lost count of the number of times she glanced over her shoulder at Lucie; despite everything that lay ahead, she experienced a pang of excitement at the thought of seeing Adam again. Even though her life had spanned many years, more years than even the oldest person on Earth could fathom, the last two and a half Earth years seemed such a long time ago. Her mind wandered back to the day he'd left. She'd wanted to go with him, take the trip back to Earth by his side, but there had been more pressing matters at home which required her immediate attention. Craft were being despatched for the invasion of Sheol daily, and the council had no intention of letting her take a trip back to the planet she'd almost lost her life trying to defend.

It had been a glorious sunny day when the two men had left. In all, they'd spent two Earth weeks on Arkkadia, and she'd hugged Adam and planted a kiss on his lips before they parted, unable to hide the tears welling up in her ancient blue eyes as the door to the scout craft silently slid closed. They'd maintained eye contact for as long as possible, but eventually all she could see was a gleaming ship's hull. As silently as the door had shut, the craft rose into the air – at approximately a thousand feet it had hung for a few long, drawn out seconds, Oriyanna straining her eyes as sunlight glinted off the bright silver craft. Then in an instant, it shot up, far faster than her eyes could track. He was gone.

Three Arkkadian days later, she was saying goodbye to her home once again, bound for Sheol. The fight had already begun, craft were on their way within hours of her coming through the Tabut, keen to strike hard and fast, leaving little chance of anyone escaping the miserable place. By the time she arrived the battle was almost done, only a few strongholds set deep into the planet's ninth level were proving difficult to take. Intelligence from the surface was grim; while many of the Elders had been captured and flown back to Arkkadia to face trial and probable execution, they believed the one they most wanted was gone, cowardly fleeing the planet even before the first strike vessels had arrived in orbit. A day or so later, she'd been on the Sheolian surface, heading deep into the bowels of the former mining outpost. Arkkadian troops had finally broken through and captured the last subterranean territory. Once every person had been accounted for, they were two Elders short, and more who had been created in the years since the Great War could also have fled. Just as they feared, Asmodeous was among the missing. It didn't surprise her or the council; he'd fled Earth just as quickly when his cities began to fall. He obviously valued his own self-preservation far above that of his misguided followers. What also struck her as odd was the craft he'd used; Arkus 2 was a long-range exploration vessel, and it had been under Asmodeous' command before the Great War. The ship was vast and could easily have offered passage to many people, but he'd fled with just a handful – proof positive of his selfish, narcissistic nature.

Once Sheol was back under the command of the Arkkadian Council, Oriyanna had been recalled. It had been a relief to leave the sun-baked planet. Sitting around two million miles closer to its large sun than Arkkadia did to hers, Sheol was a sweltering place. Despite the terraforming carried out thousands of years before, the atmosphere was hot and carried the faintest egg-tainted hint of sulphur. Below the surface things weren't much better, the purified air nasty, and almost suffocating to breath.

They had scanned the vastness of space fruitlessly, looking for the smallest trace of the vessel Asmodeous had taken. It was a pointless task, even if they'd only been a few hundred miles away from it, the Arkus 2 would be nearly impossible to detect. Plans had been found on the planet's surface which suggested any identifiable transponders aboard the ship had been disabled and replaced with jammers, making it virtually impossible to find. Even with their advanced radar and scanning systems, the situation was hopeless. It didn't stop them from trying, however.

As the weeks ticked by, it was increasingly apparent that their most wanted prize had slipped through their fingers once again. Soon after, Oriyanna approached the council, suggesting he might take refuge in the one place he longed for most – Earth. Oriyanna requested she be sent back to the planet with a small team, a team which could fly under the radar and search for signs that Asmodeous had indeed returned to Earth. The council had been reluctant to let her go, fearing her feelings for Adam would get in the way of more important tasks. Oriyanna countered that being the only Arkkadian who'd spent valuable time on Earth's surface during the modern age made her the best choice to undertake the mission. Even those who'd been in place before the four

Watchers Finch killed held little knowledge of modern living. Sadly, the ones who would have been best placed to carry out such a mission were mere names on a memorial plaque in the council's chamber, the only Watchers ever killed in the line of duty.

Shortly afterwards, Oriyanna, along with three other Elders and former Watchers from the council, found themselves Earth bound, with Oriyanna receiving explicit instructions not to contact Adam or try to see him. There was a job to do, and with no clue as to how many Earth-Breeds still languished on the planet, they were given two tasks. Firstly, to establish if Asmodeous was on Earth, and secondly, find a way to track and kill as many of the enemy Earth-Breed as possible.

On their arrival, they'd set up what Earth's security services would classify as an intelligence cell. As Earth began to find its pulse once again, they combed through the accounts of Integra Investments, identifying exactly who was on the payroll. Information on the Earth-based business had been recovered, along with a wealth of other information held on Sheol. Not coincidentally, she found herself based in London, in the borough of Greenwich, just a few temptingly close miles from Adam's home. Although she hated herself for the decision, it had been her idea to use Sam as the tool to dispose of any Earth-Breeds they uncovered. None of her team had spent any modern time on the planet, and what little time she'd spent had hardly given her enough experience to fit in. It would be an almost impossible task to blend in, and they couldn't risk the exposure if things went wrong. Sam had proven himself extremely handy in such situations and in possession of the Gift, his chances of suffering a fatal wound were greatly reduced. She'd been wracked with guilt on the day they'd delivered the first target's details to him. From a short distance away, they'd monitored the house, and just as she knew he would, Sam went to work. The recompense for such a risky job had been large sums of money, which she deposited as payment for every kill, gleaned from the wealth built up over the long years the Watchers had been present on Earth. She didn't like what they were making Sam do, and the only way she could quash some of that guilt was to ensure the three of them

– Sam, Adam and his sister, Lucie – lived through these testing times as comfortably as possible.

Over the next few months, she'd watched Lucie open her small bar,. She'd seen Adam a few times, but always and painfully from afar. Despite her longing to speak to him, she respected her orders and concentrated on the task in hand.

Then in the last six months, her cell began to pick up intelligence confirming their worst fears. Several Earth-Breeds they'd been tracking began to head to South America, taking various routes to the large continent, but it was a trend that reeked of something more sinister. There was a wealth of ancient cities which had been under Arkkadian supervision in that area during the old days, the days when they'd first returned to Earth. There were only a handful of places that fell under Asmodeous' rule, however. They'd waited patiently, wanting to gain the maximum amount of information possible before putting any plans into action – a plan that had fallen short during the last few hours. Now with five minutes to catch her breath, Oriyanna took painful stock of what had happened at their London base not an hour ago, and marvelled at how easily things could go wrong.

* * *

The house in Greenwich which had been Oriyanna's home for almost two years was a modest-sized four-bedroom property. It was one of several places owned by Euri Peterson, while he'd been alive and operating as a Watcher. The London residence had been vacant for nearly thirty months. Luckily, it had remained squatter free, and apart from needing a little dusting and airing, the place was in good shape. More than comfortable enough to house the small team which consisted of Oriyanna and three former male Watchers, who'd lived on Earth during the early years of the industrial revolution and through to the mid-twentieth century.

Rhesbon was a sturdy-looking man of broad build, with short cropped blonde hair. Bliegh was small and slight, the polar opposite of Rhesbon and the kind of person you'd pass in the street and forget within a few seconds. Taulass had the appearance of a young, dark-haired professional, despite his true age being closer to five hundred Earth years. Put together at a dinner table, the small quartet of Arkkadians would have seemed a little odd, not the kind of people you'd expect to see socialising together, but individually, there was nothing exceptionally memorable about any of them, other than Oriyanna who'd caught more than a few Earth-Human males glancing in her direction while out in public. Although all three were way out of touch with modern day society, they were far better placed to blend in than anyone else on the council.

Each of the team had a special element they brought to the mission. Taulass was very tech-savvy, despite having been absent from Earth for almost a hundred years, he'd kept himself appraised of man's developments, studying information fed back to him by those who'd followed in his footsteps. Rhesbon and Bleigh, whilst earning their spot on the team due to their previous service, were there as much for their fighting ability and physical presence as anything else. Although Bleigh was slight and unassuming, he was fast, and during his time on Earth he'd studied many variations of the martial arts. It was Oriyanna's place to oversee the team; as one of the oldest Elders on the council she had lived for longer than all three of her team mates put together.

Oriyanna had been carrying out an algorithmic style name and account number search of people they'd found to be on Integra Investments' payroll, comparing them against airline bookings and passenger lists, when she glanced away from the screen of the Apple Mac, to watch the TV broadcast with a troubled expression. U.S. President Hill was addressing a crowd of eager reporters in the press room at the White House; to Oriyanna, they looked like a hungry pack of hounds who'd just been shown the fox. Oriyanna studied the President's face, he looked as if he hadn't slept in days, and she was sure his normally dark hair had taken on some fresh grey. Usually a handsome man, his tired face seemed to be sporting a few extra deep lines across the fore-

S T Boston

head, making him look much older than his fifty odd years. His hands were tightly clutching the side of a lectern that sported the White House logo, drawing his gaze from the lights that were fixing him to the stage, he glanced down at whatever speech had been prepared for him by his people, swallowed hard and began to talk.

"Yesterday, the British Prime Minister and other European heads of states, as well as myself, were in talks with President Balashov, looking to resolve the stranglehold Russia is placing on oil supplies to the west. As industrial and domestic life is gradually restored to normal, it's important for us to secure our future and unfortunately, that future means we need to secure a certain quota of oil and fossil fuel supplies, something we've been unable to do. As you know, the original goal to be rid of vehicular fossil fuel dependency inside of ten years suffered a setback after the solar flares and virus which took so many of our friends, loved ones and colleagues." President Hill paused for a moment as a mark of respect. Oriyanna watched him, transfixed, a worried expression on her face.

"As you know," President Hill continued, *"Russian reserves which are now being mined in Eastern Siberia, as well as the ones they control in the Arctic region, represent around seventy percent of the remaining reserves, so you'll appreciate just how important it is for us to strike a deal with President Balashov. Unfortunately, it would seem there is no deal to be had."* The camera panned around the room; a female reporter in the third row had her hand in the air, and the camera angle changed to take in both President Hill and the waiting journalist. *"Yes, Sally,"* said the president, pointing to her – she was obviously a White House press room regular.

"Are you looking at military options, sir?" she asked in a heavy southern accent.

"Today, Russian naval forces were activated in the Bering Sea, it would appear they're heading south, toward the Pacific. It isn't yet clear what their objective is, however, as you already know, we've mobilised our Pacific fleet to counter any threat." His face took on an even graver expression. *"I suspect Russia is pre-empting some kind of action by us for their decision. While we do need to find an answer to this situation, I*

want to assure the American people as well as the people of the world that I have absolutely no intention of going down that route. We, as a race, have suffered enough over the last two and a half years."

"*If that is the case, Mr. President,*" came a voice from the back, and the camera swung around quickly, searching for the heckler, "*then why are you intending on bringing our nuclear defence systems and strike capability back online inside the next forty-eight hours?*" The camera's operator found the owner of the voice. A guy in a cheap suit stood at the back of the room, he had a small digital recording device clutched in his hand and thrust it forward eagerly, getting it as close to the scrutinised president as possible.

"*These are uncertain times, we need to be able to defend this nation if necessary. As you well know, North Korea and China are on the brink of coming back online. Our sources indicate that Russia will have their systems back in the next twenty-four to forty-eight hours. If I hadn't followed suit, we'd have been left defenceless. Within that naval fleet currently steaming toward the Pacific there are three K-class cruiser subs and one B-class submarine; all four will have nuclear launch capabilities when their systems go online.*" There was no retort from the floor, just a pensive and frightened silence. Oriyanna wondered how John Remy would have handled this situation, but she admired President Hill for his brutal honesty. The fact that President Hill and President Balashov would have their fingers on the trigger in the next forty-eight hours didn't trouble her too much. Nor was she overly concerned about China or North Korea. Earth-Humans had been capable of wiping themselves off the face of the planet in a hail of nuclear fire for many years, and despite some very tense and close calls, they hadn't done it.

"Another match?" asked Rhesbon, as he walked into the room carrying a bottle of water. Oriyanna studied the screen intently.

"It is, but I suspect we won't need to worry too much about this one." She pointed at the screen as Rhesbon crouched beside her.

"Mathis Laurett," he said with interest. "I'm guessing he won't be making the flight.

"No, but this points toward the fact that Asmodeous is somewhere in South America. I'm concerned they're going to use this oil situation to their advantage." She added in a worried voice, "I told the council we needed more resources."

"We still don't know for sure."

"No, we don't," replied Oriyanna. "But we've been here for almost two years and for the majority of that time, we've been scratching around in the dirt. Over the last six months, we've seen a number of suspected Earth-Breed, who were getting hefty pay-outs from Integra when they had no real link to the company, migrating to South America. We don't know much about many of them, but one of the first we tracked, Benjamin Hawker, used to work in defence systems for the U.S. Government. This guy worries me. Now Laurett was planning to fly the nest, too." She pointed at the screen and thought of Sam, who would, as they spoke, be heading to France to execute Laurett. She switched screens, bringing up a map of southern England and northern France, locating a small red dot which sat half a mile off the French coast. It represented the modest-sized cabin cruiser they'd chartered for Sam to cross the channel. Prior to him arriving to collect it, Taulass had fitted a small GPS tracker to the vessel. She hoped the red dot would be on the move again soon, heading back toward Portsmouth. "It has to be Asmodeous," she insisted. "Why else would they all be heading that way?"

"I don't know," Rhesbon answered, as the door burst open.

Bliegh rushed in, his usually pale complexion flushed with panic. "We need to move, now!" he demanded, rushing to the screen Oriyanna was using. "They know where we are." He glanced at their confused faces, pushed Oriyanna to one side and sat down at the terminal.

"Okay, explain," she said, trying to stay calm.

"We have been running this program for the past eighteen months," Bliegh began, pointing at the screen. "Taulass upgraded it to search for travel patterns of those on our radar, so we could see who was travelling where and possibly associating with who."

"That's right," cut in Oriyanna. "Without it, we'd never have identified the travel pattern 'we've been seeing of late."

"I've been helping him to develop a program to hide our activities, but it would seem someone out there on the 'net is using a seeker-style program." He glanced at them both, looking from one confused face to the other. "Basically, there's a program on the 'net searching for a program that's running our kind of searches. As in, persons financially linked to Integra Investments and those who continued to be paid by their accounts, years after the business officially ceased trading. I'm guessing that after Sam took out a few of their own they got twitchy, and started looking for ways to uncover where the information was coming from. It must be a new program, as we have alerts built in to the system to detect this kind of thing."

"When did you find out?" quizzed Oriyanna, flicking the screen back to the red dot, which still flashed frustratingly, half a mile off the French coast.

"I wasn't sure until just now," Bliegh defended, his face locked in a scowl. "The lines of code are very subtle, once I smelt a rat it took some time to figure out just what it was; whoever wrote the program is good, they almost got around our counter measures. It could have been pinging us for a few hours, maybe longer, I just—"

"Grab what you need," Oriyanna cut in, getting to her feet. "Where is Taulass?"

"In bed, sleeping," answered Bliegh. "He was in front of that screen for ten hours straight earlier, he's likely fatigued."

"Wake him, we can brief him on the move, we don't—" Before she could finish telling Bliegh that there was no time to brief Taulass, a red dot appeared on his forehead. Glancing quickly at Rhesbon, she saw an identical dot decorating his head. She didn't need a mirror to know she also had one of her own. "Get down!" she screamed, hitting the deck. As she fell the sound of three high velocity rounds penetrating the glass sounded in the room. *Pizzinkk, pizzinkk, pizzinkk.* The round that had been intended for her slammed into an antique oil painting which hung over the ornate fireplace. Twisting as she fell, she was horrified to see that the other two rounds had found their intended targets. Bliegh and Rhesbon were slumped on the cream coloured carpet, bright red stains spreading out from the backs of their heads.

Staying low, she clawed her way to the door as another round slammed into one of the walls. She had to reach Taulass; there was a chance he was still alive, likely asleep and unaware. Then the automatic gunfire began, as if those in charge of the assault wanted to make sure the only thing coming out of the house was dead bodies. Burying her face in the carpet, teasingly close to the door to the entrance hall, Oriyanna covered her ears with her hands and clenched her teeth, waiting to feel the searing pain as the melee of slugs found her body. Through her covered ears, she heard glass smashing, as if every window in the building were being broken simultaneously. The air zinged with ricocheting bullets, but she still felt no pain. Filled with adrenalin she lifted her face, finding the acrid smell of gunpowder clogged the atmosphere. Staying lower to the floor than a snake's belly, she rolled through the door into the hall. This was an old house, the walls at its heart were solid brick, not plaster like some of the others which had been added years after it had been built. Downstairs, the rapid gunfire continued, unabated. Reaching the landing she stayed low, as the shooters turned their attentions to the first-floor windows. The odd round found its way through the door frame, or a post-renovation plasterboard wall. One came frighteningly close to her ear, the air displacement feeling like a light hand wafting over her blonde hair as it sped past. She could see Taulass' room, just a few feet away.

"T!" she screamed, opting to use the shortened version of his name she'd come up with. It wasn't a thing they did on Arkkadia, but it was an earth trait she liked and used, much to Taulass' annoyance. The gunfire stopped as abruptly as it'd begun, and what remained was an eerie silence, so quiet it seemed unnatural. Not wanting to risk being heard, Oriyanna scrambled to the door, reaching up to open it and sliding inside. The room was dark, but there was a street light just outside the window, still lit before curfew. It gave enough dim glow to see his body in the blood-soaked sheets. Panicked, she stripped them back, confirming the automatic fire had found him; the left side of his torso was a mess. The sound of the front door being broken down kick-started her into action. Replacing the covers, she bolted from the room and hurried to the back of the house, hating herself for being unable to check Taulass properly and confirm if he was alive or dead. Once in her room, she crouched below the sill and with a cautionary hand, slid the sash open. Not wanting to find herself in the sights of a sniper she risked a quick look, surveying the back garden. It seemed clear, but snipers weren't in the habit of advertising their positions.

"Two dead down here!" A male voice called, the accent confirming it was an Earth-Breed.

"What about the girl!" This voice didn't carry a local dialect, it was harsh, perhaps Eastern European.

"No sign yet, sir." The accomplice didn't sound quite so confident in his reply. "I had her in my sights, I'm not sure what happened."

"Find her!" the Eastern European voice snapped.

It was all Oriyanna needed to hear – taking her chances she slid the sash window open to its fullest extent, climbed out onto the ledge and stopped. Cursing herself for not thinking of it sooner, she quickly climbed back into the room and rushed to the dresser. Opening the top drawer, she removed the Glock semi-automatic hidden there. The sound of footsteps were literally outside her door when she climbed back out onto the ledge and pushed away. There was the briefest sensation of falling before her feet hit damp grass, sending a current of pain through her ankles. Ignoring it, she sprinted across the lawn, cursing her failure to close the window. Her escape route would be obvious to the intruders, still, what was it she'd heard Adam say once? *Beggars can't be choosers.* With the peculiar Earth idiom ringing in her mind, she reached the neighbour's wall and vaulted it swiftly, landing in a dishevelled-looking flowerbed. Hurrying to the side gate, she burst out onto a back road. The night was cold and she immediately regretted not grabbing a warmer jumper when she'd retrieved the gun. The thin, long-sleeved tee would have to do; at least it was black. What mattered most was the gun she'd retrieved from her drawer. It might save her, and in the meantime, she could put up with a little cold.

Heading away from the house, she finally reached the main road. If they'd located Oriyanna's hideout so easily, it wasn't a stretch to believe they knew Sam, Lucie and Adam's whereabouts. The two boys were well out of Oriyanna's reach, but Lucie would be at work in her bar. She had no way to warn the men, but she could reach Adam's sister and in turn, Lucie might be able to contact Adam,. Having made the short trip on several occasions to check on them covertly and deliver kill packages to Sam, she knew exactly where to go. Lucie's bar was no more than five miles away; only a few minutes' drive on the quiet roads. The VW Golf they'd hired was waiting in a side street, a minute's jog away from the house. It was locked of course, and the key was back in the kitchen, but hidden a spare inside the car for emergencies. Oriyanna rammed an elbow through the driver's window. The sound of breaking glass seemed far too loud in the quiet street, and she could hear sirens from not too far away, yet another good reason to clear the area. Climbing into the driver's seat she snatched the spare keys from beneath the passenger side floor mat. Gunning the engine, she slammed the car into drive and hit the accelerator, leaving the nightmare behind her, but knowing in her heart she was likely heading straight into another.

* * *

Behind the wheel of the Juke, speeding away from London and heading toward the next nightmare, Oriyanna tried in vain to push the sight of her fallen colleagues to the back of her mind. Her long years had helped her grow stronger, almost detached from certain situations, but here, as good as alone in this car as it sped down a dark road, a single tear broke free of her right eye and streaked down her cheek.

Chapter 12

Benjamin Hawker had once worked for DARPA, the Defence Advanced Research Projects Agency. It was a US program, designed for researching projects which aided in the technological advancement of the country's military. Now, however, he found himself sitting at the main console on the bridge of a spacecraft named Arkus 2, named after the sun that feeds its warmth and light to Arkkadia. He rubbed his hazel eyes and returned his focus to the holographic screen in front of him. The plug-in he'd helped develop over the last two months was working, and currently worming its way through a back door into Kwangmyŏngsŏng, the North Korean nuclear launch and defence system, named after the failed satellite the country had attempted to launch back in 2012. The satellite's launch had been a smoke screen for the secretive nation, to test its first long range nuclear weapon, a ploy that hadn't been lost on the United States and other NATO countries. In the years following, and during the run up to the events which had seen his creators and masters fail in their attempts to wipe mankind off the Earth, the country had continued to develop its program, albeit behind closed doors and hidden from the suspicious eyes and prying satellites of the western world. Then in the year before President John Remy met his demise in a Malaysian hotel room, the secretive country had carried out another supposed test launch, only this time, there was no smoke and mirrors act. Kwangmyŏngsŏng 4 had carried with it a nuclear defence satellite, a long-range detection machine capable of spotting any threat from the point of launch and retaliating with the states' own small, yet lethal, stockpile. Much to the disgust of the western world and despite several urgent meetings held by the world's superpowers, the country had refused to halt its program, arguing that it had as much right to the deadly power as any other nation. Although on paper and as far as anyone was concerned, Benjamin Hawker was a patriotic American doing his bit for the country he loved, he agreed with North Korea, and relished watching the pathetic squabbling between those he hated and ultimately hoped to see destroyed. He held no allegiance to any country, only his own kind.

For the past two and a half years, Kwangmyŏngsŏng 4 had been dormant, keeping to a perpetual orbit around the planet among all the other bits of junk which had been fired into orbit over the years. As its parent program was readied for action once again, Ben found himself watching every step its programmers took, completely unknown to them. As well as Kwangmyŏngsŏng, his programming work of art – nicknamed Enola – monitored the US defence and launch systems, the Russian equivalent and those of the United Kingdom, as well as China and the other two NPT (Non-Proliferation of Nuclear Weapons Treaty), nations. North Korea wasn't party to this group, but they had the tools he needed to use. Once they all came online, he'd have more power at his fingertips than any Earth-Human had ever known. The thought sent a chill of excitement through his body. At his command, he could set every nuclear bird free from its nest and heading for a target of his choice.

Of course, this wasn't ideal. Obviously, the ideal scenario would have seen the Reaper do its job and kill over ninety-nine-point nine percent of the population, leaving Earth virtually wiped clean of Earth-Humans. Even the best laid plans sometimes failed, and so it had been with the Reaper. But this was no longer about preserving the Earth, now it was about wiping out a genetic mistake, one which never should have existed.

For two years, he'd been forced to live in the broken world that was left, living with Earth-Humans, and in the early days, often going hungry or needing to fight for food. Thankfully, his masters and creators hadn't forgotten him. Six months ago, just when he thought all hope was lost and they'd surely been destroyed and wiped from Sheol, he'd been contacted by Asag, one of the few Elders who escaped the war-torn planet. From him, Benjamin had learned that Asmodeous was alive. And not only alive, but on Earth. For the next two nights he'd been unable to sleep, excitement over what this might mean for him running through his head constantly. He'd waited patiently for his next instructions, laying low and only too aware that numerous of his kind had been located and killed, discovered by those who'd been responsible for the virus's failure. He'd finally received instructions and a ticket buying him passage to Ecuador, and from there he'd travelled by land for two days, meeting with Asag and his brother, Namtar in Lima, Peru. From Lima he'd been transported into the Peruvian desert where Arkus 2 had appeared before him like a shimmering mirage, temporarily de-cloaked in all her glory.

During his conditioning and education in Allentown, he'd seen pictures and images of the craft his superiors had at their disposal, but nothing could have prepared him for the real thing. The ship was colossal, almost a mile long and half as wide at the stern. The craft dwarfed him like a New York skyscraper, one laid on its side that is. Its shiny onyx-like black hull glinted in the sunlight, making it almost impossible to look at directly. The craft held the appearance of a massive triangle, only chopped off at the tip and resembling a strangely shaped, angular bullet. The top of the behemoth was gently rounded, just enough to stop it from seeming like a flat wedge, and the front, which was raised clear of the ground, hung out over the sweltering desert like a canopy. At the rear, Ben could see no propulsion system; the flawless surface ran toward the aft where it ended in a wall of shimmering black, looming some six hundred feet into the hot, unforgiving desert sky. In stunned wonder, Benjamin walked the length of the craft, sometimes, close to the rear of the ship, where the hull still met the ground, he enjoyed running his hand along the smooth, metallic surface, wishing he could connect with the spacecraft and see where she'd travelled in her long, long life. Standing where he assumed the bridge would be, the sun's relentless heat was blocked out, leaving him in a vast patch of shade. Craning his neck, Ben tried to study the bridge area, suspended a few hundred feet above his head.

For the past six months, Arkus 2 had been his home. Ben had spent hours wandering the craft's endless corridors and exploring her common rooms and quarters. In her day, Arkus 2 had been a long-range exploration vessel, designed to accommodate a crew of two thousand for an indefinite period. She had her own ecosystem, which in her operational days was capable of growing fresh plant life for food as well as sustaining a continual cycle of livestock. In essence, she was her own city, and a man could live out his life aboard her and never need to set foot on Earth, or any other planet. It was aboard this craft where Ben finally met his master, Asmodeous.

Ben had a thousand questions in his head during those first months, but he'd waited patiently for Asmodeous and the Elders who'd escaped the planet to divulge their plan, for he feared them just as much as he respected them. One evening in June, they'd gathered in one of the craft's massive auditoriums, and here what needed to be done was explained to them. Not every Earth-Breed had been selected – only a finite number who were integral to the plan had been chosen. Much to his excitement, Ben, a computer and defence system specialist had become an integral, no – a vital part of the plan. Working with him on the project was Michael Braun, an unassuming, almost geeky-looking Earth-Breed of German nationality, who had a flare for systems hacking. His thick-rimmed black glasses made him look like a young Woody Allen.

During the past five months, Ben had been hard at work, learning the advanced computer systems aboard Arkus 2. Although cutting-edge, they had one thing in common with Earth's computer systems – the language of mathematics. It was universal, and in no time, he could navigate the ship's system as easily as he'd worked with other systems in the past. From there, he'd developed the plug-ins which saw Arkus 2's computers become capable of working alongside Earth's. His first upgrade had made the ship compatible with the internet; although nothing like the animal it used to be, the web was still a useful tool to have and ultimately, the key to getting into the defence systems he needed to breach. Alongside this task, he and Braun had been asked to look at just how his Earth-Breed brethren were being traced and killed.

Navigating the web and searching under the names of Adam Fisher and Samuel Becker they had soon found 'Watchers', the book penned by Adam Fisher. It detailed just how the Earth-Humans had helped Oriyanna and aided her in thwarting the virus. It was a book Asmodeous and the Elders had studied with interest. The book got them no closer to tracking down Fisher and Becker, although it led them to believe the pair lived in the United Kingdom, somewhere in London. Fisher had been careful not to reveal too much about their location, obviously aware that people might be looking for them.

He was right, and it took more digging to locate their details, but as the 'net became increasingly functional, more and more personal information became available once again. To a systems expert such as Hawker, it had been a synch to eventually locate Fisher and Becker and place a watch over them, while they waited for the final part of the plan to fall into place. They'd also discovered it was Sam Becker targeting the Earth-Breeds who remained in hiding. Asmodeous issued orders that neither Fisher nor Becker be touched – he'd suspected a bigger player was behind the targets identification and selection and he'd left it to play out, in the hope that they could snare the bigger fish simultaneously.

Many weeks went by with the team having no luck in figuring out just how Samuel Becker was selecting his targets, but then they'd reached a breakthrough. A program Ben developed which kept an eye on people poking around in the old business files of Integra Investments had found a search program running, one that reported every payment made from the company's still active accounts, as well as old ones made before the virus. Although the originator's IP address was being bounced around the web like a rubber ball, the systems on Arkus 2 had easily traced the culprit, her advanced computer systems making it easy work to get through even the toughest of firewalls, a benefit that would also come in handy for Enola. With technical stealth he'd poked around the host computer and planted his own little bug, one which reported everything back to him and automatically copied all the system's files to his, including every update and saved file. From a distance they'd watched, waited and monitored their folly, completely unseen and hidden. The bug had found the files about Mathis Laurett and his pending appointment with Sam Becker. It gave them a time, date and location when Becker would be alone, vulnerable and easy to grab. In turn, it cemented the date on which they'd take them all. Becker, Adam Fisher and his sister, Lucie, would all be snatched at once, much the same as they'd killed the four Watchers at the World Summit.

A small team who'd been sent to London to survey the location of the host IP address sent photo files back which filled Asmodeous with rage. Four Arkkadian Elders were on Earth, operating out of an intelligence-style cell in Greenwich, London, and among them was Oriyanna. Ben's master didn't want them taken alive, he wanted them dead, out of the equation for good. A strike team would hit them simultaneously with the capture of Becker, Fisher and his sister; that way, no one had a chance to warn anyone. Once the Earth-Humans arrived on board, they would watch as Asmodeous poisoned the world, reducing its cities to nuclear dust and leaving enough radiation in the air to kill every living thing on Earth. After that, Ben suspected his master would end them himself, dole out death on a more personal level.

Once these tasks were complete, Ben and the other Earth-Breed would be given passage on Arkus 2, the opportunity to spend a lifetime travelling deeper into the universe than anyone had ever been, searching for other rare jewels of life where they might settle. The prospect filled him with nervous excitement as he imagined what wonders he would witness.

"Benjamin!" the exotic and steely voice snatched him from his daydream. "Ben, do we have any news?"

A hand clamped down onto his shoulder, twisting him in his seat, and Asmodeous' amber eyes fixed his with an expectant anticipation. Hawker's bowels dropped and he immediately needed the toilet, but he respected his master in a fearful manner, only too aware of his power and authority. "Sir," he began, clearing his throat. "From what I'm seeing, North Korea will be the first to the table, I'd say within the next twenty-four hours. The Americans are balls out trying to catch up, they have several bugs in the system preventing them from going live; same for the Russians." Ben stuck his hand into the holographic display and swiped it left, then from the bottom he pulled up a second screen which displayed a hacked satellite feed. "The Americans have been monitoring the North Korean silo closely." He pointed to a slightly grainy image, his finger disappearing into the picture. "They're reaching a state of readiness, sir."

"Let me know as soon as their systems are live," purred Asmodeous. He seemed to ooze confidence and physical presence in a way Ben had never seen in anyone else. He was dressed in Earth-Human attire, an expensive grey suit which bore a trouser crease so sharp, Ben suspected you might cut yourself on it. The black shirt beneath his matching blazer was secured to the top button and contrasted against his sandy blonde hair. "I think a little test of your abilities might be in order." He smiled and stepped back from the terminal. "And who knows, it might just set things in motion a little sooner than we expected. While I long to push the button myself, I would take a certain sense of enjoyment out of seeing the maggots destroy themselves. Proof positive they should never have been entrusted to live on this planet."

"Of course, sir." Despite his nerves, Ben relished working this close to the action. He brushed an imaginary speck of dirt from his GAP hoody, then straightened out his 501s.

"Also, have someone see if we can get any news from the field," Asmodeous continued. "I want to know as soon as we have everyone in custody and the four kills have been confirmed."

* * *

The acrid smell of gun smoke and hot metal clung to the air like an invisible fog. Nicolai Peltz, enjoyed the aroma; it was the scent of battle and death. His black Magnum tactical boots crunched across the countless shards of broken glass which littered the lounge room carpet. Crouching down, he studied the bullet-ridden bodies of Bliegh and Rhesbon, saw the multitude of hits they'd taken. The two that counted were the ones the M40A1 sniper rifle had inflicted. The pair had sizable head wounds, the rounds penetrating deep into their skulls and ending their long lives in a blink of the eye. Fresh blood still leaked from the wounds, dripping into the thick carpet which soaked it up hungrily. Peltz kicked a lump of shattered plasterboard out of the way and adjusted the belt on his black combat trousers. With the tactical boots and combat trousers he wore a tight black tee-shirt, a tactical vest zipped over the top and he knew he looked mean and purposeful. On the vest he carried some of his favourite tools, including a Glock G26 9mm handgun. The semi-automatic weapon was one of his personal preferences; at a mere 19 ounces, it was as light as it was deadly. Accompanying the Glock was a M26C Taser with four cartridges, for those occasions when he might need to take a subject alive. "What's the situation upstairs?" he called out sternly. His Eastern European accent added to the air of authority, and he liked it.

"One body in bed upstairs," the soft southern US drawl of Jim Croaker drifted down the stairs, another member of his little team and his second-in-command. His feet drummed rhythmically down the stairs, followed by the third member of the assault team, Drew Richards. Both men were of impressive stature, toned and not one of them under six feet tall, with close, buzzed haircuts. Their matching attire gave them the appearance of a private army, and in truth, that's exactly what they were.

"Looks like he took a right peppering," Richards said, a morbid smile on his face. Proudly, he flicked his phone's screen to life and present Peltz with a gruesome picture. Blood splattered the length of Taulass' body, the bullets seemed to have hit him in the legs first and then worked in a wave up his body.

"Is there a head wound?" asked Peltz, his voice completely unaffected by the image before him.

"Hard to tell," said Croaker, a vein of uncertainty in his voice. "There was so much blood."

"I'll check on him in a bit," said Peltz. "We can't leave anything to chance."

Peltz had been on the clean-up team sent to take out Xavier, and although not in charge of that team, he'd been party to the cluster-fuck. He would have staked his life on the fact the Arkkadian was hiding in the panic room, and as such, he'd used a large amount of plastic explosive to take care of the matter. For years, he'd believed they'd killed the Watcher in that house, but thanks to the account written by Adam Fisher, it seemed he and the crew he'd been with had failed. Fury had eaten at him for days after reading that Xavier escaped the property before they'd even destroyed it, and not only that, but he'd gone on and made it all the way to the Pyramid, playing a part in stopping the virus. Peltz was sure that once his master had seen this evidence, Peltz would be killed. Instead, he'd gotten a second chance, a chance he wasn't intending to throw away. "And the girl – Oriyanna?" His voice was heavy with expectation.

"No sign of her," Croaker replied, his soft southern drawl wavering a little.

"Then, as it stands," smouldered Peltz, "this mission is a fucking failure!" His usual stone-cold grey eyes smouldered with rage. "When morning comes and we make contact with the boss, what am I supposed to tell him?" His eyes worked methodically back and forth, flicking from one man to the next.

"I had her in my sights!" Richards protested. "I'm sure she was hit."

"Well, evidently *fucking* not," Peltz screamed. Richards offered no reply, although his mouth opened and closed a few times, as if he was trying to decide what to say. "What room is the third body in?"

"Straight up the stairs, first on your right," Richards answered, trying to sound helpful. The distant sound of sirens was drawing closer.

"Okay, I'll check it out," sighed Peltz. "We don't have much time, and we still have one outstanding target to find." Police attendance didn't really bother him, but it would make the situation messier. Peltz thumped his way up to the top of the stairs, careful not to pick up a splinter from the shattered bannister which had been peppered with automatic rifle fire.

The bedroom door was open, but he pushed it further back against the hinges, clicking the bedroom light on. He looked expectantly toward the bed. The grey duvet was soaked in crimson, as were the pillows and the sheets, but much to his horror, the bed was empty.

* * *

Lying on his side in the pitch-black roof space above his room, Taulass gripped at his shredded flesh in silent agony, gritting his teeth to stifle the cries which longed to escape. Just six feet below where he lay, he'd heard one of the men storm into his room. This was the third such visitor. The first two had rushed in to check the small bedroom and stood by his side, staring down at his bullet ridden body. Taulass had waited, played dead, certain one of them would discharge a round into his skull to be certain. Thankfully, their lack of attention to detail, and the sheer amount of blood on his face had seen them leave, believing him dead. In those vital few minutes Taulass had managed to roll his pain-soaked but already repairing body out of the bed and with nothing other than a strong urge to survive driving him on, he'd reached up and dislodged the small square access hatch located in the roof of his room. Standing on the antique oak desk he'd found the strength to haul himself up and into the small cavity between the ceiling and the grey slate roof, managing to wipe away a tell-tale print of blood he'd left on the rim of the hatch. Thankfully the carpet in his room was black, and hid any blood which dripped from his body as he'd crossed the room. Sliding the hatch silently back into place he rolled onto his side, wrapped his arms around his bleeding torso and lay there, shaking with pain.

The person below, the one intruding in his private quarters, was taking an age to leave, obviously fixated by the perplexing image of an empty bed, where not two minutes previously what he'd believed to be a corpse had lain. Unfortunately for Taulass, the perpetrator would understand the reasoning for his sudden resurrection. Where any normal Earth-Human would be running from the house in fear of a zombie attack, this one knew the truth. Despite suffering enough bullet wounds to kill the strongest of men, the head shot which was needed to dispatch an Elder had been missed. A clean heart shot would also have proven slowly fatal, but Taulass was confident the vital organ had been missed.

Just a few feet below his position he heard footsteps pacing the room, a cupboard being flung open, sounding as if it were done in a fit of rage rather than the need to search. Then the sound of his bed being upturned echoed up from below. Closing his eyes, Taulass prayed the intruder wouldn't look toward the ceiling and see the hatch, which would undoubtedly give away his hiding position. After the sound of the bed tipping over, an unearthly scream of frustration was followed by the sound of heavy feet stamping out of the room, onto the landing and down the stairs. In the distance, the wail of sirens drew closer; a neighbour had obviously heard the ruckus and called the authorities. Taulass hoped those responsible would be well clear of the house before their arrival. He had no doubt that if they were still at the scene, they'd dispatch the attending police officers and paramedics with no more regard than a person might swat a pesky fly. Rolling onto his back and trying to find a comfortable position, his mind raced, wondering what had happened to the other three. Were they dead, their bodies crumpled in pools of blood two floors below? Was he the only one left?

"The fucking bedroom is empty!" came a furious voice from the ground floor. Despite the distance and the timber and masonry between them, it echoed throughout the house, as if through a loud-speaker.

"Impossible," he heard a quieter voice defend, catching a definite tinge of panic to it.

"So now we're missing the girl *and* one of the males." Silence. "Do you know what they'll do when they find out about this cluster fuck?"

"It wasn't our fault," the other voice piped up, the panicked tone more evident. The loudest of the team didn't reply, and there was a brief second of eerie quiet before a gunshot rang through the building.

"Croaker, I swear, if we don't fucking find those two, we'll be headed the same way." There was no reply from what Taulass guessed was the third member of the team. It was apparent that the weakest link had been disposed of. Sucking in his lips and biting at them to prevent a much-needed gasp of pain, he heard the voice say, "They can't have gone far. We'll take the car and do a street-by-street search. If we have no luck, we might need to call the other team. Once they've secured the Becker girl, they can help." Heavy feet tramped across the old timber floorboards on the ground floor, and even from his hiding place he could hear the aged wood creaking in protest. The two intruders reached the front door and departed, slamming it shut with such force that Taulass suspected the whole building shook.

Finally allowing himself a gasp of pain, grief and relief flooded Taulass' body simultaneously, both sensations juxtaposing against each other. Oriyanna was alive and probably escaped from the house and out of harm's way. Sadly, that meant both Bliegh and Rhesbon had been killed.

In the darkness of the roof space he felt for the hatch, his trembling fingers finding the plywood lip and prying it open. The dim light from the room below cast shadows into the small space, and for a few long drawn out moments he listened, ensuring no one had stayed behind. The house remained still and silent. The wail of sirens was drawing closer, and Taulass knew the police and forensic teams would examine the house from top to bottom. He couldn't allow a certain item to fall into the hands of people who didn't understand it. Lowering himself painfully onto the desk, he staggered out onto the landing, taking in the utter devastation caused by the volley of automatic gunfire which had peppered the building. He paused, one hand clutching the bannister and supporting his weakened body. He had at least five puncture wounds in his torso and two in his left leg; another round had sliced open his right calf, making it excruciating to walk. The bleeding was subsiding, albeit very slowly. He had no idea how long it would take for the multitude of wounds to heal, but guessed it would more likely be hours than minutes. What he did know was that he needed to rest and let the Gift do its thing.

On the move again, he half walked and half stumbled into Oriyanna's room. Reaching the built-in wardrobe, he flung the sliding door to one side, letting it glide smoothly on the runner. Dropping to his knees, he located the safe and keyed in the combination – 240113. Opening the door, his eyes immediately fell on the item he was after. The recall tab. It was small, around half the size of an average mobile phone and half as thick. Grasping it, the device felt like a well-polished piece of black glass, tactile and expertly bevelled on its four sides. There were strict rules set out by the council about what Arkkadian technology could be stored on the planet, and this little device was it – nothing else was permitted. Alongside the recall tab was a Glock G42. He collected it up and closed the sliding door, not worrying about shutting the safe. The police were just minutes away and he needed to take care of his fallen colleagues; couldn't have their bodies taken by the authorities.

Using his free hand for support he traversed the stairs and hobbled into the lounge and over to the main computer, which much to his surprise, seemed to have survived the gunfire. Taulass pushed a combination of buttons which set a program designed by him into motion, one that would wipe the hard drives, leaving them as clean and blank as the day they'd rolled off the production line. The room would soon be destroyed, but computer hard drives often survived fire damage and he couldn't take that risk.

Taulass left the Swiss-cheesed lounge, not stopping to investigate the body of the executed intruder who was bleeding out on the carpet. He went through to the kitchen and spun the dials on all six of the stove's gas hobs to maximum. The invisible and noxious gas began escaping eagerly from the appliance with a gentle hiss, and for good measure he also turned on the oven's gas supply and opened the door. Leaning against the back door, he was aware that the sirens had arrived outside the front of the house. Soon they would enter the building, and if that happened, he wouldn't be able to bring himself to do what was necessary. He slid out of the back door, flashing blue lights illuminating the ground floor and making his movements appear epileptic and erratic. Taulass had no idea if there would be enough built-up gas in the kitchen to have the desired effect, but he didn't have time to spare. Moving back into the garden he raised the Glock, released the safety and aimed the weapon through the window, the muzzle lined up with the stove. Gritting his teeth and turning his face away, he squeezed off two rounds. The effect was instant, although it didn't have the impact he would have liked. A massive *whhoommppp* blew the windows out and forced the back door open, it slammed back against its hinges as it hammered against the wall, the top pane of glass smashing and showering the concrete path in a million jewel-like crystals shards.

The explosion might not have wiped out the ground floor, but it would stall the police until the London Fire Service arrived, and by then the whole place would be an inferno.

Pain stabbing every part of his body, Taulass headed deeper into the overgrown garden and scaled the rear fence. Painfully, he dropped into the back garden of his neighbour's property, and contemplated his options. He needed to rest and heal, and that was all he could focus on.

Scaling another fence and a brick wall, he found himself standing on a surprisingly well-manicured lawn. A grouping of three plum trees sat in the far corner of the garden, all three clinging to the last of their summer leaves as if attempting to deny the approach of autumn. By the gnarled trunks was a green summer house. Crossing the garden,

Taulass forced open the door and slumped into a well cushioned sun lounger, his body singing in relief as the soft fabric enveloped him. Trying his best to relax, he closed his eyes. In a few hours, once fully healed, he would need to get mobile and to the safe house. He just hoped Oriyanna would be there.

Chapter 13

There weren't many times in his life when Sam felt completely out of control of a situation; on the day he'd been shot rescuing Adam from the Afghan village, and even during the ordeal which had seen him almost die in the bowels of the Great Pyramid, there had been an element of control, the idea he was driving his own destiny. Here however, locked in a cell he had zero chance of escaping from, and with god-knows-who on the way to take him out of the inspector's hands, despair gradually crept over his body, like a cold and unwelcoming blanket. He knew things worked a little differently in this new and uncertain world, but he was damn sure the American Government couldn't have gotten an order to take him to the US Embassy for questioning past the French authorities. Not without a few well-placed people in the background, to oil the hinges of an otherwise drawn out and protracted procedure. Closing his eyes, Sam just hoped the thread of doubt he'd seen flicker across Ackhart's eyes was enough to make the man dig a little deeper and find out what was really going on. The wire-clad clock hanging above the thick metal door told him the time was almost two am; doing the math Sam worked out that it would be around eight pm in Washington, likely too late in the day for the inspector to get in touch with any of the nine to five, shiny-bummed, desk-driving agents who would handle such a case. Maybe he'd call the embassy in Paris, but then again, it was just as likely he wouldn't. Time was growing ever shorter, and if the people collecting him were on time, as he knew they would be, he was down to his last ten minutes. Sam felt like a man on death row, hopelessly awaiting a last-minute stay of execution.

The inspector just needed to make that one call; a quick trawl through the FBI's system by any agent would surely be enough to advise Ackhart the papers were fake. But then again, there was a chance they were only far too real, sped through the system by some highly-positioned Earth-Breed contact, still working away like any other member of the community, just pensively waiting for his position to be of use to them once again.

Watching the clock, Sam saw the ten minutes gradually tick down to nine, then eight, then seven. Somewhere around the four-minute mark he heard the sound of the cell door at the entry to the corridor creaking open, and he noted that it never clunked shut. With mixed emotions, he waited for whoever it was who'd come for him. Would it be the inspector, and would he actually have managed to tell those 'fucking Americans' as he'd put it, to turn around and go home? It was a slim hope, but a hope nonetheless.

Footsteps clicked their way down the cell-lined corridor before coming to a stop outside his less than comfortable accommodations. The lock was turned and the door opened. To his relief, Inspector Ackhart was standing there with the ever-faithful, yet seemingly silent Claude, who appeared to almost be Ackhart's own personal minion.

"Monsieur Becker," began the inspector, frustration still brimming in his accented English. "The men who are to collect you have arrived, they are awaiting you at the holding cells. The documents and ID are in order, I personally checked them myself." The last ounce of hope Sam had held onto seeped away. Maybe they hadn't even needed someone on the inside; he remembered only too well how Oriyanna had gotten out of the United States on a stolen passport, accompanied by an airline ticket in a different name.

"Have you checked?" he growled. "You must check, we both know this is total bollocks!"

"Do not tell me how to do my job, monsieur!" fired Ackhart. "You are a criminal, you do not dictate to me what I will and will not do!"

"I'm no criminal," retaliated Sam, shaking his head. "Deep down you know that! You were a military man, you told me that, you know I'm not lying. I understand that you find it impossible to believe me, but please... this is my fucking life!"

The final outburst was apparently Claude's cue to come lolloping into the room. He had to duck his head a little in order to fit his lummox-like frame through the doorway. He grabbed Sam roughly and pushed him against the wall, forcing his hands behind his back with one swift and well-practised movement. Sam tried to struggle against it, pushing back he managed to force his head back against Claude's chest, giving him a little room. With Claude's purchase on his wrists lost, Sam freed his hand and drove his elbow back hard into the guard's gut. Claude's foul, stale coffee-scented breath hit his cheek, and Sam grimaced when he got a lungful of it. Claude was big, more powerful than Sam, but he was on the back foot, untrained and much slower, all things which helped to level the scales. Spinning around, Sam brought his knee up, taking advantage of the fact that Claude was still doubled over, desperately trying to catch his breath. Sam's right knee contacted with the guard's nose in a satisfying, yet sickening crunch. The whole thing had gone down in a few short, game-changing seconds, but it seemed much longer. Sam spun around expecting to see the cell door closed, was surprised it wasn't. The inspector was blocking the door with his large body, eyes wide and seemingly unable to believe what he was witnessing. His body was large for the wrong reasons, too long spent at a desk eating fast food, and likely hitting the bottle. Sam knew he could take him out, but he didn't want to. Despite the disbelief the inspector had shown in his story, Sam knew he was a good man. They eyed each other for a few seconds, the way two cowboys in a sundown shootout might. There was no time for negotiations so Sam rushed at him, keeping low, like a rugby player going for the try. His right shoulder drove hard into Ackhart's gut and the inspector's body reeled backwards. Sam kept up the momentum, forcing Ackhart across the narrow corridor and into the door of the cell opposite, knocking the wind from his sails. Had it not been shut, they'd have continued until they ended up in a heap on the floor. Pinned against the wall, Sam knew he had Ackhart; he swung his fist around and contacted with Ackhart's cheek. The punch was a game ender and Ackhart went down, his legs buckling under his weight. Stepping back, Sam swung around in time to see Claude, back on his feet and making his way for the door, blood flowing from his nose. It had spilled down his white shirt, resembling a bright red child's bib. In one swift movement Sam swung the cell door closed, trapping the massive guard and taking him out of the equation. He began hammering on the three-inch-thick metal pointlessly, as if mere frustration would unlock the door. Sam treated him to a mocking wave through the small glass window, only adding to the guard's frustration.

Surveying the corridor, Sam was relieved no one else waited to take him on. He'd been so compliant up to now, he suspected he was classed as low risk, a big mistake. The inspector was coming around faster than Sam would have liked, and he knelt by his slumped body. "It's not personal, Inspector," Sam whispered in his ear. "I'm no liar; you left me no choice. I'm sorry." Raising his arm, Sam drove his elbow down onto the back of Ackhart's head, knocking him unconscious for a second time. He quickly patted Ackhart's unconscious body down, cursing inwardly when he failed to find a gun. With precious seconds ticking by he got to his feet and rushed for the barred door at the end of the corridor. He didn't know what to expect or who he'd meet, all that mattered was he now had a chance. The odds had turned in his favour for a split second and he'd gone for it.

Sam burst out into the next corridor. Stopping, he looked right and then left, unsure which way to head. Deciding any decision was better than none he broke left, hammering down the seemingly never-ending corridor, each wall lined with unused cells. He wondered if the French were hedging their bets on a second revolution when they'd built this place; certain they could never fill this massive cell block, even on the rowdiest of Saturday nights.

Reaching the end of the corridor, and almost slipping in his socks, Sam arrived in what must have been a booking-in area. The one detention officer on duty looked half asleep, but he jumped up and grabbed for something on his belt.. Rushing around the detention officer as quickly as he could, he yanked open the first door he came to. Two men, both built like the proverbial brick outhouse jumped to their feet, eyes bulging at the sight of Sam on the loose and making a break for it. They were dressed in identical long black trench coats, and their stone-grey eyes seeming to drill holes right through his chest. This was who'd been sent to collect him, no introductions needed. Sam slammed the door again before they could reach it, and span around, only to find the desk officer behind him, arms raised in a shooting position. Sam recognised the weapon and glanced down at his chest, a familiar red dot held steady between his pecs.

"Get on the floor, hands on your head!" the officer shouted in accented English. "Do it now, monsieur, or I will Taser you!"

Strangely, Sam found himself thinking how good the officer's English was. With the red dot fixed on his chest, Sam took a few drawn-out moments to consider his options. He glanced around the room desperately, searching for a way out. The only way to go was the way he'd come, or there was the other corridor, which could prove fruitful. Not for the first time that night Sam found himself at shit-or-bust stage. Gritting his teeth, he went for it.

The detention officer was quick to react, and Sam heard the rapid *click,click,click,click* of the Taser before he felt the fifty thousand volts slam through his body. He'd seen it done during testing, but he'd never experienced the pain for himself. It was indescribable, every muscle in his body went into spasm, his legs gave way and with a thump, he hit the floor, convulsing as the merciless officer kept his finger on the trigger. Sam wasn't sure just how long the lightning was pumped into him, it seemed like hours. In the end, a veil of unconsciousness slid over him, and he didn't try to fight it. Although he knew ultimately it would spell the end of his life, at this point all he wanted was for the pain to stop.

When Sam came around the first thing he wanted to do was claw at the sore area on his chest, where the barbs from the Taser had bit into his skin like some vicious insect. He could feel it healing, but it still hurt like a bitch. Someone had slid his coat over his fleece before securing him in restraints. His arms and legs were still numb. The limb restraints were binding his legs so tightly together, he suspected his balls were close to popping like a pair of ripe grapes.

Blinking against the lights, which seemed to amplify the pounding headache raging behind his eyes, he could just make out the slightly rotund figure of Inspector Ackhart standing over him. One of his eyes was rather purple and swollen. Seeing Sam open his eyes, Ackhart planted a swift foot into his gut and Sam doubled over in agony, the cuffs biting further into his already-bruised skin.

"Nice try, Monsieur Becker," spat Ackhart, his voice laced with fury. "When you come back to us, I'll be sure to add one count of assault on a police officer, one count of assaulting a detention officer and one count of trying to evade lawful custody – not that it will matter much when you're facing a murder charge!"

"I won't be coming back," groaned Sam, rolling onto his side, the air still reluctant to refill his lungs. The two men wearing the trench coats were standing next to Ackhart, watching Sam curiously.

"Once you have been interviewed by these agents at the US Embassy in Paris, you will be brought directly back to this police station." Ackhart paused. "You're going to wish you never came back," he grinned, revealing stained yellow teeth. "I might have to let poor Claude have a few minutes with you alone in the cell."

"He won't be walking out, I can promise you that," Sam retorted, and the inspector planted his foot into Sam's gut a second time. Coughing and spluttering, he felt heavy hands lifting him to his feet, way before his legs were ready to take his weight. The two men trench-coated men had him, one under each arm, and the cuffs bit further into Sam's skin, hard enough to have blood running down his hands. With all his strength gone and his body beaten, Sam had no fight left. By the time his millions of little caretakers had cleaned this mess up and put him back together, it would be too late.

"We will return him to your custody by ten PM tomorrow," he heard one of the guys say. He'd heard that accent before – deep in the Pyramid whilst just clinging on to consciousness with a bullet lodged in his chest – and his blood ran cold.

"I'll take your word for it," Ackhart replied. "Be careful, he can be a bit feisty, as you have seen." There was no reply from his new captors, they escorted him swiftly through the door which would have been his escape if they hadn't been sitting in there. His feet were trying to walk but failing to do much more than peddle the air and occasionally scrape across the ground.

Faster than he'd expected, Sam's chest started to recover from the brutal beating he'd been given. The Gift did have its uses, although the eternal life thing Sam wasn't so keen on. As they hauled him silently down one last corridor and out into the brisk early morning air, he decided that someone on Arkkadia needed to come up with a Half Gift – the ability to heal but not live for ever. That one he'd take.

Offering up little resistance, choosing instead to preserve his energy should another opportunity raise its head, Sam found himself bundled into the rear of a shiny black X5 BMW, another sign that this was exactly who he'd feared.

Chapter 14

Five minutes after Sam had left Inspector Ackhart's custody he was sitting at his desk, a fresh cup of black coffee steaming at his side. Wincing, he held an ice-cold towel to his eye, which seemed hell-bent on swelling even further. With his free hand, he knocked back two painkillers, swallowing them dry. His face throbbed and he gritted his teeth. Becker's actions had taken him by surprise – he'd been caught napping and it enraged him. In a pointless effort to take his mind from the throb of his swollen eye, he picked up the clear zip-tied bag which had Becker's mobile phone inside, noticing there was a message waiting to be read. His interest piqued, he navigated to the inbox, pushing at the buttons through the plastic. It was from a contact Becker had saved as 'AF', and the single message read **WILTSHIRE** – nothing to help him understand this perplexing situation. He closed the phone down in annoyance and turned his attention to the computer, opening his emails. He scanned and deleted various junk messages, informing him of upcoming duty changes and pending court cases the was required to attend. Staring blankly at one such email, his computer bleeped politely, informing him a new email had arrived. Closing the current screen and hitting the delete button, he cast the semi-read message to the trash folder, collected up his coffee and took a gulp, enjoying the warm, bitter liquid when it hit his tongue. With his one good eye, he squinted at the new email, which had an FBI.GOV address. Cursing at the impatience of the Americans he thought about sending this email the same way as the previous one, straight to the trash, but thinking better of it, he opened the message.

Scanning it, he froze, his blood pumping erratically in his veins. It was an automated response, but the message amplified the thread of doubt he'd experienced earlier, during his illegal, but informal and unrecorded interview with the crazy Englishman.

The message came from the international enquiries centre, thanking him for his contact and promising that someone would be in touch within twenty-four hours. It went on to say if his enquiry was of a more urgent nature he should call a number supplied at the bottom of the message, quoting their reference number.

After taking Becker into custody and searching the Interpol database for persons with a similar modus operandi, he'd come across three cases in the States which matched the events at the Laurett Chateau. Cases had also surfaced in England and Germany, and in his excitement at uncovering what he believed to be the work of some crazed serial killer, or a black ops government assassin, he'd sent Sam's details to the respective authorities.

Hands shaking, he scanned the email a second time, grabbing his pen to write down the phone number, noting the enquiry reference number as well. Becker's words echoed through his pounding head like the tolling of a bell. '*If you let them take me, I will disappear off the map.*' And when he'd lain on the floor in the custody block. '*I won't be coming back.*' Becker had honestly believed he'd be on a plane and out of the country within an hour of being handed over. Doubt growing with each passing second, the inspector began to wonder if Becker had been as crazy as he'd imagined. Ackhart still believed his story of human-like aliens and an ancient battle for Earth was nonsense, but his gut said something was going on, and he hated not knowing the full story. Shakily he grabbed the receiver from the cradle and began to dial. If the Yanks didn't have his prisoner, then who the hell did?

* * *

Special Agent Joshua Simmonds sat at his terminal on the other side of the Atlantic, reading the details of the Russian Navy's latest deployments in the Bering Sea with interest. The Washington Post website was painfully slow to load, the internet a shadow of what it had been before the solar flares which crippled the globe and left the planet in a state of disarray – at least, that was the official story. What intrigued him was how all the satellites had somehow managed to survive undamaged. Surely a solar flare would have fried those as well? Simmonds wasn't a scientist, but he felt sure there was a cover-up going on – maybe some military experiment had gone wrong, and no government would want to 'fess up to that little cock up. Whatever the truth, he knew it was way above his security clearance. Shaking his head in disbelief, he almost didn't hear the phone ring, he had the volume turned down to its lowest level, the shrill ringer had always offended his ears. Rubbing his eyes he looking away from a heading which read, '**PRESIDENT HILL IN TALKS WITH RUSSIA IN EF-FORTS TO AVOID SECOND COLD WAR.**'

"FBI international enquiries, how may I help?" he asked when he picked up the receiver. Dealing with these calls used to fall under the header of civilian duties, but with times as they were, it was all hands to the pump. The odd shift stuck in an office was bearable when mixed in with his other, more interesting investigation work, but only just. The fact it was also double time on one of his days off was both a bind and a bonus; even on his salary, trying to live above the breadline was an uphill struggle nowadays.

"This is Inspector Franck Ackhart, from Le Police Nationale, France, stationed at Le Havre. To whom am I talking?" The heavily accented English was unmistakably threaded with tension.

"This is Special Agent Josh Simmonds, what is your enquiry?" The call had disturbed his reading, and he hoped that whatever the issue was, he could deal with it swiftly and get back to reading the news.

"Agent Simmonds," the person at the other end of the line barely waited for him to finish the sentence. "I sent over a case file regarding one of your wanted, missing, identify reports – reference F2453.2025."

Simmonds changed screens and pumped the number into the search bar on the FBI's intranet. "Arrest of a male by the name of Samuel Becker, possibly connected with three unsolved homicide cases, currently in French custody," he read back from the original email.

"Oui, that is the one," Inspector Ackhart agreed urgently. "Tell me, Agent Simmonds, have you raised papers to have the prisoner handed over to your authorities for initial questioning at your embassy here in France?"

Simmonds scanned the actions attached to the file; it was only a few hours old. A contact request had been added to the notes, but it was being held over for the morning team. "Not that I can see. It's likely we would seek permission to do so if there are similarities between the cases, but there are no notes on the action yet." Extradition was becoming rarer, with countries choosing to deal with initial enquiries either at the prisoner's place of detention, or if the matter warranted it, the prosecuting country's embassy. There was a long silence on the other end of the phone. "Inspector, did you hear me? I said we have made no applications to speak with your prisoner."

"Merci," the Inspector responded, and even though the call quality wasn't great, Simmonds thought the man sounded distracted.

"Is there something I can help you with, sir?" questioned Simmonds. There was no reply, the phone went dead. Returning the handset to its cradle, Simmonds read the case file report. There was no doubt it was an interesting case, but it was in a queue for the morning, and that made it someone else's problem. Closing the report, he re-opened the Washington Post story and went back to reading the grim news about the USA bringing its nuclear defence systems back online, and how the world would once again be in a state of nuclear standoff.

* * *

Ackhart placed the phone down, his hands shaking uncontrollably. For a few long seconds he stared into middle space, contemplating what he'd learned. Sliding his drawer open he eyed a fresh bottle of brandy longingly – it had been twenty long years since he'd searched for the answer at the bottom of such a bottle. The answer was never there, but it did make life easier to deal with. Those days lost in the bottle had come at a cost; his military career, his pilot's licence and his marriage. Despite all those losses, the booze still called to him. He'd stayed dry for twenty years, and yet he still felt the need to keep a bottle of poison close by, in case things went sour – for days such as this. Deep down he knew it wasn't a matter of if he went back to the booze, but when. Pushing the growing temptation to one side, he slammed the drawer, the action making his cooling coffee slop over the brim of the mug and onto the desk.

Becker had tried to escape, and he'd given Ackhart a black eye and a pounding head which would no doubt rival the worst hangover after one of his heaviest binges, but he'd been wrong about the man. He'd released a prisoner to people who had no right to take him.

Even though the papers and IDs had looked as genuine as any he'd seen, Ackhart would be held responsible for the monumental fuck up. For a high profile murder like Laurett's, that would mean both his balls and head on a stick. Immediate dismissal and no chance of receiving the pension he'd been paying into for the past twenty years. Ackhart was certain that bottle, which had laid for years in his desk, would soon see the light of day, but not yet – first, he had things to do. Later he would drink, later he would drown his sorrows for not trusting that moment of doubt. Maybe Becker had good reason to fight for his life, to ensure those who had him didn't get the chance to do whatever it was they'd planned. Ackhart wasn't certain – it all seemed a little fuzzy – but he seemed to recall Sam Becker apologising to him, just before hitting him a second time. It was likely his imagination, but it seemed frighteningly real.

Glancing at his watch, he realized Becker had already been gone for fifteen minutes. Ackhart had to act now and he needed to act fast.

Grabbing his Sig Pro SP 2022 from the locked gun drawer, he headed for the door. What was it Becker had said again? '*I'll be on a plane and out of the country within an hour!*' The city's airport was less than twelve kilometres away, meaning Becker was probably already there. Ackhart might be too late, but he had to try.

Chapter 15

A single monotone sound, which reminded her of a droning air-conditioner, was the first thing Lucie heard when she blinked her eyes open. She was tired and achy, the kind of throbbing which went right down to the bones. Moving her neck and arms, Lucie discovered her joints were stiff. She tried to adjust her position but was held firmly in place and a momentary burst of panic welled in her chest. Managing to force herself upright, using her elbows as support, she discovered she was lying on the back seat of a car, and the droning noise was nothing more than the sound of tyres as they hummed along the concrete of the motorway. For a second fear gripped her, freezing her body to the spot. The last thing she remembered was flying down the small slope and into the orange glow of the Blackwall Tunnel; after that, there was nothing. One thing was certain, this wasn't her car. She'd kept her little Mini spotless, and the rear foot well of this vehicle was littered with snack packets and half-crushed Coke cans. Fighting the desire to avoid the answer, she craned her stiff neck around to discover who was driving. Seeing Oriyanna's glossy blonde hair flowing down the sides of the grey cloth headrest, she laid back on the rear seat and released a long, relieved sigh.

"You're awake," Oriyanna noted, keeping her eyes on the road. "And not a moment too soon. I know I'm headed in the right direction, but I have no idea when I need to get off this massive road!"

Having stolen a few extra moments to steady her nerves, Lucie found what she called the 'clunk clicker' on the seatbelt and released it, giving her full movement and the ability to swing her legs around and sit up. Initially she was a little dizzy and her head swam. Taking slow, deliberate breaths she forced herself back on an even keel. She'd found that lately she was prone to such episodes; the odd dizzy spell here and bit of sickness there. She'd put it down to nothing more than exhaustion and a bit of stress; certainly, this evening's little wobble could be blamed on either of those things.

"How long have we been on the motorway?" she croaked, "And where the hell is Mavis?"

"Who is Mavis?"

"My Mini, the car I seem to remember you blasted the back windscreen out of."

"You named your car?" Oriyanna sounded surprised and amused by the human idiosyncrasy of naming inanimate objects.

"Yeah, I did. Sam used to rib me about it, too."

"You Earth-Human's never fail to amaze me – how funny!" A little giggle escaped Oriyanna's lips, and the sound made Lucie relax a little. Underneath that tough and alien exterior, she was human after all – in a manner of speaking, anyway. "We have been on this heading– on this road," she corrected, "for just over half an hour, and my speed has been a constant eighty miles an hour."

Lucie squinted out of the window, trying to get her bearings and some idea of how far they'd travelled. Her own reflection was all that looked back at her, bouncing off the darkened glass. Amusement brimmed at Oriyanna's very clinical answer to her question. They might look anatomically similar, but there were some vast differences between the two women.

"You need to take a road called the M3, it should be coming up any-time soon. We might have already missed it."

"I don't recall seeing it, and I have studied every exit since I got on this..." Oriyanna paused, "motorway?"

"Good, then we should be just fine." Lucie climbed out of the back, slid her slight frame into the passenger seat and secured the seatbelt, her feet finding another empty drink container abandoned on the floor. "Whose car is this?"

"Just before the crash, the men chasing us down swerved to avoid it, and the driver and his passenger got out to help. It was a big mistake on their part, but lucky for us." Oriyanna offered Lucie an encouraging smile. She was pleased to have Lucie to talk to, it helped quell the memories which had plagued her thoughts since leaving the house.

They past a darkened motorway information bridge, illuminated only by their headlights. The flood lighting once used to make such signs standout had long since failed. The sign instructed them to keep left for the M3 in a few miles. "Looks like I woke up just in time," Lucie announced, not entirely comfortable with the prospect of making the long trip in a stolen car. "Take a left at the M3 and head towards Southampton, then look for signs saying Salisbury. I wonder if Adam has made it yet?" She fished her mobile from her pocket, not surprised there was no signal. For the first time since waking the sickening worry returned; Sam was still out there somewhere.

The knowledge that they'd been watched made her feel sick, they must have known what Sam was doing, and a team of them had likely been lying in wait for him at his target's house. Lucie took a deep breath to steady her nerves. "Just how long have you been on Earth?" she asked, trying to take her mind off the endless possibilities regarding what might have happened to Sam. None of them ended well in her imagination. The question seemed stupid, but it wasn't –suddenly she'd gotten an idea of what Adam and Sam, had needed to deal with when they'd first stumbled into this mess.

"I got here roughly seven months after Adam and Sam came home."

"You've been here for nearly two years?" Lucie spat, sounding disgusted. It certainly wasn't the answer she was expecting. Oriyanna eyed her, almost appearing hurt by the outburst. "In all that time, you never once came to see my brother! Do you know how he feels about you?"

"Not a day went by when I didn't wish I could see him," Oriyanna defended . "I had to beg the Arkkadian Council to be placed on this mission, and the one condition they insisted on was that I had no direct contact with Adam or Sam. "I have seen him," she admitted sheepishly. "I worked out where your house was from his description of the area when we were on Arkkadia. I saw him sitting in the park one day, with his notepad and I wanted to go to him, but I couldn't. I've seen him a few times since. Every time, it's taken all my willpower to stay away from him."

"Just what do you mean by *direct* contact?" Lucie demanded, ignoring the last part of Oriyanna's explanation. She hadn't listened to much past '*direct contact*'. She suspected she already knew the answer to the question. "You're responsible for the target packages which arrived at our door, aren't you?"

"Please, Lucie, it was hard for us to use Sam, but it had to be done."

"What 'us'?" Lucie snapped.

"Myself and three other Arkkadians; I did not come alone. We have been gathering intelligence for the past two years, fearful that the one who made the virus had escaped to Earth. After we arrived, we began to track and trace as many of the Earth-Breed as we could. I didn't want Sam to get involved—"

"You had a funny way of showing it," fired Lucie, anger rippling through her body. "He's out there, right now! Likely dead – and it's your fault!" She jabbed a finger at Oriyanna, who shrunk against the door of the Juke. "If anything happens to him, or Adam... don't you think they've done enough!"

Oriyanna glided the 4x4 left and onto the M3, flying south through the cold night before she looked at Lucie; she didn't need to touch her to feel the betrayal and anger coursing through her body. "I can't change what has been," replied Oriyanna flatly. "I had no choice, the last Watchers who lived on Earth are all dead. I brought three back with me, men who had carried out the duty before Euri Peterson, Jacques Guillard, Francis Tillard and John Remy, and now they are dead, too."

"How so?" Lucie noticed Oriyanna's complexion, she looked drained, as if she had nothing left to give and Lucie wondered if she'd been too hard on her.

"Our base wasn't far from you, in Greenwich. They figured out where we were. Ten minutes before I arrived at your bar I was running for my life, having seen my three colleagues slaughtered."

Lucie shook her head in disbelief, not only of the current situation but also hearing the names of the former Watchers Oriyanna had reeled off. Even two and a half years on, she still found it hard to believe. They were names that Lucie had known, even before hearing Adam and Sam's account, and the one that resonated most was John Remy, one of the most powerful and famous men on the planet. The fact that he wasn't even from this planet made her head spin.

"They'd returned to help me look for the one who was ultimately responsible for the virus, and now they're dead and there was nothing I could do to stop it."

Oriyanna's voice sounded a little distant, and Lucie could tell she was running through whatever it was she'd witnessed, and likely not for the first time that night. Despite that, Lucie was still angry that they'd used Sam. "Sam didn't owe you anything. Just because you gave him and Adam the Gift, it didn't put them in your debt for the rest of eternity, and I don't see how you can even call it a gift. Who wants to live forever? From what I can tell, it's left you pretty lonely." Lucie immediately felt guilty when the last few words left her mouth. She was angry, but that hit was below the belt.

"Lucie, you didn't see how badly hurt your brother and Sam were when we went through the Tabut," Oriyanna defended, sounding hurt. Although she understood Lucie's anger she tried to defend herself. "They were both as good as dead; Adam was in the final stages of the Reaper virus, hours from death. Sam had a chest wound, and I thought..." she paused, remembering how she'd believed both men were dead when the Tabut had shut down on the Arkkadian side. "I thought they were both dead. Sam had such a severe chest wound it's a miracle he survived, and before we could apply the Gift he *did* die, twice. On Earth, nobody would have been able to save him. We did what we had to, to ensure they survived – after all they'd been through I couldn't leave them to die millions of miles from home." She waited for Lucie to attack again, but all that followed was a long, pensive silence. She glanced at her new travelling companion, saw tears flowing down her cheeks.

"I'm sorry," Lucie finally said, clearing her throat before she spoke. "I'm just so worried for Sam. I know Adam's safe, that's one thing, but I'm going crazy running through all the things that might have happened to Sam." She gave her mobile phone a cursory glance; not surprisingly, there was no signal. "I don't blame you for wanting to use his expertise; I know he enjoys that line of work. God knows I wish he didn't. I know you didn't force him out the door." Lucie smiled apologetically and wiped her eyes with the backs of her hands. "By the time we reach Wiltshire, the mobile networks will be down until six AM. I just don't think I can take the worry of not knowing."

Oriyanna reached across and placed a hand on Lucie's stomach, breathing a sigh of relief to discover the accident had done no damage. "From what I have seen of Samuel Becker," Oriyanna smiled, "he can take care of himself. I take it he knows?"

"Knows what?" asked Lucie, looking confused.

"That he is going to be a father."

"I— I'm sorry?" Lucie stammered, eyes wide. "What did you say?"

"I picked up on the baby's life-force when I grabbed hold of you back at your bar. You mean to tell me you didn't know?" Lucie just gawped, eyes wide in a mixture of fear and excitement. "You're two months pregnant, Lucie; you and Sam are going to be parents."

Chapter 16

Two hundred meters, left turn. Fifty yards, cobbled road, right turn. Laying on the back seat of the X5, cuffed and with his legs bound, Sam tried to record the journey in his head. Using what little he could discern from the restricted view through the dark tinted windows he tried to imprint it into his brain. It was how he'd been trained to deal with kidnap situations during his time in the army, then a second, very similar course when he'd gone back to the Middle East on close protection work. The rule was, try to remember how far you'd been taken from the point of capture, what direction you'd travelled and for how long. Any recalled smells or sounds could mean the difference between life and death, being found or being beheaded on some fanatic's internet broadcast. Sam never imagined it would be a skill he'd put to use, it had been years since he'd practised the art. Practical training was the only way to prepare for such situations, it wasn't a skill-set which could be gleaned in the lecture room.

"So – you're the infamous Samuel Becker." The mocking voice of one of his captors came from the front seat. "I don't see what all the fuss was about; you weren't that hard to capture." His sarcastic tone made Sam's blood boil.

"It's not over 'til the fat lady sings!" croaked Sam, his throat impossibly dry. He jiggled his wrists behind his back, uselessly trying to stop the metal from biting further into his skin.

"An Earth phrase which means nothing to me." Sam had heard that particular accent before, the voice was frighteningly similar to that of Buer, the man-mountain who'd gunned him down, deep below the Pyramid. Had he not known beyond a doubt that the man who'd masterminded The Reaper was long dead, he could have mistaken this voice for the evil bastard.

"It means as soon as I get chance, I'm going to kick your fucking arse." Sam chuckled, and rolled to one side, finding a position that for a few seconds, was a little more comfortable.

"I doubt that very much," Sam could see the back of the passenger's head, it shook slightly when he spoke. "Don't worry, Mr. Becker, we are not here to kill you – although in a day or two, once you have seen what we are doing here, you are going to wish we had."

Three hundred yards... Sam realised he'd lost his train of thought; the conversation had taken him off guard. Not that it mattered a jot, he had a feeling there was no escaping this one, not yet. They didn't plan to kill him, he was being taken somewhere, to someone. What was it Laurett had said? *He is here, he has plans for you – E-N-O-L-A,* Sam cursed himself for the cold chill that ran though his body on remembering the wretched Earth-Breed's words. The important thing was that every hour, minute and second he stayed alive, gave him a chance. One had come back in the police station and he'd grabbed it, and he would sure as shit do the same if the opportunity presented itself again. "I look forward to well and truly fucking up whatever it is you have planned this time," he half-laughed and half-croaked. The passenger thrust his fist backwards, finding Sam's gut and, not for the first time that evening, winded him to gasping point. "Bit – of – a sore point?" he chuckled, gasping for air and simultaneously trying not to choke on the words. Despite how much the punch had hurt, he felt a warm glow at having touched a raw nerve.

"For a man facing a rather dreadful fate, you are far too full of yourself," the driver spat, glancing at him through the rear-view mirror.

"Maybe," Sam replied, searching for a little comfort; his former position had already started to make his arms ache again. "I'd say it's more of a strong dislike for your kind. Hopefully later, I'll have the pleasure of killing you, just like I did Finch and the other Earth-Breeds."

"The feeling is mutual, Mr. Becker, I can assure you of that," the driver's voice mocked. "Just don't get your hopes up too much about the second part of your statement. Finch was a fucking idiot."

"That's one thing we agree on," Sam muttered under his breath.

"Buer should never have been entrusted to see things through on his own, with a bunch of lab-bred half-wits. We won't be making the same mistakes again," the guy concluded, as if hadn't heard Sam's comment.

"So – as we're going to spend some time in each other's company, how about you tell me your names?"

"My name is Asag, and this is my brother, Namtar," Asag replied proudly from the passenger seat, as if the names should mean something to Sam.

Definitely Elders, thought Sam, with a chill of foreboding. "Don't you have something a little easier to remember," he coaxed, trying to keep up his show of confidence. "Like Brian and Bob?" The two brothers ignored his statement, not even casting a glance in the rear-view mirror.

"Just what do you have in mind for me, then?" Sam could hear anger brewing in his voice, but behind that confident and cocky façade he was scared, scared for Lucie, Adam and lastly himself. He'd learned to trust his gut and he knew deep down, no matter how much he tried to tell himself it was silly, that tonight's events were probably engulfing Adam and possibly, even Lucie. The thought of her being drawn into this mess enraged him. "I take it that it's not just me this guy wants."

"Very intuitive, Mr. Becker." Asag twisted around in his seat and set his stony eyes on Sam. They were ancient eyes, and momentarily Sam wondered what sights they'd seen over the years. "I wouldn't worry too much about Adam and your pretty little wife, Lucie – you will be seeing them very soon."

Sam pulled hard on the cuffs, almost oblivious to the pain. "If you harm either of them—"

"As I said, no one is harming anyone – for now!" Asag cut in, letting the last words hang for impact. "We are merely on a fetch and retrieve

S T Boston

mission, just like my colleagues across the channel." He gestured to his left, in the general direction of the English coast. "But don't be so vain as to think this is *all* about you!" Asag emphasised the *all*, letting it roll off his tongue. "We thought it only fitting that before you die, you witness our victory, and you die knowing that despite all you went through with that bitch Oriyanna, you failed." Asag paused and cleared his throat, as if speaking her name had left him with a nasty taste in his mouth.

He returned his captivating gaze to Sam's aching body, and Sam could almost feel his presence bearing down on him, putting pressure on his brain. He continued to watch Sam for a few more moments, and Sam could see the enjoyment in his eyes at the sight of him, laying there, bound, cuffed and well and truly stuffed. "Humanity has been a cancer on this planet for too long," Asag finally continued. "A cancer created by my ancestors and wrongly nurtured by the Arkkadians after the war. A cancer which will soon be eradicated, unfortunately, along with the planet. For a good few thousand years anyway. It's a shame; if we'd succeeded the first time, the planet would have merely been washed clean of humanity – sadly, now we don't have the same options." Asag smiled, revealing unnaturally white teeth. It seemed that out of the two, he was the one who enjoyed the sound of his own voice most. "Oh, don't worry, Mr. Becker," he added, seeing the confusion on Sam's face, "It will all become clear, very soon."

* * *

Inspector Ackhart gunned his Renault Mégane down Rue Clement Marical. At the Carrefour Market roundabout, he threw the car right on the Rue Irène Joliot Cure, nearly losing the rear end as the tyres screamed in protest against the roughly cobbled street, desperately searching for grip.

Post-curfew Le Havre was a ghost town, desolate and dark, quiet and ghostly. A person out at this time of night could easily have been mistaken in thinking the Reaper had killed everyone. With its residents safely in their homes, the streets seemed to take on a life of their own. Ackhart rarely ventured out, even though his position within the police force permitted him to wander the streets during duty time. He hated the deserted sensation that flowed through the city he loved. Flying through the empty streets made him feel as if he were stuck in a nightmare, fleeing some invisible foe which would reach out and strike him down at any moment. Engine screaming, his headlights sliced through the night, reflecting from the off-white walls of the buildings, making Ackhart squint and curse his failing eyesight. The situation was not helped in the least by the throbbing and swollen eye Becker had dealt him back at the station.

In his head, he ran through what might happen when he got to Le Havre airport, although in truth, he didn't know. How many of them would there be? And who the hell were they? He didn't believe for a second that Becker had told him the truth – did he? Protocol stated he should have a tactical unit back him up – hell any form of backup would be good – but this job didn't fall into protocol, this was his cock up and his alone, and it needed to be put right. Also, something about the whole situation didn't sit right. He needed to get to the bottom of it, and hopefully take Becker back into custody, saving his career and his reputation at the same time.

Weaving down the street, aiming the car along the narrow straight road he fumbled in his jacket, checking for the umpteenth time that his gun was there. The heavy, reassuring lump that was his SP 2022 met his hand. In the brief seconds he had his hand away from the wheel, the Renault hit a pothole and it pitched dangerously to the left. The front tyre found the kerb, shaking the car violently and forcing Ackhart to grab the steering wheel with both hands. Cursing under his breath, he got the car under control, and briefly he longed for the bottle of brandy sitting in his desk drawer. He quashed down the craving; there would be time for that later if things didn't work out, or if he even had the luxury of having a later. The men who'd taken Becker had been huge and there was only one of him. He reached for the SP again; no matter how big the men who'd taken his prisoner were, the gun would deal

with them without discrimination . If it came to it, he might be able
to use Becker, sure he'd jump at the chance of being taken back to
the station. He'd seen the fear and desperation in his eyes when the
two massive, supposed FBI agents had hauled him out of the custody
block, a look which had sent a chill through Ackhart's body. But why?
He didn't believe Becker's account, not one detail of it – did he?

Reaching the end of Rue Irène Joliot Cure, Ackhart wrestled the car
around another roundabout, the front end understeering dangerously,
tyres singing in chorus yet again. Throwing it into another right turn
and onto the D6382, Le Havre airport lay ahead, the runway lights
gleaming against the dark and post-power cut night sky.

The white-walled shops and buildings disappeared behind him, replaced by darkened, concrete industrial units, all empty and slowly
being reclaimed by nature. Their skeletal concrete hulks planted in
empty grounds, weeds poking through the ever-growing gaps in the
tarmac car parks, as if in defiance to man.

Like the police station, the airport would have its own generator.
The things cost a small fortune to run, but local government always
seemed to find the money to buy fuel from somewhere. The brightly-
lit complex cast an artificial white glow into the night sky, giving off
an almost halo-like effect.

Ackhart reached yet another roundabout, a smaller one this time
which he didn't bother to steer around, instead slamming the Mégane
over the raised mound of reflective white paint. Powering through the
short-stay car park he knew exactly where to head. At the end of the
car park was a small gate; usually manned, it led airside, easy access
for emergency services. Not far from the gate he hoped he'd find a
plane, a plane which contained his prisoner.

* * *

The X5 lurched around a roundabout, the inertia caused Sam to slide
across the back seat and hit his head on the rear passenger door. He
swore under his breath.

"Le Havre airport," Asag announced in a thunderous voice, making Sam jump. "Not long now and we will be heading to Portugal. From there, we will change to a slightly larger craft and hop across to South America." He sounded almost chipper, as if he was taking Sam on the trip of a lifetime and he was the tour guide.

"I'm not sure my travel jabs are up to date," Sam quipped, his body cramped uncomfortably against the back door of the 4x4. The post-curfew darkness gave way to bright lights, the sudden illumination making Sam squint. The vehicle mounted a couple of speed humps, faster than necessary. Even with the 4x4's big tyres, his body jolted painfully. The vehicle slowed abruptly, and Sam braced himself in the seat, ramming his feet against the opposite door to stop from rolling into the foot well. He heard Asag jump from the cab, then the sound of a gate sliding open. A few moments later Asag was back and they were moving again, slower this time, through the gate and to what Sam assumed would be airside. The vehicle stopped for a second time and once again the Asag got out. Sam heard the well-worn wheel supporting the gate squeak its way back across the tarmac; it was a sound he hated, like running fingernails down a blackboard.

Finding a position which offered a little more comfort, Sam felt the BMW creep forward, making a number of left and right manoeuvres before they finally came to a stop. Namtar switched off the engine and applied the parking brake, they'd obviously reached their destination. Being moved was a key time, a moment when Sam might just get that small window of opportunity. He took a deep breath, letting the air fill his lungs. Releasing it slowly he tried to slow his racing heart to a reasonable pace. If a chance did present itself he would need to be calm, not have his heart slamming in his chest as if he'd just run a hundred-meter dash.

Both of his captors left the vehicle, leaving him on his own for the first time since he'd made a break for it in the custody block. First thing on the agenda was getting his hands to the front of his body, with his hands cuffed behind his back he had no chance. At the front was bad enough, but at least he could strike out and defend himself if he could get them to the other side of his legs. Rolling from his side and onto his back, Sam lifted both legs in the air, ignoring the pain as he stretched his arms down and just about managed to slide his cuffed wrists over his backside. It was the first time the limb restraint on his legs had come in handy, it kept them bound tightly together, aiding his attempt. Gradually he eased his legs through the hoop created by his arms. The pain was almost intolerable, but his strong survival instinct had kicked in, mixed with years of hostage situation training, helping to increase his pain threshold to its maximum level. Just when he thought he could take no more, eyes shut and teeth clenched firmly together, his hands cleared his legs. The pain relief was almost instant, every muscle in his shoulders and arms singing with joy. Not stopping to savour the small victory, Sam bent forward and removed the Velcro limb restraint binding his legs together. Hands to his front and legs free, Sam half sat and half crouched in the back seat, not wanting to stick his head too far into view. Gingerly, he peered out of the passenger side window.

One of his captors was standing by the door, his back to Sam, partially blocking the view. Looking around his thick body he could just see the second male, Namtar, who'd been driving. At least he thought this one was Namtar; it was hard to tell, as the two Elder brothers were practically identical. The fact that they wore matching long black coats didn't help matters. One thing Sam was sure of, was that these two weren't Earth-Breed, they were definitely like Buer, and undoubtedly, they shared his magical healing abilities. Namtar was standing by a twin-engine propeller plane. It looked like some kind of Beechcraft, possibly a King Air, more than capable of zipping them down through Europe and into Portugal. Namtar was talking to someone, most likely the pilot. He wondered if the pilot was in on their plan, or did he also believe they were working for the government, transporting a dangerous prisoner? Knowing the long reach the aliens had, and the eclectic mixture of trades used by the Earth-Breeds, he suspected the pilot would know the score. The cab of the X5 was well soundproofed but he could hear the plane's twin engines idling, ready for action. Sam was thankful for the droning sound because it would help hide the noise created by the next section of his plan.

Moving away from the window, Sam slid over to the opposite door. Praying it wasn't locked, he grabbed the handle carefully and pulled back on it gently, trying to avoid making too much noise. To his relief, the door clicked open and the refreshingly cool early morning air rushed in. Sam breathed deeply, enjoying the fresh breeze. Casting a final cautionary glance toward Asag, Sam pushed the door open fully.

* * *

Asag watched with frustrated impatience while his brother continued to chit-chat idly with the Earth-Breed pilot who'd flown them here from Peru. Having received the 'Go' order from Asmodeous to grab Becker, they'd used one of Integra Investments' jets to hop across the Southern Atlantic. Once in Portugal they chartered a smaller plane to make the shorter trip to France. It had been his idea to leave the Integra-registered jet in Portugal; using a chartered plane would afford them more anonymity should they get tangled up with the authorities, which they had. In the end, it hadn't mattered, but Asag liked to err on the side of caution. It was a small catalogue of errors that had caused Buer to fail, and Asag wasn't about to make the same mistakes. He was eager to prove to Asmodeous that both he and Namtar were worthy, wanted to prove he'd been right in choosing the two brothers to flee Sheol when the attack came. With Samuel Becker in their custody, Asag thought they'd confirmed their worth. Even if things went wrong during the taking of Adam Fisher and his sister, they'd both done their part. As soon as they got airborne, he would call Asmodeous and tell him of their great victory.

Things had almost turned sour, and the capture of Becker had ridden the razors edge of failure for a few hours that night. In order to get full un-curfew restricted access to France, they had both entered the country on diplomatic papers. Papers that saw them as U.S. Senators on a visit to Laurett. Despite the fact that such paperwork usually got

S T Boston

the low paid security minions scurrying around in panic and saw you processed very quickly, the ones at Le Havre had been a little more cautious. In the end, and fearing that they would be discovered to be the fakes they were, Namtar had used his skills to get them through. The two border officials had still been sat, eyes glazed over, as they'd strode through customs to their waiting hire car. He'd even persuaded one of them to give him the keys to the emergency access gate, so they could get airside directly on return, making it even easier for them to get Becker to the waiting plane without any questions or killing. The delay had, however, caused them to be painfully late, too late to save Laurett and almost too late to get Becker. Thankfully Earth-Humans were easily influenced, stuffing his hands into the jacket's deep pockets, Asag removed the papers that had delivered Sam Becker into his custody. They were, of course, completely blank, but then the officers at Le Havre Police Station had been expecting two agents to collect Sam Becker, they had been expecting the two agents to be in possession of the correct papers and identification, making them see what they'd wanted and expected to see had been simple. He'd not even had the time to get the FBI identification, instead a blank wallet had done the job. Making those at the station see a badge and ID card had been no harder than making them see the paperwork they'd expected.

Asag smiled to himself, his ancient body shivering despite the long, thick coat. It was cold, so cold it bit right through to his bones. Thousands of years had passed since he'd experienced temperatures such as this. It made him feel alive and long to live back on his home world and not the subterranean, sun-baked pit that was Sheol. It was almost a blessing to know returning there was no longer a viable option. The air quality was even more blissful than the refreshing cold, and he savoured every single lungful of the natural and unprocessed atmosphere. Despite these comforts, he was looking forward to relaxing in the snug, plush cabin of the primitive aircraft which had amazingly delivered them to France without crashing. Bored of watching his brother run through things with the pilot he turned, expecting to see Becker writhing around uncomfortably on the back seat, instead he saw the overly-confident Earth-Human staging an escape from the other side of the X5. He'd somehow managed to get the cuffs to the front of his body and remove the leg restraints. Asag immediately re-alised he'd been wrong to underestimate his prisoner, and very wrong to leave him in the car alone. With a deep roar of rage Asag tore open the rear passenger side door, almost removing it from the hinges. With his massive, shovel-like hand he grabbed Becker's foot and yanked. Becker's body was like a toy against his strength, the man came eas-ily, his body threading through the rear of the X5 like a ribbon. Asag kept pulling until Becker flew from the cab and hit the tarmac like a rag doll being thrown about by an angry child.

* * *

Sam felt the vice-like grip on his ankle before he realised what was happening. His mind was still filled with a mixture of fear and eu-phoric hope when he felt himself being dragged through the cab at a swift speed. The back seat, which had been his prison for the last fifteen minutes or so whipped by, and for a few brief seconds he was in free fall, before the hard tarmac hit him like a truck, knocking the wind from his sails and causing his battered body to throb with fresh pain. Sam instinctively rolled onto his back, brought his legs up and kicked out, his shoeless feet finding their target.

Caught off guard by Sam's immediate attack Asag stumbled back-wards; not far, but enough for Sam to roll to his side and get to his feet. Things happened fast; across the brightly lit apron Sam saw Namtar, rushing to the aid of his brother. The pilot scurried back into the small plane, bolting like a rabbit down a burrow. Sam backed up to give him-self room, and when Asag reached him he ducked left, swinging his cuffed wrists high, as high as he could reach, and around in an arc. His cuffed wrists made painful, but satisfying contact with Asag's face, the metal outer blade of the cuff destroying his nose with a wet crunch. Sam heard him roar in a mixture of pain and anger, which gave him a sense of satisfaction. He didn't have long to enjoy it, however. Namtar was bearing down on him like a raging bull; he'd obviously seen the lucky shot Sam had planted on his brother and he wasn't taking any chances, drawing his gun. Sam didn't think they wanted to kill him, but he didn't fancy having a bullet in his leg. He broke left and made for a pallet of boxes around twenty yards away, his sock-covered feet smacking against the cold tarmac as he went. He heard the gun discharge but the familiar white hot pain which usually accompanied the noise was absent. He'd missed, and Sam didn't intend to give him a second chance. As he dove behind the boxes he heard another sound; it was a car, the engine screaming at torturously high revs. Rolling onto his back he watched as an old and somewhat battered Renault Mégane crashed through the gate in a hail of sparks. The rusting relic had to be pushing twenty years old or more. The Mégane weaved left, its tyres chirping on the smooth surface of the airport's apron. The driver, who Sam couldn't see, lined up the bonnet with Namtar, who was frozen to the spot, his square jaw gaping open in a mixture of surprise and horror, clearly struggling to process what he was seeing. The driver of the Mégane had time for one last gear change, teasing a little more power from the screaming engine before the car collected Namtar's paralysed body and flung it into the air like a rag doll.

* * *

Out of all the scenarios Inspector Ackhart had run through during the short, out of control sprint to the airport, none of them included the situation which met him when he closed in on the gate leading to the airport's apron. As he smashed through the gate, closing his eyes when the car made impact, he saw Sam Becker, free of the leg restraints. He was pounding across the tarmac in his socks, one of the massive, purported FBI agents thirty meters away, bearing down on him with a gun. Ackhart couldn't see the other guy, and he wasn't sure which one he had in his sights. He'd tried to remember their names on the dash to the airport, but every time his mind fogged over. Tossing the old Renault to the left, his headlights illuminated the agent, the guy truly was a behemoth. Gunning the engine he knocked it up a gear and mashed his shoe hard onto the gas pedal, ramming it down into the worn carpet. The old car picked up a little speed, but she was far from being a thoroughbred. Nothing could have prepared him for the god-awful sound that hammered through the car when he found his target. He closed his eyes for a second time, swearing under his breath as the body hammered over the roof of the car. He was sure that he even heard the sickening thwack as it hit the tarmac behind him, although he suspected that was his imagination. Ackhart jammed on the brakes, the car lunged violently, and trying to recover it he fought with the wheel. The car undertook an almost artful pirouette which traced out four ribbons of rubber from the tyres.

As the car came to a stop, reality caught up with him. He flung open the door of the wrecked Renault. Staying low, he hit the ground and in a low crouch, ran to the back of the Mégane. Forty meters behind him was the guy's body, a tangled mess on the floor, blood leaking from some unseen wound. Scanning the apron with his good eye, he saw the second agent rushing across the tarmac toward the body. Where the hell was Becker?

His question was soon answered when he heard Becker's voice, loud and urgent, shouting over the drone of a plane's engine. It was the first time he'd noticed the sound; the small, twin engine Beechcraft gleamed in the flood lights, its white fuselage gleaming as the props spun at idle speed. Becker was shouting again as he dashed toward the Mégane, "**THE HEA - SHOO - IN - TH - HEAD!**" Becker's words were disrupted by the sound of the engine, but he was closing fast. "**SHOOT HIM IN THE FUCKING HEAD!**" Ackhart heard him cry as he slammed into the side of the Renault. He was breathing hard, his breath creating vapour in air in front of his face. Becker slid around the car, flopping his body onto the tarmac beside Ackhart, and he noticed the cuffs still binding his bleeding wrists. "Please tell me you have a key?" he panted, a broad smile on his face.

* * *

Heart hammering in his chest and lungs burning from the cold air, Sam slid down the side of Ackhart's car. From his hiding place behind the pallet of boxes, he'd seen the Renault smash through the gate, then slam into Namtar's body. It was a turn of events he would never have foreseen, but welcome nonetheless.

"Please tell me you have a key?" he gasped, holding his battered wrists out. "We don't have much time." He watched the shocked policeman fumble in his pocket before retrieving a cuff key. There were only seconds to spare before Asag would turn away from the twisted body of his brother, and focus his rage on them. Ackhart, his hands shaking badly, struggled to find the small keyhole on the flat face of the cuff, but eventually the key connected. As his left hand was freed, Sam took over, deftly switching the key to the right side and clicking it open. As he tossed the bloodied manacle aside, a round slammed into the side of the Mégane, ricocheting with a loud *pzzinngg*.

"*There is nowhere to go, Mr. Becker!*" Asag shouted. "*If you and your accomplice turn yourselves over now, we won't harm you!*"

The inspector turned to Sam in confusion. "I killed one of them," he said in a hushed voice.

"Oh, I doubt that very much," replied Sam. "They're hard bastards to kill." Despite the situation, Sam took a little satisfaction in the confusion washing over Ackhart's face. He was about to get proof of Sam's story – hell, he was about to get sucker-punched by the truth. "Look!" Sam held his wrists up. The bleeding had stopped, the marks left by the unforgiving metal no more than ragged red lines, and in the bright floodlights Sam could see the skin colour improving with every passing second.

"Mère de Dieu," muttered Ackhart, shaking his head. "What madness is this?"

"I know, right?" Sam smiled nervously. "It's some real fucked up shit to get your head around. The one you ploughed down will be fighting fit again, in just a few minutes."

"*Time is running out, Mr. Becker,*" shouted Asag. "*You have ten seconds, then I'm coming for you!*"

"Give me your gun," Sam demanded, holding his hand out.

"I will do no such thing, you're my prisoner—"

"Cut that shit, we both know we're way beyond that now." Sam thrust out his hand in a stabbing motion. "And I hope you remember how to fly a plane." The inspector stared blankly at the idling aircraft, and Sam felt sorry for him. He'd been in a similar situation at one time, and there was no easy way to get your head around it. Slower than Sam liked, Ackhart withdrew his gun from the holster and handed it over reluctantly. He checked the magazine, testing the weighty black weapon in his hand before flicking off the safety.

"You really think we can take that plane?" There was no hiding the doubt in Ackhart's voice.

Sam didn't blame him, Buer had been hard enough to take out – hell, he'd failed to kill him. It was a lucky shot from Adam which finally put the bastard down, and now they were facing two of the fuckers, plus whoever was piloting the King Air. A second shot slammed through the Mégane, the bullet slamming through the car, exiting just above the rear wheel arch, spraying a deadly hail of shrapnel. They needed to move.

"On my mark," mouthed Sam, trying to be reassuring when he looked into the wide, frightened eyes of the police inspector.

"Three, two, one – MARK!" Sam grabbed his new partner and made a run for it.

* * *

Unquenchable fury burned deep inside Asag's gut as he knelt beside the crumpled body of his brother. He'd expected Namtar would dive out of the way at the last moment, was horrified when he'd stayed frozen to the spot and gotten tossed into the air like a piece of litter thrown from a car window

"*I would suggest you give up, Mr. Becker!*" he shouted again, his voice an angry snarl. He glanced briefly at Namtar, who was improving by the second, but it would still be some time before he was fully functional after being hit so hard. The Gift was a wondrous thing, but severe injuries took longer to recover from, head injuries taking days if critical enough. Thankfully it looked to be Namtar's torso which had taken the brunt of the impact from both the car and the ground.

Asag squeezed off another round and watched it slam into the car with a metallic *ping*. With any luck, the bullet would pass right through the rusty old car and take one of them out. He was under strict instructions to take Becker alive, but right now he wanted nothing more than to rip Sam Becker's head off his shoulders with his bare hands. If it was a choice between Becker escaping and being killed here and now, it would be the second option – he would face the wrath of Asmodeous when the time came. Eyes fixed on the old silver car, he watched with the nervous excitement of a cat stalking a mouse, ready to spring into action. Becker sprang from behind the front of the car, pulling the one who'd come to his aid behind him. Asag's rage increased at the sight of the police inspector, desperately trying to keep up with Becker, who was out of the handcuffs and covering the distance to the hangar swiftly. Asag stood up and raised his gun. Before he had time to fire, Becker's arm reached out, and a muzzle flash confirmed he now had a gun. Asag hit the deck, firing two rounds blindly. Becker's shot missed, and to Asag's disgust, so did his. Becker and the inspector were now closing in on the hangar, their backs to him. Rolling onto his side, Asag squeezed off another round, this one timed and aimed better. The shot found Becker's shoulder, throwing him forward, slamming his body into the corrugated side of the hangar. Asag shot to his feet and pounded across the apron, closing fast as his massive legs ate up the tarmac. He raised the gun, fixing it on the inspector this time. Becker had gotten back on his feet, hand on a small access door. Doing his best to aim, Asag fired again.

* * *

The bullet hammered into Sam's shoulder. The weapon which had fired the slug was powerful, Sam felt as if he'd been hit by a train. Helplessly, his body fell forward, and just before he slammed into the side of the hangar he heard the slug hit the metal. Thankfully, it had passed right through his body. It wasn't the first time he'd taken a bullet and in full survival mode, he didn't let it slow him down – if he did they were both dead. Getting back to his feet he turned to see Asag closing on them, his face contorted with fury as he raised the gun again. Sam gripped the freezing cold aluminium handle, praying the door was unlocked as he pumped it down. Another shot rang out through the cold night air. Instinctively he ducked, pulling Ackhart with him. As they fell the door swung inward, the momentum of their bodies sending them reeling across the threshold. Sam's shoulder radiated with pain when his body hit the floor, and looking back through the doorway he saw Asag, now less than fifteen meters away and closing. When the door swung back he kicked it shut, thankful when it found the latch and closed. It would only buy them a second or two but when you were rolling the dice between death and survival, those few seconds counted.

"You've been shot," panted Ackhart as Sam pulled him to his feet, almost wrenching his right arm from its socket. Ackhart was gulping in air, wheezing like a set of broken bagpipes.

"No time to worry about it now," replied Sam, heading deeper into the hangar. After the brightly flood-lit apron, the hangar seemed as black as sack-cloth. "It hurts like hell, but in a few minutes, it will be right as rain." Sam took them left, away from the door and Asag's line of sight. A few seconds later he heard the hangar door fly open, smashing back against the wall before swinging shut.

"We need to get to that plane," Sam whispered. He guided Ackhart toward the wall where the door was. He'd felt the handle move upward slightly when he'd flung it open, and it gave him an idea. It was a long shot but worth a try.

"*Give yourself up NOW, Becker!*" Asag shouted, his voice echoing hellishly inside the cavernous hangar. "*If you do, I'll make your deaths swift!*" A shiver snaked up Sam's spine, there was an unhinged note in Asag's voice which told Sam he and Ackhart were both dead men if they were caught. Even if they did escape the hanger, there was the not insignificant problem of Namtar, who by this time, might be regenerated and fighting fit again.

One hand stretched in front of him, the inspector holding onto his belt, and with the gun in his other hand, Sam crept toward the wall, praying his feet wouldn't find an abandoned wrench or a discarded paint tin. Any noise would surely give them away; this was a dangerous game of hide and go seek. Sam didn't think they'd gone too far into the hangar, and after shuffling for what seemed like miles in the pitch-black, his outstretched hand eventually found the cool metal wall. The darkness was both his best friend and his enemy. With every painstaking second, he expected Asag's hand to grasp hold of him like a prize. Somewhere off to his right he caught the brief sound of heels on concrete. Asag was in here, and he wasn't far away. Heart hammering in his chest, his shoulder on fire, and Ackhart's laboured breathing sounding like a steam train in his ear Sam felt his way along the wall, praying he'd locate the handle before Asag found them.

"*I can hear you, Becker. I can hear both of you,*" came Asag's torturous voice.

Resisting the urge to shout a string of obscenities back, Sam sighed inwardly with relief when his hand found the door frame, then the handle.

"I'm going to open the door," he whispered as quietly as he could to Ackhart. "Follow me out as quickly as you can." There was no reply, but Sam imagined the inspector nodding his head eagerly in the darkness. Wrapping his hand around the cool metal, he mentally counted to three and went for it.

* * *

Asag paused in the frustrating darkness, trying to distinguish anything, but even his eyes, used to the gloom of Sheol's subterranean chambers, couldn't see in the darkness enveloping the hangar. He cursed the door for swinging shut on him, cursed himself for not opening it again, but he hadn't wanted to frame himself in light, giving Becker a clean shot. He listened carefully; there was the definite sound of shuffling coming from his right. He raised the gun, trying to use his hearing to aim, but it was an impossible task. Gritting his teeth in frustration he spun around on the spot, trying to decide on his next move. As he turned a single sound echoed through the hangar, which he recognized as coming from the door. In an instant, Becker and the inspector were framed in light so bright, Asag inadvertently looked away, losing any chance he had of taking a shot. As the door swung shut he broke into a run, watching the light reced into a small bead around the frame. As it closed, he heard Becker slam the handle up. Asag raised his gun and fired, *BANG, BANG, BANG* – the sound echoed around the building, rebounding off the walls. The rounds tore through the thin aluminium wall of the hangar, and streams of light, resembling three small torch beams instantly cut their way through the darkness. Asag's body slammed into the hangar door, right where the shots had carved their way through the thin metal. He clawed at the handle but it wouldn't budge.

The door was locked.

* * *

Sam slammed the hangar door shut, throwing his body against the corrugated metal as he thrust the handle up, praying it would lock, and thrilled when it did. Thanking his lucky stars, he pulled the inspector to the right, just as three rounds punctured the door. Sam heard them whizz past on a trajectory to nowhere in particular. The door wouldn't hold Asag for long, Sam had to get them to the plane, deal with whoever was piloting the damn thing and then hope Ackhart could get his shit together enough to fly them both the hell out of Dodge. It was a long shot, but he'd survived longer shots in the past. He felt the inspector shake off his grasp; turning, he saw Ackhart frozen to the spot, gawping at the figure of Namtar who was picking up his rapidly-healing body from the ground and staring at them, anger burning in his otherwise stone-cold eyes.

"Impossible," Ackhart muttered as Sam reached out and grabbed his dishevelled shirt. As he did, the hangar door behind them shook violently, Asag slamming his body into the thin panel repeatedly. Sam released his grip on Ackhart and levelled the gun at the door, aiming where he guessed Asag's head would be. He discharged four rounds, grouping them close together. The banging immediately ceased; either Asag'd taken a head shot and was out of the game, or he was badly injured. Either way, it had bought them enough time, now they just had Namtar to get through. He was still some way off, lolloping toward them, his legs still not fully functional.

"I told you they were hard bastards to kill!" yelled Sam, grabbing Ackhart and shoving him toward the plane. Namtar was making the best ground he could on his damaged legs, but he looked like a zombie from some low-budget, Eighties B-movie. "Can you fly the plane?"

"I d— don't know," stammered Ackhart. "It's been many years."

"A yes or no is all I need," Sam shouted.

"Oui, yes, I believe I can." Sam could see doubt etched on Ackhart's face, and the closer they got to the plane, the more his doubt grew. Sam very much doubted the inspector's flying hours were in order, but he had a hell of a lot better chance of not fucking it up than Sam did.

"They have a pilot on the plane," said Sam when he reached the small craft. "I don't know if he's a charter, or one of their own." Sam turned to check on Namtar's progress, the man's legs had lost their zombie-like movements, and now he was heading their way with greater fluidity. Sam raised the gun; Namtar was still a way off and it would be a lucky shot, but he fired, and as expected, missed. Namtar stumbled to the right, guessing which way to move to avoid the shot. Not wanting to waste a second bullet, Sam climbed into the fuselage. Sitting in the pilot's seat was a lone male, his dark hair spiked up at the front with far too much product.

"I'm just being paid to fly," he said desperately, turning in his chair.

"Get your *fucking* hands in the air!" cried Sam, training the gun on the pilot's head.

"Please, don't shoot!" the pilot begged. He started to raise his hands, and Sam saw the bastard had a pistol, his finger on the trigger, ready to let one fly. Instinct took over and Sam fired, but not before the pilot got a round off.

It missed Sam but punched deep into Ackhart's gut, knocking him back against the fuselage door and making him scream in pain. Sam grabbed at him, his fingers gaining purchase on his belt loop and preventing him from falling out of the plane and onto the tarmac.

Turning his attention to the pilot he saw the guy's body, slumped over the plane's instrument panel. He was dead, Sam's single bullet right on target, just a painstaking fraction of a second too late.

Sam reached past Ackhart, who was clawing frantically at the circular pool of blood spreading out like an incoming tide on his shirt, to grasp the door and slam it shut.

"How bad is it?" he asked, dropping to his knees and pulling Ackhart's shirt away from the wound.

"Hurts like hell," winced Ackhart. "I should have worn my vest." He looked at Sam with sad, regretful eyes.

"Can you still get us in the air?" Sam hated asking the question. The wound was in Ackhart's stomach; it would hurt like crazy, and without the right medical attention he was doomed.

"I think so," he smiled, but he looked a little crazed.

Sam reached for the dead pilot and pulled his limp, heavy body over the back of the seat and deposited him into a luxurious cream leather chair.

Wincing with pain, Ackhart climbed into the pilot's seat, and Sam took the co-pilot's position, hating the sensation of the cramped cockpit. It wasn't much bigger than the front of an average family car.

Not bothering with pre-flight checks, Ackhart grabbed the throttle and punched it forward. The small eight seater craft shot away from its parked position. Namtar was in front of them, closing ground, the gun raised in his meaty hand. "Duck!" Sam screamed when Namtar discharged the weapon. Instinctively, they both stooped low, using the instrument panel for cover. The sudden movement made Ackhart scream in pain and his foot hit the left rudder pedal, sending the small plane lurching to the left as the shot pinged off the cockpit window. It cracked, creating a spider's web of lines, but it held. The sudden turn of the King Air made Namtar dive to the ground to avoid the deadly, spinning propeller, which narrowly missed his head.

Sitting back up Ackhart grabbed the yoke, and using the pedals steered the plane back on course. With no radio and no idea if he was about to enter the single runway as another plane was landing, he careered onto the long ribbon of tarmac. Two more shots pinged off the rear of the fuselage, if they found the right spot they'd prove fatal, causing the craft to crash before it even got off the ground. With no time to check, Ackhart threw the throttle fully open. The twin engines sang with delight as they received a blast of aviation fuel. The small plane built up speed quickly, bouncing down the runway. When they hit eighty knots, Ackhart pulled back on the yoke. The nose lifted and hung in the air for a split second, as if the plane was deciding whether to fly or not.

* * *

"Fly, fly, fly," Ackhart begged, his head spinning from loss of blood. He glanced at Sam, who had hold of the yoke on his side of the cockpit, helping Ackhart pull the craft into the air. There was no time to ask Becker if he'd flown before, he was weak and needed all the help he could get. Then it came, a feeling which Ackhart hadn't experienced in over twenty years, when the King Air lifted gingerly into the air. Reaching forward he hit the landing gear tab, folding the wheels up into the wings, just beneath the engines. He put them on the steepest ascent he dared, being careful not to stall the engine. Satisfied they'd gained enough altitude he banked left, swinging them level with the apron they'd just escaped from.

* * *

Sam peered down at the tarmac and saw Namtar, no bigger than a child's toy soldier, fruitlessly firing his weapon at them. "Yesssss!" cried Sam, thumping his fist against the side of the cockpit. In the moment of euphoria he'd almost forgotten Ackhart. Feeling guilty he glanced at the inspector. His face was pallid and dripping with sweat, the only colour in his complexion the purple and swollen eye Sam had dealt him only an hour ago.

"Where are we going," the inspector croaked in a voice racked with pain.

"Point us toward the English coast."

"I'm not sure how long I'll be able to fly this thing," Ackhart admitted through gritted teeth. "I fear I'm going to die with many questions unanswered."

"You're going to make it," lied Sam. He'd used a similar line on one occasion in Afghanistan, comforting one of his squad who'd strayed off a cleared path and stepped on an IED. "As soon as we reach the south coast we'll land, maybe at Bournemouth, and get you some medical attention." Deep down, Sam knew the chances of Ackhart making it even that far were slim. He hoped beyond hope that he would, as Sam had no idea how to get the King Air on the ground. *One thing at a time Sammy boy*, he told himself.

"Well, for your sake, monsieur, I hope I do make it, as I'm guessing you don't know how to land this craft." Ackhart managed a half-cocked smile and Sam could see it was a façade, hiding a wall of pain. "You weren't lying, were you, monsieur?"

"No," said Sam bluntly.

"Que Dieu nous aide," muttered the inspector.

"I'm sorry?"

"I said, God help us, Monsieur Becker. God help us."

* * *

Namtar watched as the King Air banked around the airfield, seemingly mocking him. They were out of range, but he fired until the gun clicked empty, then threw the weapon across the apron in frustration. Eyes fixed on the blinking red tailfin he stood, smouldering in anger and watching until it vanished into the early morning darkness. Shoulders slumped, he strode across to the hangar to reach his brother. As he approached, dread swept Namtar's ancient body – there was no sound coming from inside. He noticed the four closely grouped holes decorating the top of the door with mounting horror. Grasping the handle, he tried the door, discovering it was still locked. Cursing himself for wasting his bullets, he grasped the cold handle and in a mixture of rage and anxiety, ripped the door open. It gave easily in his adrenalin-fuelled rage, and when it swung open his worst fears came to fruition. Asag's body moved with the momentum of the door, spilling out over the threshold. Two of the rounds had torn the side of his skull away, just above his right ear, while the other two rounds had torn open his throat. The two headshots had killed him, instantly shutting down the tiny nanobot maintainers as the electrical signals in his brain died.

Namtar's legs weakened and he fell to the floor beside his brother's body. Grasping his bleeding skull, Namtar let out a cry of pain and anger which echoed across the small airport and out into the night.

Chapter 17

"I think it's best if you tell Adam how long you've been here on Earth as soon as you can," said Lucy, turning toward Oriyanna who had her eyes fixed firmly on the narrow, dark country lane. Unconsciously she ran her palms over her stomach, still unable to believe there was new life growing inside her.

Oriyanna drooped her eyes to the floor and looked at her feet, "Yes," she replied sounding somewhat reluctant. "Then we need to figure out just what's happened to Samuel."

The mention of his name made Lucie's heart skip a panicked beat in her chest as the icy tendrils of worry crept over her; she left her hands on her still-flat stomach, as if protecting the tiny foetus.

"I'm sure he is just fine," Oriyanna reassured the young woman, sensing Lucie's worst fears, but at the same time not quite believing her own words. Lucie grabbed her phone from the small cubby-hole on the dash and brought the device to life. "Still no news?"

"Nothing," she replied soberly. "The network coverage is never great out here." Lucie squinted at the road ahead, making the most of the Juke's powerful headlights. "Go straight across this roundabout," she instructed. "We're very close now." It had been a good few years since she'd last visited the old cottage, but the route was imprinted onto her brain. Adam always took a right at this point, preferring to drive through Pewsey – it was slightly more picturesque but she wasn't on a sightseeing tour. Lucie noticed that the Woodbridge pub, where she'd often eaten at as a child, was looking a little worse for wear. Two of the ground floor windows were smashed, and the old net-curtains hung limply through the jagged gaps, fluttering in the light breeze like spectres in the headlights.

Oriyanna guided the Nissan across the roundabout and picked up speed along yet another dark and impossibly narrow lane. Lucie peered out of the window, fruitlessly trying to take her mind off Sam and the terrifying thought that he may never hear her news, and even worse, never get to meet his son or daughter. They passed the looming, tree-lined top of Woodborough Hill , completely unchanged in all the years she could remember, it created a bloated shadow against the darkened sky. "Slow it down a little," she commented a few miles later as they passed a sign that read 'Honey Street'. "It's just on the right, before the canal bridge and sawmill."

"Sawmill?" questioned Oriyanna. "What's that?"

"Never mind," smiled Lucie. "Here, turn right." Oriyanna slowed the stolen Juke to walking pace and swung them into the gravel drive. Lucie was relieved to see Adam's quirky little RX7 parked at the far end, close to the gate. A dull orange glow flickered in the front window, a welcoming light after their long and danger-fraught journey. "Well, he made it, that's one thing," she sighed, a little of the stress leaving her shoulders.

"This is a good place," Oriyanna commented, killing the engine. "I think we will be safe here, for now."

* * *

"It won't make her get here any faster," groaned Maya, as Adam crossed the small lounge for what seemed like the hundredth time. She tried to stretch her legs out on the cramped, floral two-seater sofa. The piece of furniture was well worn, and the springs pushed against the bottom of the cushion, biting into her backside. Making his way to the grubby window, one pane of which he'd wiped clean, Adam peered out into the darkened driveway, cupping his hands around his face to block out the candle and firelight.

"It's easy for you," he snapped. "It's not your family, is it?" He turned away from his vantage point and fired a terse look at Maya, immediately feeling bad for the way he'd spoken.

"I'm sorry," she sighed. "It just might be better if we both try and get some rest. Your sister will be here as soon as she can."

"Yeah, unless she's been..." He couldn't bring himself to say it.

Since arriving at the cottage half an hour ago, they'd checked the building thoroughly, moving from room to room, the flashlight app on Adam's phone guiding the way. Apart from a few spiders and other house-dwelling creepy crawlies who'd scurried away when the light from the phone found them, the cottage was empty. Having cleared the building, Adam found some old candles and matches in the walk-in pantry. The once brightly-glossed white door had succumbed to three years of human absence and damp, the paint peeling away in strips and revealing the aged pine beneath. It made Adam sad, and at the same time guilty, that he hadn't taken time to come out here and give the place a once-over. His grandparents had been very house proud and it would have broken their hearts to see their life-long home in this squalid state of disrepair. In the days after the virus things like property were not the prized possessions and investments they had once been, however, so like his Aunt and Uncle's, it had sat empty.

The matches Adam found were, like most things, a little damp and frustratingly hard to light. He'd broken more than a few trying to spark a flame. As the contents of the box grew dangerously low, one which had been buried nearer the bottom fired, crackling and popping reluctantly to life. Once he'd got the candle wick to take, he'd used the flame to light a further four candles. He'd taken four of his grandparents' old saucers from the crockery cupboard and dripped a little wax onto each, making a safe base for the candles, then positioned them around the lounge. Scavenging through the pantry and cupboards, he searched for any tinned food left behind after he and Sam had last used the place. That hadn't been long before he'd headed off to Malaysia to cover the

World Summit, if memory served him correctly. Thankfully, they'd left a couple of tins of beans and sausages, as well as a tin of orange segments. It hardly qualified as a feast, but it was better than finding the cupboards bare. The dust-covered tins were a welcome sight, and although a few months out of date he was sure they'd be safe enough to eat. His stomach rumbled at the thought of food. If it was no good they'd have to go hungry; it was a good five miles to the nearest shop unless the village's pub, the Barge Inn, was open for business in the morning, but he doubted it. Times had changed, the days of people taking nice canal walks in the morning, then stopping at their local for a bacon and egg sandwich were gone. Normality was gradually returning, but it would still be a good few years, if not decades, before life was anything like it had once been.

Having located food and some basic lighting, he made his way to the old asbestos-sheeted garage and under a waxy tarpaulin, located the pile of firewood. Thankfully, it was still dry and well-seasoned for the most part, having been inside for god knows how long. The tarp had helped hold the relentless damp at bay. With the help of some kindling, which was still in its Honey Street Sawmills' hessian sack, he'd got a fire burning in the lounge's hearth. The heat instantly began to remove the musty smell of damp from the air and gradually, one degree at a time, the room had grown warmer, making the run-down cottage more homely and habitable.

"I hope Sam picked up my text," he said absently, turning away from the window. "I got it out just before I lost signal."

"I'm sure he will be just fine," Maya lied. She knew only too well that they'd been aware of his every move since he'd cast off from Portsmouth. The two who'd been sent for him were not to be messed with, a matter she hadn't broached with Adam yet.

"If and when he picks it up, at least he'll know exactly where we are." The sound of an approaching engine drew his attention back to the window. Peering out, he willed it to be Lucie's Mini, but as the sound drew closer e disappointment washed over him. It was a diesel for sure, much too loud to Lucie's little Mini Cooper. He watched as the lights traced along the hedge outside, throwing shadows across the overgrown front garden as they pierced through the wiry hedge. They slowed to a crawl before swinging into the drive. "Get down!" he hissed, as the lights illuminated the lounge. Waving his arm frantically at Maya, he dropped below the old glossed sill, his heart thundering in his chest.

"What is it?" Maya questioned.

"A small four by four just pulled up, it's not Lucie's car!" Behind him, he heard Maya release the safety on her gun and slide to the floor.

"What can you see?" she asked in a tense whisper.

Adam poked his head above the sill like a wary meerkat, searching for a predator. "Two on board, both in the front— Wait a sec!" In a state of relieved disbelief he watched as his sister jumped down from the passenger side, followed by a second female who'd been driving. "Impossible," he muttered to himself.

"What?" Maya's urgent voice came from behind him.

"It's her!" Adam beamed, taking his attention away from the window. "And she's with Oriyanna!" He spun back to the window and watched them file past the front of the Nissan Juke they'd arrived in, feet crunching over the pea-shingle drive. As they rounded the corner of the cottage he made for the door, his body wracked with a burst of nervous excitement. Behind him Maya remained standing, a worried look creasing her tanned smooth skin.

Adam was far too caught up in the moment to notice her expression.

* * *

Lucie gripped the cold handle of the cottage door and depressed it. It was locked. No sooner had she started to knock than she heard the key turn in the barrel and the door flew open, her brother revealed in the dim orange glow of the room behind, a wide smile of relief on his face. They'd last seen each other at breakfast that morning, but it felt as if a week or more had passed since then.

Adam flung his arms around her as the door opened. "You're safe, thank god!" he exclaimed. Lucie didn't have time to cross the threshold before he was gripping her tightly. After a few long seconds his grip relaxed, and he held her at arm's length, smiling madly. He reminded her of how a proud grandparent might look before saying, '*My, haven't you grown!*'

"There's someone with me that you'll want to see," Lucie smiled, aware that Oriyanna was hanging behind. Lucie stepped aside and beckoned Oriyanna to join her at the top of the step..

Oriyanna moved to Lucie's side, smiling. "Hello, Adam Fisher," she said. "I told you we'd see each other again."

"I don't understand," Adam said. Seeing Oriyanna alight from the Juke with his sister had taken him by surprise, he hadn't yet had time to figure out what he wanted to say, or work out how he should greet her. It all felt a little awkward, like unexpectedly bumping into a girl you'd had a holiday fling with, except in this case, it had been no holiday. It had been a bitter fight for survival which had brought them together, and he felt as if the dice was about to be rolled for a second time.

"There is much to tell you," replied Oriyanna. She made to make the first move and slid past Lucie to embrace him warmly. Adam melted into her arms, just as he had on the beach in both the lucid dream, and then later, for real.

"It's so good to see you," he sighed, enjoying her warmth.

Lucie snuck past them, eager to get in out of the cold. There was a warm fire burning in the hearth and she was keen to flop out in front of it and get warm. It brought back fond memories of staying in the cottage with her parents; before bed she would sit by the fire, nursing a hot chocolate while her mum read her stories. Times had changed, and not for the better. "Who the hell is that?" she gasped, seeing Maya sitting on the sofa, hands on her knees, watching the reunion with interest.

"This is who I owe my life to," Adam answered, reluctantly turning his attention away from Oriyanna and feeling unaccountably guilty at being found alone with another woman. He cursed himself inwardly for being so stupid, Earth females might react with jealousy but he hoped Oriyanna was above that. "Her name is Maya," he continued, letting Oriyanna enter the cosy lounge. His skin was warm, and he suspected he was flushed. "She was at my book talk, in Brighton," his voice sounded rushed to his ears. "She warned me about what was happening and got me to call you and get you to leave the bar." He turned to Oriyanna who was standing with her back to the door, her head tilted to one side, regarding the unexpected visitor with interest and more than a little suspicion.

Oriyanna turned to Adam. "Just how did she know all this?" There was no malice or betrayal in her voice, and why would there be? He hadn't done anything wrong.

"Before I tell you," he began tentatively, sensing how easily the situation could get out of hand. "Just remember that without her help, I'd have been taken, hours ago." There was an awkward pause, the kind which happens when no one really knows who should speak next.

"I am Earth-Breed," Maya interrupted matter-of-factly, as if keen to break the awkward silence.

"You brought an Earth-Breed here?" Lucie fired, fixing a disbelieving glare on her brother. Lucie turned her attention to Oriyanna, who pushed the door shut, and it creaked on its aged hinges.

"I think we need to give Adam a chance to explain," Oriyanna cut in, raising her eyebrows at him in a *please explain* fashion.

Adam explained the events that led to him arriving at the cottage. Both Lucie and Oriyanna remained on their feet, listening to his account in interest. "She has photos on her phone of the team she killed," he finished up with. Lucie looked at Maya, then back to her brother, disbelief on her face. "I doubted her at first, too, but then she showed them to me. Maya, can I have your phone please?" He held his hand out, gesturing for her to hand it over.

Maya dug into her pocket and removed the handset, "It's all true," she said earnestly, passing the mobile over. "I wanted out of the whole situation, I can't help what I was born into, but I can try to make amends."

Adam opened the image gallery on Maya's phone. It wasn't what you'd normally find on a young woman's phone; there were no pictures of her out having fun with friends, no photos of pets in amusing situations or baby showers or family shots. All the gallery contained were the gruesome, bloodied images taken in his aunt and uncle's kitchen. "See, Lucie," he encouraged, holding the phone up for her to look at. "That's Aunt Sue and Uncle Brian's kitchen, I know you haven't been there in ages, but you know what it looks like."

Lucie studied the images, with Oriyanna watching on beside her. When Adam reached the last picture she let out a sigh and said, "Okay, I'm not saying it's an ideal situation, but it would appear she's telling the truth." She looked at Oriyanna. "That is my aunt's old house."

"Then it would appear we owe you a debt of gratitude," Oriyanna said, smiling. There was something that didn't feel right about the woman, despite the pictures. Oriyanna couldn't get an accurate read on her mood or feelings, something she could usually do naturally, thanks to her highly-evolved brain. For the time being, she decided to play nice and treat this Maya woman as you might a dangerous animal – carefully, while trying not to provoke it. She hoped she was wrong – after all, she had apparently killed three other Earth-Breeds to save Adam. If she had an ulterior motive Oriyanna couldn't grasp what angle it was coming from, yet.

Lucie flopped down onto a single chair near the fire, enjoying the way the flames warmed her legs. She turned her attention to the fire, mesmerised by the flames as they ate at the charred wood. She decided not to tell Adam he was going to be an uncle for the time being,. She owed it to Sam, to tell him first. To be brutally honest she wasn't sure that this crippled and crazy world was any place to bring a child into at all, but if they came out of this with their lives, she'd do the best she could. "Have you heard from Sam?" she asked, looking at Adam hopefully. "I'm worried sick."

"Nothing," he sighed, throwing another log onto the fire. "I got a text out to him before I lost signal, with just a single word. 'Wiltshire'." He picked up a well-used brass poker and jostled the wood into position, sending a hail of embers fluttering up into the chimney stack.

"You think he'll understand that?"

"You did."

"Let's hope," sighed Lucie. She turned her attention to Maya, who had stretched her legs out on the small sofa once again. "Do you have any idea what might have happened to him?" she asked, trying hard to mask the venom in her voice.

"I think our new friend might be a wealth of information," cut in Oriyanna. "Once she has told me what she knows, I need to speak with Adam." She crossed the room and sat beside him on the dusty carpet, enjoying the fire's warmth.

"I will do all that I can to help you," began Maya, twisting slightly to face Lucie. "You are facing a grave situation, they knew all of your whereabouts last night, Sam's included. They knew he was planning to kill another Earth-Breed, they knew the target. They have been watching you for weeks."

"And you didn't notice!" Lucie snapped, glaring at Oriyanna.

"No," she replied apologetically. "We had no idea. It would seem they were also aware of our presence, they traced our server and got into the program we used to study the travel patterns of the Earth-Breeds we were tracking."

"I don't understand," said Adam, switching his attention between Lucie and Oriyanna.

"I'll let her explain later," said Lucie, anger still brewing in her voice. "Right now, I just want to focus on Sam. I'm sorry, Maya, please continue."

Maya smiled awkwardly. "They were going to be waiting for him at the Chateau. Unlike Lucie and yourself, they sent two Elders for Sam. They were aware of his abilities and talent for killing. The two they sent are brothers, the last Elders to escape Sheol after the invasion began.

"Namtar and Asag," said Oriyanna, almost as if she was speaking to herself.

"Yes, you know them?" Maya questioned.

"Once, like I knew Buer and – him, Asmodeous. Many lifetimes ago. They are truly both here on Earth?" Oriyanna's concern for Sam's welfare grew. The two Elders, like Buer, were big, much bigger than he was and together they would prove very difficult to defeat, even with the Gift.

"Yes, and they are the ones he sent to get Sam. As I told Adam, his intention was to take you all alive, he wanted you to witness the end of days. After that," her eyes fell to the floor. "After that I don't know what he planned to do with you."

"I'm guessing he didn't intend on taking us out for a steak dinner," Adam laughed nervously. The joke fell flat on the room.

Maya told them everything she'd revealed to Adam in the car on the way to the cottage. Having already heard the story, Adam watched Oriyanna. She sat silently, a grave expression on her face as she digested every detail.

"We suspected he was in South America," she said when Maya finished. "So it's Peru, then?"

"Yes, in the Nazca region."

"And he still has Earth-Breeds infiltrated into locations of importance?"

"No, he doesn't need them," Maya replied. "He has the ones of use to him in Peru; even I do not know how many of us there are left. From what I understand, the numbers are lower than you might think. The events before the Reaper, along with the assassinations carried out by Sam hit them hard. I do know that those who didn't win a place on Arkus 2 are going to be left to burn with the rest of the world when those weapons launch. He has lost Sheol, his people, and with it, any hope of taking this planet as it would have been after the virus. He doesn't care about that anymore, this is the end game," said Maya solemnly.

"I feared that something like this was in play," Oriyanna said, a thoughtful look on her face. "We don't have a whole lot of time until those systems come online. The question now, is just what can we do about it."

"I think we all need to get some sleep first," Adam suggested after a lengthy silence. "In the morning, we'll figure out what we're going to do." He glanced at his watch; it was almost two thirty in the morning, and they'd been listening to Maya talk for over an hour. His eyes ached, and it seemed as if someone had sprinkled gravel into them.

"I think that would be best," Oriyanna agreed. "I would like to speak to you first, Adam; you need to know why I am here." She stood and beckoned him through to the kitchen, leaving Lucie and Maya in the lounge.

Lucie collected up the small footstool and placed it in front of the chair. Stretching her legs out she tried to get comfortable and closed her eyes. She could hear Oriyanna's voice, low and exotic, coming from the kitchen, knew she was running through their escape from London and the brush with death in the tunnel. Just as the first waves of sleep crept up on her they came back into the room. "Is everything okay?" she asked, half opening her eyes.

"Yes," Adam replied. "Oriyanna brought me up to speed. What she's done, was done for a reason."

"As long as you're happy, I'm happy," Lucie said in a sleepy voice.

Adam took another two logs from the wicker basket and carefully placed them into the flames. With luck, the oak logs would last the few hours until first light. Immediately the flames began to lick at the dry wood with a multitude of hungry red and orange tongues. On the other side of the room, he picked up two largish floral cushions which matched the dated furniture. Thankfully, the fire had warmed the musty fabric enough for it to lose the damp stickiness. He placed them on the floor by Oriyanna, who set them up like pillows and tried to make herself comfortable, like a cat in front of the fire. She removed a gun from her waistband and placed it on the floor by her side and beckoned for Adam to join her. "Tomorrow, I promise you we will figure out what happened to Sam," Adam said to Lucie, settling onto the floor next to Oriyanna. Maya, it seemed, was already sleeping, her breathing deep and relaxed.

"He should be here, with us," came Lucie's sleepy response. "I miss him so much, Adam."

"I know. We'll find him, I promise."

Adam just hoped it was a promise he could keep. Stretching out on the floor his tired bones relaxed and he let his head sink into the soft cushion as he enjoyed the fire's warmth. Oriyanna laid next him, and after he closed his eyes he felt her turn and cuddle up next to him, her body fitting perfectly against his. Instantly, he felt better, but worry for Sam kept niggling away in his mind, threatening to rob him of the much-needed sleep he craved. As the fire crackled away he finally felt sleep creeping over his body, and he welcomed it gladly.

Chapter 18

"Wiltshire," croaked Ackhart. Another wave of nauseating pain erupted from his punctured stomach and broke over his body, leaving a sheen of sweat on his brow.

Sam turned to him, his face deeply lined with confusion. "I'm sorry?" he asked, taking his attention from the ominous darkness of the English Channel, which lay six thousand feet below. Off to his left he'd noticed a single ship, its light acting like a beacon, a single star in an otherwise black abyss.

"Wh— When I was examining your phone," there was no hiding the pain in Ackhart's voice, it spewed forth with every word, "there was a single unread message. I do not remember who sent it, but it just said 'Wiltshire'. I. . ." he paused as another wave of pain-filled nausea hammered his body. "I don't know – if – it helps." He removed his hands from the controls and clutched at the sticky red stain on the front of his shirt. He'd lost too much blood now, could feel it trickling down his gut and into his trousers. It had flooded his lap and he knew he was sitting in a warm, concealed puddle of the stuff. Ackhart wasn't afraid to die, he just wanted the pain to end. If he hadn't been in the plane, and the only qualified pilot on board, he would have ended it himself by now.

"I don't know," said Sam thoughtfully, the county's name tumbling over in his head. Then the penny dropped. "Adam!" he said, "It had to be from Adam. Wiltshire." The name sounded good on his lips. He finally knew where to go, and more importantly, that Adam was safe. Or had been, when the text was sent. It meant things were happening at home, too. Adam had reason to flee to the small cottage near Pewsey. He hoped to god Lucie was safe – she had to be, or there would have been more in the text, wouldn't there?

Sam brushed his worse fears aside and tried to recall the last boozy weekend he'd spent at the quaint little place, his train of thought broken when Ackhart growled in pain. His face was already a death mask, pallid and drawn. Sam was sure if he glanced into the back of the small corporate twin prop, he'd see the Grim Reaper, scythe in hand, waiting for his next customer. Sweat drenched Ackhart's brow and matted his greying hair to his head.

"You're going to… need… to land… th— this plane," Ackhart stammered.

"Just get us as close as you can," said Sam, "I'll do the rest, I've survived one plane crash." Ackhart gave him a confused look. "Another story for another time," Sam concluded, knowing he'd never get the chance to tell it. "Just run through what I need to do, as simply as you can."

Sam listened intently as Ackhart ran through the most basic of ways to get the small twin prop on the ground without killing himself in the process. "You're going… to… want to land on grass… or soft Earth. Shallow… water is also good." Sam nodded, his attention fully focused on the dying man. "At about t— two hundred meters… put the gear down, but bring it… up… before you land."

"Bring the gear back up?" Sam questioned. "Why the hell would I do that?"

"Monsieur, please," Ackhart's brow creased, deeper still as he fought to hold on to consciousness long enough to get the job done. "You are… not a pilot, use the gear to help lose speed, it… creates drag. Not before two… hundred meters, or it will destabilise the plane. You stand… a… much better chance of landing… if you go belly down."

Sam understood where Ackhart was coming from; he had zero chance of landing the plane on a conventional runway. A gear down, off-balance touchdown could see him flip the plane and career off the tarmac. He knew where Adam was and he had a bloody good idea where he was going to land— well, crash the plane. Finding the location he had in mind from the air and over a darkened landscape would be another matter.

Ackhart took his bloodied hands off the yoke and let Sam experiment with gaining and losing altitude, as well as scrubbing off speed. "Piece of cake," Sam said, his voice caked with nervous uncertainty. "I can do this." Sam wasn't quite sure who he was trying to convince, it wasn't as Ackhart could just spin around and ask the Reaper to hold off for an hour or two; his scythe pressing firmly into the inspector's back and the deadly blow was about to be struck.

Ackhart offered up a grimacing smile that was creased with pain, his body convulsed and he went into a coughing fit, a fine spray of blood painting the hand covering his mouth and the instrument panel in front. Helplessly, he pawed at his ruined gut, as if his hands could magically heal the life-sucking wound. Sam wanted to turn away, but his morbid curiosity held him firm. Finally, the coughing subsided, and Ackhart swayed woozily from side to side before slumping forward against his harness. Reaching over, Sam pushed two fingers into the crease of his neck, searching for his carotid pulse. His skin was cool to the touch, the sheen of sweat making Sam's fingers slip across Ackhart's pallid flesh. Much to his surprise, he found a weak pulse; his heart was still working inanely, and pumping what little blood he had left around his body. Sam breathed a shaky sigh of relief through his teeth, making a whistling sound. Taking his fingers away and wiping them on his dirty cargo trousers he hoped, for the inspector's sake, that he wouldn't regain consciousness.

Turning his attention from the dying man he surveyed the array of dials and switches, most of which he could ignore for his haphazard landing. Suddenly, the dark cabin seemed like the loneliest place on Earth. He might as well have been on his own, orbiting the planet in a tin can. With unsteady hands he gripped the yoke and wiggled it left to right. The aircraft responded immediately, its port and starboard wing tips mimicking his movement. "Good, good," he reassured himself. Checking the altimeter, he noticed he'd dropped a couple of hundred feet while his attention had been on Ackhart. He didn't bother to rectify the slight change, it would be tough enough getting the plane down to terra firma as it was, and the shattered windscreen had prevented them from climbing too high in the first place.

Leaning forward, he surveyed the black expanse laying like an endless darkened lake before him. Navigating the craft to Wiltshire in the dark and with the country in blackout mode, would be a virtually impossible task – no points of reference, no landmarks and no roads to follow. Like a slow incoming tide, the magnitude of what he needed to do dawned on him. Chewing some skin on the inside of his bottom lip, as he always done in tense situations, Sam ran through his options. The plane was heading due north and that was fine, he would undoubtedly pass over the British coast very soon – it was setting the plane on the right north westerly heading that would be the issue. With the gentle thrum of the twin turbo props as a soothing soundtrack, Sam had a eureka moment. It all depended, once again, on Inspector Ackhart, but thankfully, he didn't need to be alive for it to work.

Leaving one hand on the yoke, Sam reached across and patted Ackhart's trousers pocket. When he'd first met Ackhart, those dark grey trousers had been well pressed and freshly laundered; now they wore a variety of battle scars from the night's events. The first pocket was useless, just the outline of a wallet made itself known under Sam's hand. Leaning further left and running his hand over the other pocket, he found his quarry. Ackhart had a phone. With more than a little difficulty, Sam teased the device from its blood-soaked home. He tried not to think about how the red liquid had congealed and darkened the sodden material, like molasses left out too long on a cold day.

Praying the device was one; not wrecked from the blood, and two; modern enough to carry out the task in hand and three; charged enough to last the trip, Sam wiped the screen clean against his trousers. The Samsung Galaxy was a few years old, with a badly-cracked screen. Blood had found its way into the microscopic cracks, and when the screen came to life it seemed as if a network of tiny red veins had been sown into the glass. Sam immediately checked the battery level, it was green and sat somewhere between half and three quarters full. Not ideal, but it would have to do.

Using his spare hand, the other keeping the plane steady, Sam flicked though the menu. Naturally post-curfew and lights out there was no coverage, but he didn't need it. Like most people who had phones in the old world, and those fortunate enough to have one in this new, broken version of society, Ackhart had a GPS mapping application which was easily accessible from the front screen. Hitting the application tab, Sam was greeted by a request that read, *activer le GPS*. The last time Sam had anything to do with the French language had been back in school, but he could figure out the device was asking if he wanted to activate the GPS. He pressed the part of the screen that said *Oui* and hoped.

After what seemed like an age, the map loaded and pinpointed him at a location somewhere in the suburbs of Le Havre. Sam guessed it was Ackhart's home address, and the last place he'd used the application. Unfazed, he waited for the small device to locate enough satellites to reveal his current location. Another painful minute passed as the Samsung clunked its way to life, the phone slow and out of date. Finally, the map sped by and much to Sam's relief the arrow blinked into view, about ten miles off the coast of the Isle of Wight. In the old world Sam had always cursed car drivers chatting on their phones and for some reason, he felt a pang of guilt at not having his full attention on the path ahead, as if a momentary lapse of concentration would see him crash into some unseen object at over five thousand feet.

Flicking his eyes from the phone to the altimeter and back to the windscreen, he located the search function and typed in *Pewsey, England*. The Samsung thought about the request before a small pin appeared over the tiny village. Finding his landing site was one issue he didn't have to worry about any longer, the only issue now was the very minor one of landing, which he would worry about when the time came. *One thing at a time, Sam,* he reminded himself. *One thing at a time.*

Sam propped the Galaxy up in a natural right angle behind what he was calling the power handle, the control Ackhart had shown him for adjusting airspeed. The small arrow that represented his King Air crept slowly over the channel until it broached land and began to crawl over the small island below. Sam gazed out of the window at the black expanse, here and there, small pinpricks of light showed from the ground, places which had their own generators. It amazed him that anyone could afford to run such an item with fuel prices as they were, and it would only worsen, thanks to the Russians.

The King Air flew over the Isle of Wight, just west of Cowes and powered across the Solent, the small stretch of water separating the island from the mainland. As he once again flew over land, he adjusted the plane's course very slightly, pointing it toward Salisbury.

As the New Forest slipped by unseen below him he started to descend. Pushing the yoke toward the clocks and dials, his stomach pitched slightly as the twin prop lost altitude. He watched the dial spin around; five thousand, four thousand. As he descended he noticed the airspeed creeping up. Just as Ackhart had shown him, he compensated by scrubbing the power back. The engines responded and their smooth hum dropped in tone. As the plane passed three thousand feet, somewhere just north of Salisbury, Sam steadied his descent out as best he could. Heart hammering in his chest, and with the sound of his blood rushing in his ears, he scanned the instrument panel, trying to remember where the adjusters were for the flaps which would apply the air brake. Calming himself with deep breaths, he found it and at two thousand feet, engaged it. A small, mechanical whine met his ears and casting an eye out to each wing he saw the small strips of metal rise from the top of the wings. The effect on the airspeed was instantaneous, the dial slowly creeping down.

A variety of strange village names swept by on the phone's map, he was getting close to Pewsey and even recognised some of the names – Manningford Bruce being one he often found amusing.

At eight hundred feet Sam flew over the village he'd been aiming for. He'd engaged and disengaged the air brake several times, trying to get a speed which felt right, but in truth he had no idea and imagined any instructor would be hiding his face in his hands, or more likely, crying with fear of his impending death.

As he swept north of the small Wiltshire village, the first tendrils of light crept into the sky as night began to lose its battle with the dawn. The early autumn sun, although still hidden over the eastern horizon, offered a better view of the ground below.

Sam surveyed the view below, casting a glance at the altimeter. Five hundred feet. A sudden blaring alarm made him recoil in shock, searching frantically for the source and found that the landing gear alarm had kicked in to life. Evidently the King Air knew he was below a certain height and thought it was time for the wheels to go down. Sam silently thanked the small plane, because he'd forgotten Ackhart's instructions. He hit the control and felt the wheels locking into position. The yoke immediately reflected the extra drag and began to vibrate gently in his hands. His attention flitting between far more tasks than he felt comfortable with, Sam located the small ribbon of tarmac which threaded its way through the Vale of Pewsey and into Alton Barnes. Banking the plane slightly to the left, he dipped below the hills which lined the ploughed fields. Two hundred feet. Sam knocked the power all the way back; he had no idea if he was right or wrong and a mistake now might cost him his life, Gift or no Gift. The propellers died and began to spin down, and he re-engaged the air brake, cursing himself for not doing it sooner. As he slipped below a hundred feet, he took the gear up, and the alarm immediately scolded him for doing such a ridiculous thing. Nonetheless, the plane complied and Sam heard the wheels clunk back into place, beneath the wings.

As he sped by the cropless fields beneath him, Sam carried out the inspector's final instruction and threw the engines into reverse, reducing speed further. Before the plane could slam down into the ploughed field, Sam cut the engine and switched off all the electrical systems, lessening the chance of a fire. Gripping the yoke so tightly his knuckles turned white, the King Air glided into East Field, lost the last forty feet of altitude with a gut-wrenching drop, and just slightly faster than Ackhart would probably have liked, if he'd been alive to witness it, the plane slammed down onto its belly, sending a hail of debris behind it in a frenzied wake of clumpy brown earth and stones.

The shock of the haphazard landing jarred every bone in Sam's body, rattling him to his core. Stupidly, he was still gripping the yoke, as if he could steer the King Air in off-road mode. He closed his eyes as dirt from the field hammered the windscreen, the small stones ricocheting off the thick glass. The section of windscreen damaged by the bullet gave way, showering the cockpit in glass. Sam felt the tail start to lift as the nose dug into the soft dirt, and the lifeless body of the Earth-Breed pilot he'd killed was flung forward. His body, moving with more speed than Sam thought possible for a corpse, slammed into the back of his chair.

Ironically, as Sam would later realise, the dead pilot had the last laugh. Despite being dead he still managed to hit Sam's seat hard enough to catapult Sam into the instrument panel and knock him unconscious.

Chapter 19

Adam stood in the shade, his slender figure protected from the unforgiving desert sun. Nonetheless, the heat was sweltering, and his white cotton polo shirt was wet with perspiration and stuck uncomfortably to the nape of his neck. Walking back a few steps, he craned his head upward and looked toward the sky. Towering some three hundred feet above was the black underside of a colossal spacecraft. He tried to focus on the perfectly flat, black surface, but his head began to spin. Lowering his gaze to the ground he took a few seconds, waiting for the nausea to pass. Gradually feeling better, he walked for what seemed like an age, shielded by the massive hull of the craft that loomed ominously overhead. Despite pounding his way hurriedly over the highly-compacted sand and his laboured breathing, there was no sound, all he could hear was the steady *thump, thump, thump* of his own heartbeat. Reaching the edges of the shade, he walked out into the sun.

Thump, thump, thump.

With fresh sweat pouring from his hot skin, Adam walked along the side of the massive craft until he reached a point where the hull swooped down from the sky and met the ground. He stopped and placed a hand against the ship's onyx-like surface; surprisingly it was cool to the touch and seemed to vibrate very gently beneath his fingers as if it were a living thing.

Thump, thump, thump.

Nauseous once again, he rested his back against the cool surface and relished the slight chill that ran through his hot body, and slowly turned toward the merciless sun. Only now the sun was gone, replaced by two hungry, amber eyes which regarded him from a god-like height with both hatred and interest. Adam shrank back, as if the craft would absorb his body and shield him from the heavy gaze of those hateful eyes. Inch by inch, Adam slid down the hull until he was on his knees, cowering on baking, compacted sand. As the fiendish eyes continued to drink him in, he noticed them almost smile at him. It wasn't a pleasant sensation, rather the idea of the eyes smiling installed a fresh fear in his gut. Those eyes knew something, something he didn't, and it terrified him.

Thump, thump, thump.

With the eyes still mocking him, he saw something else from the corner of his eye, in that watchful sky. A small pinprick of black, a floating speck of dirt speeding across the skies. Unable to draw his gaze away from the swiftly growing speck he remained transfixed, and tried hopelessly to focus on it. Just as he thought he could make out its shape it burst and gave birth to a new sun, which spread with ferocious speed across the sky. A burst of pain erupted in Adam's eyes, and suddenly everything was in darkness. As a thunderous roar filled his head, his flesh began to boil against his bones and he opened his mouth to scream, but instantly his throat turned to fire. Then he was ash. Fire and ash.

* * *

Adam's eyes snapped open, his breath coming in quick pants that over-oxygenated his blood and made him woozy. The first tendrils of morning light were creeping in beneath the floral drapes, the shafts of autumn sun picking up swarms of busy dust motes which floated around the room on invisible air currents. The fire had died down during the night and Adam's skin was chilled. He shivered, removed Oriyanna's hand from his waist and sat up. For a few moments he watched an ugly black spider, busily weaving a web between the worn red bricks of the fireplace and the overhanging oak ledge above. Everyone was still asleep, Lucie snoring gently, still sitting in the seat with her legs stretched out on the foot stool. Maya was face down on the small sofa, cocooned into a foetal position with her arms wrapped around her slight body in an apparent attempt to keep warm. Oriyanna, who'd been wrapped around him not moments before was murmuring something in her sleep. Adam tried to focus on her words, but the strange and exotic dialect was lost on him. Digging his phone out of his pocket he saw it was almost six AM. In a few minutes the power and phone networks would be up, and he hoped there would be news from Sam, but the chance of getting a signal out in the sticks was slim to none. He'd probably have to drive to the nearest town to stand any chance.

Getting to his feet he retrieved the poker from the hearth. As quietly as he could, he tried to stoke the fire but the wood he'd fed it hours earlier had been devoured and reduced to nothing more than a few hot embers which glowed dimly, barely hanging on to life. Laying the implement gently back onto the grate he straightened out his sweater and tutted at the dishevelled state of his trousers. He'd been smartly dressed for the book talk, but that now seemed like a lifetime ago. He needed a long shower and a change of clothes, but doubted he would be getting either.

Making his way through to the kitchen, he collected up a glass from the drainer and turned on the cold tap, letting it run for a while before placing the glass into the steady stream of water. He shut off the tap and drank deeply, his mouth and throat resembling the scorched desert from his dream. The water, although chillingly cold, carried a nasty, metallic taste; the taste of old, seldom used pipes and age. Setting the glass onto the side and wiping his mouth with the back of his hand, he surveyed the abysmal selection of tinned food he'd found last night. Shaking his head, he wondered how a couple of tins of beans and a tin of preserved oranges would feed four people. As if sensing the lack of food, his tummy offered up a protesting growl of hunger.

Ignoring it, he glanced out of the window. It had been hard to gauge the exact condition of the back garden in the darkness, and in the dim first light of morning he could see much more. Long strands of ivy had latched themselves onto the wooden shed, strangling the dilapidated building and setting it slightly askew. The grass could almost house a small Amazonian tribe and looked more like a jungle. Tangled through the various overgrown bushes and weeds were some angry, knotted thorns which seemed to belong to one of his grandfather's old fruit bushes. Left unchecked for the past few years, they'd set about on their own mission to take control of the whole garden. They were winning.

"Trouble sleeping?" came a soft female voice from behind him. Stolen from his thoughts, Adam turned to see Oriyanna leaning against the off-white door frame, her blonde hair glowing in the early morning sunshine.

"Bad dream," he replied, smiling back at her. "I seem to get those when you're around."

"The desert?" she asked curiously.

"How did you—?"

"I had the same dream – the eyes and the explosion?" Adam nodded solemnly, not bothering to try and figure out why they'd shared the same dream. With Oriyanna, that kind of madness was normal. "That ship, the large black one," she paused, eyeing Adam to ascertain that he knew exactly what she meant. "That's Asmodeous' vessel, the Arkus 2. At least, that used to be her name."

"And he's out there, right now. Waiting for us?" The acceptance in his voice surprised him. Oriyanna nodded and crossed the room, wrapping her hands around his waist she kissed him deeply on the lips. When they parted, Adam looked down at her and said, "You know, it would be nice to spend some time with you and not be fighting for our lives."

"Well, maybe when this is all over," she said temptingly, her deep blue eyes dazzling with promise.

Before he could tell her they might be dead before it was all over, the sound of someone clearing their throat drew his attention. Maya stood in the doorway, almost exactly where Oriyanna had been not a minute before. Yawning and trying to get control of her dark, sleep-tousled hair she said, "Are you planning on cooking that food we found?"

"Sure, once Lucie is up. Let me go and check on her." Adam made his way back through to the lounge to discover his sister had moved, ever so slightly. A bead of sunlight was making itself at home on her face, and in her sleep, she seemed to sense it and turned her head slightly, causing it to loll off the edge of the seat. The resulting movement snapped her awake. Frantically, she looked around for a few seconds, as if she was still caught up in whatever night terror she'd been suffering.

"Is there any news?" she asked, sitting up and stretching.

"It's almost six, sis," replied Adam. "The networks aren't back up yet – I'm sure once they are you'll hear from him." Adam wasn't sure how convincing he sounded. "Why don't you come through to the kitchen, we're going to crack open the cans of food I found yesterday. If there's nothing growing in them, we might just have ourselves some brekkie!" He raised his eyebrows in an encouraging fashion.

Lucie followed Adam through to the kitchen, and collected up one of the two tins of baked beans with sausages. Turning the can over and searching for a use by date, she glanced at Adam, who was fishing a tin opener out of one of the drawers. "Are you certain these are going to be okay?"

"Only one way to tell," he replied, finding the tool he needed and waving it triumphantly in the air.

"I'll do the honours," said Maya, taking the tin opener out of his hand and turning to the sink. The sharp point on the utensil had seen better days and no matter how hard she pushed down, it just wouldn't breach the thin metal. Turning to the drawer she recovered a sharp kitchen knife and tried to pierce the top of the can.

"Careful it doesn't slip and..." Lucie began, looking over her shoulder, but her warning was too late. The can toppled over and Maya drove the knife down into her left hand, slicing open the skin between the top of her thumb and index finger.

"Shit," Maya hissed, snatching her hand away. The tin of beans spun across the drainer before tumbling to the floor.

Lucie grabbed Maya's hand and put it over the sink. "Best wash it out," she encouraged as blood began flowing steadily from the wound, dripping into the metal sink with a dull *plink, plink* sound. Manoeuvring Maya's hand under the tap, Lucie turned it on. "Those knifes have been in that draw for God knows how long."

"It's okay, really," Maya protested, struggling to free her wrist from Lucie's grip. "Just get me an old towel or something, in a day or two it will be just fine."

"Nonsense," Lucie fussed, "If it gets infected..." Lucie's voice trailed off as the water, which had been coloured a very light shade of pink from Maya's blood, turned clear. Eyes wide, Lucie watched as beneath the water's flow the damaged skin turned pink, then healed completely. Lucie dropped Maya's hand and stepped back a pace. Neither Adam nor Oriyanna had seen it, and neither were ready for what happened next. "She can heal!" Lucie gasped.

In a flash, Maya grabbed the knife from the drainer and pulled Lucie backwards by her untidy brown ponytail. As Lucie stumbled back, Maya grabbed her around the shoulders and whipped the knife to her throat. In a mixture of panic and surprise Lucie screamed, the sound piercing the otherwise still morning and resonating through the walls of the old cottage.

Oriyanna was first to react, a nanosecond before Adam. They both rushed toward Maya who had the knife pushed painfully against Lucie's neck. Her eyes darted from Adam to Oriyanna as she tried to weigh up which side the threat might come from. "It wasn't meant to happen like this!" she growled, the soft and mystical edge to her Eastern-European accent gone. "If either of you take another step, I'll bury the blade so deep into her neck, it will pop out the other side."

"Just take it easy," said Adam, holding both palms up to show he was no threat. "What's all this about?"

"The... cut," Lucie choked the words out, "it healed. She... said she was Earth-Breed!" Maya tugged her hair painfully, and Lucie shrieked.

179

"I should have trusted my instincts," Oriyanna said in a low voice. "I sensed something was off about you, but as you'd saved Adam, I gave you the benefit of the doubt."

"I don't understand," said Adam, his mind spinning. He glanced toward Oriyanna, who slid her hands behind her back. She huffed out an annoyed breath when she realised the Glock was still in the lounge by the fireplace.

"Really!" Maya spat. "There is nothing remotely familiar about me?" she scolded in a venomous voice. Her accent was gone, replaced by another familiar one that she couldn't hide beneath her aggression. It wasn't a million miles away from Oriyanna's, but it had a slightly different twang to it, a twang that he'd heard once before, deep below the pyramid. The memory was clouded thanks to the feverish state Adam had been in, but it was there.

"You're no Earth-Breed," growled Oriyanna, her body tensed. Like a lioness, she was poised and ready to strike at the first opportunity.

"You get full points," Maya said scornfully. Her hauntingly beautiful eyes burned with fury, and Oriyanna realised with horror why her eyes seemed so familiar. Buer had fixed Oriyanna with an identical stare when he'd had hold of her in the Tabut Chamber, two and a half Earth years ago.

"You took everything from me!" Maya shrieked, looking hatefully at Adam, the knife's blade pushing into Lucie's neck. "Between you, you have left me with nothing!" She turned and glared at Oriyanna. "Thanks to your book, Adam, I know exactly how my father died and who pulled the trigger. Soon after, in the invasion of Sheol, my mother was killed. Maybe you didn't cause the explosion which killed her," Maya hissed at Oriyanna. "But you are high on the council and there is no one else here to blame."

"Buer was your father?" Adam said shakily.

"Her real name is Lilith," Oriyanna cut in. "I never had the pleasure of meeting her, she is a child of Sheol, after the war. It was always rumoured that Buer had a wife and daughter, but never confirmed.

Let alone that she possessed the Gift. Typical of his kind, to bestow such a power upon their kin."

"And the penny finally drops!" Lilith turned her face upwards toward the dirty white ceiling, as if relishing the revelation. "A thousand years I lived on that shit stain of a planet, then after my father and mother were killed and Sheol was taken I escaped with Asmodeous on Arkus 2."

"But you killed your team to get to me, to make sure I wasn't taken?" Adam protested.

"Don't you get it!" she shrieked, her voice an octave higher. The blade had cut Lucie's skin, a small trace of blood running from the tip of the knife, and like a lone red tear it ran down her neck, paused momentarily as it navigated the slight hump of her collar bone before disappearing below her sweater. "This was never about getting you to Asmodeous, this was about my own revenge. I didn't plan on *her* showing up." She shot her fiery gaze across to Oriyanna. "But things don't always go according to plan. I wanted you to suffer like I did, to have someone taken away from you, then once you'd seen your sister killed…well, I hadn't decided what I was going to do with you! Once those nukes fly, you're all dead anyway. The radiation poisoning will be far more unpleasant than anything I can do. As for me, I knew that doing this only bought me a one-way ticket, but when you've got nothing left to lose, who cares?"

"Just let her go," Adam encouraged, taking a tentative step toward Lilith. "You can have me, you can do what you want to me. Just let Lucie go."

"This isn't about killing you!" Lilith retorted, her hand steady on the blade. "This is about taking something *away* from you! Come to think of it, I can make you pay twice— no, three times!" The thin, reptilian smile spread yet again across her once-pretty face. "You can watch me kill your sister," she paused, seeming delighted by her discovery. "She is with child," she finally declared. "You're going to be— oh, sorry, I mean you *were* going to be an uncle, Adam!" She laughed maniacally, letting her words sink in. "I thought I detected something strange about her, and this explains it."

Adam stared into Lucie's frightened eyes. Tears began to well up against her lashes and she tried to blink them away, which only caused them to streak down her face.

"I was going to say you could watch me kill your sister, and then her!" She nodded toward Oriyanna. "But now I get to take three things away from you – it's almost too perfect to be true."

"If you harm either of them, I will kill you with my bare hands." Adam's fear was swiftly replaced by a red-hot fury. He glanced at Oriyanna, hoping she'd figured out a way to overwhelm Lilith. Unfortunately, with both of them unarmed and Lucie with a blade to her neck, they were well and truly on the back foot.

"Enough of the chatter," Lilith growled, her eyes sparkling with rage. She took the knife away from Lucie's neck, ready to drive the blade home.

Chapter 20

Sam sat back against the seat and ran his dirty hands over his face, trying to detect any trace of injuries. Of course, there was nothing to find, the Gift had taken care of the split lip and broken nose he'd suffered on impact, an impact which rendered him unconscious for a short period. As the memory of the crash caught up with him, he looked about frantically, searching for any signs of fire. Thankfully there were none, and the only sound in the cabin was the soft *ting-ting* of broken glass as it dropped from the spider-webbed windscreen.

Consciousness fully regained, Sam unclipped the safety belt and reached across to Ackhart's body. He searched for a pulse, if the inspector was somehow still alive he owed it to him to get medical help. After thirty seconds or more of searching, Sam gave up. Ackhart was dead. He silently thanked the inspector for what he'd done and hoped he had no immediate family who were going to mourn his loss. Climbing over the pilot's seat, he navigated the ruined fuselage. The overhead lockers had come open, spilling their contents over the eight large seats. The body of the pilot, after slamming into Sam's seat, had ended up halfway down the cabin, his skull jammed into the bottom framework of one of the seats, his torso contorted into an angle that made him look like a strange piece of modern art. Kneeling down Sam felt under the opposite seat. The pilot had been toting his own gun, and Sam wanted it. A few minutes later he found his folly; the Beretta Px4 9mm had been thrown to the back of the cabin and was buried under two orange life jackets. Sam turned the weapon over in his hand and checked the magazine. The weapon was missing only one round from its seventeen-shot capacity, the one which would have been in the chamber had slain the inspector.

Scouting the wrecked fuselage for other useful items he located a small backpack. Taking the SP2022 from his waistband he deposited it into the pack and slid the pilot's gun into its space, and then shouldered the pack on his filthy jacket.

In the fridge at the rear of the cabin he located six small cans of Pepsi and three sealed packs of prawn salad sandwiches, which he deposited into the pack along with two packs of dry roasted nuts. Satisfied that he'd picked the cabin clean, he stopped one final time at the body of the dead pilot and removed his shoes. They weren't a style Sam would have chosen, but they were just one size too big and far better than being in his socks. Taking the dead man's socks, he slid off his filthy grey ones and tossed them aside. The new shoes were black and shiny, and looked odd with his dirty cargo trousers, but it was nice to have something on his feet.

With a last cautious glance around the cabin, Sam pulled the emergency handle on the cabin door. It gave immediately and fell away into the field, coming to rest on a divot of ploughed earth. Sam sat on the edge of the cabin, dangled his legs over the side and dropped down to the field below.

He wasn't sure how long he'd been out for, the sun was peeking over the easterly horizon. The sky was clear, apart from some light tendrils of cloud which formed unfathomably long lines across the sky. The autumn chill bit into his shirt and he zipped up his jacket. Clearing the King Air's wreckage, he surveyed his landing site. The plane had come to rest halfway across East Field, which had found fame in 1990 when Led Zeppelin used a picture of a crop circle formation which had appeared the field for their Remasters album cover. Sam was impressed that he'd ended up almost precisely where he'd intend to land, although crash would have been a more accurate description. Nonetheless he'd survived and was now well and truly back in the game. Perhaps he'd been wasted as an infantry sergeant, maybe he should have joined the air force.

Sam crossed the roughly-ploughed field as fast as he could, reaching the hedgerow he followed it for around a hundred yards before finding an aluminium five bar gate, which he scaled easily. He wasn't surprised no one had come to his aid; this was a sparsely populated area, even more so after the Reaper – proof positive that the deadly virus had dealt its hand in every corner of the globe.

With his new, shiny shoes smacking rhythmically on the tarmac, Sam pushed on, walking the short distance from the crash site to the cottage. As he crossed the old canal bridge he stopped momentarily and shook his head at the sight of the semi-sunken narrow boat which jutted out from beneath the bridge like a massive splinter. The local duck community had taken up residence and two of the web-footed creatures were wobbling unsteadily along the breached side of the boat.

Jogging down the other side of the bridge he noticed that the Barge Inn sign was still in place, and it even looked clean. Sam hoped the quirky little pub, which had a games room ceiling decorated with hand painted crop circles was still in business. Around fifty yards further up the lane he reached the cottage's gate post. Parked on the shingle drive were two vehicles, one of which he recognised as Adam's old RX7. The Nissan Juke he'd never seen before, and it filled him with a slight sense of foreboding. Moving his hand to the back of his trousers, he removed the Beretta and clicked off the safety, but before he had chance to take another step a shrill scream punched through the air.

Chapter 21

Asmodeous paced impatiently across the bridge of the Arkus 2, his large, strong hands balled into fists. Clutching the bottom of his Armani suit, he creased the material endlessly. Although he despised humanity on Earth, some of their tailoring and fashion appealed to his narcissistic nature. As such, he'd purchased numerous suits and other highly priced items of clothing while he still could. "So, Sam Becker is gone?" he boomed, the sentence as much a statement as it was a question.

On the other side of the world, standing on the top deck of a car ferry, Namtar gripped the mobile phone in his right hand so tightly he thought he would crush the small device. Taking a deep, chilled lungful of the early morning air he responded. "And Asag, my brother is dead."

There was a pregnant pause at the other end of the line before Asmodeous replied. "Do you have any idea where he might be going?"

"Did you not hear me, sir? I said Asag is dead. Becker killed him while making his escape."

"Yes, I heard you!" Asmodeous snapped, the bark almost reaching down the phone and biting Namtar's ear off. "This is war, Namtar, and in war there are casualties."

"Is that all you have to say?" Namtar fumed, he knew he was on dangerous ground being so insubordinate but the loss of his brother sat hot in his gut. "Almost seven thousand years we have served you, been faithful to you, and all you can say is that he's a casualty of war!

And this is not a war, this is a *fucking* personal vendetta, a vendetta that my brother just paid for with his life!"

"You'd do well to remember who you are addressing," screamed Asmodeous, his face contorting into geometric lines of rage. Back on the bridge of the craft, sitting invisibly in the Peruvian desert, Namtar's voice filled the room, Asmodeous utilising the hands-free calling system Ben Hawker had designed and enabled with one of his many programs which made Earth technology compatible with the Arkkadian equipment. The small group of Earth breeds present, who were either working with Hawker or part of Asmodeous' small private army, stopped what they were doing to watch the fireworks, but at the same time tried to remain unobtrusive. "I'm surrounded by incompetents!" Asmodeous continued. "You let Becker escape in the plane you took to transport him in! And I have heard nothing from Lilith's team, who were retrieving Fisher! The same goes for the team sent to retrieve his sister!"

"What about the team taking care of the Arkkadians?" Namtar paced the length of the deck, as the ship sounded its horn and with a small jolt, pulled away from the port.

"They killed two, and two are outstanding. Oriyanna is one of them." His voice had relaxed slightly but there was a tension in it which told Namtar Asmodeous might erupt again at any moment. While the situation was indeed grave, there was a small part of him relieved to discover he wasn't the only one to have come up short. "How hard can it be to snatch three Earth-Humans?"

"Becker was extremely well trained, sir. He was hit several times but it would appear he is in possession of the Gift." There was a silence on the line, the carrier signal clicking a few times before Asmodeous spoke.

"Then Fisher must also be in possession of it. This was not mentioned in his account."

"When I catch up with them I have the means to disable it." Namtar reached into his deep pocket and removed a flat black disc; once activated it would dig itself into the skin of the subject and pulse the body, immediately disabling the nanobots which made healing possible. "That is, if I don't kill Becker first."

"They are to be delivered to me alive, do you understand?"

"Absolutely," Namtar replied icily, uncertain he could trust himself not to tear Sam Becker's head from his shoulders at first sight. He placed the flat black disc into his coat pocket and removed a small tablet-style PC. Bringing the device to life he looked at the green dot which was stationary, sitting in the middle of nowhere, in a small village in Wiltshire. "I took the liberty of bugging him with a small GPS tracker while he was in my custody, it's in his jacket pocket. It's one of ours and small enough for him to miss, for now. I'm sending you the feed."

Back aboard the Arkus 2, Asmodeous paced the bridge and reached Hawker. "Can you bring that feed up on the main holo-display?"

Hawker closed the current screen by placing his palm over the display and closing his fist, before flicking his hand to one side as if he were tossing away a piece of garbage. He was proud of his work and the way he'd made the two technologies speak to each other. He'd been one of the best during his time at DARPA, a trait which had followed him through to his new duties. His shabby appearance didn't quite fit with his intellect. His clothing of choice was a pair of faded blue jeans, a GAP hoody that had seen one too many winter, and a pair of retro Nike Air Max trainers.

A small green holographical dot began to blink in the bottom left of his display. He touched his finger to it, making the dot turn from green to red as he dragged it to the centre of the display area. Once in the centre it changed back to green and expanded and the GPS read unfolded before him. "There you go, sir."

"I monitored him throughout the whole flight," Namtar's voice came over the speaker system. "I think he landed about ten minutes ago, he was mobile and on foot, but he's been stationary in this position for the past two minutes."

Asmodeous watched the green dot, amber eyes squinting in frustration. "If I don't hear from the other two teams in the next hour, I am going to assume they have failed," he said. "I don't know how or why and as impossible as it seems, I am afraid it's very likely."

"I will be on British soil in four hours," Namtar cut in, watching the French coast steadily disappear behind the ferry and thinking that if the teams were not dead and had indeed failed, then they were likely to have gone to ground and be taking their chances, rather than facing almost certain death at the hands of Asmodeous.

"Good, once you are there you will be working with Peltz and Croaker, and any of the others if they check in. Wherever Sam Becker is, I can almost guarantee you will find Adam Fisher and his sister, and more than likely, the two Arkkadians, too."

"My thoughts exactly, sir."

"You will control the operation. I have dispatched the Gulf Stream jet to you from Portugal, the co-pilot, as you know, stayed with the plane. He tells me there is still some hardware on board that you may find useful – tranquilisers and such."

"How long do I have?"

Asmodeous looked at Hawker, who opened a number of smaller screens within the large one; the GPS read shrank and adjusted to the same size as the others, and all still retained the visually pleasing holographical 3D layer effect that Earth's computer scientist had not yet managed to perfect. "North Korea will have Kwangmyŏngsŏng live in around ten hours. The United States, Russia, China and the European Alliance will be live by this time tomorrow."

"Thirty hours," Asmodeous boomed. "You have thirty hours to secure them and get them here. The jet is going to RV with you at a place called Netheravon, it's an old military airbase, decommissioned now. From what my team here can tell it's used, or was, up until recently for skydiving and pleasure flights, so the runway should be in good shape. It's about ten miles from Becker's current position. When you get to the UK, meet up with Peltz and Croaker and make your way up country, it should be there waiting. That's your first stop."

"Understood."

"Oh, and if you fail, don't bother coming back to the Arkus. I hope that gives you enough of an incentive to do a good job."

The line went dead. Namtar wanted to launch the handset into the channel, but he resisted the urge and clenched his teeth tightly together, trying to force his anger to recede from boiling point. Placing the phone into the pocket of his jacket he paced to the rear of the ship and stared down into the broiling, churning water. He had no desire to fail and he was certainly not planning to have a front row seat for the coming apocalypse.

Chapter 22

A persistent blackbird, perched among the twisted branches of the plum trees, serenaded Taulass with a pretty, yet somehow annoying song, rousing him slowly from his deep, restful sleep. For a few brief moments, in the period between awake and asleep, the birdsong seemed to form part of some twisted dream, in which he thought he was in his bed, safe. Then like a train emerging from a tunnel, reality hit. He sat up in the reclining sun lounger which had acted as his bed for the night. His body still thrummed with dull pain, although it was nothing like what he'd experienced the previous night. Standing up and looking down at his ruined clothing, he ran his hands over his body in an exploratory fashion, checking his wounds had healed. Much to his relief, they had. The Gift was a wondrous piece of technology, however Taulass couldn't help but feel that he'd tested its effectiveness to its limits, and then some. Despite its miraculous ability to heal, it had done nothing to stifle the initial pain of the injuries, and being shot to shit hurt – a lot.

Stretching his aching limbs, he crossed the small timber building, his bare feet making the wooden floor creak. Drizzle dusted the thin glass door, grey clouds filling the dawn sky, as if someone had thrown a blanket over the sun. He shivered and looked across the garden toward the house he'd fled. His view was obscured by several pine trees which lined the adjoining property. He'd made good his escape from that direction last night, but didn't recall seeing them. Nonetheless, behind the trees he could still see a solitary plume of smoke tracing its way into the damp sky, seemingly eager to join the cloud which had placed a lid on the morning.

Momentarily energised at having both escaped and survived, Taulass ran through what he needed to achieve in his head. Firstly, he needed clothes. His loose fitting jogging bottoms and shirt were wrecked. Although the shirt was red, it did nothing to hide the massive, dark crimson pool of blood which had congealed and dried into the material overnight. He needed to wash, dried blood was caked onto his skin. Catching a watered down, ghost-like reflection of himself in the drizzle-powdered glass he imagined he closely resembled what could only be described as the walking dead. Last year, a number of boisterous children dressed as zombies had trick-or-treated at the house, and his current state of dress and appearance wasn't a million miles away from their costumes. With it still being a good six or seven weeks until the unusual Earth festival, he doubted he'd pass as a reveller on his way home after an evening's fancy dress party.

After cleaning up, he needed to get to the safe house. The small, two-bedroom property in Kingston upon Thames had been rented by them for the past two years. Although furnished, it had never been used. It was nothing more than an emergency backup plan to be used in the event of things going south, which over the last twelve hours, they undoubtedly had. Stabbing his hands into his pockets he clutched the recall tab, relieved that he had a way out – even if the worse happened, he was not stuck on Earth. He had no intention of pulling the plug on the operation yet, though. Oriyanna was alive and if she hadn't gone to the safe house, he needed to find her.

* * *

If there were a headstone in a cemetery somewhere, commemorating Taulass' life on Earth as a Watcher, it would read *Richard Blake 1840 – 1950.* Richard was his Earth name; it was an unassuming name, and he'd held a very unassuming position in society, hence his longer than normal one-hundred-year service. During those years, firstly in London, then moving further south to the safety of the country, he'd witnessed humanity at its darkest hour, twice over. The second time stuck in his memory more clearly, for by the time World War Two broke out, Earth tech had developed enough to allow death to touch every country on the globe. Working as a reporter for the Daily Express – a paper which on his return to Earth he'd proudly discovered was still in publication – he'd kept a low profile, yet easily kept up to date with news from around the world. In those days, information hadn't been so readily accessible and television wasn't the main medium for news. On September 7th 1940 he'd almost lost his life, when on the very first night of the Blitz, a high explosive German bomb had detonated near his small terrace house on Union Street. The blast had stripped the front facing wall from the property and caused the roof to cave in. Thankfully, he'd taken shelter in a cupboard under the stairs, crouched next to his old iron bath and string mop. That one occasion had been enough to convince Taulass to relocate to a quiet part of Surrey, where he lived out the rest of the war. Although he'd regularly find himself in war-torn London for work, it was far safer to live in an area not targeted by relentless waves of German bombers which seemed hell bent on burning England's capital to the ground. Despite the Nazi threat being great and the death toll during the war unthinkable, it wasn't his job to protect Earth-Humans from each other. Wars between men were not his concern, he merely had to endure them and hope humanity would learn from its mistakes.

It had pained him to witness both the world wars, but when his time on Earth came to an end in 1950, he couldn't help feeling a new hope for the Earth-Humans. The winds of change were coming and he was certain those bleak and death-filled days would never be repeated on such a wide scale, a foresight which had proven correct. After returning to Arkkadia, he'd kept a close eye on information provided by the next generation of Watchers, keeping himself abreast of Earth technology and advances in medicine. He'd been astounded by how quickly technology had developed and how fast things progressed during times of peace. Unfortunately, war seemed to come naturally to Earth-Humans, and despite the atrocities he'd lived through and witnessed, smaller wars and conflicts continued to break out on the planet he'd left. As soon as one ended, another crisis seemed to arise. Eventually this led to John Remy's time, and after much deliberation the council decided to try and steer humanity away from conflict and toward peace. It was a plan which worked until the night when all four Watchers were killed by Finch, the start of the events which plunged humanity into unprecedented times of hardship and death. A small part of Taulass suffered the odd pang of responsibility for what had happened. After all, Buer had been on Earth for some eighty years before the plan was put into action, and those eighty years spanned back to his time as a Watcher, but neither he nor his two dead colleagues had known. Buer had been cunning, the Earth-Breed program designed to keep this new army unknown and untraceable. A sleeper-cell style attack on a massive scale, one that had taken decades to nurture into fruition.

* * *

Shaking the memories aside, Taulass left the summer house and padded across the manicured lawn which was home to a well-maintained pond. The Glock seemed ridiculously heavy in his pocket and he kept having to haul the material up, in order to prevent his joggers falling down around his ankles.

Kneeling by the water's edge, giant golden fish began to surface from the depths of the dark water, their scaly bodies revealing an odd flash of dazzling orange, despite the lack of sunshine. As the fish grew braver and hunger took over, they got closer to the surface, until the first brave, hopeful diner stuck his mottled orange and silver head above the water and opened his mouth, as if he expected a tasty treat to be dropped right in. Fish were one of the few species Earth had in common with Arkkadia, although the variations were vastly different. It was a fascinating evolutionary quirk that appealed to Taulass' meticulous desire to understand and learn.

Feeling bad because he didn't have any food for the hungry creatures, he cupped some cold water into his hands and washed his face. He was hoping to avoid seeing anyone until he could make himself presentable, but the blood on his face would have anyone racing to call the authorities at first sight. As it was, with blood-soaked clothing and a Glock which was too large to fully hide in his pocket, he looked like a maniacal killer on a relentless spree, stalking around in search of his next victim.

Using the dark water to catch a glimpse his reflection, he saw his pale complexion staring back, displaced by the gentle ripples lapping across the pond's surface. Blood still tinged the tips of his dark brown hair, but the worst was gone. Crossing the garden, his feet cold on the wet grass, he reached the back door. Gripping the handle, he was met with a resistance that confirmed the door was locked. In frustration, he paced down a small path between the red brick wall of the house and the matching brickwork of the garage. Halfway down, the garage had a door, which was positioned directly opposite the house's side entrance. He tried the property's door first – locked. He turned his attention to the garage, and to his delight the handle depressed with a well-oiled fluidity and let him in.

The painted grey concrete was chilly beneath his bare feet, and when his eyes adjusted to the gloom he located a light switch and flicked it on. The presence of electricity confirmed it was past six AM. Scanning the garage, he realized it was more of a utilities room than a garage, which could prove beneficial. On the far wall was a sink, beneath it a washing machine and dryer. He went straight for the dryer. Much to his frustration, the first few items he found were feminine. Panties and a small pair of jeans, a pink blouse with delicate roses embroidered on the front. Shaking his head in frustration, he reached deeper into the drum and heaved the full load out onto the concrete floor. Scanning through the items, he located some things that were designed for a male, and on first appearances, looked as if they might just fit. Shaking some of the creases from a pair of grey Chinos, Taulass removed his own blood stained joggers. The gun made a dull metallic clunk when it dropped onto the floor. He wriggled his way into the clean trousers, they were a size too big, but looser was better than too small in his book. Next, he did his best to smooth the creases out of a white Polo shirt. The emblem on the left breast was a man on a horse, the label in the collar read Ralph Lauren. He slipped it on, discovering the shirt was a tiny bit tight under the arms but the freshly laundered cotton felt good on his skin. He needed a shower, but that would have to wait until he reached the safe house. Turning his attention to a rack of shoes, he found some dirty, off-white, Nike trainers that were a good match to his feet. He used a stiff, blue towel which hung over the sink to dry between his toes and dust away some of the damp grass which clung to his heels before slipping them on. Above the shoes, he saw a dark green jacket hanging on a hook, it bore the same emblem as the shirt and was heavily lined with soft fleece. Heat started returning to his chilled skin as soon as he slipped his arms into the sleeves.

Returning to his ruined clothing, he removed the return tab from the pocket of his joggers and the half-exposed Glock from the left, secreting both items into the deep pockets of the padded jacket. Standing at the sink, he turned on the hot tap and held his hand under it until the water turned from cold to tepid, then warm. For a few seconds, he kept his hands under the torrent of water, until it was so hot it almost scalded his skin. He didn't care; the heat felt good. Aware that time wasn't on his side, he filled the steel sink with water and rinsed his hair and face, watching as the water quickly turned from pink to red. He pulled the plug and repeated the process twice more until the water stayed clear. Grabbing the same towel he'd used on his feet, he ran it over his face and hair before tossing it to the floor and slipping out of the building.

Out on the pavement he doubled back and with some trepidation, followed St. Austell Road to its junction with Eliot Park, where he took a left and walked back toward Oakcroft Road, where the house was. Standing at the junction of the two roads, he could see blue and white police tape, cordoning off half the street. Crossing over, he could just make out the burnt-out shell of the four-bedroom house which had been his home for the past two years. He suffered a pang of grief when he thought about Rhesbon and Bliegh, and wondered if their charred bodies were still inside, waiting whilst investigators pawed through the evidence and tried to figure out what happened. They never would.

After a few long minutes of silent reflection, he turned around and left the scene. He had fifteen miles of London streets to navigate in order to get to the safe house; he needed to get moving.

Chapter 23

The scream momentarily froze Sam to the spot, and he knew instantly it was Lucie. Hurriedly he squeezed down the side of the Nissan Juke, which was nosed into the driveway, its bulbous rear end level with the aging, lichen-mottled concrete gate posts. Sam squeezed through the gap, the spiny branches of the hedge scraping the back of his jacket. Staying low he rushed to the lounge window, his ill-fitting patent leather shoes practically announcing his arrival as he crunched over the pea-shingle. Drawing the dead pilot's gun, he checked the safety, confirming it was already released and ready for action.

The bright morning sunlight fell on the dirty, single-glazed windows. Reaching the ledge, Sam peered into the building, discovering the front room was empty. He could hear voices, the speech undistinguishable but one of them was Adam's. Scooting around the crumbling brickwork he passed the RX7 and pushed the gate open, wincing when it creaked on its rusting hinges.

Overgrown grass, weeds and brambles filled what he remembered as once being a picturesque display of flowers, set off by a well maintained and mown lawn. Gun in hand he ducked down again, creeping under the kitchen window. He could hear another female voice screaming, but with adrenalin thundering through his veins, and a horrible feeling that if he didn't act now something unspeakable was about to happen, he couldn't make out what was being said. He grabbed the cold, terracotta-tiled ledge and risked a glance inside.

The sink and drainer were situated in front of the kitchen window, and his view almost completely blocked by the back of a slender, dark haired woman he didn't recognise. She had her left arm fixed tightly around another female, and this one he did recognise. It was Lucie. The stranger's held a knife, and it was pressed tightly against Lucie's neck. Fear and fury washed over Sam simultaneously. Directly in front of the two women was Adam, who appeared poised and ready to strike out, but he was unarmed. Sam was sure there was another body in the room, too but with his restricted view, he couldn't identify if it was friend or foe. Clarity came when he heard a rapid exchange of words from inside the kitchen.

"If you harm either of them, I will kill you with my bare hands," he heard Adam shout. Sam admired his spirit, but unarmed and facing a knife-wielding maniac, he didn't much fancy his chances.

"Enough of the chatter," the dark-haired female screamed. Beneath the rage, Sam picked up on her accent, it was a direct female equivalent of the two who'd come for him in France. Not stopping to think he stepped back from the window, confident he was out of everyone's field of view. He watched, his heart hammering in his chest like a drum, as the dark-haired woman adjusted Lucie's position and held the knife high above her head, in an angle that would drive it deeply into his wife's throat. As the knife curved its way above Lucie's head, Sam settled his feet into a shooting stance. The window was filthy, restricting his view but he was confident from this angle he could take the back of her head off and not hit Lucie. Praying he'd gotten it right, his breath caught momentarily in his throat when he squeezed the trigger.

* * *

Time seemed to slow down, as if the very fabric of the universe wanted Adam to witnessthe death of his sister frame-by-frame. He lunged forward in a futile, involuntary reaction which his brain ordered his limbs to attempt before he really knew what was going to happen. Then came the blood, and the blood brought the nightmarish scene spinning back into real time. Somewhere in the confusion, there was the sound of an explosion and breaking glass. When his brain caught up with his eyes, he saw the crimson liquid was flowing not from his sister, but from Lilith. Her head snapped violently to one side, contacting with Lucie's as she twisted free of Lilith's grasp. His brain processed a gaping wound in Lilith's neck which she clawed frantically at with the hand that not a second ago had been gripping his sister. With his focus entirely on his quarry, Adam reached Lilith and with a fury unlike anything he'd experienced before, he snatched the knife from her other hand. The wooden handle was warm in his grasp when he brought it up rapidly and buried the blade deep in Lilith's head, penetrating her skull at the softer part of the temple. For the briefest of moments her skull offered up resistance before it gave way with a nauseating *pop*. He thrust the blade home until his fist, still clutching the handle, stopped against the side of her head and grew sticky with blood. With his chest pressed tightly against Lilith's body, Adam felt her spasm as a gurgling, chilling cry spewed from her lips. She twitched a couple of times, her eyes filled with fear and anger, before her weight slumped against him. Leaving the knife where it was, he stepped back and let her body fall to the faded linoleum floor.

Slightly dazed and more than a little confused, Adam's stomach churned. Bile rose in his throat and he grabbed the roll-top edge of the aluminium sink, vomiting up what little food remained in his belly. Before he finished retching, the back door came crashing in.

* * *

Sam heard the shot leave the chamber, but the sound of the bullet penetrating the glass was lost to the ringing in his ears from the discharge. Through the dirty glass he saw the dark-haired woman's head snap to the left. He'd missed the perfect headshot he wanted, , but the slug had found its mark in her neck. Rushing toward the back door he glanced at the window once more and saw Adam was on her, locked in a struggle. Sam hit the door like a freight train, smashing the lock free of the woodworm riddled frame. He hadn't expected it to give quite so easily and spilled into the kitchen, grabbing the counter to prevent himself sprawling across the floor and crashing into Oriyanna as she jumped in alarm.

"Oh my god! Sam!" he heard Lucie cry, and before he had to chance to steady himself she threw her arms around him, clinging so tightly he could hardly draw breath. He stumbled under the extra weight but kept his feet. "I thought they'd caught you, or you were—"

"What, dead?" he asked, grinning. "I'm a hard bastard to kill, you know I have more lives than a cat, right?" Sam planted a kiss on her head and noticed her eyes were welling up with tears. One escaped and ran down her pale cheek, and he scooped it away with his forefinger. "How many times am I going to have to save your arse?" he joked to Adam, as Lucie continued to cling to him. He glanced down at the woman's body which was lying face down with a knife buried into the side of her head. "Nice work, though," he added, turning his attention back to his friend who was wiping vomit from his lips with the back of his hand. "But you're still soft as shite!"

"Fuck you very much," Adam replied, without a hint of malice. His mouth tasted like a sewer, and Lilith's blood coated his right hand, slick and warm on his fingers. Gripping the tap he turned it on and washed his hands, although he suspected that just like Macbeth, no amount of water would clean the blood away.

Sam managed to prise Lucie from around his waist and planted a kiss on her lips. They were chilled, probably from the shock of her ordeal. He glanced at Oriyanna. "Well, I see the gang's all here – which probably isn't a good thing."

"It's good to see you too, Samuel Becker," Oriyanna smiled. Sam's quick wit never failed to amuse her and it was good to have him back. Despite the danger and drama they'd experienced during those days when they'd struggled to save humanity last time, she'd enjoyed their time together.

"Sam," he corrected. "How many times do I have to remind you?" He shook his head and laughed. "I'm guessing by your presence and the hellish few hours I've just had, that the shit has hit the proverbial fan. I don't imagine you've dropped by on a planet-hopping holiday for tea and cake."

"Don't you take anything seriously?" Adam asked as he refilled the glass he'd used earlier with cold water and rinsed his mouth out. The liquid still tasted metallic, but it was better than the aftertaste of puke.

Sam chuckled and glanced once more at the body on the floor. "You can start by telling me just who the fuck this is, and how she managed to get here?"

"Her name is Lilith," Oriyanna answered before Adam had a chance to reply. "She was on the team which was sent for Adam, but she killed them in order to help him escape."

"So, she saved your arse and then turned on you? Now I am confuddled," Sam admitted.

"It's a long story," Adam cut in. "She told me she was an Earth-Breed who wanted out, but turns out she was no such thing."

Oriyanna crossed the kitchen, and avoiding the pool of blood on the floor, put a comforting arm around Adam. "She was Buer's daughter and had her own agenda. She'd gone rogue to accomplish her own goals."

"Shit," said Sam, shaking his head in utter disbelief. "You'd better hope she's the end of his family line, or they might all be after you." He smiled at Adam, who shot him a dirty look. "Let's get her body out of here, it's making the place look untidy. Once that's sorted, I think we need to sit down, preferably over some grub, and tell each other what we know." He unwrapped Lucie's arm from around his waist, and placed his pack on the benchtop before bending to Lilith's body and searching for a pulse. "I'm guessing she has the Gift?" he asked, looking to Oriyanna.

"That's what gave her away," Lucie answered. "She was opening a can when she cut herself, and I saw her heal as I was helping her to wash it clean."

"And that's what put you in the firing line," he speculated, nodding. "I wonder just when she planned to show her true colours?" He stood and wiped some dust from his hands. "Well, she's a goner alright. I guess a knife into the head works just as well as a bullet."

"Yes, it will have the same effect," Oriyanna agreed. "Anything which kills the electrical signals from the brain disables the nanobots and renders them inactive."

Sam stepped over the body and opened the back door fully, it had bounced back against the wall and partially shut again. He turned back to Adam. "You take the legs, I'll take the torso. I don't want you chundering again if you get a bit of blood on you." He shot his friend a wicked smile. "I don't suppose you've checked to see if the boozer is still in business?"

"Not yet," Adam replied, bending down and grasping Lilith's legs under his arm.

"I passed the sign on the way in and it looked," he paused, "maintained. Let's hope, as they've always done a good fry-up. I don't know about you guys, but I'm famished. I have a few bits in my pack but nothing I'd class as breakfast." Sam picked Lilith's body up beneath her limp arms. "And those tins on the side musta been here since we last came up."

"We'll clean up here," added Lucie, opening drawers and searching for a rag. She was only too aware of the trade her husband worked in, but from the safety of her own home she always felt detached from its ugliness. Seeing just how easily he could brush off the sight of a dead body slammed the reality home. She was under no illusions that she'd been in a situation where Lilith would have killed her, but Sam's nonchalance was still hard to swallow. While she respected and almost envied his blasé attitude, it also chilled her. Finding an old threadbare tea towel in a drawer, she watched the two men heave the body up into their arms, and navigate it out of the kitchen. As soon as it was gone, she felt better.

"So, that hulking sack of shit had a family," Sam said, careful not to fall over the doorstep. "I guess she must have studied that fucking book you wrote, and knew exactly who was to blame for her father's death."

"I think on that particular day," Adam began, almost losing his grip on Lilith's legs, "that it was me who did the arse-saving by shooting him, although it was more luck than judgement. And that book needed to be written – how was I to know this was going to happen?"

Sam nodded and smiled. "Trust a reporter to fuck things up for everyone." He offered Adam a wink which took any sting out of the sentence. "Book or no book," he continued, walking backward down the crumbling concrete path leading to the garage, "they'd have found us."

Shuffling along, Sam reached the door first. He partially rested the body on the ground and reached back, opening the door. The dark interior of the garage smelt of dust and old oil, and cobwebs hung from the cracked timber beams.

"Put her over by the wood pile," Adam instructed. "We'll use the tarp to cover the body. We'll be long gone before she starts to smell and people come looking." Placing the body on the dusty concrete, Adam stripped the faded green tarp from the timber stack. A few large black spiders scuttled from their hidden homes and scurried into the wood, their bulbous bodies moving with a swiftness which sent a chill down his spine.

"Almost a shame," Sam said as they settled the tarp over Lilith's face, her dark, tanned skin already pale.

"How so?"

Sam shrugged. "She looked quite hot. Pity she was – one of them."

"You're sick," Adam groaned brushing his polo shirt down and standing back. "Don't let my sister hear you say that," he added.

"That's a bit rich, calling me sick. I'm not the one who's lusting after an alien. Maybe I should call you Avatar from now on!"

Adam flipped him the bird. "Oriyanna hardly looks alien."

"Let's see. For one thing, she wasn't born on Earth, and secondly, she's over six thousand years old. So yeah, I'd call that pretty fucking alien. Admittedly, she doesn't have a big grey head and black eyes, but…" he chuckled, enjoying the banter. "But I have to admit, on the grounds that there wouldn't be a straight guy on the planet who wouldn't have a crack if they got the chance, I'll let you off."

"You're a dick," said Adam light-heartedly.

"I know, sorry. Too many years being around squaddies does that to you." Sam rounded the tarp and walked out into the overgrown garden. "Your old granddad would be turning in his grave if he saw this mess." He gestured to the invading brambles which snaked their way through the other unkempt plant life.

"I know. It's gone to rats, hasn't it?"

"Bit like everything else, then," Sam concluded, heading back into the kitchen where Lucie was wringing out a blood-soaked tea towel into the sink.

"Right, time to learn what needs to be learned," announced Sam, looking at Oriyanna. "I guess you guys are pretty much up to speed?"

"Yeah, thanks mainly to Lilith," Adam answered when he stepped into the kitchen. "She disclosed everything in a bid to win my trust."

"And you think she was telling the truth?"

"I wish I didn't, but I do, yeah."

Sam shook his head, "That bad, then?"

"Pretty much," Adam replied solemnly.

"Shit. I feel like that guy from the Die Hard films – what was his name?"

"Bruce Willis," Adam answered, a little unsure where Sam was going with this.

"I know that, I mean the character he played."

"John McClane."

"That's the one. You know, when he says about the same shit happening to the same guy twice. That line."

Adam chuckled. "You remember some useless crap, don't you? Unfortunately, for him it happened like five times."

"Well, balls to that," Sam replied. "I don't even want to be a part of the sequel." He looked at Oriyanna and enjoyed the expression of sheer confusion on her face. "I guess we don't have any teabags for a brew, so let's go to the lounge and talk this through, then, if I still feel hungry, we eat. But in the meantime..." He bent down and retrieved his pack from the floor. Opening it, he took out the small cans of Pepsi and the packs of nuts. "There. That should keep us going, and there are some prawn sangers as well, but I don't think I'd trust those unless it's a food emergency."

In the lounge, with the curtains still drawn, the sun cast a pinkish light over the room. Adam perched on the small sofa with Oriyanna at his side. Sam slumped into the chair Lucie had slept in, the well-worn springs enveloping him in a welcome as he tried to relax. Lucie perched herself on the arm of the chair and rested a hand on his shoulder.

Sam let the others go first. Adam, Lucie and then Oriyanna spoke, each running through their accounts as succinctly as possible, being careful not to leave out any important details. Lucie chose not to tell Sam about his impending fatherhood; it was something to tell him when they were alone. She wasn't sure when that would be, but the baby wasn't going anywhere yet, so she had time. Despite the short amount of time she'd known Oriyanna she trusted her not to mention the subject. Talking in low voices, they nibbled on the snacks Sam had provided and sipped the warming soda. Just as she had in the RV, Oriyanna took a swig from the can and complained at how bad it tasted.

Sam listened with interest when she explained about her small intelligence team and how they'd secretly been on the planet for almost two years, certain Asmodeous would eventually turn up like a bad penny. "I'm not in the least surprised that you're here," he said, leaning back into the armchair. "I actually had my suspicions from the start."

"And you never said anything?" questioned Adam.

"No, I didn't want to get your hopes up as she'd never broken cover,"

"Like I said, Adam, many times I wanted to come to you, but the risks were too high." Oriyanna smiled apologetically.

"Strategically it makes perfect sense that she'd be here. Oriyanna is the only living Arkkadian who had direct dealings with the Earth-Breed. Not to mention that she'd been here recently and had a bit of knowledge about the modern age."

"I'm sorry, Sam, that we used you as we did" Oriyanna said. "I knew you'd be up to the job, and I also knew it would be unlikely you'd turn it down. With the Gift, you stood a smaller chance of anything bad happening."

"You don't need to apologise," Sam reassured her. A wicked smile flashed across his hazel eyes. "Well, apart from that last job – that was a cluster fuck!" He leaned forward and clasped his hands together. "That bastard, Laurett. He knew I was coming, kept looking around his room before I gave him a nice dose of Pancuronium. He also told me there were plans for me, and he muttered a name, ENOLA. Now I know what he was referring to, although I wish to fuck I didn't."

"The feeling's mutual on that one bud," Adam agreed.

"It was like he was waiting, thinking someone was about to save his arse. I guess they meant to nab me before I'd done the deed. I don't know what went wrong at their end, but if it hadn't been for the French Police, I'd have been out of there and on my way home hours ago." Sam gave them a brief rundown of his ordeal. As he spoke, they listened in silent amazement as he recounted his time in the cells and the daring escape from Le Havre airport with the inspector's help. "If I hadn't had Ackhart's assistance, I would be dead or on my way to Peru by now."

"So, do you know if you killed either of them?" Oriyanna asked when Sam finished speaking.

"I'm not sure," he replied, his stomach gurgling with hunger. "Possibly one, but I didn't stick around to confirm it, sorry."

"Asag and Namtar will not stop until they find you, or us." Oriyanna added. "I believe we are safe here for now, but we need to get things moving soon."

"So," Sam began, sounding slightly exasperated. "You really think they can do what Lilith claimed, all that stuff about taking control of the launch systems when those crazy bastards turn them back on?"

"I have no doubt," Oriyanna replied. "It will take some work, making the Sheolian and Arkkadian tech work together with Earth's, but it can be done, and he's done it. We tracked one Earth-Breed from the US to Peru – a guy named Benjamin Hawker. From what we could learn about him, we believe he was a government technology and programming specialist. I just know he will be involved in Enola."

Sam groaned and rubbed his face with his hands. Looking through his fingers, as if he didn't want to face reality, he spoke. "Only a person who had spent time here would know to give the program that name – it's sickening."

"I don't follow," said Adam, sounding confused.

"Enola? As in Enola Gay – the B29 Superfortress that dropped the first atomic bomb, Little Boy. And I thought you were the educated one."

"Of course," sighed Adam. "The name did sound familiar."

"So, what do we do? Peru is on the other side of the world, and no offence, but last time I stepped onto a commercial airliner with you, it didn't end too well," Sam grinned.

Oriyanna chuckled, admired Sam's ability to make light of any situation. "Don't worry, there will be no need for planes this time."

"Good, 'cos I've already crashed one before breakfast."

"I need to get back to London," Oriyanna continued, eyeing them in turn. "There is something in the house I need."

"You do know that the place will be crawling with police?" Sam warned.

"Not necessarily," Adam disagreed. "Once they've completed the initial scene investigation, the place will be locked up and put on cordon for a few days while they come and go as they please. By the time you turn up, there'll just be one or two uniformed officers at the front of the place with a log." He grinned at their surprised expressions. "I've been to enough crime scenes to know the score."

"Okay," said Sam, thinking carefully. "So, say you get there, say you get in; what the hell do you have stashed away that we can use?"

She glanced around the small group and leaned in as if she was about to reveal a big secret. "We weren't dropped off here on Earth," she began. "We travelled as a four."

"Are you telling me you have a fucking spacecraft squirreled away somewhere?" Sam asked, his voice tinged with childish excitement.

"Not here, but in a way, yes. Let me explain."

Sam grinned, leaning back in his seat and crossing his arms. "I'm all ears."

"There is a device in the safe at the house. Once used, it will recall the craft to my exact location."

"And just where is this craft?" asked Adam, feeling a pulse of nervous excitement.

"On the dark side of the moon." Before anyone had a chance to cut in, she added, "As soon as we recall it the craft will enter lunar orbit. Once there, it will jump directly into Earth's orbit by opening a small, short wormhole tunnel to bridge the two hundred and forty thousand or so miles. When it is in orbit here, it GPS locks to the return tab and comes directly to its location."

"Shit," cried Sam, his smile almost spreading from ear-to-ear. "Us Earth skivvies really are under-evolved. Just how long will it take to get to us?"

"No more than five minutes from the point of activation," Oriyanna answered proudly.

Sam stood up and thrust his hands into the deep front pockets of his jacket,. "It's just past eight o'clock, I don't know what time the pub opens, but if they are opening, and they're serving food, it should be anytime soon."

"Is that all you can think about?" mused Adam.

"An army marches on its stomach," Sam defended.

"We are no army."

"We might be facing one," he grinned. "Let's trundle down there in the Juke; as it's not legit we need it out of sight. We can just dump it in the pub's car park."

"That leaves us with the Mazda which only just has four seats – not that the two in the back count for shit. How the hell are we going to get back to London? There's no way you can have two people in the back seat all that way." Adam followed Sam to the front door as Lucie retrieved the keys for the Nissan from a dusty side unit.

"We don't all need to go," Sam stated, stepping out onto the shingle drive. "That's like putting all your eggs in one basket. Look, it should be a simple enough trip, there and back. Five hours max. You can go with Oriyanna, you know, give you guys a bit of quality time." He punched Adam's arm in encouragement.

Climbing into the 4x4, Lucie reversed out onto the road. Secreted in the deepest corner of Sam's left hand jacket pocket, lost among the usual pocket lint and fluff, was the small GPS tracker. Sensing that it had moved more than a few feet, it woke up.

Chapter 24

Nicolai Peltz stood on the quayside and watched with trepidation as the black speck on the horizon gradually became identifiable, at first merely as a large ship, then morphing into a car ferry.

Failing to locate either of the outstanding Arkkadians in London, he'd received instructions over the phone to head south and get to Portsmouth. He'd been told he needed to meet Namtar who, it seemed, had experienced some issues of his own. To make things worse, Namtar was alone, having lost his brother Asag in the attempt to take Becker. Peltz wasn't sure if the fact that Namtar had also failed would go in his favour or not. On the one hand, Namtar couldn't berate him too much, to do so would be hypocritical, but on the other, he'd be so furious at the loss of his kin and having failed himself, he would be in desperate need of venting some anger, and that anger would be heading his and Croaker's way.

Jim Croaker stood next to him, glancing around nervously, obviously thinking the same thing. Enjoying the warmth of the disposable coffee cup which was clenched in his right hand, he swilled the liquid around and took a sip, the steam from the drink escaping in a small vapour trail through the hole of the carry-out lid. Despite being a sunny day, there was a nasty chill in the air and the bright sun reflected off the ripples in the water, producing countless mini-suns which shimmered on the surface. He was as keen as Peltz to get the job done and make it to Peru; it felt like he'd been in the field for weeks.

Croaker swallowed the hot, bitter liquid and said, "So he knows where Becker is, then?"

"Yes, he managed to bug him while they had him in custody." Peltz spoke without taking his gaze from the horizon, his eyes squinting against the low sun. To the north behind them, clouds were building, threatening to turn the day dank and miserable. "Once we have Namtar we will be heading to Wiltshire. The location that the GPS tab is pinging is in the middle of fucking nowhere. He's been holed up in one place for the past few hours. Two things make me believe the others are there, too."

"And they are?"

"Namtar said the plane carried out a direction change while in flight and over the channel. The line to the point where he suspects the craft to be was straight, meaning Becker was aiming for a specific location. Also, there was plenty of fuel in it to go further. The bastard was heading somewhere specific. Secondly, he walked on foot from the landing site to one location where he's remained for some time. Lastly, it's remote, just the kind of place you'd expect no one to find you."

Croaker nodded in agreement, it seemed a reasonable and rational theory. He didn't want to mention what he knew Peltz was thinking; that Becker might have found the tracker and be leading them on wild goose hunt, or worse – a trap. Instead, he drained the last of the coffee and tossed the cup over the quayside where it floated on its side, nudged back and forth by the gentle waves. The P&O car ferry was nearing port, close enough now to see the small breakers crashing against the hull as it glided through the water.

* * *

Namtar watched impatiently as the English coast steadily grew larger on the horizon. The clock was ticking, but he still had time. Time to get this done and get back to the Arkus 2 before zero hour. He wondered if Asmodeous would stick to his thirty-hour deadline, or afford him some breathing space. Mulling it over for a few minutes, he concluded that he probably wouldn't. Running the timescales in his head, Namtar worked out that he'd taken the call from Asmodeous four hours ago, at six AM, which meant he was down to twenty-six hours. Noting the number in his head he started the countdown timer on his phone. The flight back to the Arkus would take somewhere in the region of twenty hours aboard the Gulf Stream, and that was allowing for a fuel stop in Portugal on the way. So his window of opportunity was down to six hours. Six hours to find Becker, who he hoped would be with the others, and get them to Netheravon to meet the jet. It was cutting things close but it was achievable – yes, if things went to plan, it was definitely achievable. He would be in Wiltshire within an hour and a half of rolling off the boat, plenty of time if Becker stayed put. He removed the tablet computer from his coat and checked. A few hours ago, Becker had been on the move, his original location, which Namtar had seen on street view as a small brick cottage, had changed. For some reason, he'd moved half a mile away, down a small track to a building which Namtar could only get an aerial satellite view of. He couldn't make out what it was, the place looked to be of moderate size and sat on the banks of the river or canal which wound its way through the tiny village. Having stayed in one spot for just over half an hour, Becker had returned to his original location, where he'd been for the past hour and a half or so.

A bored-sounding voice came over the speakers and politely requested all car drivers go below decks to their vehicles and prepare for docking. As if being first to his car would make the process faster, Namtar thrust the handheld computer into his pocket and rushed downstairs to locate the French-hired X5. He'd received word that everyone else, apart from the team sent to take care of the small Arkkadian cell, were suspected to be dead. Even Lilith's team had dropped off radar, which wasn't good news. Earth-Breed were expendable, and with his brother dead and Lilith missing that just left him and Asmodeous, two out of the hundreds who had been killed and captured during the Sheolian raids. Finding the vehicle with ease, he climbed into the driver's seat and clutched the steering wheel, his blood boiling in anger. He respected his orders and wouldn't kill either Becker, his wife or Fisher – but he would make them hurt. Oh yes, they were going to be in a world of hurt when Namtar got his hands on them. They'd beg for death, but he would not give it to them. He relished the prospect of making them watch as he killed the two Arkkadians, particularly the female, as he knew Fisher had feelings for her. He'd make Fisher watch as he cut her flesh repeatedly, giving her time to heal between each, making each new wound more painful than the last. Then if she begged for death enough, he'd show her mercy, but not before he'd had his fun. A thin smile formed on his lips as his imagination ran wild with the possibilities, his body experiencing an excitement that bordered on sexual when he played out each wondrous scenario in his head.

Lost in bloodthirsty thoughts, Namtar almost missed the slight nudge as the boat docked. Blinking away the images of Oriyanna beneath his blade, and with the imaginary echoes of her screams slipping from his twisted mind, he checked his watch impatiently and started the engine. Many of the other motorists shot him disapproving looks, but then like sheep they followed suit, all fouling the air with pollution when there was nowhere to go and nothing to do but wait. He hated them. Hate wasn't even the right word… more despised – hated and despised – yes, that was it. Soon they would pay. He was relieved when the front of the bow dropped, finally producing a ramp leading onto the port. After beeping at a few idiotic humans who seemed hell bent on slowing him down, Namtar rolled down the ramp and onto British soil.

* * *

Six thousand two hundred miles away, Hawker paced down the long corridor that led from his very ample quarters to the bridge of the Arkus 2, his Air Max moving silently on the hard, metallic alien flooring. Despite being Earth-Breed and technically a child of this advanced alien race, and having never been on such a craft before, it amazed him how very human it felt. The general design and layout of the craft could have come straight from some Earth-Human's concept pad. The lengthy corridor he currently paced was around seven feet high from floor to ceiling. The walls had a brushed metal effect while the floor was onyx-black, like the outer hull. Intermittent lighting donned the ceiling, but there were no visible light fixtures. The bright white material created a natural luminescence every ten or fifteen feet, but the light somehow didn't seem artificial. It even radiated its own subtle heat which kept the craft at a perfect twenty degrees centigrade. Every thirty feet the outline of a door broke the brushed metal wall, spaced out on either side of the passage. These doors led to the living quarters for the more senior members of the crew, and this particular section he'd come to call the Bridge Approach. The thirty or so private state-style rooms were designed to house those essential to the running of the craft, ensuring that in an emergency, any member of the bridge crew could be called upon and in post within two minutes. Nowadays, though, Arkus 2 wasn't quite so well crewed.

Hawker's quarters consisted of what was akin to a two-bedroom, moderately sized apartment. In her day, Arkus 2 had been a long-range exploration craft, much bigger than conventional short trip scout vessels, she was designed to carry whole families, allowing her crew to spend longer away from home.

For most of the past six thousand years, her many rooms had been empty spaces, a reminder of a time when the Arkkadian people had been as one, before planet Earth hammered an immovable stake between them.

Reaching the end of the corridor, Hawker placed his hand into a recess in the wall, and the door hissed open.

"I trust you are rested?" Asmodeous asked when Hawker reached his terminal and brought the holo-display to life.

"As rested as you can be at five AM," Hawker replied, wishing that somewhere on this hulk of a vessel there was a coffee machine. "I've only had a couple of hours' sleep."

"It's overrated, anyway." Asmodeous stood next to him, his suit fresh, clean and ready for a catwalk show. His sandy blonde hair still looked a little messy, yet somehow stylish. The first thing which had struck Hawker on meeting his boss and master, was that if he lost those very alien, yet somehow captivating amber eyes, and let his blonde hair grow a little, with a vest and a pair of boardies he'd almost look like a surfer. However, with his well-tailored look he was a formidable character who oozed a magnetic charisma that could charm the birds from the trees.

Hawker blinked, his eyes feeling as if they were full of desert sand. His Woody Allen look-a-like colleague was busy monitoring chatter on hacked government phones while he studied the news and tracked the progress of the American and Soviet submarines and ships, as they played a deadly game of standoff in the northern Pacific. A stupidly risky game, considering it was all over the supply of oil. The location of the boats was of interest to him, for they held a bunch of nukes that he would be using. At zero hour he would need to know the exact location of each craft, to make sure Enola didn't target its weapons on a city too far out of reach. He trusted she wouldn't; once he set her free she would be fully automated, but like any expectant parent with a child going to school for the first time, he wanted to be there to hold its hand.

"How is Kwangmyŏngsŏng, coming along?" Asmodeous asked, watching Hawker work, bringing various screens to life with the ease of a person who'd been using holo-screens for years.

Hawker found the screen tab he needed and flicked it to life. Frowning, he studied the 3D image with interest. Turning away from the screen he looked at his boss. "Looking at the lines of code that they're running I would suggest they're in the start-up phase. The system will go live and reboot a few times before it's online and working, but I'd estimate no more than five hours."

"So they really did beat the others to it," Asmodeous summarised.

"Looks like it. The others won't be far behind, and every system should be back in the next twenty hours or so."

"If we wanted to raise the tensions a little in the East, what city would you target?"

"Tokyo, sir," Hawker replied immediately. "That will stir up a hornets' nest."

"Alright. In five hours, as soon as Kwangmyŏngsŏng goes live, be ready to launch a strike. I think we need to test out this program of yours."

Hawker snapped the screen closed and opened a fresh one. Within a few seconds, he had a satellite view of Tokyo before him, and allowing himself a tiny smile he nodded in agreement.

* * *

Thirty minutes after docking in Portsmouth, and with time slipping away from him faster than seemed possible, Namtar watched as the English countryside whipped by. He'd abandoned the rental X5 at the port, instead favouring the Volvo XC90 driven by Peltz and Croaker which had its steering wheel on the correct side for this country – another oddity of the Earth-Human world which pissed him off.

"We will meet the Gulf Stream at Netheravon," he said to Peltz, who was concentrating on the road ahead. "There are more weapons on there."

"Very well, sir. We are pretty well armed already, however."

"If you're so well armed, how did two escape?" Namtar boomed, fixing his eyes on Peltz who instantly shrunk back into the cream leather seat. "Just what firepower do you have with you?"

"One Colt AR15 machine gun, one USMC M40A1 sniper rifle, three Glock G26 9mm semi-automatic handguns, a M26C Taser and a few knives," Peltz offered with a smile.

"You were on a kill squad; we need to take Becker and the others alive, not pepper them full of lead. Do you have any tranquiliser rounds?"

"No, sir, just killing machines. I do have the Taser."

"It may be of use," Namtar said thoughtfully. "There should be a secondary tranq-pistol in the Gulf Stream; we had two but I couldn't find the other so I'm guessing it was left behind."

"We should be there in about an hour, sir." Peltz left the motorway and pointed them north toward Salisbury.

"Excellent," Namtar praised. He fired up the hand-held computer and was relieved to see the green dot representing Samuel Becker was still in the same place, a cottage just off Honey Street in a tiny village in Wiltshire, which appeared to be the back end of nowhere. He closed the window and brought up the street image of the cottage, studying it with interest, wondering what the link was that connected Becker, and hopefully the others, to this out-of-the-way place.

Chapter 25

Sitting around a table in the lounge of the Barge Inn, Sam popped the last mouthful of toast (his third slice), into his mouth and washed it down with the last of the lukewarm, sweet tea. Putting the cup onto the lacquered pine table, he exhaled in satisfaction and said, "Now I think I can concentrate on the task in hand."

"Are you sure you don't want to finish off my scraps, too?" Adam asked, still not able to believe Sam had managed the Gut Buster breakfast and an extra three slices of toast. His plate still had half a sausage on and two grilled tomatoes. He'd been as ravenous as he could ever remember, but the portion had beaten him easily.

"Nope, I'm good thanks," Sam smiled, patting his belly proudly. "It's good to see the old place is still in business, and it's lost none of its kooky charm." He gestured to the ceiling which was beautifully hand painted in a mosaic of crop circle designs. It had been like this for a long as he could remember, although the paint was starting to show its age now, it was still an impressive bit of artwork. Matching the ceiling, the walls were decorated with countless photographs of the local phenomenon, many of them dating back years.

"It's fascinating," said Oriyanna, standing up to study some of the more impressive designs.

"It's amazing what a few guys with some rope and a few planks of wood can achieve," Sam said sceptically.

"I'm not so sure," said Adam. "I think the majority are fake, yes. But a few I'd say are a real mystery."

"It's not your lot, then?" Sam said to Oriyanna with a laugh. "Landing your spaceships here and leaving pretty pictures in the corn?"

She looked at him, not certain if he was serious. Unable to work it out she shrugged. "There are still many things in this universe that we will never know the truth behind. This whole area is naturally rich in Earth energies, there are numerous sites like this around the planet. I'm afraid I have no answer for you. I just don't know."

"We need to get moving," Adam announced. In the pub, eating the much-needed breakfast and rehydrating, he'd felt safe and detached from the events unfolding outside. He didn't know why, but it felt different to when they'd been together in the States. Maybe it was because this time they were on home turf, in places they'd grown up in.

"I'm still not certain splitting up is such a good idea," Lucie complained, slipping out from behind the table. Sam opened the door leading out onto the canal towpath and ushered her through. "I mean, we only just got everyone back together."

"We don't need to go," Sam reassured her. "Let Oriyanna and Adam handle it. Besides, I haven't slept in over twenty-four hours and if I don't get some shuteye, I'll be fit for nothing." Up until he'd sat down for food, Sam had been running on adrenaline, bolstered by the caffeine in the Pepsi. Now with a belly full of stodgy food, exhaustion was hitting him hard. "I need to grab a few hours' sleep while they're gone. As soon as they get back, we'll figure out what to do next. Just like I said, one step at a time." He offered her an encouraging smile, turned and nodded his thanks to the bartender, who looked far too old to be working. The aged man raised an arthritic hand in appreciation and Adam and Oriyanna slipped past Sam onto the towpath.

Outside the morning had warmed a little, but not much. If you ignored the wreck of the partially sunken, narrow boat resting under the road bridge, in this part of the world it was almost possible to forget that anything had ever happened. Unlike London, which was still littered with the remains of burnt out and looted shops, here, where people enjoyed a more relaxed pace of life and the hoodlum population was virtually non-existent, it had been left almost unchanged.

The walk back to the cottage took them five minutes. As planned, the stolen Nissan Juke remained parked at the rear of the pub, in a field which had once been used as a campsite. Before leaving for the pub they'd searched the boot of the little 4x4, but the only thing of any real use had been a pair of tatty old Reebok trainers which Sam had laid claim to immediately when he discovered they were his size. They looked more fitting with his dirty, battle scarred clothes.

As they crossed the crumbling forecourt of the old sawmill, Sam held them back for a few seconds and studied the cottage. Satisfied that things looked to be as they'd left them, he beckoned the others on.

At the front door, he studied the jamb, relieved to find the small pin still wedged in the bottom of the frame. It was an old trick he'd learned years previously, to tell if anyone had been in while you were out.

A few minutes later Adam had the engine in his Mazda ticking over, listening to Lucie telling him to be as quick as he could and not to stop for anyone unless he was sure it was a police car.

He smiled and kissed her on the cheek, pleased to see she had a little more colour in her face now she'd slept, eaten, and had her husband back. They were all in desperate need of fresh clothing and a good wash, however. Lucie's brown hair was still in an untidy pony-tail, smudges of dirt visible on her cheeks. "See if you can get the old boiler fired up," he suggested as he prepared to leave. "It would be nice to get clean when we get back."

"I'll get Sam on it after he's had some rest," she replied. "He was beat, he's already in bed."

"And remember to tell him about—" Adam eyed the region of his sister's belly.

"I will, I just need to find the right time. If I tell him now, he'll just want to wrap me up in cotton wool."

"Maybe he should," Adam said seriously.

"Be quick," Lucie encouraged, forcing a smile onto her lips.

Adam planted a last kiss on her forehead, "I plan to be." He gave her a wan smile and walked to the car, his shoes crunching on the gravel. Oriyanna was already in the passenger seat, waiting patiently.

Lucie watched as her brother carefully reversed the Mazda out between the two concrete gate posts and onto Honey Street, revved the engine and vanished behind the overgrown hedgerow. It was just past nine AM. They should be back by half past three, four at the latest. She checked her phone – no service. *Great,* she thought, *I won't know about it even if they do need to call me.* Not relishing the prospect of six more hours' of nagging worry, Lucie turned from the door and closed it. Inside the cottage, Sam was already lying on top of the damp double mattress in the master bedroom, sound asleep. Leaning over, she kissed her husband on the cheek and brushed some of his sandy blonde hair back from his forehead. When he began snoring lightly she collected up his jacket, which he'd hung on the floor. *No change there then,* she thought, and draped it over an occasional chair in the corner of the room. The two handguns he'd arrived with she left in place, on the old oak bedside table, where he'd left them before climbing onto the bed.

With anxiety running riot, Lucie knew there'd be no more rest for her, so she left Sam to sleep and went to the boiler cupboard. If she could get the thing started, at least she could enjoy a nice relaxing bath and get clean. If only she had some casual jeans and a fresh top. Her work skirt was battered and grubby and her blouse looked as if she'd scooped it straight out of a bin. Her thin blue jumper also looked like a charity shop reject which annoyed her, as it had been one of her favourites. With a sigh, she began to work on getting the boiler running.

* * *

Adam whipped the poky little Mazda away from the cottage, over the canal bridge and began the climb up into the hills, following the road which would eventually bring them to the town of Marlborough. In a field below them he caught a glimpse of the King Air Sam had escaped in. The broken plane was halfway across East Field and a single police 4x4 sat beside the wreck. He could just make out two more yellow jackets by the main gate, which was some three hundred yards away across the roughly ploughed ground.

As the road rose higher and the small village dropped further behind he lost sight of the crashed plane and focused his attention on the road ahead. It was narrow and twisty, but he knew it well and could drive it fast. Pushing the accelerator to the floor he spoke to Oriyanna. "So, what do you plan to do when you get this device?"

"Ultimately, I need to recall the craft and we need to head to Peru."

"I was afraid you were going to say that." Adam chuckled. "I'm guessing there's no one else here and by the time you get a message home—"

"It will already be too late," she cut in. "I'm not sure what kind of timescale we are working to here, but I doubt very much Asmodeous will hang around. As soon as he can gain control of those live launch systems, he will use them." Oriyanna eyed him with a serious expression before continuing. "Last night, just before we were attacked, President Hill was giving an address to the American people. He believed their nuclear systems would be going live in the next twenty-four to forty-eight hours, but they could be faster." She watched him with her wide blue eyes. "If we can stop this now, Adam, it's over. Do you understand that? Sheol is under Arkkadian control, there is nothing left of his army or his people, other than that ship out there in Peru. Nothing! Unfortunately, that's also what makes him so much more dangerous. He has nothing to lose."

Adam didn't reply immediately, concentrating on throwing the RX7 around a corner. He navigated it confidently, and the tyres chirped nicely as the back end of the car drifted slightly and held. Back on a straight section of tarmac he said, "That doesn't make me feel any better. If we can end this now, and there's no chance of a reprisal from his people, we need to make sure we don't fail. Simple."

With one stop for fuel just on the other side of Reading, Adam arrived in Greenwich in bang on two and a half hours. If there was one positive to be taken from the events which had changed the world, it was the sheer lack of congestion that had once troubled almost every arterial route in the country. The unfortunate mixture of death and ridiculously high oil prices had seen a fifty percent drop in traffic. Consequently, on a Saturday morning which had grown more overcast and dull the further north they'd pushed, Adam hadn't been stuck in a single traffic jam getting into the nation's capital.

"You'll need to direct me," he said as they entered the London district. He set the wipers on the Mazda to intermittent, as light drizzle dusted the windscreen.

"It's on Oakcroft Road," she replied, staring intently out of the front windscreen and trying to get her bearings. "I think it's off Lewisham Hill, do you know it?"

"Yeah, I think so. One sec." Adam had a good idea where the road was, it was a main route through the area, and living relatively close by he'd used it several times. He swung the car left and slowed down. "Anything look familiar?"

"Yes, the large beech tree." She pointed to the landmark, the beech was on a camber which hung it slightly over the road, and as a chillier and earlier than usual autumn set in, its leaves had dropped onto the tarmac in an almost perfect outline of the canopy above. "Take a right here!"

Adam followed her instructions and crept along Eliot Park. In a few hundred yards Oriyanna pointed out another right turn, which he took. As they drew level with the junction of Oakcroft Road, he saw what he'd been expecting; about a hundred yards down, near the larger detached houses was a line of blue and white barrier tape. He couldn't read the single word printed repeatedly on it but he knew it would say 'Police'. Scanning the road for somewhere to park he spoke. "Nice area this, not cheap, or it wasn't before the virus."

Oriyanna was leaning forward, trying to understand what she was seeing. "Oh, no," she gasped as Adam reversed into a space just down from the road closure. "That can't be possible."

"What?" he asked, leaving the car's nose poking precariously out into the street as he looked to see what she was staring at. The ground floor window glass was gone, leaving gaping holes that revealed the foreboding dark interior. In the top two windows, which Adam guessed would be bedrooms, one had a pane of glass semi-intact, although it had been punctured by what he knew, from Oriyanna's account, was automatic gunfire. The glass had somehow held, but was spider-webbed and stained smoky brown from the fumes and flames. More police cordon tape ran the length of the front wall and closed off the driveway, just to get the message home that there were to be no visitors today.

"That looks bad," said Adam, not quite sure what he should say.

"I don't know how it happened, why would they burn it down?"

"To get rid of evidence?"

"I doubt it," she answered, her eyes wide and drinking in every detail. "I'm sure they wouldn't be worried about that." She paused for a moment and said, "Unless..."

"Unless what?"

There were a few long, drawn out seconds of silence which ticked by slowly. Finally, Oriyanna spoke. "Taulass."

"You said he'd been killed." Adam took his attention away from the burnt-out building and parked the car properly. The two uniformed police officers, one burly looking male and a female who looked far too small to be in a position of authority, paid him casual attention before returning to their conversation. They were both soaking wet and pissed off, it appeared to have been raining for a good few hours and Adam wondered just how long they'd been left on post. He knew it wasn't unusual for people to rubberneck a scene of destruction or tragedy, and as long as they didn't pay too much attention to it, the cops wouldn't be interested.

"He looked dead, I mean, he was covered in blood – but..."

"We don't know yet, don't torture yourself over it." Adam placed a reassuring hand on her leg.

"We need to get inside, there's one way to know for certain." Oriyanna cracked open the car door and stepped out into the light drizzle, Adam followed suit, and taking her by the hand he walked away from the scene.

"What are you doing?" Oriyanna protested.

"We can't just walk in, the place is a crime scene. We need to get around the back and hope they don't have an officer in the rear garden." He spoke in a low voice, leaning toward the side of her face.

"I can get us in, remember?" she grinned at him.

"Far too risky, what if it goes wrong? Do you want to spend the day locked up in a cell? I sure as hell don't. If we have no other option we'll have to try, but just for once, let's try and fly under the radar." Adam knew she was more than capable of influencing the two PCs on the front door, but it was a risky move, and a skill they might need to fall back on if they were caught. "We'll garden hop," he explained. "The house is..." he counted the buildings from their position, "six down."

"I imagine it should be obvious," Oriyanna smiled. "Once we reach the burnt-out shell, I'd say we are there."

"That's why you're the superior race," he said, flushing red with embarrassment.

"I've told you before, not superior, just a little more evolved." She offered him a joking smile.

"Many of these places are empty now," Adam explained. "That aside, they all have massive back gardens, you can tell from here." He pointed to a line of trees at the rear of one of the properties. "If we're careful, we won't get seen." He gestured to the house sitting opposite them; in its day, before the virus it would have no doubt been home to some London professional earning a hundred thousand euro a year. Now it looked abandoned. The metal boarding on the windows was decorated with graffiti, the unreadable purple and yellow tags filling the aluminium boards as if they were canvasses put there for the sole purpose of street art. In a few places, the paint had strayed from the boarding and encroached onto the painted rendering. There were numerous examples of these now-ownerless houses scattered across the city. For many unlucky families, the Reaper had taken them all, leaving no one to inherit their prized worldly possessions. The long-range plan was that these abandoned houses would be renovated and sold cheaply to people in need, or taken under council ownership. The utopian idea was that now, in a population reduced nation, no one need be on the street or homeless. It was a nice, idealistic plan, but Adam knew it was still many years from coming to fruition. They hadn't even managed to lift curfews yet, or have a 24/7 power supply.

He took Oriyanna by the hand and led her down the unevenly paved side path. The faded cedar panel gate was closed, but with a tug it opened, the swollen wet timber offering up resistance as it ground its way across the brindle paving blocks. Slipping into the rear garden Adam lifted the gate, to make its passage easier, and closed it engaging the latch. The garden was almost a carbon copy of his grandfather's, overgrown and unloved. At the far end a greenhouse was losing its battle with the grass that now climbed halfway up every wall. The building was also being attacked from within, plant life filled its interior, pushing against the dirty wet glass as if eager to join its kin outside. In the centre of the garden an old rigid swimming pool held back the vegetation, one side partially collapsed when a ladder had fallen over and into the pool. Stagnant, foul smelling water filled it to half depth, a variety of autumn leaves in various states of decay floating on the surface, and where the light rain hit the manky water, tiny rippling circles radiated out from the point of impact, setting the leaves to bobbing up and down.

Turning away from the pool, Adam battled through the long grass and tested the fence at the far end of the garden, which still seemed quite sturdy. He guessed it belonged to the house next door, which appeared to be inhabited. Reaching the end of the garden he gave Oriyanna a boost and she scaled the larch lap panel with the grace and speed of a feline. With much less grace, and a little more struggle, Adam heaved his body over and joined her on the other side.

"Only five more to go," Oriyanna encouraged.

"Maybe you can give me a boost next time," he suggested with a wink. "You might also want to take care of that." He pointed to the gun and holster which had been tucked under her long-sleeved top; the climb had exposed the gun for any prying eyes to see. Oriyanna pulled her top down to conceal the weapon before heading across the lawn. This property was definitely occupied. Although it would never win any awards for best garden, a little care had been taken, the grass was cut and a few toys were scattered here and there. Whoever lived here had been one of the lucky ones.

It took them a couple of minutes to reach the final fence, which thankfully was a good foot shorter than the previous ones they'd scaled. Crouching down, to avoid any police who might be in the garden, Adam gingerly poked his head over the top and surveyed the scene. "The back door's open," he said in a hushed voice. "I can't see anyone on point at the rear, come on!" He used his right hand as a pivot and vaulted the low panel in one jump, Oriyanna following closely behind.

"How long do you need?"

"A minute, two at most," she whispered, studying the soot-black interior. "The device is in the safe, it's fireproof but it is up on the first floor."

Adam gave the building a surreptitious once over and said, "I hope the stairs are intact, then."

"Only one way to find out." Oriyanna kept to the fence line and rushed the length of the garden, not stopping before she entered the kitchen. Adam followed behind, praying that no police would be inside.

The housed stank of ash, burnt timber and water, the combination nauseating. Adam followed Oriyanna through the kitchen and she paused by the breakfast bar. People, likely scene examiners, were working in the front room. Between bursts of quiet conversation, Adam could hear the sounds of a camera snapping photos.

S T Boston

"Any identity on the two who were in the lounge yet?" a softly spoken female asked the question, her voice slightly muffled by the face mask she wore.

"Nothing, nada, zip," a male voice replied. The rapid click of a camera taking pictures followed. "It's a fooking mystery alright. Even the guy we have ID for, Richards – he's a yank. What was he doing here?" More rapid shutter clicks interrupted their conversation.

Adam had waited for the camera sounds to start up again. Moving quickly he drew Oriyanna up the stairs to the first floor, using the camera sounds to mask their footsteps on the damaged stairs, and praying there would be no one up there. On the landing, he surveyed the damage. Bullets had blasted the bannister rail into splinters, and the walls were peppered with bullet holes. "These guys really did a job here, didn't they?" he whispered as Oriyanna passed him and hurried into her room.

Adam watched as she rounded the bed, which apart from being smoke damaged, appeared unscathed. She crouched down and went to work on the safe at the bottom of the built-in wardrobe, its mirrored door hanging precariously from the runner.

"It's gone," she said, louder than he would have liked. "The device is gone."

Adam held a finger over his lips and hoped the symbol for *shut the fuck up* was a universal one. Oriyanna came back to where he was standing, by the door. "Taulass must be alive, the safe wasn't forced."

"Where the hell is he then?" Adam hissed.

"We need to go to Kingston upon Thames," she announced, bounding down the stairs as if she'd completely forgotten the scene examiners in the lounge. Adam followed her, expecting to hear voices challenging them at any moment. He peeked around the wall and into the lounge, discovering it was empty. He hoped the two examiners had gone out via the front door and weren't taking five in the back garden. Oriyanna was waiting for him in the kitchen, and Adam signalled for her to stay put. Deftly, he moved to the door and peered into the garden, which thankfully, was empty. He signalled her to hurry and

229

they left the smoky-smelling kitchen. Staying low, they covered the length of the garden and vaulted the fence.

Crouched in the wet grass in the neighbouring property, Adam caught his breath before he spoke. "What's in Kingston upon Thames?"

"The safe house. It's where we planned to meet if things went wrong. Unless he's been caught, that's where he will be."

"Best we get moving then," said Adam, glad to be out of the crime scene. He stayed low and crossed the lawn, eager to reach the car.

Two minutes later, Adam cleared the final fence and found himself back looking at the dilapidated swimming pool. With Oriyanna following behind, he made his way down the side of the house and out onto Oakcroft Road. Reaching the safety of the car he finally allowed himself to relax. The windows immediately steamed up, affected by the combination of wet clothing and the warm cab. Adam cracked his window open and turned the fans on full. "Well, that was intense," he laughed. "Why can't we do things that normal couples do?"

"I don't think we could ever be classified as normal," she said, running her fingers though her long blonde hair and flicking excess water into the footwell. "Let's get moving, I'll direct you once we get closer."

Ninety miles away. a dark grey Volvo XC90 pulled into the small visitor's car park at Netheravon Airfield. The passenger in the front seat checked a handheld computer and smiled.

* * *

Steam gradually built up in the small bathroom, fogging up the mirror on the glossy white medicine cabinet and taking some of the chill out of the air. Feeling rather proud of herself, Lucie dipped her right hand into the deliciously warm water and stirred. Satisfied with the depth and temperature, she shut the water off. Making her way through to the bedroom she checked on Sam; he'd hardly moved in the last two and a half hours, and was still flat on his back with his arms spread either side, breathing deeply. Almost looking like someone who'd come in from the pub after have a few too many beers. On her way back to the bathroom she cracked open the boiler cupboard door and checked the pilot light. A bright blue flame was still burning away happily, emitting a steady and satisfying hiss. It hadn't taken much work to get the old girl burning again. The gas had been switched off at the main stopcock, a problem that was easily fixed. Then she just had to re-ignite the pilot flame, which had proven simple, once she'd found the ignition switch on the base of the unit. In the airing cupboard she'd also discovered a couple of blue towels and a matching dressing gown which she seemed to recall had belonged to her mother. Taking it from the slatted shelf, Lucie had buried her face into the material, hoping to smell her mother's perfume still on the robe – but it just smelt a little stale.

She'd also discovered an old bar of Dove soap, still in its wrapper, in the medicine cabinet. Sure, the stuff was a little dried out and cracked, but as soon as she put it in the water it created a lather which would make her feel a whole lot cleaner than she did currently.

Lucie placed one of the light blue towels and the dressing gown by the bath, both within easy reach. She stripped off, quickly realising the steam and the warm water hadn't taken quite as much of the chill from the air as she'd thought. She shivered and glanced down at her flat tummy. *Well, I guess pretty soon that's going to be a thing of the past*, she thought, running her hand over her bare skin, still not quite believing there was a tiny life growing inside her. Climbing into the water, she did her best to relax. As soon as Sam woke she'd tell him about the baby; she hated the idea that he was the last to know, but things didn't always turn out the way you wanted them to. Working the soap in her hands she washer her face, body then took her long brown hair out of the ponytail, placing the hairband to one side so she could use it again later. Hand soap wasn't the best thing in the world to wash hair with, but beggars couldn't be choosers. Having built up a good amount of lather, she worked it into her hair.

Satisfied that she'd cleaned her locks as best she could, she slipped down in the bath and submerged herself completely.

At first, she thought the figure which suddenly loomed above the tub was Sam, until a strong hand reached into the bath, grabbed her freshly cleaned hair and heaved her upwards.

It wasn't Sam – and the stranger was grinning.

* * *

The small country cottage was uncared for when compared to the image Namtar had seen on Google Street View, but it stood to reason. Watching the building from a safe distance in the sawmill car park, Peltz had explained that imagery on Google was out of date, taken way before the Reaper had swept its scythe over the land. Now the place looked abandoned, and there wasn't even a vehicle in the driveway.

"Are you sure this is the place?" asked Peltz, not hiding his uncertainty.

Namtar passed him the tablet computer, revealing that the green dot blinked steadily in the same position, right over the aging building. "We passed the wrecked plane back there, didn't we?"

"Yes, but – what if he found the device and this is a trap?"

The thought had crossed Namtar's mind, but he didn't want to tell his subordinates that. There wasn't a back-up plan. He'd hoped to arrive at the building to discover either the small sporty car they knew Adam Fisher used, or the Mini Cooper that his sister and Sam Becker owned. Finding neither was a little disconcerting.

Croaker fidgeted anxiously in the rear seat, using the gap between the two front headrests to watch the cottage. "So, how do you want to play this?" he asked, keen to get on with the job. Namtar had explained Asmodeous' threat to proceed with the plan, whether they returned or not. "The clock is ticking."

Namtar was about to speak when a steady flow of steam emitted from a vent pipe on the side of the building. He stared at it in confusion. "What's that?" he asked pointing it out.

A grin was forming on Peltz face. "Someone is home," he announced, glee threaded into his speech. "That's either the heating, or hot water being used. I doubt the place has central heating, so someone is there."

It was all Namtar needed to hear. He opened the car door and strode around to the boot, unzipping a bag and taking out the tranq-gun. It was loaded with one dart, and he helped himself to a further five, stuffing them into his deep pockets. His fingers touched the small disc that could strip the Gift away from anyone in an instant, a useful tool which he might well need to stop Becker or Fisher from thinking they should attempt any heroics. Beside him, Peltz zipped up his favourite tactical vest, his usual weapons of choice affixed to the front, each within easy reach if needed. By his side, Croaker did the same.

"We have as many as six targets in there," Namtar explained, not taking his eyes from the building. "It's not only possible, but highly likely, that the two Arkkadians have tried to make contact with the Earth-Humans, and most certainly Oriyanna."

"Understood, sir," said Croaker.

"They can be killed if necessary, but try to take the girl alive. I have special plans for her." His lips spread into a thin grin as brief snippets of his thoughts from the ferry flooded back. "We can use her, so only deploy lethal force as a last resort. The others need to stay alive." Not waiting for a response, he pushed the boot closed and using the overgrown hedge as cover, crossed the road and trod carefully up the shingle drive. At the door, he paused, flashing Peltz and Croaker a brief nod before he tried the handle. It was unlocked.

* * *

Sam was in a deep and restful sleep, but no matter how deeply he slept, he had the uncanny ability of keeping one ear alert, no doubt honed from years of practice. The part of his psyche which was constantly on guard heard the front door latch turn and in an instant, his eyes snapped open. At first, he remained motionless, completely awake and alert. From the bathroom, he could hear splashing water.

Lucie obviously got the boiler working, he thought, his ears scoping deeper into the property and zoning out the aquatic noise. Then he heard it: footsteps in the lounge, two— no, three pairs. In an instant, he dismissed the chances of it being Adam and Oriyanna; a quick glance at his trusty G-Shock watch confirmed they'd only been gone for three hours, an impossibly short time to do the round trip. Rolling over, careful not to let the aged bedsprings creak he slid to the floor, reaching up for the either the Glock or the Beretta that he'd left on the nightstand. Getting to his feet he mentally followed the direction of the quiet footsteps; in the kitchen, then the hall. Lucie was in the bathroom and his first instinct was to rush to her, warn her – but he had the element of surprise on his side, and once that was gone, it was gone for good.

The yellowing oak bedroom door was half closed, forming a natural V shape between the jamb and the side of a darkly stained antique wardrobe. Staying clear of the door's aperture, he secreted his body in the small space and peered through the thin crack between the frame and the door. The sight of Namtar made his blood run cold, and behind him were two other males Sam didn't recognise. They were both dressed in combat style clothing, black cargos, black tees with tacvests over the top. The guy behind Namtar had a holstered Taser and a very lethal knife. His gun – Sam couldn't distinguish the make and model – was in his hand, held low and ready. He searched for the other one – Asag – but he was nowhere to be seen. Sam hoped he'd made a corpse of him in France, but there was always the possibility he was waiting outside, intending to scoop up any potential escapees fleeing the building.

His heart racing, he watched Namtar pause by the open bathroom door, firing a meaningful look at his two colleagues before he went in. *Why hasn't Lucie seen them?* he wondered. Half of him wanted to spring to her aid, but three against one wasn't good odds. He could easily kill one of the intruders, but the other two would be on to him before he could switch his aim. The tactically trained part of his mind won the battle, and he decided it was better to stay hidden and wait for the right opportunity to present itself. The teams which had been sent to get them had all wanted to take them alive, so he hoped their plan wasn't to kill his wife on sight. A fraction of a second after Namtar went through the bathroom door Sam heard a scream of terror which sent a chill through his body. Gritting his teeth, forcing himself to stay hidden, he watched as Lucie's naked body was heaved through the door and into the hall.

"Where are the others?" Namtar bellowed, his large hand clutching Lucie's wet brown hair and forcing her head back at an unnatural angle. Sam flicked his eyes to the guy without the Taser; his eyes were taking in every detail of Lucie's naked body, and a small grin of satisfaction was etched on his features. Sam felt his blood begin to boil.

"I'm alone," Lucie said in a shaky voice.

Good girl, Sam thought as he ran options through in his head.

"I don't believe that for a second. Peltz, search the house," Namtar demanded.

"My pleasure," the Taser-toting guy said, a thick Eastern-European accent lacing his words. Holding the gun low, Sam watched the guy throw the spare bedroom door open, bringing the gun up. "Clear," the guy said when he reappeared.

The cottage was too damn small, Sam fretted. They'd checked the kitchen, bathroom, lounge and second bedroom, there was only the main bedroom left and Peltz was headed Sam's way. In two long strides Peltz covered the distance, his body eclipsing Sam's view. When he entered, Sam slid the Glock into the back of his trousers and turned to face the room's interior. He had a clear view of the perpetrator, his back facing him, sweeping left and right with the gun tracing an almost perfect arc through the air. Wasting no time, Sam sprung from his hiding place and slammed his open palm over the guy's mouth; reaching around his head with his other hand and working in opposite direction, he snapped his neck swiftly, then dragged the body out of the way. The man had attempted to cry out, but before he had the opportunity, he was dead. The weighty body twitched once in Sam's grip before he lay the body quietly on the faded red carpet.

Pressing his body into the V section between the door and the wardrobe he waited, trying desperately to figure out his next move.

Namtar spoke. "If you kill another one of my men, Mr. Becker, I'll snap your wife's neck like a twig! While I am under orders to take you all alive, you're the main prize. You have ten seconds to decide. Either turn yourself over without a fight, or I'll kill her, and we take you anyway. Ten seconds, Mr. Becker. Your time starts now."

Chapter 26

The TV was on, and the sound was down. The screen switched between shots of American warships cutting through a broiling, angry Pacific Ocean and a brightly lit CNN News Room somewhere in Washington. Taulass changed the channel to the BBC Word News who were showing almost identical footage taken from a variety of angles. Half watching the footage and half lost in thoughts regarding what his next move should be, he stared at a point past the screen, his eyes unfocused. The heavy drapes were closed and blocking out the small amount of natural light supplied by the dull grey day outside.

He had no phone with him, and no idea if Oriyanna had hers. Even if she did, he couldn't remember the eleven-digit number. He'd have to rely solely on the chance of her coming to the safe house. It had been around twelve hours since the attack. Even if she'd had to walk the distance, which he doubted because their hire car was missing, she'd have been here by now.

Feeling the first rumbles of hunger stirring in his belly, he blinked the world back into focus and went through to the kitchen, turning on the LED lights. The blind was down, the window obscured, just as every window in the house was, hiding the interior from any prying eyes. In the cupboard was a variety of dehydrated ration pack-style meals that they'd stocked the place with months ago. Enough dry, tasteless and unexciting food to feed the four of them for two weeks, without having to break cover. In the adjoining cupboard were a number of five litre water bottles and various Earth fruit flavoured liquids which made it a little more interesting to drink; raspberry was his favourite.

As he cast his gaze over the unappetising options, the sound of two car doors slamming outside drew his attention. Rushing through to the lounge, he grabbed up his gun and waited between the lounge and the hall, his back pressed into the wooden door frame. He knew he was overly jittery and bordering on paranoia; he knew the car doors probably belonged to a neighbour's car and were nothing to do with him. Nonetheless he was ready, poised and aiming the gun at the black Georgian-style door. As he heard the rapid sound of feet on the concrete path outside, heading his way, he took up a little of the trigger pressure and prepared to shoot.

* * *

The sixteen-mile drive across London had taken them forty minutes; electrical repair works on several of the roads saw them having to take a number of frustrating detours. The city was a bizarre patchwork of new and old. The new took the form of shiny fresh shops and buildings, signs of the government's Fresh Start initiative beginning to make a real difference. But there was no hiding the masses of boarded up buildings, many with black finger-like tendrils of discoloration visible behind the metal shutters bolted to their masonry, signs of fires started by looters during the seven days of hell which had taken over a billion lives. In those seven days, a fire had raged across the city, one that almost rivalled the one started at a certain bakery shop in Pudding Lane in the seventeenth century.

As Adam pulled up, the drizzle started to develop into a heavy rain, which splashed heavily in the numerous puddles which littered the quiet street, rippling their dark surfaces and making them swell.

"This is the place, then?" he asked, looking at the Georgian style detached home. "Do you think he's there?"

"The safe had been opened, not forced, and the return tab is missing. He must be here. Unless he thought I'd been killed and has already used it to call the ship and return home."

"He'd do that?"

"No – I don't think so, but that is the worst-case scenario. We need that ship, Adam."

"Only one way to tell," he replied. Opening the car door, plump drops of rain splattered on his arm. He shivered as his shirt started soak up the water, quickly soaking the already damp material. Adam cursed his lack of jacket or appropriate clothing. Oriyanna led him up the concrete path, which was lined with a miniature picket fence. It looked as if it had been whipped from some model village. At the glossy black door she turned her attention to a key-safe affixed to the buff brickwork just inside the porch. Adam squeezed into the narrow space, sheltering from the rain.

"Two, four, one, one, three," she muttered to herself, spinning the small metal wheels on the safe. She turned her attention to Adam as the safe's door clicked open. The key was inside, but that didn't mean a thing. If the team were split and arrived at the house separately, the key was to be returned to the safe as soon as the door was opened. Her hands trembled as she slotted the brass key into the lock and turned it.

* * *

Taulass heard the key safe being opened and a little of his paranoia subsided, replaced by hope. All the same, he kept the gun trained on the door, although he did release the pressure off the trigger. As the door swung open, Oriyanna's slender frame was silhouetted in the dim light from the world outside his hideaway.

"T!" he heard her cry, relief in her voice. "Put that gun down before you shoot someone." She paced over to him as he lowered the weapon and embraced him. "I thought you were dead, I'm so sorry!"

"To be honest I thought I was dead, too," he admitted, holding her at arm's length, a broad smile on his face. He turned his attention to the male she'd brought with her. "Adam Fisher," he smiled warmly, having met Adam briefly during his short stay on Arkkadia. "I'd hoped Oriyanna had gone after you when we got attacked." He looked down at Oriyanna again. "Why did you come back to London?"

"The return tab – I had no idea you were alive until I saw the safe was open. "Please tell me you have it?"

He gave her a knowing grin. "It's safe. Now, please tell me you know what's going on?"

"I do," Oriyanna replied, walking past him and into the lounge. She frowned at the darkened interior and the drawn curtains. Her attention turned to the TV, which was still running a story which carried the on-screen headline, 'Crisis in the Pacific'. She turned her attention back to Taulass and said, "That," pointing to the television.

"They are behind this?" Taulass replied, sounding confused. "Then there must be far more Earth-Breed still in deep cover than we estimated."

"No – they're not behind it, they are going to *use* it. Those ships are just a show of strength, the USA and Russia flexing their muscles, but currently, they are only good for close quarters combat. It's the nuclear cargo, as well as all the weapons waiting in silos and bunkers all over the planet that they intend to use, just as soon as the launch and defence systems come back online."

"But that's going to be," Taulass checked the time on the TV screen, "in less than twenty-four hours, according to the news reports."

Oriyanna nodded, a grim expression on her face. She glanced anxiously from Taulass to Adam. "Possibly sooner, it just depends on who manages to boot up their launch system first. I know it's a race to be the first to the table, those ships prove that."

Adam checked his watch. They'd been gone over three and a half hours, but it was pointless texting either Sam or Lucie back in Wiltshire to inform them of the delay. Alton Barnes had always been in a dead spot for cell service, even before the EMP. "We need to get moving," he said urgently, "we've been in London much longer than we estimated." He glanced at the return tab which Taulass had produced from his pocket. "I guess we don't have to worry about driving back." He'd seen such devices during his time on their home planet.

Oriyanna shook her head., "We can't use it, not yet."

"Why?" Adam protested. "Correct me if I'm wrong here, but a space-craft is going to be a lot faster than my knackered old Mazda."

"Oriyanna is right," Taulass cut in, "we can't call the craft, not yet. Arkus 2 has her transponders deactivated, which is why it was impossible for us to locate her. We'd have to be within ten miles to detect the craft, maybe closer. On radar, she is like a ghost, invisible. The Niribus has her transponders on, and as soon as she is activated her systems will reveal to Arkus 2 that she is there."

"And?" sighed Adam, raising his eyebrows. "We can just jump on board, be in Peru in seconds and blast them out of the desert. Simple!"

Oriyanna placed a hand on his shoulder and smiled at the naivety of his comment. Trying her hardest not to sound condescending, she said, "You saw that ship in the desert, how big it was?" Adam nodded, already feeling foolish for his optimism and for even one second thinking it was going to be an easy ride. "Our craft, Niribus, is a planetary shuttle craft, like the one you came home on. It holds a maximum of twenty crew and was designed to spend no longer than three weeks in space with a full complement of personnel. She is fitted with defensive weaponry, but it's only really intended for blasting asteroids and the like."

"So, what you're saying is," Adam began, sounding disappointed, "that if we try to shoot at the Arkus 2, it'll be like standing on the dock and firing a handgun at a battle ship."

"Pretty much," Taulass agreed regretfully.

"So, what use is the craft, if we can't use it to get there?"

"There might be another way," Taulass said, his eyes narrowing in thought. "But I need to work on it. As an absolute last resort, we can use the craft to get you and your family off planet before the fireworks start."

"That's a last resort I'm not planning on getting to," Adam said, not feeling the slightest relief that he, Lucie and Sam would be safe. "Before we hit the road," he continued, "I don't suppose you guys have any spare clothing here?" He pointed to his shirt which was untucked, creased and resembled something stolen from a vagabond, and his dress trousers weren't faring much better.

"Sure, upstairs in the bedroom at the end of the hall there is a wardrobe full of stuff, just grab what you need," Taulass offered.

"I'll just go and change," Adam said, wishing he had time to grab a shower. He paused in the doorway, turning to Taulass. "I'm out of my depth here – if you say we can't use that craft to get us there I trust you. Just tell me you have some other plan cooking in that head of yours."

"As I said, I have an idea, but it will take some work."

It wasn't the answer Adam was hoping for, but it was better than nothing. He hurried upstairs and into a large double room decorated in a neutral magnolia. The bed was covered with a plastic sheet to keep dust at bay. In the modern white wardrobe he found a pair of Rab Stretch walking trousers, a grey and blue Toggi polo shirt and a Rab fleece, which matched the trousers. There were numerous examples of the same pieces of clothing in a range of sizes, all still with the labels on. The team had obviously purchased a job lot from the local outdoor pursuits store. In the bottom of the wardrobe he found a range of Salomon walking shoes. The closest match was a half size too big, but with the laces secured they felt like a pair of comfortable slippers compared to his dress shoes, which had seen better days. Leaving his chinos and shirt in a neatly-folded pile at the end of the bed, he headed downstairs feeling better thanks to the clean clothing. Oriyanna had also changed, and it seemed her wardrobe consisted of similar items to what she'd already been wearing. She sported another pair of leggings, identical to the ones she'd changed out of, and a blue tee-shirt worn beneath a zip-up, lightweight black Marmot jacket. On her feet she wore nondescript flat-soled boots which covered the bottoms of her leggings and reached part way up her calves. The clothing hugged her figure amazingly, considering it was designed to be practical and hardwearing.

"Not much of a wardrobe, then," smiled Adam.

"It's light and functional," she replied matter-of-factly.

"If we get out of this alive, remind me to take you shopping," he grinned at her. "I don't think I've ever seen you in a dress."

She scowled at him, before it morphed into a bright smile.

Taulass tucked the Glock into the back of his trousers and pulled his top over the weapon, hiding it from view. He reached the door, paused as if expecting someone to be on the other side, then swung it open. "Let's get moving, we can discuss the details of the plan on the way."

Chapter 27

Namtar had his first clenched so tightly in the girl's wet hair that his knuckles began to throb with a dull ache. He pulled back slightly, her body responding to his every move, as if she was a puppet on a string. The thrill of the hunt was almost over. Soon he would get to avenge his bother.

"Five seconds, Mr. Becker," he growled, the urge to snap the woman's neck almost too tempting to ignore. In his mind, he could already feel her delicate bones cracking and splitting beneath his hands. He focused his attention on the bedroom door, partially obscured by a slight kink in the line of the hallway. He knew Peltz was dead, his highly-tuned hearing had heard his bones break, just the way he longed to break Lucie Becker's neck. Namtar wished he'd sent the other guy, Croaker instead of Peltz. Out of the two, Peltz seemed more professional, and he didn't like the way the last member of his team was leering at Lucie Becker's naked body. It made him feel unclean. He knew only too well what would happen if he left the girl in Croaker's care and as much as he had no duty of care toward her, he wouldn't let that happen. He deplored acts of sexual violence, it was a nasty, grubby trait of Earth-Human psyche that he was disappointed to see one of the Earth-Breed displaying. *Too long living among the maggots,* he thought, feeling repulsed. Acts of pure, unadulterated violence of a non-sexual nature, on the other hand, were more than okay. That's what gave him his kicks.

* * *

Sam cursed under his breath. He might be able to take out the guy perving on Lucie, but as soon as Namtar saw him spring from his hiding spot, gun in hand, he'd kill her. It took all his willpower not to act. From experience, he knew while they were both still breathing they had a chance, you never knew what hand fate might deal you. He scanned the corpse on the floor again, searching for a weapon he could hide somewhere on his body, but the Taser and knife were both too large. Cursing again, he removed the gun from the back of his Craghoppers and held it at arm's length, by the butt, between his thumb and forefinger. He rounded the edge of the door and dropped the Beretta to the floor, kicking it aside reluctantly. The other firearm remained on the nightstand.

"Hands to your sides, Mr. Becker, and palms facing out," Namtar commanded.

Sam did as instructed, focusing his attention on Lucie's frightened eyes as he carried out the order. "It's okay," he reassured her. It was a lie – their situation was pretty fucking far from okay; in fact, things couldn't be much worse, but who told the truth in a situation like this? "Just one request," he added, chancing his luck, "let my wife put some clothes on, there is a robe in the bathroom."

"Just stay right where you are," Namtar demanded as he seemed to ponder the request. He looked at the other male and said, "Go see if there is a robe in there, if there is give it to her?" motioning with his head toward the bathroom.

"Shame," the other guy said, sighing. "I was enjoying the view." He flashed a knowing look at Sam which made his blood boil, it was all he could do to hold himself back from launching at the lecherous bastard. The guy disappeared into the bathroom and a second later he was back, a light blue towelling robe clasped in his right hand. He cast one last lascivious look over Lucie's naked skin, his eyes lingering on her breasts long enough to make Sam furious. He decided that when the time came, he was going to kill the bastard as slowly and painfully as possible.

"Put it on," Namtar instructed, continuing to grip Lucie by the hair but allowing her enough room to slide the garment over her shoulders.

Lucie wrapped the robe around her body, covering as much skin as possible and quickly tied the cord around her waist. Sam was dismayed to see the fear in her eyes, the look that suggested she felt dirty and unclean under the guy's disgusting leer.

"Slowly now, Mr. Becker – walk with me through to the living room." Sam watched as Namtar guided Lucie backwards, tugging her thick hair harder than necessary. He had taken hold of her left arm and twisted it behind her back, and Lucie shrieked in pain. Reaching the lounge, Namtar guided Sam's wife to the rear of the room, kicking the door shut. He fixed his emotionless gaze on Sam. "My colleague is going to handcuff you. I don't need to remind you what will happen if you resist."

"Just let her go," Sam said calmly. "You can take me – I won't put up a fight."

"That's not the deal, Sam," Namtar replied. "I need you both, and Adam Fisher. I suspect he's with Oriyanna and the other Arkkadian."

Sam's mind span. Who was Namtar referring to? "Adam and Oriyanna are gone," he said truthfully. "They left a couple of hours ago." He thought quickly. "I wanted out, I've given all I can and then some. Our run-in over in France was the final straw, I'm a married man now and I've got too much to lose. We're not a part of this. Just let Lucie go; if you must, you can take me." He eyed Croaker who was clutching a set of rigid cuffs in one hand. He was regarding Sam with a wary expression, as he if couldn't decide whether to approach or not. "They've gone to Liverpool to meet the other Arkkadian, I don't know what they plan to do from there. If I was still in, do you really think I'd be here?"

"A half-truth, Mr. Becker," Namtar said suspiciously. "I don't believe that you're out, not for a second. Nice try, though!" He gestured for Croaker to stop procrastinating and get on with the job.

Croaker glanced uneasily at Sam and approached cautiously, as if Sam was a dangerous animal.

"What I think," Namtar continued, "is that they have gone to meet with the Arkkadian, maybe in Liverpool, maybe not, and that you'll be expecting them back."

"It's the truth," smiled Sam. Sounding genuine, he held his hands out, wrists together and allowed Croaker to slip one of the cuffs on, and watched as he disengaged the second from the ratchet and got ready to clip it over his other wrist. "They're not coming back here, if you want them, you'll need to get to Liverpool. Waste your time if you like, but I can promise you they're not coming back."

"But they might come after you, if they know we've got you," Namtar smiled. There was a smouldering fury building in his gut; he had no time for this shit, he needed to be back on the plane, and soon. It drew his attention away from Lucie for a split second as he pondered the problem. It was the break Sam had been waiting for.

Before Croaker had a chance to secure the second cuff, Sam whipped his handcuffed wrist around, the disengaged blade flaying dangerously through the air in an arc. The end of the cuff buried itself in Croaker's left eye and hooked in behind the bridge of his nose. Sam tugged at the cuff, the blade bit at his wrist but the pain was nothing compared to the agonised expression creasing Croaker's face. He let out a shrill scream of surprise and panic as Sam tugged him forward, the curved cuff blade acting as a hook, latching itself into the cavity between the eye socket and nose bone. Croaker stumbled but the cuff broke the bone and peeled though his skin before he went down. The cuff completed its arc, the disengaged end dripping with blood and sporting a fresh flap of skin that covered the tip.

The attack caught Namtar by surprise and his grip on Lucie's hair and arm faltered, only for a split second, but it was long enough for her to react. She drove her right elbow back, deep into his ribs, making him double over in pain.

"Run!" Sam shouted, as Namtar quickly recovered from the blow. Lucie paused for a second, caught between the fight or flight response.

In the end, Sam's command and her fear took over and she bolted for the door, crashing into it and keeping it closed with her body. Desperately, she clawed at the handle and finally managed to wrench it open. With a burst of adrenalin she sprinted, feeling the tips of Namtar's fingers run down the back of the bath robe, failing to find purchase when he grabbed for her. Barefoot, Lucie fled down the shingle drive, unaware of the stones as they cut and stabbed at her feet.

* * *

Sam watched in relief as Lucie made the door; suffering an agonising second of panic when she slammed into it, but she found the handle and opened it, escaping out into the sunlit afternoon as Namtar fruitlessly tried to grab hold of her. Sam seized the opportunity and slammed his weight into Croaker, who was clawing desperately at his punctured eye, shrieking in agony. Off balance, Croaker crashed to the floor, hitting a small lacquered table, on the way down. He continued to writhe and shriek, and the few seconds of delay allowed Namtar to reach into his jacket and remove a pistol. Before Sam could cover the ground to his quarry, the gun went off with an unusually quiet *ssnnapp sound*. Sam felt the impact on his chest, but it wasn't the pain of a bullet. Inertia kept him moving for a second or two, before his legs turned to jelly. Falling to his knees, he glanced down at the impact point and registered the small yellow-feathered dart which protruded from his chest. The world spun, the floor became the ceiling and the ceiling became the floor, and then the walls tumbled. He buried his head in the faded carpet as waves of nausea broke over him. He fought to remain lucid, but it was a futile struggle. Rolling onto his back, Sam watched five blurry versions of Namtar heading for the door and chasing after his wife.

* * *

It was the kind of fear you experienced as a child, running up a darkened staircase, almost certain that if you looked back, the boogieman would reach out from the darkness and grab you. Only this time, Lucie knew someone *was* in pursuit, and it was even more terrifying.

She fled across the cracked tarmac road at the foot of the canal bridge, and into the front yard of the sawmill. The desire to sprint the few hundred meters to the pub was overwhelming, but she knew that this particular pursuer wouldn't be worried about the general public, he would very likely kill everyone to get to her.

With her wet hair flying behind her and holding the dressing gown with one hand, she reached the front door of the mill. Her heart sank at the sight of the large chain affixed through the purposeful but rusty iron D-handles, locking it in place. She glanced behind her, not registering the Volvo C90 she'd sprinted past. Across the street, a few hundred yards back, she saw the guy who'd hauled her out of the bath. He reached the cottage gate and paused, his soulless eyes scanning for her. It didn't take long for him to see her and he wasted no time in careering toward her at a full sprint. Lucie screamed and broke to the right, rounding the old mill building. The prefabricated concrete building was showing its age, dirt streaking the cracked and peeling white paint, giving it a ramshackle appearance.

Lungs burning, and her heart slamming against her ribs, she reached the rear wall and cut to the left, escaping his line of sight. Another locked door halted her escape, and she kept running along the wall until she saw one of the iron framed windows which was slightly ajar. Stopping, her breath coming in deep, oxygen-hungry gasps, she clawed it open. The white paint flaked away on her fingers and turned to powder as the window reluctantly opened, creaking on rusted hinges. Wasting no time, she hauled herself up and threw herself into the building, rolling over a dirty work bench before tumbling to the floor. Pain flare =in her right shoulder as it struck the cold dusty concrete. Ignoring the pain, she shot to her feet and tried to heave the window closed, but to her frustration she couldn't get it completely shut. Abandoning her efforts, she headed further into the gloomy, cavernous building. Stacks of twisted, aged timber were dotted about, some half-collapsed, making Lucie think of a massive game of Pick-Up-Sticks. The air was thick with the smell of damp, dust and old machine oil.

Lucie examined her surroundings, searching for a place to hide. Her survival instincts fired up, and she suddenly remembered the band saw. She'd only been about four or five when her father had brought her into the building to get some firings cut for the shed roof, but she remembered the enormous saw the men had cut the timber on. Squinting in the diffused light, she saw it, silent and decaying at the other side of the mill. A massive spare blade was hanging over two hooks on the wall next to the sleeping giant, which looked like a rusty metal shark's jaw. The saw wasn't what she was after though; it was the pit beneath it she sought. Bending down, Lucie removed the plywood cover and peered inside; the remnants of the last piece of timber to pass through the band saw's hungry blades still covered the bottom of the pit. The sawdust was partially obscured by a mass of cobwebs, which hung like dirty silken drapes. Spiders were one of her least favourite creatures, but given the choice of the guy perusing her and a few harmless arachnids, the arachnids would win every time.

Glancing toward the window she heard the man's heavy footsteps pounding outside; they went past the window, faded a little, and then paused before growing louder again as he returned to the open frame. He'd obviously seen the gap. Lucie jumped into the pit and hauled the cover into place, plunging her into thick, black darkness.

* * *

Namtar dashed across the gravel drive, his feet crunching loudly on the shingle. He paused momentarily at the gate, scanning left and right before spotting the girl, a few hundred yards in front of him. She'd reached the front of the building opposite and was at a standstill, looking at a chained door. Then she saw him. They held each other's gaze for a split second before she broke into a sprint and pounded across the concrete with amazing dexterity and speed for someone lacking footwear. Namtar ran, fishing another dart from his jacket pocket as he went. He lost sight of her for no more than ten seconds, but as he rounded the back wall of the mill she'd disappeared. He stopped, gulping cold air into his lungs. He scanned left and right, before deciding to follow the building's rear wall. It ran for about sixty or seventy yards, Namtar suspected she would have had enough time to clear that and double back down the other side of the mill. The first door he passed was secured and locked, the same way the front one had been. *Would she really have gone to ground in there, trapping herself like an animal in a cage?* He doubted it. He was certain she must have doubled back down the other side of the building and returned to the cottage. Namtar smiled at his own deduction and was about to turn back and head the way he'd come, when he saw the window.

* * *

In the darkness, Lucie waited, sure that the sound of her laboured breathing could be heard from a good half a mile away. She wasn't unfit by a long shot, but swimming was more her thing. Running always made her lungs want to burst, and consequently it was a physical activity she avoided at all costs. Now she wished she'd partaken in it a little more often and conditioned herself. Still, no one ever planned to actually be running for their lives, did they? She held her breath, desperately trying to hear what was happening in the world above her subterranean hidey-hole. She tried not to gasp the halted breath out as the sound of the window being opened echoed through the dilapidated mill. Carefully, she exhaled and drew another much-needed breath, trying to shallow out her breathing as much as she could.

Heavy feet slapped down onto the floor, halted, then began to pace patiently through the building, searching. As if working in alliance with the pursuer, in some attempt to make her give up her position, a spider dropped onto her chin from one of the silky webs above. She couldn't see the creature but she knew what it was, and it was big.

Half of her warned her to lay still, this was southern England and although there were a few large species of domestic arachnid, none were dangerous. The other, irrational half screamed at her to escape the bug-ridden hole before it bit her and sucked her brains right out of her head. Screwing her face up in disgust, she felt the agile legs scurry over her lips, they navigated over her nose and tightly closed eyes, brushing her eyelids and making her want to retch, before scuttling across her wet hair. Her new companion drew her attention away from the real threat for a few tense seconds, but with the spider now gone and no doubt planning how he could devour such a large and juicy meal, she heard feet on the concrete once again. Fear coursed through her veins like a paralysing elixir, one that wouldn't allow her to spring from the sawdust pit if a Camel Spider happened to drop onto her face.

He was close, six feet away maybe, now five. The steps drew closer, until those eager shoes almost stepped over the plywood cover, but then they stopped. Lucie waited in despair for the board to be lifted – it was all she could do.

Chapter 28

Sanderson McCormack, or Sandy as his friends called him, sat in the pleasantly cool Tokyo night air. The roof garden bar at the Palace Hotel afforded him a spectacular view over the city, a network of tiny lights sprawled out in every direction like countless twinkling stars. Intermingled with them were toy-sized vehicles, scurrying about like a multitude of self-illuminating bugs, fireflies negotiating a maze that had no end.

A light gust of wind rustled his dark hair and a small shiver carried through his slightly inebriated body. To counter it he took another sip of his gently-warmed saké and instantly felt the liquid chase the chills away. Autumn was well on its way and in a few more weeks the temperature would start to drop, making nights like this a little more uncomfortable without the addition of a heavy jacket. Tonight however, his knitted cream sweater and blue jeans were just enough, with the aid of a little booze, to keep him feeling toasty.

Sandy had been residing at the luxury hotel for three weeks now, studying the efficient way the Japanese had rebuilt the capital's electrical systems and infrastructure. There were no curfews here, not like back in DC. Here in Tokyo life was virtually beating at a regular pulse – no one turned the power off at one AM and then back on at six, which seemed to be the rule for the entire western world; and the local police patrolled the city street, not backed up by the army, like in Washington, New York and many of the European cities. There was a lesson to be learned here for the whole western world, and he was learning it. Once back in DC, he'd have to pen a lengthy report for presentation to the city council and ultimately President Hill himself, on just how Japan had done things so quickly and efficiently.

Placing the warm beverage onto the metal coaster, he lazily thumbed through his passport, his return ticket tucked neatly into its centre pages. The ticket was dated for tomorrow and with a morning flight he really should be heading to bed, or at the very least starting to prepare his report. He shouldn't be drowning his sorrows and attempting to bury the past in saké, which he doubted would be any more effective than any of the poisons he regularly turned to at home. It was a sad fact that at only thirty-three years of age, Sandy now lived only for his job. It was a good job; it had brought him on an extended visit to this magnificent city, in a time when most of the population couldn't even afford a holiday in the next state. But in truth, Sandy's life ended on the day which had changed the modern world for ever. His beloved wife Sarah, whom he'd met in college aged just seventeen and was no doubt the only woman he'd ever love had died – not killed by the Reaper as so many others had been, but in a far crueller manner.

Sarah had been working as a teaching assistant for a history lecturer at George Washington University and was on her way to a field study trip in Egypt when the EMP struck. It was a trip she'd been brimming with excitement over for the best part of a year. The group of fifteen students and two teaching assistants, of which his wife had been one, along with two lecturers, had been in the air when it happened. Their 747 was on approach to Cairo when the EMP hit, and the craft had crashed into the city streets below, killing over half the passengers. Two of the students had survived, and then remarkably, also managed to evade the virus and return home. If it hadn't been for them, he'd have never known just how his beloved Sarah had died. He'd had three agonisingly long months of not knowing before the two students managed to make it back to the USA and report to the college, confirming his worst fears. He'd hated himself for wishing one of the two survivors had been his wife, but he suspected most people would have felt the same way. It didn't make things any easier. At one time, he'd been a man of religious belief but now he hated God, because if he did exist then he'd well and truly turned his back on humanity, and in return, Sandy had turned his back on him.

Being young and busy with their respective jobs, they'd delayed planning a family; both believing they had all the time in the world to become parents. They'd been wrong. Now Sandy was alone, nights in their formerly cosy two-bed apartment in Penn Quarter were long, and often spent trying to find solace in a bottle of bourbon.

Sliding the ticket from the passport he glanced at the date again and experienced a desperate urge to add a week's leave to his trip, just to delay that moment when he'd arrive home to a silent and cold apartment. Gripping the ticket tightly Sandy glanced to the west, out over Chiyoda, where the city lights diminished slightly thanks to the more rural parklands. The sky was clear, beautifully so but the city's ambient light blocked out many of the stars. He caught sight of a moving dot of an aircraft, another stark reminder that tomorrow he'd be heading back to reality. He followed it with his eyes and began to question if it was a plane at all, it seemed to be far too high, and as it drew closer and lost altitude, he could see a tail of flame streaking along behind it. Was it a meteorite? Or could it be an aircraft in trouble? The thought sent another stab of pain through Sandy's chest. As he watched, the falling object exploded and in an instant Tokyo was bathed in a daylight created by a new, but deadly, sun.

* * *

Ben Hawker closed several of the screens on his control panel, the ones monitoring the western world's launch and defence systems, and concentrated on Kwangmyŏngsŏng, which had just finished running through its start-up process and was live. From over nine thousand miles away, he watched the engineers run through a few test targeting procedures and smiled when he thought about how the United States Government would give just about anything to see this information. Their systems selected targets for each of their rather meagre, but nonetheless deadly, twenty-five megaton nuclear warheads. The vehicles which carried the deadly payloads were a close copy of the R-36 Russian missile, but unlike its Russian ancestor, each rocket only carried one nuke. It wasn't the greatest nuclear arsenal in the world, but it was the most primitive, and that meant it was the simplest to get ready and re-program. The nukes Hawker was most excited about were the Russian fifty megaton babies, the ones the USA thought had been dismantled in late 2017, before the virus – but more than a few remained and formed part of the stockpile that he would very soon be putting to good use.

As the programmers on the other side of the world finished their targeting program, Hawker scanned the list.

Seoul, Tokyo, London, Paris, Berlin, New York, Washington DC, LA, Chicago and San Francisco were the ten honey pots they'd selected. Of course, there was no launch planned as far as Hawker knew, but they were pre-loaded targets so that in the event of an attack, the birds would know just where to fly. He only needed one for now, the other nine Enola could use as she saw fit when the rest of the world's nuclear powers came back online. Even if the North Koreans tried to shut it down in panic, they'd fail; his systems now had primary command and they didn't even know it.

He smiled and turned to look at Asmodeous, who was sitting in the bridge's main control chair, surveying the small Earth-Breed team at work. "We're ready to test, sir. On your command, of course." Hawker watched a smile, broader and more charming than any he'd ever seen form on Asmodeous' youthful, yet knowledgeable face.

"This is good news," Asmodeous beamed. "Earlier than we expected, too!"

"By an hour, sir," Hawker replied smugly. He pointed to the list of targets on the screen and said, "This is what they've pre-programmed. You can take your pick, or I can re-program one of them if you prefer?"

"You recommended Tokyo, earlier," Asmodeous said casually, as if they were picking a fine wine in a restaurant.

"I did," Hawker grinned. "It's almost poetic seeing as Japan is the only country to have been nuked in anger in the modern world, and with the name of the program being Enola, it just seems right. Not to mention the political shit that will fly when it goes down. They won't be able to retaliate, either, not even when the rest of the world comes out to play," Hawker added. "Japan has always had a non-weaponization of nuclear technology policy, so it's a good test target."

"Make it happen," Asmodeous commanded, watching the holo-display with interest.

Hawker nodded and went to work. Enola was already running silently inside their defence systems, they wouldn't know about her until the launch codes went in, and then they would be able to do nothing except sit back and watch as their nukes launched. Two minutes later, Hawker was ready. He'd re-jigged the targeting on the Japanese bound nuke to test that part of Enola's programming, not moving it by much, just a few miles, centring the twenty-five megaton bird of death over Chiyoda, an older part of the city that used to lie in the centre of Tokyo. It didn't matter either way, the blast would still be strong enough to flatten the entire Japanese capital.

Working swiftly, Hawker reached the final screen, knowing this test was only a fraction of Enola's capability. Just a simple eight-digit nuclear launch passcode was all that stood between him and the ability to kill around eight million people instantly, with a further two million being sentenced to death as a result of the radiation fallout. He hit the execute button and Enola went to work, decoding the password. The North Koreans would know something was wrong now, and suspect that their system was either malfunctioning, or someone had their hand well and truly down its pants. Hawker glanced at Asmodeous who was watching intently, a satisfied grin on his face. In less than then ten seconds the bird would be in the air.

* * *

Sung-Jae watched nervously from the secret underground nuclear launch bunker as Kwangmyŏngsŏng finished running through the start-up phase. It was live. From the capital in Pyongyang, at the headquarters of the nuclear program, those in charge of the system had been working around the clock to make sure his beloved country could defend herself against any oppression from the Western World. Although only twenty-five years of age, he was not stupid. If he were, he wouldn't have been given such an important role. Sung-Jae knew that the Kwangmyŏngsŏng program was a show of power to the West and nothing more. The chances of them ever actually using their meagre stockpile of nukes was remote, because their main enemies could literally wipe them off the map if the mood took them. At this point in time however, and if only for a few short hours, North Korea would be the world's only nuclear power and the prospect filled him with pride. He was part of a team of twenty-eight men who worked in pairs around the clock, monitoring for any signs of nuclear attack and guarding the launch codes, which refreshed and changed their configuration every two hours. If it happened, it was their job to send the ten nuclear weapons toward their preordained targets. Although an important job, it required no special intellect, but Sung-Jae was proud of his role nonetheless.

He sat back and glanced as his crew mate, Jun-Seok, a more experienced officer in his late thirties. They'd been buddied up three days ago, after arriving at the bunker which lay some fifty kilometres from the nuclear research facility at Yongbyon. Sung-Jae hadn't really managed to figure out if Jun-Seok liked him or not, he seemed to regard him with an air of subordination that was not uncommon within the North Korean military. Aside from that he seemed like a quiet and brooding man who carried every trouble in the world on his shoulders. It was fair to say that Sung-Jae thought he'd drawn the short straw when he'd been paired up and wished he'd been buddied with one of the younger officers closer to his age.

The urgent blaring sound of the launch alarm grabbed his attention away from unimportant matters and fixed him solely on the job he was being paid to do.

Jun-Seok sprang into action, staring at him in alarm. He spoke in a tone about as far removed from his quiet and brooding nature as it possibly could be. "The launch system is initiating, who gave the order?"

Sung-Jae's hands flew over the keyboard, trying to log into the command system to see just where the computers were being operated from. The only place which could remotely command the systems was in the capital, but that didn't make sense because they'd passed control over to the launch bunker not an hour ago. He hit the escape key frantically, but he may as well have been slamming his fist on the desk – the keyboard was useless. He glanced at Jun-Seok, whose face had turned pale and said, "I don't know, I'm locked out. We don't have control."

With panic spreading through his body like an unwelcome wave, he watched the launch code screen flash onto his monitor. One by one, the numbers blinked into the eight boxes. As the third one turned from red to green Jun-Seok snatched up the emergency phone, a direct line to the capital and headquarters, and almost immediately began shouting down the mouthpiece to whoever was manning the other end. By the time the seventh digit was accepted, Sung-Jae had heard enough of the one-sided conversation to know that the launch had not been initiated from headquarters. As the eighth digit blinked onto the screen and turned green, Jun-Seok stopped talking and sat in stunned silence, watching the outside camera feed. Deep rumbling growled up through the floor as the R36 inspired ICBM roared to life. The powerful engines created a deep vibration which thrummed through the concrete walls. Sung-Jae watched his paper cup of water dance across the control desk and fall to the floor; he didn't move to stop it. On the outside feed, one single rocket emerged from its tube, a sleeping giant rousing itself to life.

"Where is it heading?" Jun-Seok asked, his voice thin and taut.

Sung-Jae looked at his screen, which had switched to target and track mode. "Tokyo," he responded in a hollow voice.

* * *

Sandy McCormack had less than half a second to ponder the artificial daylight brought on by the fiery-tailed object he'd seen heading toward the city. For half a second after the nuclear sun rose over the Japanese capital, Sandy was blinded. The blindness was of no real concern however, as a nanosecond later his entire body was vaporised and scrubbed from the Earth as if he'd never existed. The heatwave spread out in an unrelenting circle, annihilating almost every structure for a seven-mile radius, leaving only the strongest of reinforced concrete foundations as evidence that anything had ever existed there. Ten miles from ground zero, the windows were blown out of every building, and many others just crumbled to the ground, as if taken down by an invisible demolition team. The blast's sound wave rolled across the country like thunder and for a further hundred and fifty miles, windows shattered and the boughs of trees bent in a uniformed direction as if succumbing to a violent, one-directional storm.

Before the Reaper, Tokyo had been home to almost fourteen million people; after, and according to the census conducted by the Japanese Government, nine and a half million were left. In less than a minute, and far more efficiently than the Reaper had managed, the vast majority of those remaining nine and a half million souls were eradicated from the face of the Earth.

Chapter 29

Adam had trouble remembering the last time he'd been stuck in a traffic jam. The roads in this brave new world – a world which offered a strange mixture of the new and promising, juxtaposed against the ruins of that fateful week – got busy, but never offered the total gridlock of the world before the Reaper. He utilised an empty stretch of motorway to ease the RX7's accelerator pedal to the floor, and the car cruised easily past a hundred miles an hour as it raced through Hampshire and on toward Wiltshire. He glanced in the rear-view mirror at Oriyanna, who was cramped uncomfortably into one of the two tiny back seats. Adam had never had the need to take a third person in his car and now he realised just how impractical it was. The small back seats seemed to have been thrown in almost as an afterthought, by a designer who'd wanted to appeal to males suffering a mid-life crisis, who needed to transport kids around but still wanted a sporty car. Short of a five-minute spin to the local shops, no sane adult would want to ride in the back.

Taulass occupied the front passenger seat, and for the past hour his face had been locked in a stern expression of concentration. Adam was almost bursting with the need to get him talking about the idea he'd mentioned back in London. Finally, as Adam caught up with the next small block of flowing traffic and backed the speed off a little, Taulass glanced at him and spoke. "Okay, hear me out on this, it's very rough around the edges, but I believe the old human adage says that three heads are better than one."

"It's actually two heads are better than one," Adam corrected, mildly amused at the alien's misuse of the term. "But as you can probably count me out, I'd say you were half correct."

Taulass nodded, the humour completely lost on him. He edged around in his seat so he could see Oriyanna as well. Satisfied that he had their attention he began. "Now, as I said, we can't call the craft back and fly to Peru, because as soon as we move the ship from the dark side of the moon, they will know we are coming. They will be tracking us." He paused, but no one offered any comment so he carried on. "We need to find a way of getting to that ship, without having to take our craft to it."

"The transportation hub?" Oriyanna questioned, leaning forward slightly as she realised what Taulass was alluding to.

"I'm lost already," Adam said in frustration.

"Each Arkkadian vessel, is fitted with a transportation hub, much like the ones you both saw and used while on Arkkadia," Taulass explained. "They are designed for short space transportation of personnel between craft in a fleet." He watched Adam nod doubtfully. "It's cheaper and less labour intensive than having to move crew around via shuttle craft. They also use them to move ground crew from Arkkadia to craft in orbit, once again, to save us having to use expensive shuttle craft. It's also much safer."

"I get it," Adam defended himself, and this time Taulass was sure he did understand. "So, we can use the hub on your craft to move us directly to Arkus 2, in effect by dialling up its hub?"

"Yes. But there is one problem."

"I had a horrible feeling you were going to say that," Adam groaned.

"The hubs," Oriyanna chipped in, leaning forward, "are only designed for very short journeys, no more than a thousand miles. Plenty of distance to allow for movement between craft in fleet, or from the planet's surface to a ship in orbit."

S T Boston

"But Peru must be over five thousand miles away," Adam said, not quite sure why they were wasting time on a plan which obviously had no hope of succeeding from the off. "Two questions," he added. "One: why can they only be used for a trip of that distance? And two: why don't we just get in range, we can still separate the two craft by a thousand miles?"

"Both good questions," Taulass said as they flew past a large truck, its massive tyres throwing a barrage of spray over the wipers. "As you know, to create a bend in space needs a massive amount of power, and the larger the bend, the larger the amount of power needed."

"Yeah, I remember that one," Adam cut in, pleased he could at least grasp the concept in layman's terms. "Hence why the Tabut used the Earth's power and took two hours to charge."

"Exactly," Taulass agreed enthusiastically. "Now, the originating hub, the one on our ship, will take its power from the anti-matter engines that power the whole craft. Unfortunately, if we push the hub to a greater distance than a thousand miles, we won't have enough power to generate the first wormhole to return home." He glanced at Adam who was, once again, looking confused. "It takes a tremendous amount of power to generate that first hole, but as we pass through, it also expels a tremendous amount of power. The ship's hull is made from Taribium, just like the hub and the Tabut. As that energy is expelled, it's re-harnessed by the hull and used to create the anti-matter for the next wormhole. It's a perpetual cycle of fuel expenditure and creation. But if we can't produce that first jump…"

"Then you can't refill the engines for the next one," Adam completed the sentence, grasping the idea.

"Exactly. Only the power generated by a jump can be captured by the hull and used to refill the engines. Even if we could jump the six and a half thousand miles to Peru using the on-board hub, the ship would be useless – heck, it can't even jump us halfway."

"Then we fly within range," Adam protested, sure he was about to be shot down in flames by some bizarre reason that his underdeveloped brain could not figure out.

263

"No!" Taulass said promptly. "If we do that, we may as well fly the whole way there. They will be tracking us, see us land and guess our plan. As we pass through the hub they will be waiting. We may as well just walk up to Arkus 2 waving white flags."

"Then really, there's no plan, is there?" It was a despairing statement more than a question. Adam squinted through the spray as he approached another truck, this one a fuel tanker. He backed off the speed a little; with the ludicrously high oil prices, more than a few tankers had been hijacked in a Mad Max style display of thievery. Now they came with a police or army escort, in an effort to ward off would-be highway pirates. This tanker was obviously empty and on her way back to one of the refineries on the south coast, as it was alone. Satisfied that the vehicle was Fuzz-free, Adam got them up to speed and watched the tanker shrinking in size in the rear-view mirror.

"We need to find a way," Oriyanna protested, "to get enough power into that hub to span the six and a half thousand miles, but not drain too much power from the ship's engine."

"Exactly," Taulass agreed. He looked across at Adam and said, "The hubs on Arkkadia all use the planet's energy grid, just as the Tabut did. It's a very powerful and completely clean energy and it has more than enough power to do the job."

"So if we can get the hub on our craft to use the Earth's energy…" Oriyanna began.

"Then you can make the connection," Adam completed, suddenly seeing a glimmer of light at the end of the very long tunnel.

Taulass saw the spark in Adam's eyes and nodded. "Indeed," he said, feeling more confident that between them, well, more between himself and Oriyanna, they could work the problem. "The ship's hull is made of Taribium, as I said, so I would need to re-calculate the way she takes power in through her hull to feed from the Earth, then re-program the computer to allow it to happen. It's complicated, but possible."

"As you have no planetary grid established here," Oriyanna said, "we will need a small amount of power from the ship's engine, but as long as we don't leave the window open too long, or open it too many times, we should be fine."

"If we can find a natural energy point, a place where the Earth's energy is naturally high, then we can minimalize the amount of power we need to take from the ship."

"Are you saying we have to go back to Egypt?" Adam groaned. If he never visited the pyramids again it would be too soon.

"No, we can't move the craft from the point it's recalled to, and we need to work fast or they will know what we are doing," Taulass said thoughtfully. "I can run the calculations on paper before we bring it back, that way, I'll just need to run the completed calculations through the ship's computer when we board. It will save hours."

"Hours," Adam groaned. "I'm not sure we have that long."

"We don't have a choice," Taulass defended. "It is what it is. I will work as fast as I can, but it's a complicated process. First, we need to reach a point naturally rich in Earth's energy, as I mentioned."

"That won't be a problem," Oriyanna cut in. "There is such a place within a half hour's drive of Adam's cottage."

Adam glanced into the mirror. "Stonehenge?" he suggested, certain he must be right.

"Not just a pretty face," Oriyanna smiled. "Yes, Stonehenge."

"I'm guessing you can shed a little light on that particular mystery then?" he asked hopefully.

"It's not as fantastical as you might think," she replied, a sly grin on her face. "Back before the war, when we were studying this planet and the various cultures which had sprung up in the many thousands of years we'd been absent for, we used several of the naturally rich energy points to build hubs. You see, we need some hubs set in areas of higher power, this helps to feed the entire grid, creating a kind of circuit. Stonehenge was the site of one such hub; it was a much smaller version of the system we have on Arkkadia. The Neolithic Agrarians built the stones as a monument to the hub, they believed it to be a portal to the heavens, from where their gods came down to Earth."

"I always thought the Druids built it," Adam commented.

"It was build a good thousand years before the Druids came on the scene," she answered. "This isn't the time for another lesson in your misinterpreted history." She winked when she caught his eye in the mirror.

"Just how long will it take you to work the calculations?" Adam asked as the radio, which had been playing Chic's 'Le Freak' quietly in the background, went silent for a second, drawing his attention from the conversation. Leaning forward in his seat, Adam fiddled with the volume button. The BBC radio news jingle suddenly blasted though the cab, making them all jump. Adam glanced at the clock in panic; it wasn't the top of the hour, or even half way through the hour, which meant something big had happened somewhere.

A very sombre news reader began to speak. "*We interrupt this scheduled show to take you to a live broadcast by the British Prime Minister, Richard Cole, live from ten Downing Street.*" There was a slight crackle as the engineers in the studio switched feeds, this was followed by another unexpected silence, which almost had Adam adjusting the volume again. As he reached for the knob, Prime Minister Cole's voice blasted thought the car.

"*Ladies and gentlemen,*" the Prime Minister began, his Midlands accent laced with tension, "*it is with deep sadness and regret that I must inform you that at ten past twelve GMT the nation of North Korea launched a nuclear attack on the Empire of Japan. The blast, which early indications tell us was a twenty-five megaton warhead, detonated over the Chiyoda district of Tokyo.*"

"Dear God," Adam said in a hollow voice. An icy hand of horror ran its bony fingers down his spine, clenching hold of his gut and twisting sharply.

"*We are not yet able to talk about the death toll, but it is my belief that we would be naive not to think it will be in the millions. Myself, President Hill, as well as other NATO and European Alliance leaders have condemned the attack as a barbaric act of war and one that will not go unpunished.*" There was a pause and the sound of Prime Minister Cole taking a sip from a glass, the microphone picking up the clink as it caught on his teeth, and the sound of him swallowing distinguishable before he continued. *"As you know, our world is in a fragile position. Our sheer dependence on oil and fossil fuels began this new and now-deadly race back to a nuclear era that we had a chance of leaving behind. It would seem North Korea wished to make the most of being the new world's first nuclear power, and like cowards, they struck out before the rest of the world could answer. I can assure you that the rest of the world will make them answer for what they have done."*

There was another pause and then another male voice, a reporter, Adam assumed, shouted a question. *"Are you planning to retaliate with nuclear force, Mr. Prime Minister?"*

"I was elected on the back of honesty and integrity, and a hell-bent will to get this nation back on its feet," the Prime Minister fired back, his voice tainted with a little annoyance at the question. *"And I will keep those values when I answer your question. I believe that the human race has suffered enough over the past two and a half years, and it is my hope that we can resolve this matter without the further use of nuclear weapons. As you know, at this time nuclear weapons are not an option for us, but we are continuing, along with the United States and nuclear European Alliance members to develop our launch and defence systems, a system that we all hope will be online in the next twenty-four hours."* He paused again, his voice taking on an octave of dread as he said, *"We know very little of the North Korean nuclear arsenal; we do not know who they've targeted, or if indeed their weapons can reach our shores, but we have to be prepared for the worst. At the moment, Great Britain is completely defenceless against an attack."* There was a worried murmur that spread across the soundwaves, it reached out across the air and broke like a wave in the Mazda. *"If you're currently outside of the country's major cities, I would urge you to stay clear. If you are in one of our cities then please, at this time, do not try to evacuate. We have no direct intelligence to suggest we will be a target and I have no desire to needlessly clog the arterial routes in and out of London, or any other city, as the result of panic."* Another pause, and it was clear that the last part of the broadcast had been improvised, it had sent a

mixed message and Adam suspected that very soon London would be in gridlock for the first time since the Reaper. "*That's all I have for you, ladies and gentlemen. Please stay tuned to your local news channel for the latest news. As a result of events in Japan and the need for the public to know what is going on, there will be no power cut tonight. The curfew, however, will remain in place.*"

The radio broadcast cut back to the BBC news room. Adam had heard enough; he cranked the volume down, and turned to Taulass . "I have a horrible feeling that however long it's going to take you to do those calculations, is going to be too long."

"It will take several hours to work the calculations," Taulass said, matter-of-factly. "Then around half an hour to reprogram the ship to those calculations. It's a complicated process, I have to make the ship do something it was not designed to do."

"This is a test," Oriyanna said, her voice flat. "They are testing Enola, and it looks like she works. We have until the other systems come online to stop this thing. If that's still a day away, we might just have time. I suspect the other nations will up their game now, so… I just don't know."

"And let's just say we can use the hub to jump us to Peru, that we manage to get aboard Arkus 2 – what the hell do we do then?" Sweat had formed on Adam's brow and was rolling down his back.

"I don't know," Taulass said, sounding a little helpless. "I hadn't got that far."

No longer worried about the possibility of passing a police car or army patrol, Adam slammed the accelerator pedal to the floor. He needed to get them back to Wiltshire and fast. He glanced in the wing mirror, half expecting to see a mushroom cloud forming in the distant sky.

Chapter 30

Just over three and a half thousand miles away, deep below the White House in the PEOC, (Presidential Emergency Operations Centre), President Hill sat at a large oval mahogany table and cradled his head in his hands. Looking up, he surveyed the eclectic mixture of personnel who had accompanied him into the bunker, one that had been built on the command of President Franklin Roosevelt during the dark days of World War Two. The bunker was designed to withstand all but a direct nuclear surface impact, and there were those who wagered it could even survive one of those, if the yield of the nuke wasn't too high. With developments in the East, President Hill suffered an uneasy feeling that the bunker's durability might well be tested in the next few hours, and the thought was making him nauseous. The White House had stood virtually undamaged and un-attacked since President James Monroe moved in back in 1817, after the repairs were completed following a fire set by the British – and he was damned if the universally-recognised monument was going down on his watch.

Maintained and kept up to date with the latest technology, the bunker had only been seriously used twice in the last few decades. The first September the 11th 2001 had been the first such time, a day which changed the world forever, and not for the better. The Vice President of the day, Dick Cheney, and several other important members of the presidential staff had utilised its safety, while President Bush, who had been visiting a school when the first plane hit the North Tower, had taken to the skies in Air Force One, the government running a country in crisis from both above and below the Earth.

The last time the operations centre had been needed was almost thirty months ago, when the Reaper raged across the surface of the globe. On that occasion, the newly sworn-in president, Marshall Baines – who until the death of John Remy in Malaysia had been Vice President – had taken shelter with his staff for the full seven days, only daring to go topside after the strange deluge which seemingly halted the virus had stopped, leaving Washington's streets flooded and in ruins. The deluge had been so fierce even parts of the White House roof had started to leak.

A year after that week – a week that just like the events of 2001, had changed the world, but on a far greater scale – the American people elected Hill to power. There had been civil unrest due to Baines' non-existent ability to pull the country back together, and in the end, he'd called an emergency election, stepping down from power. Americans knew that whoever followed John Remy would experience a tough presidency, but trying to fill those shoes – along with running a nation on the brink of collapse, with many cities in outright anarchy – had been an almost impossible task.

President Hill, who'd been planning to stand in the election at the end of John Remy's administration, was a republican. Baines was a democrat. President Hill was certain that in a time of crises, his kind of politics was what the damaged country needed. Baines had been reluctant to spend the dollars required to kick-start the economy, delaying the regeneration which was badly needed if the United States was to become even a shadow of its former self. Spending the public dollar, and a harder-nosed style of politics was what the country required, and having won the election and been in power for close to eighteen months, President Hill had exceeded the limits of what he'd set out to do. In his mind, he'd done enough to secure a second term in office, and cement his place among the greatest leaders of his beloved country. He would be remembered as the man who got the pulse of America beating once again. Now, sitting in the PEOC, he was experiencing something that no leader of the free world wanted to experience, and only a handful of his former colleagues had needed to endure. A true life or death national emergency, and one whose outcome would shape the entire course of human history. He suspected he should be wearing a shirt that read 'The Buck Stops Here!'

His staff, made up of military top brass from the Army, Navy and Air Force, as well as senior members of his administration, took their places at the long, polished table, lines of stress and worry etching every face. At the head of the table, President Hill cleared his throat and took a swig of chilled water, which felt good on the back of his parched throat. He stood and dusted down the front of his dark grey, double-breasted suit. This one, although just one of many suits he owned by the designer, was his favourite. He only hoped it wasn't going to be the one which reminded him of the day his country was attacked with nuclear weapons.

He cleared his throat again, a little louder this time and brought the bustle of the room to order. The fifteen or so grim faces turned their attention to him and waited to hear what their Commander-in-chief had to say about the dire situation in Japan. At six foot two, with ice blue eyes and dark hair that month-by-month, grew increasingly more grey, President Hill more closely resembled a handsome, ageing Hollywood actor than the leader of the American people. It was his film star looks, coupled with his natural ability to build rapport with anyone he met which won him both votes and respect. He was what they called a *down-to-earth kinda guy*, someone who knew what it was like to be at the bottom, but through sheer guts and determination had worked his way to the top. At fifty years of age, with a background in the military, he also had the hearts and minds of his troops. Back in the day, he'd been one of them, had fought and got his hands dirty. To them, this gave him a vital foresight in matters of conflict and he took great pride in being able to talk with his military leaders as if he was one of them and not their boss. The same went for troops on the ground, who he took great pleasure in visiting on a regular basis. In this troubled world however, , his troops were on active duty on American soil, helping restore order and working with the overstretched law enforcement agencies.

He cast his eyes over the seated group. "As you know, fifteen minutes ago, the Empire of Japan was attacked by North Korea. The attack came in the form of a single nuclear blast which early indications suggest had a yield of twenty-five megatons. We don't know how large their nuclear arsenal is, but at this point in time they're the planet's only nuclear power, a situation which should never have been allowed to happen!" He fixed his eyes on Chuck Leading, the head of the CIA, who shifted uncomfortably in his seat and fiddled with his tie. "What intelligence we do have, suggests that their launch, targeting and defence systems are primitive compared to the other nuclear powers, thus making it easier for them to bring their system back online swiftly. A fact which would have never give them the upper hand, except in a situation like this." President Hill turned his attention away from Leading, who looked down at his hands in shame. "Do we know any more about what capability they may have?"

"We believe they've got a maximum of fifteen, twenty-five megaton yield birds, sir." Chuck Leading piped up, trying to sound confident with his rather shady intel. He paused, but when President Hill didn't comment, he continued with his report. "We've had no word from North Korea yet, but our channels are monitoring them where we can. As soon as we have any news, you will be the first to know."

"And what of Isamu Kato, the Japanese Prime Minister. Was he at Kantei?"

"We don't know, sir," Leading replied, sounding like the kid in class who hasn't done his homework, and consequently can't answer any of the teacher's questions.

"I hope to God he was on a visit somewhere – Kantei is in Chiyoda, right at the centre of ground zero. I think we have to assume the leader of the Japanese Empire is dead." A murmur of solemn agreement spread through the room. "And what of our own systems? What's the latest? We're like sitting ducks here."

The Secretary of Defence, Liza Sherwood, stood up to present her report. "Sir, we've stepped up our efforts to be back online within the next twenty-four hours. By this time tomorrow, we should have full strike and defence capabilities." At a meagre five feet two inches, Liza Sherwood had a reputation as a pit-bull, small but vicious and the kind of woman who got the job done. "I don't need to remind you that if President Baines had immediately re-instigated the nuclear program when he came into power, we wouldn't be in this situation."

"Thank you, Liza," Hill said with a tiny smile over her loyalty to him and this administration. She'd overlooked the fact that he hadn't wanted to re-instigate the program either, and ended up having his hand forced by congress. "However, regardless of what happened in the past, we need to work the problem we have now. What's happening in the Pacific?"

"Both US and Russian fleets are at a standoff, separated by a hundred miles of ocean. Our navy is on an 'engage only if engaged' order; we don't want to be the first ones to fire and start a third world war. We were trying to open a channel of negotiations with the Russian President, but this latest turn of events has halted our attempts. We believe they're going to be live and nuke ready an hour or so either side of us. We're monitoring their news channels and we do know the Russian government has condemned the attack on Japan."

"Let's hope it's the right side of that hour then," he said, trying to hide the nervous tension in his voice. He was about to speak again when an urgent knock came from the thickly-framed glass door to the conference room. President Hill experienced a pang of nervous energy as he beckoned to the young, fresh-faced communications operative waiting outside; whatever news he was bringing must be extremely important.

"Sir," the young African American male began, his wide, dark eyes nervously surveying the country's leaders. "We have an incoming call from the Dae Wonsu – the North Korean Army's Grand Marshal. He's requesting immediate talks with you, sir."

"You'd best put him through then," President Hill replied, not quite sure where this turn of events would take them.

Chapter 31

Lucie wasn't certain how long she'd been hiding in the band-saw pit. The guy who'd pursued her from the cottage had stood on the seam of the plywood cover, and she'd been certain he would look down and tear the sheet away, exposing her hidey-hole, but he didn't. He'd come so close, been no more than five feet from her position when he'd suddenly moved away. Lucie listened to his footsteps pacing the building for a second time before the window creaked again when he left. Time had no meaning down among the wood chippings and creepy-crawlies – the sound of the window could have been just five minutes ago, or it could have been five hours; she really didn't know. She'd stopped noticing the scurry of arachnids and bugs which occasionally kissed her skin or disturbed her hair, behaving like tiny invisible fingers.

In the darkness of the pit the one thing she did feel were the warm tears which streamed from her eyes and touched her chilled skin. They came almost rhythmically, like a constant drip from a leaking tap. Sam was either dead or taken, and she hadn't even had a chance to tell him he was going to be a father. Now she suspected it was a job he might never have the privilege of fulfilling, and it filled her with as much intense sadness as the thought of losing him herself. She'd known Sam for most of her life, knew what a wonderful person he was, but it seemed increasingly likely their child would never have a single memory of the man Sam had been to hold dear.

A distant voice, carried on the slight breeze outside drew her attention away from her grief, and when she focused, it came a second time, from somewhere closer. "Lucie!"

She stirred in the pit, her bones and joints protesting the movement. "Sam! Lucie!"

Closer again this time, and Lucie recognised the voice – it was Adam, he'd made it back from London and gone to the cottage. She knew there was a strong chance the small team of men who'd attacked her and Sam were still close by, watching and waiting to snatch Adam and Oriyanna. She had to warn them. Driven on by fear of losing the only other person she loved, Lucie threw the cover from the pit and clambered out, frantically brushing herself down, fully alert now and recalling all the nasties which had shared the space with her. She combed her fingers frantically through her hair, almost certain any number of spiders had set up home.

"Lucie!"

Adam's voice was closer again, and she could hear panic in his tone. She dashed across the mill, noticing for the first time just how much her feet hurt after the mad dash across the gravel and rough concrete.

Lucie clawed open the old window frame, more of the paint flaking away under her fingers as it moved reluctantly. The freshness of the air was wonderful as she painfully hopped down into the rear yard. The day had turned cloudy, a light mizzle drifting on the breeze which made her shiver and realise how cold she was.

"Lucie!"

She wanted to call out, but she was afraid, afraid that as soon as she did the massive guy who'd held her hair so cruelly would spring from behind one of the old wood piles and snatch her. Instead, she hobbled to the end of the building, taking the same route she'd used earlier. Peering around the corner, and scanning the building toward the cottage she could see her brother. He was standing by the mottled concrete gate posts, frantically searching up and down the road, and then he saw her.

* * *

Adam was frantic, he'd known something was amiss as the second he'd swung the RX7 into the gravel drive. The front door to the cottage was open. Rushing inside, he'd located the body of an unknown male in the bedroom. There was a large amount of blood in the lounge, near the internal door which led to the hall. More worryingly, both Lucie and Sam were missing. The presence of a dead body offered him a little hope that they'd won whatever battle had gone down in his absence and fled – but to where? When Oriyanna and Taulass returned from the outbuildings wearing similar worried expressions, he knew it was more likely they'd put up a fight and either been killed or taken. While it appeared that they'd managed to take one down in the process, he took no comfort in that thought.

Not wanting to give up hope that Sam and Lucie had fled, Adam rushed to the front door, calling their names, hoping if they were close by they'd know it was safe to come out – or was it? Could the ones who'd done this still be nearby? He was certain the team who'd carried out this attack would want Oriyanna and himself just as much, and with the added bonus of Taulass – or 'T' as Oriyanna called him, much to Taulass' disgust – they were practically sitting ducks.

Sliding past the Mazda he reached the end of the drive and scanned the road, calling his sister's name, and Sam's, over and over. Then he spotted Lucie from a distance, at the far end of the old mill building, wearing nothing but a dressing gown. Hope sprang in his gut and he rushed toward her, expecting to see Sam's grinning face join her at any moment, but it didn't. When he drew closer he noticed how painfully she was walking, limping on both feet to try and reach him quickly. When they were close enough she threw her arms around him and clung tightly, seeking comfort.

"What happened here?" he demanded, already knowing the answer, but wanting to hear it all the same. He held Lucie at arm's length, breaking her embrace and staring down into her teary brown eyes.

Lucie sniffled slightly. "They came not— not long— after you left. I was in—in the bath. They've taken Sam. He put up—up enough of a fight to— to give me a chance."

Adam took her back into his arms and wrapped her in a reassuring hug, for what it was worth, and silently thanked Sam for his selfless act. He would either grieve for his friend or attempt to work out a rescue plan later, but for now Lucie was alive and that counted for something. '*Thank heaven for small mercies,*' his grandmother had always said when he was a boy. There was a certain amount of irony to that statement now, and it made him smile. He broke away from Lucie and took her by the hand. "I think they're gone now, but I'm not taking any chances. We need to leave here ASAP. Get dressed and grab anything you might need."

"I was going to say the same," Lucie croaked, managing to pull herself together a bit. The mizzle was fast turning to a thick drizzle that would no doubt be a downpour in the next hour, and she was keen to get into some warmer clothing before she caught a chill. "Did you find what you were after in London?" she asked as they stepped into the cottage.

"We did," Adam replied, striding into the lounge. "And we found a little more than we bargained for, too." Taulass who was searching a dresser drawer frantically with Oriyanna, and he turned around and smiled warmly. "This is Taulass."

Holding the warm smile Taulass spoke. "You found her then. What about Sam?"

"It would seem they've taken him," Adam replied glumly, and the words started Lucie sobbing again. "I think we're going to have to work a rescue plan into our overall plan," he added, feeling completely beaten by the situation. "What are you guys looking for?"

"Pens and paper," Taulass replied, returning his attention to the task at hand. "I need to work the math to reprogram the hub, and I need to get it all written down so that when we bring it back I can re program the computer swiftly. Once they pick up that craft, we're in a time-sensitive situation. Now they have Sam, they'll be expecting us even more than before."

Like we aren't already in a time-sensitive situation, thought Adam. "It's not safe here, we need to relocate," he said.

Oriyanna placed a faded old blue tin box, , back in the drawer and crossed the room. Adam felt sure his grandfather had used the box for storing rubber bands in, many years before. "Sam won't be dead," she reassured Lucie with a warm smile. "They went to far too much trouble to think they would have killed him. They'll be taking him to the Arkus 2, and it's highly likely they'll be relying on human transport. Although massive, there are no shuttle craft on Arkus 2 that I'm aware of. If he's that desperate to get his hands on us, we might have more time than we thought. It must be an eighteen or nineteen-hour trip door-to-door, as you say. Just how long ago did it happen?"

Lucie wiped her eyes with the backs of both hands and sniffed loudly before she spoke. "I have no idea, it wasn't long after you guys left, so maybe four hours... six at the most. I completely lost track of time.

"So that gives us thirteen hours or more before they reach Peru," Oriyanna summarised, talking more to herself than anyone in particular.

"You think we can get him back?" Lucie asked, making no attempt to hide the hope in her voice.

"We need to get to that ship, Lucie," said Taulass, giving up his search of the drawer. "I believe we have a plan regarding how to do that and if it works, of course we will try to get Sam back. But it will take some time to work out the details. I'll let the others explain it to you; we have no time to waste, especially after what just happened in Tokyo."

Lucie stared at Adam in confusion. "What just happened in Tokyo? And what the hell does that have to do with us?"

"I'll tell you in a minute, but first we need to get out of here. I don't think they're coming back, but I'm not willing to risk it. We'll head to the Barge Inn – they always used to have a room or two for guests to rent, and we can haul up there until Taulass has figured out what he needs to figure out."

"Lucky for you guys, I am a genius," Taulass grinned, trying to lighten the mood. "I just hope I can get hold of a notepad or something – I have a lot to do if this thing is going to work."

Chapter 32

Roughly seven hundred miles south west of the Cornish coast, and just before the pilot began a steady descent through Portuguese airspace for their refuelling stop, the Gulfstream broke free of the thick blanket of cloud which covered half of northern Europe. The cloud base had been so thick, it seemed as if they were rushing across a snow-covered Arctic. It was certainly impossible to tell that they'd been jetting over towns and fields, followed by the Bay of Biscay and then northern Spain.

Inside the fuselage, in the plush passenger lounge, Namtar sat watching Sam Becker with interest, rolling a black disc about the size of a guitar plectrum over the backs of his knuckles. First one way, then the other, repeatedly. He never looked down to check his dexterity, the movement was fluid, natural and consistent.

Since leaving the old RAF base at Netheravon, he'd kept Becker sedated. The Gift had cut the time that the ketamine in the tranq-darts was active by a good half of its normal knock-out period. As such, Namtar had plugged Becker twice more since take off, and he would no doubt be coming around again soon. This time, Namtar was going to allow him to stay wake, but not for long. He had a gift for him… well, more of an anti-gift really – a little something that would strip his healing powers away, an ability he should never have had in the first place. Then if Becker thought about trying any heroics, he'd be a damn sight easier to take down and deal with.

"If he tries anything else," Croaker grumbled, "I'll kill that mother-fucker myself." He was sitting in the seat opposite Namtar. Sam was on the opposite side of the aisle, lying across the large grey leather seats, his head pushed hard against the side of the fuselage, beneath an oval window with the blind pulled down. He was a smidgen too tall to fit neatly and as such his legs hung out into the aisle. He was held in place by the lap belts of both seats. One over his torso, the other his knees. Sam's hands were cuffed and zip tied behind his back and his legs were fixed together with both Velcro limb restraints and large, thick plastic zip ties, one at the top of his chunky calf muscles and a second at his ankles.

Each set of seats was separated by a beautifully polished mahogany table which was fixed to the floor of the cabin, allowing four passengers to face one another, and conduct business meetings and conference calls from the air. Upon reaching the jet Croaker had used the first aid kit on board to fashion a dressing for his ruined eye and nose. The bandage was fixed diagonally over his head, and resembled a skull cap which had slid off at an angle. "He took my fucking eye out!" he added, sounding pissed, before knocking back a cocktail of Ibuprofen and Paracetamol.

"Stop being so pathetic," Namtar snapped. "Maybe if you hadn't been leering at his wife so much, he'd have left you with two good eyes. Besides, you're in a better position than your two colleagues. Peltz will be turning in his grave – well, I doubt he'll ever actually get one to be honest, but you know what I mean – if he knew you were being such a… what is it the Americans say? That's right – a pussy."

Sam released a small groan of discomfort and they both watched as his head lolled from side-to-side, at the same time as his legs began to move. Namtar got up from his seat and slid in between the table and the seats Sam was secured to. The whole cabin was built for comfort, not like a commercial airliner, but Namtar still had to crouch a little to stop from knocking his head on the top of the fuselage. Reaching down he used a thumb to open Sam's right eye, and as he did the pupil dilated and Sam tried to blink. "I think he will be back with us very soon," Namtar grinned, glancing at the last remaining member of his team.

"Is it going to hurt?" Croaker asked, a flicker of hope flashing in his one remaining eye.

"It's not pleasant, I know that much." He reached down and slapped Sam across the face a few times, further rousing him from the drug-induced sleep.

* * *

Sam's mind was dark, an abyss-like pool that he'd been submerged in for longer than he could recall. On two occasions, he'd been certain he was about to break free but as he'd felt himself rising to the surface he'd been plunged right back in again, sinking to the bottom and fearing he would be unable to ever break free. This time he felt closer than ever, and as he experienced the welcome pain and numbness of his body once again, the perpetual darkness was stripped away in bright, eye-assaulting light. This happened for only the briefest of moments and then it was gone, leaving dazzling red and green sparks dancing behind his eyelids.

Someone was slapping his face now – too hard for it to be Adam, or Lucie. He suffered a wash of nauseous confusion as his drugged brain tried to remember what had happened, and just where he was.

"Time to wake up, Mr. Becker," he heard a male voice say. It was a voice he knew – Namtar.

"Yeah, and maybe when he's done with you, and you can't heal quite so good, I'll cleave your fucking eye out," said another voice. The mention of the eye was the trigger which caused his struggling synapsis to fire. The events back at the cottage flashed though his mind, like a movie on fast forward. What had happened to Lucie? The last time he'd seen her she was fleeing out the door, and he'd watched Namtar go after her.

Sam struggled to get his eyes open, blinking slowly and deliberately, giving himself time to adjust. He quickly processed the fact that he was on an aircraft, and he had a strong suspicion he was the only captive, which meant either Lucie had escaped, or she was dead. The thought filled him with cold fear, a fear he would quickly need to stifle so he could focus on the situation at hand. Craning his stiff neck forward, he saw the guy whose eye he'd put the cuff blade though. The eye was bandaged up and the guy looked about as pissed off as a person could. Namtar was standing beside him, looking impossibly tall. "Look on the bright side," Sam croaked. "If things don't work out for you here, you can always get a job as a pirate at Disney World."

"Fuck you," the guy jeered. "I'm just sorry your little wifey got away, or me 'n her, we'd have had some fun. Might have even let ya watch." A perverse smile turned up the corners of his mouth, revealing off-white teeth.

Sam felt two emotions instantly from his retort; immense relief, and a burning desire to cut the guy's cock off and choke him to death with it. If it was big enough to choke him, that is, which Sam doubted. Didn't matter though, he'd quite easily finish the job by pulverising his head until he was so smashed up, he couldn't draw breath. For now though, the only thing he could do was ignore the statement. He turned his attention to Namtar. "I don't suppose you're here to take these cuffs and restraints off and give me a club sandwich."

Namtar smiled, and Sam watched him produce a flat, disc-like object from between his right thumb and forefinger. "No, not even close," he smiled. "It has been very clear from the moment you evaded us in France that you were a liability—"

"Your brother," Sam cut in. "You missed the part where I killed your brother." He managed a smile and saw a flicker of rage ignite in Namtar's cold eyes.

"You should be very careful, Mr. Becker," he growled. "You are in no position to be such a wise ass. Both of us would love to kill you; push us too far and it might just happen, and be damned with the consequences."

Sam mentally scolded himself; at the moment his voice was his only form of defence, but if he didn't keep his mouth in check he'd push one of them to breaking point. Although his current position was dire, his survival instinct was strong. While he was breathing, he still had a chance.

"As I was saying, you're a liability, and what do we do with risks and liabilities?" Namtar asked.

Sam bit his lip and refrained from saying something smart.

"We manage it," Namtar continued. He brought the disc down in front of Sam's eyes, so he could get a good look at it. "I'm not sure how familiar you are with the Gift, Mr. Becker, or if you know that it can be taken away faster than it is given."

He paused again, but Sam didn't give him the satisfaction of a reply, nor did he feel remotely like begging Namtar not to do what he knew was coming, because in truth, he didn't give a shit about it. Other than its ability to make intense situations more survivable, Sam had no use for the Gift. He would let Namtar have his fun, believing that what he was about to do was paramount to torture. "This disc will send an electrical current though your body, and within that current is a signal that shuts down every single nanobot inside your blood. You will be returned to how you should be – mortal."

"I guess I'll have to start buying anti-aging cream again," Sam blurted, unable to keep a lid on his mouth.

"I can assure you that you won't find it the least bit funny the next time you get shot," Namtar hissed, leaning forward and placing the disc on Sam's forehead. "Just relax. I'm told this hurts like a bitch."

Sam watched a wicked smile spread over Namtar's lips, before he felt the cool disc on his clammy forehead. At first it seemed as if a coin was being pushed against his skin, and then the pain began. A multitude of tiny barbs bit into his flesh, securing themselves for whatever came next. He didn't have long to wait. A split-second later, Sam felt as if he'd just stuck a fork into an electric socket – his body convulsed, his back arched, but he was held down by the lap belts securing him to the seats. He wanted to cry out in agony but he held it in, clenching his teeth down so hard he thought they'd snap. The shock ended after what seemed like ages; Sam was sure it had only lasted a second or two, but it seemed much longer. He didn't even notice the barbs retracting.

"Now, unfortunately for you, there is only one way to test if this has worked," Namtar grinned.

Sam was certain he didn't need to test a damn thing – Namtar wanted to do it, but he didn't give him the satisfaction of showing any weakness. "Do what you must," he said, trying to sound confident. Sam watched Namtar take a small switch blade from the one-eyed guy, Croaker. Standing over him, Namtar held it in front of Sam's face, and for purely dramatic effect, flicked the sharp blade out.

"Don't worry," Namtar said. "I won't go too deep." He rolled up the sleeve of Sam's tee-shirt, exposing his shoulder – somewhere since the cottage he'd lost his fleece, which pissed him off as it was one of his favourites. Using the tip of the blade he pushed down, puncturing Sam's flesh. The pain was worse than the shock and much to Sam's embarrassment and Namtar's delight he finally let out a gasp of pain. Sam felt the metal slice through his skin, and blood leaked down and ran under his armpit. True to his word, Namtar didn't do nearly as much damage as he could have done and soon he was back, waving the dripping blade in front of Sam's eyes.

"Now let's see if it's worked, shall we?"

Sam could just see the wound by straining his neck. He didn't need to watch, he knew that this time he would need a bandage, possibly stitches. After five minutes, blood was still oozing steadily from the cut.

"I think we can call that particular procedure a blinding success," Namtar announced. "No pun intended, Mr. Croaker," he mused. "Can you fetch me the first aid box, that is, if you haven't used all the dressings yourself?"

A few minutes later Sam's wound was cleaned and dressed, a small red blotch, like ink on blotting paper, already blossoming on the white of the bandage. He tried to get comfortable but all the sensation in his hands and feet was gone. A few minutes later Sam's ears popped and he felt the familiar plunge of his stomach as the aircraft began descending.

"This is our first stop," Namtar announced. "Portugal for a top-up of fuel which will allow us to complete the trip to Nazca." Sam watched Namtar hand the knife back to Croaker, before he bent down and grabbed a pistol from one of the empty seats. Sam had seen this gun before, it was the weapon he'd been shot with in the cottage. "I'm going to keep you sedated for the rest of the trip, Mr. Becker; unfortunately, I don't have any kinder way to administer the drug."

Sam watched Namtar grin as he raised the barrel, there was a soft *pffssttt* and the dart bit into his flesh. The thought of being knocked out for the rest of the trip was a welcome one, in fact. Gradually, the world began to grow dark, and yet again Sam began to sink to the bottom of that black abyss.

Chapter 33

President Hill listened to the Dae Wonsu with more than a little trepidation, and a healthy dose of scepticism thrown in for good measure. As the Dae Wonsu spoke, Hill glanced at the senior members of his administration and the ranking members of the armed forces. He could tell they were all thinking the same thing as him. *What a crock of horse shit.* The Dae Wonsu spoke perfect English and from the intelligence they had on him, which had flashed up onto their individual tablets during the call, Hill could see he'd attended Oxford University as a young man. It amused him the way countries which disliked the western way of life opted to use its education systems before heading home to fight against their western oppressors.

As he finished his in-depth account of how Tokyo had been wiped from the map, President Hill sat in silence, allowing a little tension to build. He wanted whoever was with the Dae Wonsu to feel it, too.

He sipped some water before he spoke, further increasing the tension. "Just where is your supreme leader?"

It was clear the question took the Dae Wonsu off guard, because it took him a full minute to answer. "I'm sure your intelligence is aware that Kim Jong-un died over two years ago from the virus you call the Reaper, along with any successors he might have had, so the military has taken over governing the country."

"I'm sure that suited your plans very well," Hill suggested coldly. The country had always maintained a closed-door policy and was

S T Boston

tough to get intelligence from, but since the Reaper, getting information from them had been like trying to get blood from a stone. "I think it's fair to say he was merely a figurehead, controlled by his military leaders anyway."

"Our nation's political arrangements are of no concern to your government, Mr. President," the Dae Wonsu replied tersely.

"I would beg to differ," Hill fired back. "You've just unleashed the first nuclear weapon to be used in anger, in close to a century. You've opened a door that could well lead humanity down a path from which it can't return."

"Mr. President, I have told you we did not launch that attack! Our systems were compromised, someone took control of Kwangmyŏngsŏng and launched the weapon."

"I trust you can provide tangible evidence to support your claim," Liza Sherwood announced, her brow just managing to crease into a frown against the pressure of her tightly drawn back hair.

"We can send you the feed from the launch bunker, you will see the reactions of the two crew who were on station when it happened." It was clear from the Dae Wonsu's tone that he didn't appreciate being addressed by a woman.

"A video that could easily have been staged, or recorded before the event using actors," Sherwood replied, only too aware of the nation's ability for propaganda and spin. "We need to see evidence of your system being hacked. You will send us everything you have on file, from the moment you went live. If you are speaking the truth, this shouldn't be an issue. I don't need to point out to you what could happen if you don't."

"Miss Sherwood, we are only too aware of the dire situation at hand, but we currently have no control over Kwangmyŏngsŏng. We can neither audit, nor gain access to our systems," the Dae Wonsu explained. He turned his attention back to Hill. "Mr. President, at this time we have no control over the nine twenty-five megaton weapons we still have in our arsenal."

Hill's guts churned – there was a sincerity in the Dae Wonsu's voice which made him uneasy. "Just who does have control of your systems?" he barked.

"We don't know, but we have a theory and it's vitally important that you hear me out."

"I'm listening," Hill snapped.

"We lost Kwangmyŏngsŏng as soon as it went live; whoever took control apparently only wanted to fire one weapon, when they could have easily launched the other nine."

"Your point being?"

"I fear this was a test, a test of a program they plan to put into action when you and your allies come online in the next few hours. Mr. President, you need to think very carefully before you bring your launch systems live. I bring this to you, and you alone, as I know you have the ear of many leaders. I am terrified that once the rest of the world comes online, something unthinkable is going to happen. Our nations have their differences, but ultimately, none of us want to see weapons of mass destruction used, none of us want to see our children's futures destroyed."

"Send me what you have," Hill commanded, "but you must appreciate that I'm treating this with a great deal of scepticism."

"I understand," the Dae Wonsu said. The line cleared and a second later, a video file arrived at the bunker. The tech team played it through to the large screen in the conference room.

Everyone watched in interest as the black and white clip played out, and Hill was pleased to discover it also had sound. He ordered a translation be made as soon as practicable, but even without the benefit of hearing it in English he could see what happened. The reactions of the two officers seemed absolutely genuine, but as Liza had rightly pointed out, it could have been filmed before the event. When the clip finished, Hill ran his hands through his greying hair and released a long sigh. "So – what do you think?" he asked his team. There was a long tentative pause, as if no one wanted to be the first to offer their opinion.

It was Chuck Leading who spoke up. "I think it's a load of shit, sir, if you'll pardon my language. If you want my opinion, they intended to use every nuke, but there was a problem with their antiquated systems and now the other birds in the nest are useless, and they're back-pedalling because they know what will happen when the big boys come back into the playing field. Even if they were hacked, which I very much doubt, their systems and firewalls aren't a patch on ours. It would be virtually impossible to hack every launch and defence system on the planet, and who the hell would want to do such a thing? No terrorist group that we know of is capable of such a thing."

"Possibly," President Hill commented, thinking back on how his intel teams had also been damn sure that no terrorist group had the technology to produce the Reaper. Ultimately, it was going to be his call – once again, he suspected if they survived the next twenty-four hours he really should get that 'The Buck Stops Here' shirt. "There's no way I'm going to leave this nation defenceless against nuclear attack. We continue as planned." His voice sounded more convincing than he felt. Had it not been for the Reaper, the world would be well down the path to ridding itself of its fossil fuel dependency. It was still a road he was committed to, but they were a long way off. He cursed Russia for the stranglehold they had on the world, a stranglehold which had ultimately led to this shithouse situation. He had a horrible feeling that the Dae Wonsu was telling the truth, or there was a partial amount laced in with a cover story. The thing he had trouble getting his head around, was just who would have anything to gain by burning the world. It had to be a mistake, and he hoped to God it was.

Chapter 34

The first-floor room at the Barge Inn was small and functional, but most importantly, clean and tidy. Taulass had managed to negotiate a bundle of old copier paper from the bearded guy behind the bar, the same one who had served them breakfast earlier in the day, although to Adam it seemed like a week ago.

Once in the room, Adam ordered more food and drink – steaks with chips, and over the chips the cook had melted some vintage cheddar cheese. Despite the food smelling delicious and the steaks being cooked to perfection, none of them felt like eating much.

Lucie managed to consume the most food, although she'd mainly opted for the side salad, claiming that too much red meat was bad for her baby. She'd seemed intent on not letting her unborn child go hungry, despite how nauseous she felt with every bite. As the first few hours ticked by she'd started to come out of her shell a bit, although she was still visibly shaken by the idea that for a second time in a day, she'd potentially lost her husband. The rollercoaster of events was starting to show in her delicate features.

In conjunction with picking at the food, Oriyanna and Taulass started work, spreading blank sheets of paper out on the bed and scribbling notes in a language Adam had no hope of understanding. Long scrolled out equations formed on various sheets, which Taulass moved into positions which were either some chronological order, or the most advantageous positions for him to read them from. It became clear, early on, that his intellect in this matter outshone Oriyanna's by a considerable margin. On more than one occasion Adam saw her clasp her head in her hands, her blonde hair falling over her face. The pair spoke hurriedly in Arkkadian, the language strange and exotic and it felt like oral silk, even if he couldn't understand it.

Several times a full sheet of script and math was screwed into a ball by Taulass and launched in anger across the room, the way an angry student might treat an unsatisfactory dissertation. He seemed to be growing increasingly frustrated with the task in hand, leaving Adam wondering if he really could work out the computations required to make the plan of using the ship's transportation hub work. Adam couldn't really see how it could be so difficult to change the way the ship took its power feed, but he also accepted he knew diddlysquat about the subject. All he knew was that the process seemed painfully slow.

Around two hours after eating, and with both the Arkkadians still deep in consultation, Adam saw that Lucie had fallen asleep, propped up against a warm radiator. He took a pillow from the bed, having to move two sheets of paper covered in heavy scribbles, much to Taulass' disapproval. Carefully he shifted Lucie's slight frame and laid her out flat on the floor. In the small built-in wardrobe, he found some sheets and covered her with them.

As the light of the day gradually faded, Adam felt a growing need to grab some rest himself. Making himself comfortable in a small chair, he watched Oriyanna and Taulass with interest, feeling more than a little useless. His anxiety was growing by the minute, building up like the steam in a pressure cooker and he was sure it would eventually explode. In one corner of the room a small radio played, the half hourly news broadcasts filled with the story of the bombing of Tokyo, again and again. He'd filled Lucie in on the developing events before the food arrived, and despite not knowing anyone in the ruined Japanese capital, she'd wept all the same. Each time the news jingle played Adam fixed his attention to the radio, half expecting another city to have been hit. The news he feared never came, and as light from the small single-glazed window faded from a wet, drizzly grey to black, Adam drifted into a deep, dream-disturbed sleep.

His visions were filled with fast-changing scenes; in one he was back below the Great Pyramid, his body racked by fever. He was climbing down the rope, toward the hidden chamber which held the Tabut, and he could hear Oriyanna screaming, somewhere from the bottom. Only the rope had no end and the black pit below him seemed eternal, a perpetual fall with no bottom. At the top, a fire was burning, eating hungrily at the rope, as if it were a fuse wire. No matter how fast he descended, the flames kept coming. When they reached his hands, the searing heat scalded his skin and he let go. As he fell the fire consumed his hands, spread up his arms and engulfed his torso. Opening his mouth to scream, flames flooded his throat, turning him to dust. Then the scene changed.

He was standing on the Arkkadian beach with Oriyanna, her golden hair fluttering in a light breeze, the way it had when he'd kissed her that evening over two years ago. It was an evening which had been the most perfect of his life, now though, something felt off, not right – almost foul. Above them the native bird species flew in large flocks, shrill cries filling the air, as if they were fleeing some unseen danger. The sky, which had been a stunning blue and framed Arkkadia's twin moons beautifully, was now blood red. Out across the crystal-clear ocean, Adam discovered what the birds were fleeing from. A wall of fire swept relentlessly toward them, boiling the sea as it came. He turned to run, but noticed Oriyanna's deep blue eyes had changed, replaced by a pair of evil amber irises. Those eyes fixed him to the spot and as her face distorted into a scream, she gripped his hands as he once again became enveloped in flames. He watched as she held him on the spot, and he saw her hair begin to burn, then her flesh, until all he was left holding were her blackened, skeletal hands. When he looked at his own hands they were the same, and then their bones burnt fiercely, turning to dust.

His next dream found him back in the RV, sitting in the passenger seat. The vehicle was lumbering along Trail Ridge Road, rain hammering onto the cab, hitting the windscreen like a spray of ball bearings. John Denver was on the radio, 'Annie's Song' drifting through the cab, but John's voice and his guitar were off-key. It all sounded out of tune, making Adam think of a bag of cats mewling in fear as they were cast into an icy lake. Adam didn't make it as far as finding Oriyanna this time, before once again the world around the RV was bathed in fire. This time he watched Sam burn before he, succumbed to the flames. Everything turned to dust.

Adam snapped awake. The first signs of dawn were filling the small window, light blues mixed with warmer oranges as the sun started to rise. His back was stiff and when he eased himself out of the chair, he noticed Oriyanna was curled up comfortably in the bed which had been covered in their paperwork when he fell asleep.

Taulass was clutching numerous sheets of slightly crumpled paper in his hands. It seemed he hadn't had the luxury of any sleep, but there was a broad smile on his face. "I was just about to wake you," he announced excitedly. "I think we are ready."

Any residual aches or remnants of sleep left Adam instantly. "Are you sure?" he asked, his body washed simultaneously with relief and dread.

"There was a time, not long after you went to bed when I thought it was going to be impossible. The power from a space jump and the power which can be gleaned from a planetary grid are so vastly differ-ent. But, yes – I believe I can alter the way the Taribium in the ship's hull transfers the energy to the hub, thus bypassing the anti-matter engines for the most part. We might need to take a little juice from them, but nothing which will jeopardise their use at a later date."

"You lost me in the first sentence," Adam said, attempting to smile. "If you say it'll work, I'll go along with it. What time is it?"

"Just gone seven AM," Taulass answered, pointing to the small red LED clock on the night stand. "I took the liberty of setting the correct time when the power came back on."

"If they've taken Sam to Peru, will they have arrived by now? What time will it be there?"

"It depends on how they transported him," Taulass said thought-fully. "Lucie seems to think it was around one PM when they attacked, so that was eighteen hours ago. I'd imagine they will be there, or close by now. The local time in Peru will be just after two AM currently."

"Will you need long once we get the ship here?" Adam leaned over and gently shook Lucie awake.

"A half hour at the most, I hope. I have all the changes I need to make to the craft's systems here," he gestured to the papers he clutched in his hand. "I'll work as quickly as I can, I'm aware that they will be watching to see what the ship does when they pick it up on their scanners, and I don't want them to second-guess us."

"We're ready," Adam said to Lucie, when she quickly came out of her deep sleep. Her eyes still looked red, as if she'd been weeping most of the night.

"To get Sam?" she asked, sounding hopeful.

"Yes. And to put a stop to this once and for all." It was a tall order, and Adam realised they hadn't even discussed what would happen once they got aboard Arkus 2. He felt sick thinking about it.

By the time Lucie was up and straightening her clothes, Adam had woken Oriyanna, who seemed a little embarrassed at having nodded off.

"I thought it best if you rested," Taulass defended. "I have been thinking about how we are going to play this once we are aboard. You two are going to need all the energy you can muster."

"Care to share what the plan is?" Adam asked, not sure he wanted to know the answer. He watched Taulass rip up several sheets of paper and throw them into a small bin, which was lined with an old Tesco carrier bag. Once the room was tidied to his satisfaction, he folded his precious plans and placed them in the pocket of his trousers. He grabbed the small backpack off the floor, the one Sam had brought with him. Before they left the cottage, they'd collected up what weapons they could find. Unzipping it Taulass moved to the bed and shook the contents out onto the wrinkled duvet.

"This is our rather meagre armoury," he announced, looking over the items. "We have one Taser, thanks to the dead man at the cottage. One round in it and four spare." He placed it back in the bag. "We have my Glock, fully loaded," he checked the safety and placed it in the bag, "and we have Oriyanna's Glock, minus one round. They must have taken the other firearms with them." The second Glock joined the other items in the bag before he zipped it closed. "Now, on board Niribus, we have several hand weapons."

"Arkkadian ones?" Adam questioned, hope flittering in his chest.

"Yes, of course," Taulass answered. "They work on the same basic principle as your weapons, a point and shoot affair, but what they do is somewhat different. We are past the stage of using physical projectiles – bullets as you call them. Our weapons create something akin to a very nasty energy pulse."

"In layman's terms please," groaned Adam.

"Point it at your enemy, using the red laser point – just like your primitive guns have – to make sure you're aiming directly at your target, pull the trigger and it sends a shock of electrical power through them which literally shuts down every organ in the body."

"That should do the trick," Adam said, giving the room a once over to make sure they hadn't left anything important behind. He felt a little cheated that the Arkkadians didn't have laser guns, as so many science fiction movies had portrayed over the years. "You can fill us in on the rest of the plan on the way to Stonehenge."

"Yes, agreed," Taulass answered. "It's time we got moving."

The pub was shut when they filed down into the lounge bar, the air smelt of cleaning products, and everything was prepared for a new day's custom. Adam felt a certain satisfaction in knowing that despite everything that had happened over the past few years, the old place was still in business. He had many fond memories of playing on the rope swing in the back field as a child, which had always been packed with campers during the summer months. He'd spent hours as a teenager, marvelling at the hundreds of crop circle photos decorating the lounge bar's walls like some new-age, glossy wallpaper.

Now, standing in that same lounge bar, he was a little sentimental and wondered if this would be the last time he'd ever see the place. As the others filed out the rear exit and onto the canal's towpath, he took one last wistful look around and with a heavy heart, followed them out.

The late September morning was strangely cold, , as the last week had been, and a fine sheen of ice covered the front and back windscreens of the Mazda. Oriyanna placed the bag of weapons in the tiny boot, or *trunk* as she called it = much to Adam's annoyance, before climbing into the back seat.

With the engine running the icy glass soon cleared and he bumped his way down the small unkempt road leading away from the pub and down the side of the abandoned mill, coming out opposite his grandparents' cottage. At the narrow junction, he took a left and went over the canal before taking another left down what appeared to be yet another non-descript British country lane.

"Do you know the way?" Taulass asked.

"Sure, it's no more than half an hour's drive, so we should start figuring out how we're going to do this." Adam paused, still not believing he was going into the hornets' nest once again. "I wish Sam was here, this kinda thing is much more his cup of tea."

Oriyanna leaned forward from the cramped back seat that she shared with Lucie, and placed a hand on his shoulder. "Last time, Adam, in the Great Pyramid – you saved us all, and you shot Buer. You are a different man to the one you were back then, I can feel it in you. You're stronger."

Adam felt it, too. He'd survived the Egyptian ordeal by the skin of his teeth, and even though he still wished for Sam's greater experience, he fully accepted that he needed to go ahead and do whatever needed to be done, to stop this new madness.

Adam expertly navigated the twisted, treacherous Wiltshire country lanes, while Taulass turned in his seat to address everyone. "This is how I see this happening," he began, removing the ship's recall device from his pocket. "Oriyanna and I ran though it briefly last night, before I persuaded her to get some sleep." He flashed a smile at Oriyanna before continuing. "Once we have the ship here and I've made the necessary alterations to allow the hub to work from Earth's energy grid, Oriyanna, Adam and myself will go through to the Arkus 2. Lucie, you will be staying on our ship."

"But—" Lucie started to protest.

"No," Taulass said, cutting her off. "I need someone back at the ship, and in your delicate condition, it has to be you. I'm sorry." He offered her an apologetic smile before continuing. "Once we gain a connection to the hub aboard Arkus 2 we'll have fifteen seconds to go through. It will then shut down, so if anyone figures out how we got there, they won't be able to come the other way and compromise our own ship. I'll be setting a little program to prevent a return dial from the other end. I'll set up a timed return window for a half hour after we go through." He fixed his attention on Lucie. "You won't need to do anything, everything will happen automatically. The return window will also only be open for fifteen seconds, so it's imperative we watch the time closely. If we miss that window, a second opportunity will happen ten minutes later." He paused for a second. "After that, well, we'll have a problem. That second window will be the final chance; I can't risk subbing any more power from our ship's engines. I for one, don't intend on spending more than forty minutes aboard the Arkus 2. Our situation is extremely time-sensitive; I suspect Enola will be going live today, and all indications suggest that in the next few hours, Earth's nuclear powers will all be back in the game. Asmodeous won't waste any time – the moment he can use those weapons, he will."

"How do you intend on stopping the nukes?" Adam asked.

"I'm getting to that bit," Taulass said, sounding a little impatient. "Although the systems on Arkus 2 pre-date ours, they are fundamentally the same. Enola will be designed to work alongside the alien technology=. I need to find a server room on the ship. Our craft will have the schematics for every craft ever built stored in its systems. It also has the codes for all the transportation hubs, hence why we can call any of them up. I can copy that information onto one of our portable tablets. If I can gain access to a server room, I will need thirty to forty minutes to find Enola and copy the program over to my systems. I'm hoping that if I can get a copy, I can control the launch systems and override their commands."

"That sounds like a long shot, with lots of room for failure," said Adam, sounding doubtful.

"It's the only way I can see it working," Taulass defended. "I am good at what I do – have faith in me." He eyed Adam sincerely. "But you are correct. It is a long shot, and ultimately, we may not be able to stop it."

Adam swallowed hard and nodded. "I understand, I know you'll do your best."

"Now's this is where you and Oriyanna come in," he continued. "While I am working on Enola, you will have forty minutes to find, secure and recover Sam. Arkus 2 is a vast ship, but from the server room I should be able to access her life support systems. It will show us just where the crew are, and it will also allow me to track them. That craft can carry in the region of two thousand crew, but from what we know there are only a handful of Earth-Breed on board, just the ones who were advantageous to Asmodeous' plan, the ones he needed. I'm hoping we will be able to identify the part of the ship Sam is being held in, negating the need for a room-to-room search." He grimaced. "Let's face it, we won't have the time to do a room-to-room search anyway. Once you have Sam you need to get back to the hub. If I get a copy of Enola before you two get back and I can return to the ship, I will. You have the second return window if you need it. I hope we can all get in and out together and the first half hour will be enough."

Adam let out a long breath through clenched teeth. He was experiencing a strange acceptance of the situation he was about to enter, and it made him wonder if it was akin to the way a soldier feels when he's about to go into a battle with a high probability of failure and possible death. "He who dares wins, huh?" he said nervously.

"We are going to take a mixture of Earth and Arkkadian weaponry with us," Oriyanna cut in. "Adam, you will take the two Glocks, and I'll use our tech. One of the weapons is for Sam, *when* we find and recover him. Taulass will also have one of our weapons, but we hope he can stay out of the fight; he is too valuable to risk in any conflict. Above all else he needs to get a copy of that program and get back to our ship." Her face was deadly serious. "You need to be prepared for the fact that we might not be coming back. None of our lives are worth more than the job we need to do."

"I know," Adam answered in a low voice. "I can do what needs to be done, don't worry."

"I never doubted you for a second," she concluded with a smile. "This is where you come into it, Lucie," she continued. "If the worst happens, if none of us make it back and Enola is successful, then you have your own job to do."

Lucie fixed her attention on Oriyanna. "I'm listening," she said in a voice laced with fear.

"The Niribus has an auto return program, it's designed to kick in if the ship gets into difficulties or the crew are incapacitated. Basically, it will take the ship directly back to Arkkadia. If we don't come back, and those nuclear weapons launch, I want you to manually activate the return program."

"On my own?" she asked, her eyes wide.

"You will be taken to Arkkadia and we will make sure we encode a message into the ship's systems explaining what has happened here on Earth. You will be given asylum on Arkkadia by the council."

"No offence, but that's not really much of a Plan B," Lucie said.

"You have more than yourself to think about now," Oriyanna said seriously. "If the worst happens, you will die here on Earth, and your child will never be born."

Lucie nodded in understanding, a little shocked at the directness of Oriyanna's statement. "I know," she said solemnly. "But I don't like it."

"Promise me," Adam cut in. "You promise me that if we don't come back, you'll use the ship and go to Arkkadia – you can have a life there." Adam saw tears welling up in Lucie's brown eyes, building up until they ran down her pale cheeks.

"I promise," she said in a broken voice. "I'm scared, though."

"We all are," said Oriyanna sympathetically. In the rear-view mirror Adam watched as she placed her hand on Lucie's shoulder. His sister instantly relaxed and he silently thanked Oriyanna for using a little of her *hocus-pocus*, as Sam called it.

The rest of the short journey was made in silence, with even the two Arkkadians needing a little quiet time to take stock and prepare for what they were about to do.

All too soon, Adam found himself taking a left off the A303 and bringing his trusty old Mazda to a stop on an unmade road, next to a footpath sign which read 'Long Barrow'.

"Where is the stone circle?" Oriyanna asked when he levered the driver's seat forward and let her out.

"It's a five-minute walk down this track," he said, pointing the way. "You can get closer on the main road, but if we stop on the verge and hop over the fence we're going to draw attention to ourselves." He suddenly realised that what your average person would refer to as a UFO was about to swoop down over the local countryside, so perhaps a few people climbing a fence wouldn't be such a big deal. "How close do you need to be?"

"The energy source is richest at the henge," Taulass replied, shouldering the backpack and starting off down the path.

"Alright," replied Adam as the group crunched their way up the gravel road. "It's not far.". Yesterday's rain had given way to a bright but chilly morning, wisps of ground mist floating lazily on the light breeze, partially obscuring the grass in the field to their left. They cleared a small rise and when they did, the ancient circle of stones appeared.

"I'm amazed it's stood for this long," Oriyanna commented, stopping momentarily and placing her hands on her hips.

"It's time," Taulass said, a little unease in his voice. He cut to the right, vaulting the fence which separated the path from the field containing the ancient monument. The others followed suit, falling into line behind him. "As soon as the craft arrives and we are on board I can cloak it, but I fear we might create a bit of a stir to begin with." He pointed toward the main road which was visible, a couple of hundred meters ahead of them on the other side of the stone circle. Taulass produced the return device from his pocket and pressed his thumb to its surface, and the entire thing glowed green as it read his biometrics and fingerprint information. When the light on the device faded, they all craned their necks toward the crystal clear blue sky and waited.

Chapter 35

"May I be the first person to welcome you to Peru, Mr. Becker." Sam heard an overly-confident voice announce as he opened his eyes. His head was hammering to a beat of its own and it seemed as if he'd been out of it for about a week.

"Is that your natural eye colour?" Sam asked, as the first thing he noticed about the man was his strangely haunting amber eyes.

The stranger grinned. "Yes, it's a rare pigmentation which affects less than half a percent of my people. Magnificent, aren't they?"

"Bit freaky, if you ask me," Sam replied, suddenly realising that his hands weren't bound, nor were his legs. His shoulder hurt like a bitch, a stark reminder that he was back to normal again.

"I must say that it's an honour to finally meet the infamous Samuel Becker," the guy said, his smile still covering the whole of his face. "It's cost me many men and resources to get you here. I had hoped to meet Adam as well, but you know what they say about best laid plans."

Sam propped himself up on his elbows and shimmied into a seated position, then swung his legs over the edge of the bed he was on. He took a moment to survey the room. It was around fifteen feet by ten. Everything seemed to have been created simultaneously, the bed rising out of the black, onyx-like floor, as if it had grown there. Near the end of the bed was a sofa, which also seemed to be an organic growth from the floor. There was a desk-like fixture, recessed into the metallic wall. Just to the left of this was what on first appearance seemed to be a food dispenser, almost like a vending machine without the glass display cabinet. Sam didn't need to be told where he was –this had to be Arkus 2. Just like the Arkkadian craft he'd travelled home in almost two and a half years ago, where everything was alien, yet at the same time, strangely familiar. "Best laid plans are all very well," Sam said, turning to look at the amber-eyed stranger, "until someone comes along and fucks them up for you."

"Indeed," the stranger beamed. "But I wouldn't go getting any ideas, Sam. You're on your own here, and we are so close to the completion of my plan that to think you can intervene in any way would be utter foolishness." The guy perched on the end of the bed and turned to look at Sam. There was a charismatic nature to the stranger which made him cautious. The guy's overconfident and relaxed posture was unnerving. "I thought you might be interested to know that not half an hour ago, China was the last of the world's nuclear powers to come back online. Europe, American and Russia are already operational, which means we are almost ready. Just have a few last-minute tests to complete before the final show. Although after we nuked Tokyo yesterday, there's so much political tension that I'd bet a dollar that you Earth-Humans would push the button yourselves if I left you to it."

"You did what?" Sam cried.

"I'm sorry, I forgot that for the best part of a day you've been indisposed." He grinned and Sam had an overwhelming urge to rip his head off. The amber-eyed stranger hadn't introduced himself but Sam knew only too well who he was dealing with. "Our secretive friends in North Korea managed to get their systems up and running first, and we thought it only right to test our little program. It worked, and it worked extremely well. It's fair to say that Japan is in need of a new capital city."

"You crazy fucking bastard," Sam groaned, feeling sick.

"That's nothing compared to what is going to happen in the next hour," Asmodeous said cheerfully.

Sam shook his head. "Your name has been used to depict the very image of evil for thousands of years," Asmodeous smiled, obviously pleased with his legacy. "But now that I've had the unpleasant fortune of meeting you, I can tell that you're no different than any Earth-Human tyrant our history has ever seen." Sam watched as Asmodeous' smile turned into an ugly scowl. "You're a narcissistic bullyboy with far more power than any one person should have."

Asmodeous got to his feet and hammered his fist into Sam's face, knocking him back onto the bed. Sam tasted blood, but didn't mind, pleased to know he'd struck a chord.

"You're going to wish you were dead, Sam Becker," Asmodeous growled. "When we are ready, you are going to come to the bridge and have a front row seat for the biggest fireworks display in history. When you watch it, you can think of your friend, Adam, out there somewhere, along with your wife, Lucie. There isn't a corner of the globe that won't be affected by the radiation. Maybe they will die quickly, or perhaps they will die slowly. Whatever the outcome, I'd wager Lucie will be dead long before she gives birth to your bastard child."

Sam did a double take and saw the hateful grin spread across Asmodeous' face once again.

"I'm guessing from your reaction that you didn't know she is with child. Namtar told me; we have an uncanny way of picking up on such things. Call it evolution if you like."

Before Sam could jump from the bed and reach him, Asmodeous crossed the room and left, the door sliding closed behind him. Sam sunk onto the bed, buried his face in his hands and screamed.

Chapter 36

The Niribus arrived precisely four minutes after Taulass had activated the return device. From the cold, clear blue sky, the bright silver craft had first appeared as no more than a speck, which glinted brightly in the sunlight. As the craft descended rapidly, the glinting Taribium hull was almost too bright to look at.

Passing out of the direct sunlight it swooped silently down, across the A303, and over the ancient stone circle, coming to a stop in a graceful hover just a few feet above the glistening, dew-covered grass, not ten feet from where Taulass stood.

The sudden appearance of the alien craft, which resembled a jumbo-jet sized triangle with a domed, bulbous top, caused two cars who happened to be passing Stonehenge at the time, to veer across the road and collide head on. Adam heard screaming brakes and grinding metal from across the field as the craft touched down and felt bad for not being able to rush to the aid of the occupants.

After the craft settled, a crack appeared halfway along the otherwise seamless hull, and from this opening a gangway extended, forming a gentle slope which led into the magnificent ship. The whole process was silent, automatic and happened in less than a minute. The craft was identical to the one which carried Sam and Adam home, but the sight still made Adam's breath catch. He turned his attention to Lucie, who was standing with her mouth open, her brown eyes fixed in wonder at the sight before them.

Taulass wasted no time in shaking her into action when the gang-way appeared, tugging Lucie by the arm he said, "We need to get in and get the ship cloaked. We can't have a visible craft when the authorities arrive at the scene of that accident." Taulass led Lucie into the craft, gently guiding her the way a parent might assist a reluctant child into the dentist's surgery.

Once inside and on the bridge, Oriyanna activated a large holo-display which projected from a three-foot square cube in the middle of the floor. The cube glowed cool neon blue beneath its white surface. The vivid holo-display projected a complex mixture of glyphs and graphics in stunning high definition 3D, real enough to seem as if you could physically wrap a hand around them and carry them away. Oriyanna navigated it with ease and a few seconds later the craft seemed to shimmer slightly, a tiny vibration shuddering through the hull. "Cloak is active," Oriyanna confirmed, as Taulass began work-ing on the other side of the display. Each side of the cube projected a separate screen, allowing four crew members to work on separate tasks simultaneously. To the front of the cube were a trio of chairs. Each chair rose smoothly from the bridge's stark white floor, and each had its own small holo-display, projecting from a smaller computer in the right armrest. The small computers sprang to life as the ship's main life support systems came online. Adam watched as Oriyanna closed one screen and opened another, running her hand along what appeared to be a projected, sliding fader. This action brought the lights to full brightness. Behind the terminal where Oriyanna worked, two passageways led away from the bridge.

"Where do they lead?" Lucie asked, staring around in amazement.

"Sleeping quarters and what I guess you would call a mess," Oriyanna replied. "There is also a small medical bay. If the worst hap-pens, you will find enough food for the seven-day journey in the mess."

"Why are there no windows?" Lucie questioned, not sure what to look at next.

Oriyanna smiled, swiftly swapping screens and punching a few holo-tabs. In a flash the blank wall in front of the seats lit up and displayed a live image of the field in front of the craft. The image was so realistic, Lucie was sure she could feel a light breeze drifting in from outside. "It's a video projection," Oriyanna explained. "Glass and other similar substances can't handle the pressures and energy releases caused by travelling through large bends in space. We use these video projections instead of windows. Each of the ten living quarters has a smaller version, as does the mess. I find they make the ship seem a little less claustrophobic."

"Can you call the hub?" Taulass asked, starting to thumb through his sheets of paper.

"Affirmative," Oriyanna replied. She looked at Lucie. "Could you stand back a little, please?"

Lucie shifted as the floor beneath her feet began to glow a deep magenta. Stepping further to the right, she watched as a seven-foot-high arch rose from the floor. It clicked into place, instantly seeming as if it had been there all along.

Taulass was working swiftly at his terminal, issuing orders to Oriyanna as he went, and Adam rounded the centre seat to stare out across the field. A police car had arrived at the accident, and the two drivers, as well as two passengers from one of the cars were pointing excitedly across the field towards their position. With the craft cloaked, he wondered just how the copper was going to handle their outrageous story.

"We need to be quick," Taulass commented, not taking his eyes or fast-moving hands away from the screen. "Asmodeous will already know we are here."

* * *

Over the past five hours, spurred along by the attack on Japan, the superpowers of the world had swiftly brought their nuclear launch systems online. Not twenty minutes ago, China had joined the select club, and the set was now complete. From the moment they went live, Ben Hawker had inserted Enola into their systems, and now he was waiting patiently while Enola began her first phase – reading and scanning the world's weather patterns and predictions. Once this phase had run its course, she would lock out every country's ability to control their own system, retarget the weapons, and set them free. From here on in Enola could run self-sufficiently, a little failsafe he'd engineered, just in case the worst happened.

Hawker turned to Asmodeous stride onto the bridge, his face framing a scowl. "I'm going to enjoy watching Becker die when the time is right," he growled, pacing over to Hawker's station. "It's just a shame we didn't manage to secure the others."

"With more time, it might have been possible," Namtar commented casually.

"One is better than none," Asmodeous said, casting his gaze over Croaker's ruined face. "You both gave a great deal for the cause. When this is over I too, will mourn for the loss of your brother, Namtar. Asag was a great friend to me for many years."

"Have you thought about what you are going to do with Becker after the Earth is destroyed?"

"Not yet, no. To just kill him will be too swift, and no real punishment for his actions. There is no rush to deal with him, his life will be torturous enough by the end of the day, knowing his family is dead."

"I understand," Namtar said, nodding. "When the time comes, I would respectfully request that I be permitted to avenge my brother."

"The deed will be yours, and yours alone," Asmodeous agreed.

"I hate to interrupt, but we've just picked up a signal from an Arkkadian vessel, it's entered Earth's atmosphere.

"Location," Asmodeous barked urgently, spinning around to study Hawker's screen.

"One hundred thousand feet and descending over northern France," Hawker paused, tracking the green dot on the screen. "Thirty thousand feet, southern England."

Namtar studied the map display with interest as the craft settled in Wiltshire. "This is very close to the location where we recovered Becker," he said.

"Keep the craft tracked," Asmodeous commanded. "As soon as they start heading this way, you will notify me immediately." A thin smile broke out on his face and he said, "It would seem we may be having more guests attend, after all."

* * *

Time does odd things in situations of extreme stress and anxiety. To Adam it seemed both an age, and far too soon, when Taulass finally punched the last few calculations into the main computer terminal of the Niribus, stood back and announced with a relieved breath, "I think we're ready."

In all it had taken him a little over twenty minutes to reprogram the way in which the Taribium hull captured energy from a wormhole and fed it back into the antimatter engines. Now it could tap into the Earth's energy grid, virtually bypassing the engines and feed the power directly to the hub.

"It's not perfect," he commented, as if berating himself. "I'm going to need ten percent power from the ship to top it up, and that will cover both windows."

"But that won't cause us any problems?" Adam asked as he tucked one of the Glock's into the back of his waistband. He held the other by his side, ready to use.

"If we all get back in the two return windows I've set, no. If you miss the second one, I'm afraid you're stuck, to open a third will use too much power. Power we don't have."

"We best not miss that second window," Adam smiled, although inside, he didn't feel much like smiling at all. He watched Oriyanna check the Arkkadian weapons that she and Taulass were taking. Resembling Earth guns, perhaps a mixture of a real gun and a plastic imitation, they were light grey and completely smooth. Adam wasn't sure what substance they were made of, but when Oriyanna had given it to him to examine it felt too light, not heavy and reassuring like an

Earth weapon did. He was confident, though, that it could do the job at hand.

Taulass worked quickly at his side of the terminal, and what Adam had come to assume was some type of home screen switched to a very realistic 3D image of a massive ship. It looked to be a greatly increased version of the one they were currently in. Adam recognised it from his dream and a chill ran through his anxious body.

"This is Arkus 2," Oriyanna announced, as Taulass reached into the display and moved the ship around with his hand. He touched something on the body of the main cube and it changed to a schematic. "The ship is vast, but with this map, and once we get on board, access to the life support systems, we should know where we are going." Taulass fiddled with the glowing blue block of the main computer. Adam could see he'd removed something – two somethings, in fact. He handed one to Oriyanna and kept one for himself. He unfolded the material and it formed into a tablet PC which was hand sized, made of a clear, glass-like substance which seemed amazingly flexible. Oriyanna placed her palm onto the surface of the one she held and a screen sprung to life. On the brightly lit display was a smaller computer image of Arkus 2.

"We both have these portable screens with us, Adam. You and Oriyanna are going to need yours to find Sam, without the use of a map you could wander that ship for hours, not knowing where you are. I am going to use mine to copy Enola, as discussed earlier." Taulass glanced from Adam to Oriyanna, and finally to Lucie. "As soon as the hub closes down, the thirty-minute countdown will begin to the first return window. After that closes, the ten minute countdown will begin." He pointed to a three-dimensional spinning globe in the corner of the holo-display. "If we don't come back Lucie, you touch that with your hand, and it will manually activate the ship's program to return to Arkkadia."

Lucie nodded uneasily. "I understand," she said.

Taulass switched his attention to Oriyanna. "Activate the hub."

Oriyanna worked deftly at the holo-display for a few seconds before a gentle hum filled the small bridge. The hub glowed ever so slightly, it still appeared to be a regular arch but to look through it now was like peering through thick glass. Adam thought he saw small, cotton-thin flashes of blue electricity in the glassy surface.

"Hub is active," Oriyanna said, looking up. "Fifteen seconds."

Taulass wasted no time; holding his weapon out in a ready position, he approached the glowing arch and vanished. Adam heard Lucie gasp in surprise. When Oriyanna went though he gave his sister a quick peck on the cheek, and her eyes filled with tears.

"I'll see you soon, and I'll bring Sam," he said reassuringly, before turning and vanishing through the arch.

* * *

The transportation room they'd arrived in was pitch black. It was in a lower part of the vessel, one which had not been used for a long time. It was instantly clear they were missing one vital piece of kit – a torch.

Adam stumbled from the hub, bumping into Oriyanna who was trying to bring the screen of her handheld to life. Taulass managed it first, and the glow from the display lit up the small room.

"Well, no welcoming party," he said uneasily, moving to the wall and locating a pressure pad which he pressed with his thumb. The room's lights flickered to life and Adam saw that on this vast ship, a hub room was exactly what it said it was; nothing else but a glowing arch in the centre of the small ten by ten square room. Just along from the pressure pad Taulass placed his hand into a small recess in the wall, and a door, which had been all but invisible started to slide open.

The three of them filed out into a dark corridor, using the light from the handheld displays to navigate with. The air was chillingly cool and carried no smells whatsoever. The whole place appeared desolate and abandoned.

"The nearest server room is four decks above; there are access stairs just along this passage," Taulass said in a low voice. "Keep track of every turn, you might need to remember them later."

"This ship has stairs?" asked Adam, not sure if he could believe such a technical marvel would have something so antiquated on board.

"Yes. We don't want to risk using the elevators," Taulass responded. He stopped at another small recess and opened another door. "This way," he whispered.

The dark stairway seemed to have no end, and obviously reached from the bottom of the ship to the top. Adam couldn't begin to fathom just how far they plunged into the abyss below. Taulass had mentioned that the hub room they'd used was on a lower deck, but the dark stairs seemed to plunge on forever beneath them. Having climbed four flights they exited into a lit passageway, all blinking owlishly in the bright light. Oriyanna held her hand up in a '*be very careful*' fashion, but this passage was as empty as the one they'd been in not two minutes ago.

"I'm guessing they only have basic support systems turned on for the top half of the ship," Taulass commented, scanning the screen on the handheld. "The decks below the hub room were mainly used for cargo." He halted by another hand sized recess in the wall, studied his handheld a second time and said, "This should be it – here." As with the previous two doorways, Taulass placed his hand into the opening and a door slid open. "Server room two," he announced as they stepped into darkness once again. Before the door closed he located the pressure plate on the wall and turned the lights on.

The place looked like no server room Adam had ever seen. Instead of housing banks of tall, whirring machines, there were six of the solid cubes, similar to the one aboard Niribus, only these were black, rising like a pre-cast mould from the floor to a height of around three feet.

"Our one cube has more power than all of these," Oriyanna pointed out, when she saw the expression on Adam's face. "This is very old tech now, although it is still highly functional."

Taulass hurried to one of the cubes, bringing a holo-display to life by pressing his hand to its top surface. Unlike the rich, high-definition display aboard the Niribus, this model seemed dated, much the way an old 90s computer might look when compared to one running the latest operating system. To Adam's untrained eye, the rich colours and realistic 3D imagery didn't look nearly as convincing. Taulass quickly located the life support systems, and requested a report of where all personnel currently were on the ship. A mere second later, he had the information he'd requested. Once again it was in the form of a three-dimensional image, and Taulass zoomed in on it, revealing the front section of the craft. The crew showed up as tiny green dots, scattered about the few upper and forward decks.

"We are here," Taulass noted, pointing to their three signals. "I hope that no one is monitoring this, or they will be wondering where the three extra guests have come from."

"Do you think they would be?" asked Adam.

"No, not for a second. I hope not, anyway." Taulass paused, fixed his attention on the display and continued. "This is the bridge, there are five crew there. One of them will be Asmodeous." He scanned down the ship, surprised at how sparsely populated it was. "This ship can hold a couple of thousand personnel. I know we never figured out how many Earth-Breed there were, but I'd wager he hasn't saved many of them, only the ones he could use to his advantage."

"You sound surprised," chuckled Oriyanna.

"Wait a second!" snapped Taulass, holding his hand up, as if to cut her off. "Look at this." He pointed to a room one deck below the bridge, there was a single green dot inside, but outside in the corridor were two more green dots.

"Seems almost like two people standing guard," Adam commented with a broad grin.

"My thoughts exactly," agreed Taulass, with a nod. "That has to be where they are holding Sam." He checked the timer on his handheld screen. "Just twenty-five minutes until the first window opens – go!"

Oriyanna copied the life support schematic to her handheld before grabbing Adam's hand and heading for the door. "It's going to take us about five minutes to reach Sam," Oriyanna said in a low voice as they rushed down yet another seemingly never-ending passage. At the first turn, Adam made a mental note of the direction they'd taken.

"This place is massive," he muttered, relieved that they hadn't taken more turns than he could possibly remember.

"I served on this ship thousands of years ago, before the war," Oriyanna said.

"And you can remember the layout?"

"Not really," she said, smiling nervously. "Bits and pieces, yes – it's this way." She led them into another stairway, and once again, it was black as night. This time they climbed a further ten floors. Adam had always thought he was in reasonable shape, but by the time they stepped out into another identical passageway, he felt as if he'd run a marathon.

"How... much... further?" he asked, gasping in air and realising with horror that the ship was a three-dimensional labyrinth.

"At the end, we take a left, then we should see the room they're holding him in. We must proceed with caution now, we are very close to the bridge." Adam nodded his understanding. He visually assessed the Glock making sure it was in order. He hated guns, hated shooting – but he'd have no issue using it if needed in these circumstances.

Carefully, at half the speed they'd navigated the lower levels of the ship, they both arrived at the corner of the passage. Adam peered around tentatively. About fifty yards ahead were two stern men, both toting handguns. Adam had no doubt Sam would have been able to tell him the exact make and model, even from this distance. To Adam though, all guns did the same thing, and the sight of these two was enough to know they'd found his friend. Now they just had to get to him out.

* * *

"No movement," Hawker said, his eyes fixed on the mapping display.

"What the hell are they doing?" Asmodeous growled. "Why aren't they heading this way?"

"I can't answer that, sir. The ship hasn't moved since touching down."

"I don't like it, not one bit!"

"Weather monitoring phase is now at fifty percent," Hawker said, changing the subject. He couldn't afford distractions at a time like this. Enola was busy, reading Earth's weather patterns and the potential forecast for the next five days. Once this stage was complete, and the targeting phase initiated, the world's superpowers would know something was very wrong. For now though, Enola was still undetectable.

"If that ship doesn't move before Enola is ready to launch, I want you to target a weapon to its location."

"I can do that, but—"

"No buts!" Asmodeous snapped. "You will alter the targeting of one weapon to the location of that ship – is that clear?"

"Crystal," Hawker grumbled. Enola was fully automated; her main program was running and needed no further input from him. Messing with the targeting now only left more room for error.

* * *

Fifteen decks below, and almost half a mile away, Taulass remotely connected his handheld to the mainframe of Arkus 2. He scanned swiftly though the ship's systems, seeking the plug-in which allowed an Earth-designed program to run in unison with the Arkkadian tech. It was buried deep, and a lesser programmer might not have seen it, but he was not a lesser programmer. A few screen changes later and he was copying Enola's files across to his system. After the file copied he took a moment to get a grip on how it worked. The coding was complex and beautifully designed. Although deadly, as a fellow 'geek', as he would have been known on Earth, he could appreciate the beauty and ingenious architecture that had gone into it.

On the face of it, Enola was nothing more than a rootkit-style hack, although to say that wasn't really doing her justice. This was rootkit hacking on a level which deserved an award, if they gave them out for acts cyber-terrorism such as this. Where a standard rootkit hack would give the user access to the system it was targeting, Enola completely locked anyone else out, giving the hacker full control. Not a massive deal on the face of it, but when you considered the systems it had its claws in, it most definitely was.

To add to his dismay, Taulass discovered the program was well into its start-up phase. One of his screens was now a mirror of the one on the bridge, giving him a remote view of what the operator was seeing, although from here he had no means of controlling it. It took him a moment or two to realise what Enola was doing. *It's reading the weather patterns*, he thought in horror. *Figuring out where best to target the weapons.* For the time being, he was helpless to do anything about it.

As the files copied across, Taulass switched to the life support system screen, confirming the two greens dots which represented Adam and Oriyanna were on the same deck as the room they suspected Sam was being held in. He watched, his heart thundering in his chest as they reached the corner of the passageway and paused.

* * *

Asmodeous paced the bridge of Arkus 2 uneasily, the presence of the Arkkadian vessel in southern England worrying his gut. Why hadn't they made their move? He paced the length of the bridge and studied the holo-screen where Benjamin Hawker had been stationed for the past few hours. He stared for a few moments at the solid dot on the screen – there was something about the craft's location which didn't sit right. His uneasiness grew when he noticed a small systems notification alert blinking away in the top corner of the display. "What is that?" he asked, his voice laced with agitation.

"It came around ten minutes ago," Hawker replied, sounding disinterested. "We get them all the time. It's a big ass ship, sir, and she's a little old and creaky. Likely a life support fault or a power fault."

"I need to see it," Asmodeous snapped, leaning on the back of Hawker's chair. He watched Hawker select the tab, revealing the systems notification was from the main power grid.

"It's showing a power surge in the..." Hawker paused and suffered a sinking feeling in the pit of his stomach. This was one particular notification he should never have overlooked. "A power surge in the lower transportation room," he finished, his voice sounding a little sheepish.

Asmodeous grabbed Hawker around the throat from behind and bellowed. "The reason that ship hasn't moved is because they are already on *fucking* board!" He lifted the Earth-Breed from his chair and only just resisted the urge to snap his wretched neck. Getting hold of himself, he let go, and Hawker fell back into the chair awkwardly, pawing at his painful throat, coughing and spluttering.

Asmodeous whipped around to Namtar and shouted furiously. "Take a team down to Sam Becker, that's where they will be heading. Do it *NOW!*"

* * *

In the server room, Taulass kept one eye on the two stationary dots, which represented Adam and Oriyanna, and watched the download of Enola impatiently with the other. *Why aren't you moving?* he thought. Three dots suddenly rushed from the bridge and made their way down the long passage leading away from it. In dismay, he watched as they dropped a deck and headed straight for the room where he suspected Sam was being held. *They know,* he thought. *I don't know how they know, but they do.* If they'd figured out the ruse then it would only be a matter of time until they scanned the life support system, just as he was doing. They would be able to see just how many uninvited guests were on board in an instant. His mind racing at a thousand miles an hour, he got into the life support systems program. In a few minutes, they would come face-to-face with Adam and Oriyanna, and there was nothing he could do to warn them – coms hadn't been an option for fear of them being picked up too easily. Taulass had only one option, to stay hidden. He navigated his way deeper into the system's operating procedure as swiftly as he could, hoping to find a way to shut off the monitors in his section of the ship. There were still twelve minutes before he'd have all of Enola's files, and a further three before the return hub activated.

It was going to be close. Too close.

* * *

Adam glanced around the corner for a second time and eyed the two men on duty outside the room. He turned to Oriyanna and whispered, "How the heck are we going to play this?" He adjusted his grip on the Glock, his hand clammy and his shooting arm felt about fifty pounds heavier than the other. He was sure that as soon as he lifted the weapon to fire, it would slide from his fingers.

"Leave it to me," Oriyanna said, although she sounded unconvinced. Before he had chance to question her she broke cover. He'd expected her to run, but she didn't. Instead, she sauntered along the corridor, acting as if she should be there. Forcing himself into action, he followed.

"We are so lost," he heard her say, as they closed the gap. "We only arrived a few hours ago and—"

"Stop right where you are!" one of the men shouted, his accent Hispanic. Adam knew the play she was making – hoping to influence one, or both – but it wasn't going to work, and Oriyanna realised it, too. In a flash, she whipped up the Arkkadian weapon and fired. Adam watched as the guy who'd issued the command convulsed as if he was having a seizure. The sight caught his partner off guard and spurred Adam into action. He sidestepped Oriyanna and levelled the Glock, discharging two rounds. He'd never been the best of marksmen, but one round hit the guy square in the torso. The recoil from the weapon made his hand sting as though he'd just whacked his palm against a brick wall. When the second guard doubled over, Oriyanna discharged her weapon at him. His whole body appeared as if it had been struck by lightning. Bright green flashes of what Adam guessed was some type of electricity raked over his body, and he stood bolt upright, his face contorting for a second before his hair began to smoulder. Less than a second later he hit the deck, dead.

Wasting no time, they stepped over the bodies and Oriyanna placed her hand into another recess, and opened the door.

* * *

Despite the gravity of the situation, Sam was knackered and with nothing else to do other than worry and run through a never-ending list of what-ifs, he began to drift off to sleep. His mind had been locked in a torturous quandary of unanswered questions. Was Lucie truly pregnant? Why the hell did they know, and he didn't? In his semi-awake state, he heard a female voice outside the room and thought nothing more of it, dismissing it as part of a dream leading him into the land of nod. The second voice, much louder, shouted, "Stop right where you are!" It chased away his on-coming sleep in a flash. Following the command, he heard two deafening shots ring out – someone had discharged a firearm. The next few seconds seemed to pass at the speed of minutes. Sam bolted from the bed and stood in a ready position by the door. The idea of rescue flashed though his head, but he quashed the thought as quickly as it came, fearing he was setting himself up for a fall. When the door slid open he had to do a double take at the sight of Adam and Oriyanna when they rushed into the room, both with their weapons out, ready.

"Don't fucking shoot me!" he shouted, and he was only half joking. He knew how trigger happy even the most well-trained soldier could be under pressure, and although he'd trust Adam with his life, his friend was far from well-trained in the field of combat.

Adam lowered the gun and embraced Sam, almost choking the air out of his lungs and he winced with pain when Adam crushed his shoulder. "Glad to see you too, bud," he laughed. "You saving my butt – now that's one to remember."

Adam broke the bear hug and grinned. "A wise crack? Guess that shows that you're more than alright."

Sam smiled. "How the hell…"

"We don't have time now," Oriyanna cut in, sliding the handheld from her belt and checking the display. "We have less than twelve minutes before the first return hub opens."

"Return hub?" Sam questioned.

"Later," Adam urged. "We need to move."

"You don't have to ask me twice," beamed Sam. "Just one question – Lucie?"

"She's fine, safe and back in good old Blighty," Adam replied. Before Sam had time to question his friend about the baby Adam continued, "Thought you might want to use this," and slid the second Glock from his waistband.

Sam took the gun and gave it a quick onceover. At the door, he watched Oriyanna operate the bizarre opening mechanism again. The door slid open, only to reveal three armed figures on the other side, their weapons raised and ready to fire.

* * *

"Well, isn't this nice and convenient," Namtar snarled, as he trained his weapon on Sam Becker. The surprise on the faces of the trio had been nothing short of priceless. "Just when I was beginning to think we'd only have the pleasure of Sam's company for the big show, you two literally fall into our laps."

"How's the eye?" Sam grinned when he saw Croaker. The third guy was a new player to the equation. He stood almost as tall as Namtar and his stature was equally as impressive. His black tee-shirt appeared to be a size too small and highlighted the bulging muscles beneath. His sandy blonde hair was close to the same shade as Sam's, but that's where the similarities ended. Next to the two giants, Croaker seemed almost weedy. All three were toting lethal Diablo tactical handguns.

"I'd shoot you dead here and now if I could," Croaker snapped. "Now if you'd please lay down your weapons, that'd be appreciated."

S T Boston

Sam lowered his gun reluctantly, motioning for Adam and Oriyanna to do the same.

"There is a certain someone on the bridge who would just love to make your acquaintance," Namtar grinned, watching Adam. "And it's been many years since you last met," he added, switching his attention to Oriyanna as she placed her weapon on the floor. "Now kick them towards me," he ordered. They did as instructed and watched helplessly as Namtar collected them up. He stopped to admire the Arkkadian gun. "Isn't this a little against your code of conduct?" he asked, turning it over in his hand. "Alien technology on Earth... tut-tut!"

"If you'd care to hand it back, I'll demonstrate the latest in our weapons developments," Oriyanna offered in a low voice. "Not even the Gift can save you from this."

Namtar smiled coldly. "You might want to ask Sam about the Gift, when you get the opportunity. Let's just say the pair of you might need to offer yourselves up first for a bullet. Now, let's get moving."

* * *

"Excellent news!" Asmodeous beamed when Namtar reported in on the ship's com system that he had both Adam Fisher and Oriyanna in custody and they were on their way to the bridge. He turned to Hawker who was eyeing him warily from the control console he was working at. "Please excuse my outburst," he said, patting Hawker's shoulder. "It was inexcusable."

"Don't mention it," Hawker grunted.

"Now let's see if we have any other gate-crashers. If you'd be good enough to call up the life support systems. It might help us flush out any more *rats*.

* * *

From the mirror on the main control panel, Taulass watched as the operator called up the life support system and ran a scan. Just seconds before, he'd successfully managed to shut down the censors which would have given his position away. If the user searched hard enough, he'd easily discern that this particular part of the system was not functioning, but Taulass hoped they would only carry out a quick scan and he'd be in the clear.

From the bowels of the ship he watched as the screen come to life, reporting a total of eleven crew, including Adam, Sam and Oriyanna. With bated breath he waited, not wanting to see the operator delving meticulously deeper into the system. After a few tense seconds, the screen swapped back to Enola, still busy doing her thing.

Moments before, he'd watched the two green dots outside Sam's room blink out of existence. Foolishly, he'd allowed himself a moment of hope, thinking Adam and Oriyanna would have time to snatch Sam and get clear before the other three dots, heading relentlessly toward their position, arrived. Much to his dismay the trio had stalled, likely caught up in a rapid question and answer session. The delay was just long enough to ensure their capture. He'd been so anxious, he'd had to reel himself in from screaming pointlessly at the screen, shouting useless warnings to the three. It had been torturous to watch. There were just seven minutes now until he had Enola in his possession and he was fast coming to terms with the fact that he'd be heading back to Niribus on his own.

* * *

Oriyanna stood silently in the elevator as it swiftly carried them up one deck and toward the bridge approach passage. The two men with Namtar were Earth-Breed, she was almost certain, which meant there was a possibility she could use one, if not both to her advantage. It was a tall ask, and a display of mind control the likes of which she'd never attempted before. The taller of the two males glanced at her, the way she knew men often regarded women they found attractive on Earth.

Instead of shunning his look she met his eyes and smiled. Liam Granger, that was his name, she'd plucked the knowledge from his mind. Liam held her gaze, and he could do nothing other than look at her, because she'd ensnared him. Now was not the time to push herself though: she'd need all the energy she could muster when the time came. Instead she looked away, allowing Liam Granger to have his thoughts back.

* * *

Adam was numb, his legs hung like two lumps of dead meat from his hips, yet they still carried him forward as if operating on their own agenda. The walk from the elevator to the bridge seemed miles long. His mind wandered to Lucie, who was no doubt watching the timer tick down on the display aboard Niribus, foolishly hoping that when the time came they would appear, slapping each other's backs triumphantly. It was a nice thought, but it was a fool's assumption.

Adam had figured out that at least two of the three escorting them were responsible for Sam's capture. He was certain one was an Elder – the other guy, who wore a badly-fashioned bandage over his right eye was Earth-Breed, because if he wasn't he would have healed by now. He hadn't had an opportunity to question Sam regarding what the Elder had said, about him not being able to take a bullet. What had they done to him during the trip to Nazca? Had he really been stripped of the Gift? Sam had a strange marking on his forehead which Adam also hadn't had a chance to ask about.

Like a group being led to their execution – and that's exactly how it felt to Adam – they arrived at the main door to the bridge. The guy with the one eye pulled him roughly out of the way and used another recess to open the door. The bridge of Arkus 2 was vast compared to that of Niribus. Instead of three control chairs, Arkus 2 had a bank of ten. Only two were currently occupied. It was an odd scene, while the bridge seemed completely alien, the figure sitting at the largest chair wore a dark brown hooded top, jeans and a pair of Nike trainers. He was a man, probably no older than forty; the kind of person you'd pass in the street and not look at twice. For some reason, it was the trainers which struck Adam most, they looked completely out of place. Next to the man, sitting at a slightly smaller console was a second guy. He was of similar age, perhaps a little younger, and he wore thickly rimmed black glasses. His clothing, also exceptionally casual, seemed to hang from his scrawny body. When this guy went to school, Adam had no doubt he would have been the kind of kid who was president of the chess club.

The vastness of the room only seemed amplified by the lack of crew. On a plinth behind them, closer to the door stood a third male. Smartly dressed, his suit looked expensive, and his shoes were so well polished they might as well be made of patent leather. His blonde hair, which fell in messy waves, still seemed to compliment his formal attire. When Adam looked at his strange amber eyes, an icy hand clenched around his heart. He didn't need any introduction, Adam knew instantly who this was. The thing which really struck him was how young the man looked, perhaps in his late twenties at most.

He watched a warm, almost welcoming smile form on the man's lips. "Adam Fisher," he announced in a loud voice, his eyes glinting charismatically. "It really is a pleasure." He almost bounded over to where Adam stood, taking his hand and pumped it vigorously up and down, behaving like an overly-familiar game show host. His fingers were as cold as ice. "You know, I was so disappointed that my friend here," he gestured to the one Adam had pegged as an Elder, "didn't manage to bring you back with Sam." The grin faded and turned a little reptilian, cold and not as welcoming as it had initially appeared. "But I shouldn't have been such a pessimist, because your own stupid fucking tenacity, and inability to leave things alone, meant you made it here all on your very own." He turned and stared at Oriyanna. "With a little help from your friends, of course. I mean, credit where credit is due, right?"

Asmodeous glanced from Adam to Sam and then back to Oriyanna, as if he expected one of them to respond. "But one thing is bugging me." His eyes fixed on Adam, boring into his soul. "Why would you two lovebirds run a suicide mission to rescue good old Sam, here? Something tells me you know exactly what we're intending to do, and if that's the case, what would be the point of saving Sam Becker when the rest of the world is about to go to hell in a hand basket? I'll tell you why, because this is merely one part of your plan. Although we're merely minutes away from all systems being ready to go, and far too late for any heroics, I would ask you to humour me."

Adam watched him stride over to the guy with the bandaged eye and snatch his handgun from his fingers. "I would suggest, either you tell me right now what the other part of this plan was, or I shoot her in the head!" And he thrust the gun against Oriyanna's left temple.

* * *

Asmodeous' speech was nothing more than a distant voice to Oriyanna, similar to when you hear two people talking in a nearby room, and you can distinguish the voices, but not what's being said. With Asmodeous taking centre stage, no one had noticed the vacant expression on her face, nor had they noticed a similar vacant expression on the face of Liam Granger. With every passing second, Oriyanna could feel her strength depleting, and she knew this task was going to take all of her energy reserves.

Getting into his head had been easy; for as soon as he'd had the opportunity he'd given her another one of those looks, and she'd accepted it, snaring him like a spider in a web. She didn't know how Enola worked, but she was certain the two Earth-Breeds at the control console were the ones running it. Asmodeous was calling the shots, but he wasn't the brains behind the program.

'All you need to do, Liam, is raise your gun and shoot the man at the main console. Once you have done that, shoot his friend, and if you are still alive, shoot Asmodeous,' she suggested in his mind. *'It's alright for you to do this, for this is your destiny. You want to fulfil your destiny, don't you, Liam?'*

Through the conflicting white noise in his head she felt him say '*Yes*,' but his own thoughts and subconscious were still getting in the way, screaming at him to ignore her pleas.

'*Then what is stopping you? Just raise the gun and shoot – the gun was built to shoot, that is the gun's destiny, just as your destiny is to pull the trigger. Don't deny yourself that, Liam. Time is short. Shoot, Liam, shoot the gun.*' Oriyanna was so far gone that she didn't even register Asmodeous as he thrust the Diablo against her temple.

'*Liam, time is short, you know this is the right thing to do, shoot the gun, Liam, shoot it NOW!*'

* * *

Adam knew he couldn't tell Asmodeous what he wanted to know, despite the gun aimed point blank at Oriyanna. The task at hand was of greater importance than any of their own lives, but it still ate at him like a rabid animal, every fibre of his being wanting to scream the truth at Asmodeous. *There is someone else, he's copying your fucking program right now, and he's going to stop you, no matter what happens to us!* Despite the overwhelming desire, he bit his tongue, and held back the admission. He glanced into Oriyanna's eyes, and noticed that while she was here in body, her mind may as well have been on another planet. Before he had chance to question it, one of the team who'd confronted them in Sam's room, the largest of the ones he'd pegged as Earth-Breed, whipped his handgun up and shot the guy in the brown hooded top through the back of the head. In a flash, he dispatched the second male with the same finesse, and the man's goofy glasses tumbled from his ruined face. The cubed console in front of them got splattered in a grotesque mixture of blood and brain matter, breaking the projection up into a series of crazy lines like a broken barcode. Pirouetting on his left leg he twisted toward Asmodeous, but Asmodeous was faster. The gun was whipped away from Oriyanna's head and he fired, obliterating the left side of his face. He swayed on the spot for the briefest of seconds, what was left of his face staring at Oriyanna in confusion, before his legs collapsed and he hit the floor. A split second later Oriyanna went down, blood flowing from her nostrils. Well trained on how to react in such situations, Sam threw himself onto Namtar, struggling to get the upper hand. Adam sensed the weight of Asmodeous' gun as the muzzle bore down on him, but before he had a chance to react the lights went out.

Chapter 37

Despite the ventilation and air-conditioning systems humming away in the background, the PEOC smelled of perspiration, mixed with a healthy dose of tension. America's nuclear launch capability had been live for a little over an hour, and to no-one's surprise, it had shown no signs of malfunction or hacking.

President Hill was more certain than ever that the Dae Wonsu had lied, which made the task at hand even more critical. Since the call from North Korea, they'd offered up no further evidence to support their claims that their systems had been overridden and controlled by some unknown third party, other than the questionable video feed. The decisions which needed to be made now, regarding how best to deal with such an unprovoked and heinous act against humanity, could not be made lightly.

"I say we strike them hard," suggested Roger Stanbrook, General of the United States Army. He slammed his fist down on the conference room table, which was littered with an array of half-finished mugs of cold coffee and the occasional discarded plastic cup from the water coolers. "We have vested trade interests with Japan and they'll be looking to the western world for support."

Hill buried his face in his hands and let out a long, stressful and tired sigh. "If we do that, we face retaliation from China. While they've condemned the attack, we all know they're in bed with the North Koreans.

Despite their dislike for North Korea's nuclear program, it's one heck of a risk."

"We have the firepower to manage such risks," Stanbrook responded coldly.

"I'm not going to be the president who is remembered for turning half the civilised world into a nuclear wasteland," Hill spat. "The fact that one nuke has been used, is already one nuke too many in my book. And just how do you think Russia will respond, if we get trigger happy?"

"With respect, sir," Stanbrook argued, "there's no point having one of the largest nuclear arsenals in the world if you're too frightened to use it!"

Hill fixed him with a venomous look, and stood up. "With respect, I never wanted to re-sanction the nuclear weapons program in the first place! Congress forced my hand into it, and you know that."

"Because if they hadn't, we'd have been a sitting duck!"

"I understand that, but we need to look at alternatives. While congress forced my hand into initiating the program, the decision to launch lies with me." Before Stanbrook could voice his side of the argument, a deep noted alarm vibrated through the whole of the PEOC. "What the hell?" yelled Hill as one of the two nuclear launch operators barged into the room, his brow clammy with a sheen of sweat.

"Sir, we have a problem," he panted. "Our targeting systems just went live, and the same goes for our other NATO allies."

"Who the hell sanctioned that?" Hill cried, kicking his chair out of the way and heading for the door.

"No one, sir! We've lost control. We're trying to shut it down now, but everything we try fails."

"Dear God," President Hill gasped. "How long do we have?"

"Five minutes at most, sir, maybe less, before every single one of our launch-ready birds is in the air."

Chapter 38

Taulass tried his best to keep an eye on which green dot belonged to who on the life support system, a difficult task and it had him almost seeing double. As the Enola files finished copying to his handheld, he snatched it away from the server cube and prepared to leave, but as he turned he watched two more lights blink out – two more people dead. Something was happening on the bridge. Frantically, he watched the other dots, sure that those belonging to Adam, Sam and Oriyanna were still in play. Cursing he placed the handheld back on the console. He knew he was of no use to them in person, it would take far too long to reach them, and he was about as good in combat situations as he was at dancing the tango – not proficient at all. He was a tech nerd, and tech nerds had their place, and he was in it.

Instead he accessed the ship's power grid, quickly locating the lighting control and hoping that what he was about to do would help, rather than hinder. He knew the other team had zero chance of making the first return window, but if he could buy them a distraction, it might give them time to get away and make the second and final one. He paused briefly as he weighed the options in his head, but he quickly reassured himself it was the best option and killed the lights to the bridge. He simultaneously turned on all the lights in the lower section of the ship, making it easier to navigate back to the hub. He stole one last glance at the mirrored screen from the bridge, Enola had chosen her targets and switched to launch mode. Not wasting any more time, he bolted from the server room and pounded down the passageway. Reaching the stairs he bounded down them, taking two at a time. Running at full sprint toward the hub room, he glanced at the handheld. The first return window was seconds away from opening. If he didn't make it, he had no chance of stopping Enola in time.

Arriving at the door he thrust his hand into the recess; waiting impatiently as it slid open. The arch was live, humming softly to itself as cotton-thin flashes of blue danced occasionally across the glassy surface. Not wasting another second, he threw himself forward and vanished.

* * *

Sam grappled with Namtar in the darkness, feverishly hammering his fist into the man's gut, and felt his hot, rancid breath on the side of his face. Pain raged in his damaged shoulder but good old adrenalin kept him fighting through it. In the darkness, he heard the Diablo drop to the floor and with his free hand he scrambled for it, but the move allowed Namtar to get the upper hand. Using his immense strength Namtar lifted his large body over Sam's, gripped his head and pull forward. In the brief seconds before Sam's head was going to slam into the floor, his fingers touched the gun. Snatching it up, Sam moved his arm forward and fired. Namtar's body flew backwards, the blast at close range knocking him off kilter. Sam thrust himself upward and unloaded three more shots in the area where he gauged Namtar's head would be. The gunfire was deafening, but a satisfactory spray of blood splattered over Sam's face and across his hands, confirming he'd hit his target.

Getting to his feet, he searched in the gloom for Adam or Oriyanna. He didn't have the first clue as to what had happened, or why the guy in the tight tee-shirt had suddenly gone on a shooting spree, but he didn't care.

"Adam?" he called, the dim glow of the holo-display casting enough light to see.

"Here," he heard his friend shout. "Can you see Oriyanna?"

Before Sam had time to react he was knocked sideways, punches raining down on his abdomen and face. In the partial light, he caught a glimpse of the white bandage covering Croaker's eye. Adrenalin pumping, Sam brought his knee up, connecting perfectly with Croaker's groin. The blow was hard, but the determined son of a bitch kept his grip, pinning Sam to the floor and knocking the Diablo from his grip. Cursing, Sam thrust his arms upward, groping at Croaker's face until he located the bandage. Using his thumb as a guide, he worked out roughly where Croaker's ruined eye was located and sunk his thumb into the cavity, as hard as he could. Croaker screamed, the sound loud enough to break glass, and gave up his struggle. Sam managed to get to his feet and Adam joined him. Before Croaker had the opportunity to get up, Sam slammed his boot down hard onto the side of his head, lifted it, and then repeated the action with just as much gusto.

"Thanks for the help, bud," he grinned, his eyes fully adjusted to the pale green light from the holo-display.

Adam ignored the wisecrack. "I can't find Oriyanna," he said in a panic. "Asmodeous is gone, too."

* * *

Asmodeous knew the tables were on the turn the second the lights went out. None of it mattered to him as long as Enola was live, she no longer needed Hawker to hold her hand and she would do her job no matter what. For reasons unknown, his unusual eye pigment had always afforded him better than normal lowlight vision, and when the bridge plunged into darkness he snatched Oriyanna's unconscious body from the floor and made his escape. In the melee, no one had seen him slide out of the door. To his satisfaction, the lights in the long passage were also out.

Pacing down the darkened passage with Oriyanna's limp body over his shoulder, he grinned wildly to himself. The fact that almost his entire small team were dead didn't bother him, not in the least. He didn't care what happened to Fisher and Becker either; the ship was vast and he doubted they would find their way back off the Arkus 2 before zero hour. Later, he would enjoy hunting them down and killing them. Oriyanna, though, if left to run free, could cause him issues. She knew the ship and the technology, and out of all of them, she was the one who needed to be dealt with first.

Switching left at the first crossroads, he accessed one of the living quarters and threw Oriyanna onto the floor before calling up the ship's computer. He wasn't going to miss the launch, not for anything.

* * *

"We can't just leave her," Adam protested as he guided Sam down the corridor and away from the bridge.

"Listen, you've just told me we only have two return hubs to get home, you're sure we've missed one, and if we miss the second we're stuck here!"

"I know, but—"

"But nothing, we have the square root of fuck all time and a ship the size of three cruise liners." Sam stopped and took hold of his friend, looking him in the eye. Despite the gloom he could see tears glistening in Adam's eyes. "Only you know the way back to the hub room, I can't find it on my own!"

"I'm not sure I can either," Adam replied, trying to remember which turns they'd taken.

"Sure you can," Sam prompted. "Once we get off this ship, we'll see what's happening, make some plans and then we can come back for Oriyanna." Sam wasn't certain he believed his own statement, but he needed to get Adam moving. "I need to get back for Lucie," he concluded and he heard the desperation in his voice.

Adam paused for longer than he would have liked. "Okay, but I *am* coming back," he announced firmly.

"Agreed, now let's get moving – which way?"

"We need to drop one floor, pass the room they held you in, then it's two left turns, down ten decks and straight down the lower corridor, past the server room, four more decks down and then, I think, five doors along." Adam led the way, feeling like shit and suffering a stab of betrayal for leaving Oriyanna behind. *This task is greater than any one of our lives,* he heard her repeat in his head. It was easy to say and agree to at the time; but when it came to the crunch, it was a different matter.

They rushed down one deck, passing the room where Sam had been held. The two dead guards were still slumped on the floor, one of them had his right eye closed, as if he was winking at them. Adam found the first stairway and opened the door. The pair hammered down the ten decks, Adam guessing it was Taulass who'd turned the lights on, and he silently thanked him. The handheld was with Oriyanna and without it, they'd have been fumbling around in the dark. The ten decks passed much more quickly on the descent than they had during the ascent and they soon found themselves on the floor housing the server room.

"Are you sure it's this way?" Sam asked urgently.

"Certain," Adam raced along the corridor. "This is the server room," he announced, coming to a stop. He activated the door and peered inside; the lights were on and one of the server cubes still had an active holo-display. Taulass was gone. "He must have made the first return window," said Adam, glancing at his watch, but he wasn't certain how much time they had. "Let's get moving." They broke into a run, located the next door and dropped the last four floors. "This is the passage, just five doors along."

"I hope to God you're right," Sam said.

Adam counted the doors in his head, arrived at the fifth and thrust his hand into the recess. "We must have missed it," Adam said, and he couldn't hide a hint of hope in his voice at the sight of the hub, which was silent and dull. "Now can we please..." Before he could finish the sentence a low hum filled the room, and the centre of the hub flickered with blue current.

"No, we didn't," Sam beamed. "Talk about in the nick of time – do we always have to cut this shit so bloody close?" He glanced at Adam and guessed from the expression in his eyes that he wasn't intending on making the jump. "Sorry, old buddy," he said, grabbing Adam's arm.

Adam fought back, using his weight to counteract Sam's grasp, but Sam was stronger and had the advantage of having caught him off guard. With one final, desperate effort which caused his shoulder to scream in protest, Sam swung Adam around and pushed him though the arch, then dashed through himself.

* * *

For the first half hour, Lucie had been unable to do anything other than watch the clock on the holo-display tick down painfully slowly. As the final two minutes ticked by her anxiety grew to a point where she was sure she'd throw up. Bang on the thirty minute mark the hub began to hum as it went live. Once live, the fifteen second window started its own countdown – more torturous seconds for her to endure. With five seconds to spare Taulass fell through the portal and into the bridge, his breathing rapid and his face covered in sweat. Before he'd had chance to steady himself, the portal shut.

"Where are the others?" Lucie asked in dismay.

"They— they are— alive," he panted, placing one hand on the server cube to steady himself. "The— they—– ha— have— Sam, I think. But th— there was a problem."

"What problem?" she shrieked.

"No time to explain now," Taulass said, his breath coming a little easier. "Enola is live, the launch system has already begun."

"Dear God," Lucie said shakily as Taulass placed the handheld onto the server cube and connected it. Lucie watched the second timer start its countdown – ten more minutes of torture, and then what? Not knowing was horrendous, her nerves shot.

* * *

Taulass needed to work fast. He swiftly synced Enola with his own systems, giving him access to the main control panel. He switched off the automated program and assumed manual control in the same split-second as Enola released every launchable nuclear warhead. "Launch is go," he muttered, more to himself than Lucie.

"Can you stop it?" she asked urgently.

"No. Not the launch, anyway," he said. "I have an idea, though." He located the primary command screen and pumped in a single line of code, telling all but one of the weapons to abort. Pushing execute he held his breath and watched to see if they would accept his new command. The screen froze for a second before acknowledging the abort command. "Done," he said in a relieved breath. "That was too close."

"What's happening now?"

He sat back and smiled. "I've de-armed the entire human race, that's what's happening. I altered the targeting systems on each weapon and they'll jettison harmlessly into space. Except for one. I need one of them."

"What the hell do you need a nuclear weapon for?" Lucie cried.

"This needs to end now," Taulass spoke in a voice fractured by the stress he'd been under for the past two days. "I'm re-targeting one weapon to the coordinates of Arkus 2."

Lucie tried to pull him away from the holo-display, screaming at him. "But you'll kill them! How can you even consider doing such a thing?"

"The nuke has launched," Taulass said firmly, wrestling her aside. Lucie fell awkwardly to the floor and he felt terrible, but the situation needed to be controlled. "The next window opens in less than a minute, and that weapon will take fifteen minutes to reach the target. If they're going to make it back, they'll be safely here by the time it detonates."

"And if they don't make it?" she demanded, tears streaming down her pale cheeks.

"They knew before they left this was likely to be a one-way mission, Lucie. Even if your brother didn't voice the knowledge, he knew. Your brother and Sam are two of the bravest people I've ever met – you should be proud of them both."

The hub was now less than a minute from opening. Taulass hid it well, but inside he felt like shit. Every ounce of his being wanted to turn that nuke around and let it fly off into space with its other deadly brethren, leaving time to launch a hare-brained rescue mission. But Asmodeous was in his sights and the task needed to be completed. To let him escape would just lead to another situation like this, of that Taulass was certain. He glanced at Lucie and it was clear the young woman had endured all she could, she didn't even have the energy to pick herself up from the floor. As the hub began to hum softly, she rolled into a protective foetal position and began sobbing fiercely.

* * *

Adam was still fighting against the momentum of Sam's shove as he reeled out of the hub and onto the bridge of the Niribus. Sam followed swiftly, catching him before he had the opportunity to spin around and return to the Arkus 2.

"You had no right," Adam shouted, throwing himself against Sam and fighting to get back to the hub. "It was my choice, not yours!"

Oblivious to Lucie and Taulass, Sam grappled with his friend, placing one leg behind his knees and dropping him to the floor, holding him in place until the portal blinked out of existence. Adam struggled inanely for another few seconds before all the fight went out of him. With the risk of Adam throwing himself back though gone, Sam let go and stood up, only to find himself grappled by Lucie, who threw her arms around him in a bear hug.

"Sam, Sam!" she cried, smothering his face in kisses. He took her into his arms and kissed her back, her body shaking uncontrollably beneath his hands. Lucie broke away and embraced her brother, who had picked himself up from the floor, his eyes awash with tears.

"You have to open a new window," Adam demanded. "He took her when the lights went out, she's still on that ship!"

"It's impossible," Taulass said, his voice wracked with regret. "If we do, we will cripple our own craft. We have taken as much power as we can out of the engines, even with the aid of the Earth's energy it won't be enough, and that ship is too vast to mount a search in the time we have available."

"Fuck the engines!" Adam shouted. "Do it now!"

Taulass took him by the shoulders, holding him firmly. "I have stopped the attack, but I have one nuke targeted at Arkus 2. I'm sorry, Adam but you knew the risks, as did Oriyanna. This needs to end now. There is no chance of return. In ten minutes, that ship will be destroyed."

"Then you take this ship up now and take us there! What's stopping you? You can jump the craft there in an instant! There's no need for secrecy now, and nearly everyone else is dead!"

"But the chances of finding her..." Taulass began, but in reality, he was already preparing to launch. As the Niribus lifted silently into the air he turned to Adam. "Hold on. Without being in space, this might shake the old girl a little."

Chapter 39

The strain of influencing Liam Granger to make him shoot two people had rendered Oriyanna unconscious. When the murkiness lifted from her mind and she regained lucidity, she found herself lying on the cool floor on her back. Opening her eyes, she twisted her head and noticed Asmodeous. He was perched on the end of a bed, his eyes fixated on the screen of the ship's computer, which displayed itself on the wall of the room. The whole situation struck her as odd, and her struggling brain couldn't quite compute what was happening, or how she'd come to be there. He must have sensed that she was awake because he turned his attention to her, a big, charismatic, but slightly unhinged smile spreading over his face.

"You're awake. Marvellous, and just in time, too," he chirped. "The launch is just about to begin, come take a look."

Begrudgingly, Oriyanna propped herself up on her elbows. Her body still felt weak, but strength was returning to by the second, allowing her to get up onto her feet. She glanced around, realising she was alone with him in one of the crew's living quarters. Her memory treated her to the image of Liam Granger shooting the two operators dead – if that had happened, then why the hell was the launch still going ahead?

On the screen was a box, and inside the box was a number of small graphics, each representing a nuclear weapon. Gradually, one-by-one, the graphics swiftly changed from green to red.

"We have lift-off," Asmodeous shouted in delight, jumping off the bed as if celebrating a goal scored by his favourite football team.

Oriyanna didn't know what to do. She had no idea what had happened to Sam, Adam and Taulass, the plan had obviously failed, and as a result, over the next twenty-five minutes every major city on the globe was going to be reduced to ash. Not able to drag her gaze from the screen she watched, eyes filling with tears until suddenly, the word 'ABORT' flashed across the display.

"No! No!" Asmodeous screamed, getting up from the bed and rushing to the display, but there was nothing he could do to stop it. He gripped the edges of the monitor, his eyes close to the screen, as if he couldn't believe what he'd seen.

Oriyanna snatched the opportunity and crossed the small cabin, ramming his face into the monitor, and she heard his nose break with a nauseating crunch. Turning away from Asmodeous she reached the door, opened it and fled out into the passageway. With no weapons at her disposal she didn't like her chances against him, and she needed to get off the ship fast.

Reaching the end of the first passage, Oriyanna hit the stairs and she glanced back, only to see Asmodeous rounding the frame of the cabin door and breaking into a run. His bloodied nose formed a streak of crimson down the lower half of his face. She threw herself into the stairwell and hurried down into the bowels of the ship, taking the steps four or five at a time.

She could hear him behind her, his feet slamming on the metallic stairs as he pounded down them in pursuit. Oriyanna delved deeply into her memory and tried to recall where the emergency access door was. She was certain she knew and with no other options available she stuck to her only plan.

The descent seemed to take forever, and all the time Asmodeous' feet pounded on the stairs above her. She was certain they were growing louder with every flight. Not once did she dare look back, positive a moment of lapsed concentration would surely lead to a fall, and that would be the end of any hope.

Reaching the very bottom of the ship, her feet found the landing; now she glanced back and saw how close Asmodeous was. Just a floor above, two at most, and descending as fast as a cheetah might chase down its prey.

Struggling to draw air into her chest, Oriyanna took off down the passageway, her legs burning and her muscles on fire. She reached the access hatch, threw her hand into the recess and waited anxiously. Opening the emergency access hatch would require the ship to de-cloak, meaning it took seconds longer to carry out the command, seconds she didn't have. A hundred yards behind her, Asmodeous was closing in, his amber eyes insane, the bottom of his face covered in bright red blood.

The hatch finally opened and cool desert air hit Oriyanna's sweaty face, the surrounding mountains ignited in a bright halo of light. Fork lighting laced its way across the sky, behaving like a crazed, electri-fied spider's web. Throwing herself down the access ramp, heavy rain instantly soaked her to the skin and her feet slipped treacherously on the metal ramp. She fought for purchase but it was too late, her body twisted and she went tumbling down, her body landing in a crumpled mess at the bottom of the ramp.

The few seconds it took to recover allowed Asmodeous to close the gap, and when Oriyanna got to her feet, she peered back toward the ship. Asmodeous was only twenty yards behind her now, and judging from the triumphant expression on his face, he knew he was going to catch her. He'd slowed his rushed approach and almost stalked down the access ramp, his lips locked in a jeering grin. More lightning ig-nited the sky, silhouetting the gigantic hulk of Arkus 2 against his predatory body. Oriyanna knew there was no point in running, she would only be burning valuable energy, energy she'd need to defend herself. She took a step back, buying a little more room and prepared to fight.

* * *

In the Earth's atmosphere, the short wormhole jump created a sonic boom five times louder than that of a plane breaking the sound barrier. Four miles away, in the small town of Amesbury, every window in every house, shop and car shattered. Less than a second later, the Niribus arrived above the giant structure of Arkus 2 in Peru, the smaller craft zipping along the length of the craft before dropping down beside it.

"I'll run a scan of the craft," Taulass said, as lightning flashed across the horizon. The ship was uncloaked and impossibly huge against the darkened sky.

"Down there, look!" cried Sam, pointing out of the window. Twenty feet below them, out in the open ground, two bodies were locked in a bitter struggle.

"Get us on the ground," Adam ordered. "I need your weapon, ours were taken."

"No offence, mate, but I think I'll do the honours," Sam said, as Taulass touched the ship down less than fifty feet from where the pair were fighting. Before Lucie could protest, Sam took the weapon from Taulass and gave it a once over. When the door to the craft slid open, both Adam and Sam rushed out into the pounding rain.

* * *

Asmodeous hit Oriyanna like a steam train, instantly knocking her off her feet and sending her sprawling onto her back. Before she could react he was on her, pinning her to the wet ground with the weight of his body. Oriyanna stared upwards, registering the arrival of the Niribus as it blinked into existence high above them. The small craft sped along the length of Arkus 2 and for a moment she lost sight of it, before it swooped down the side of the hull and came back. Oriyanna made a futile effort to toss Asmodeous from his positon, but he fought back, slamming her head against the ground. Oriyanna saw stars and nausea flooded her stomach.

"I might not be able to shoot you, but I'm going to smash your pretty fucking skull to pieces," Asmodeous raged as he yanked her hair, adjusted his grip and slammed the back of her head again, then again. The nauseating crunch of her skull breaking reverberated through every muscle and bone in her ancient body. Once again, Asmodeous drew her head up, but thankfully oblivion took her before the next blow came.

* * *

Sam raced across the wet ground, his shirt plastered to his skin, the weapon raised. "Hey, asshole!" he shouted as more lighting chased hot lines through the sky, followed by a clap of thunder so loud it shook the ground. Asmodeous turned to stare at him, puzzlement on his crazed face. His hands were covered in blood despite the incessant rain, and Sam realised why – the back of Oriyanna's head was mush, resembling a hardboiled egg in a shell which had been dropped from a kitchen counter. It made him want to gag. Before Asmodeous had the chance to slam her skull down again, Sam raised the gun. A red targeting dot highlighted a spot on Asmodeous' head for a nanosecond before Sam pulled the trigger. There was no recoil, and no sound – just a small vibration through the handle which lasted half a second at most. Sam watched Asmodeous' body convulse, green lightning dancing over his wet clothing, face and his hands.

Before Asmodeous' body hit the ground, Sam saw Adam slam into him, and push him away. The dead body slumped onto the wet ground with a splash. Sam watched Adam collect Oriyanna's limp body in his arms, his movements frantic. He had a horrible suspicion that they'd been too late – her skin was pallid and her lips an unhealthy shade of purple. The whole scene gave Sam a horrible flashback to when they'd first found Oriyanna, battered and shot on the riverbank. As they hurried toward the Niribus, more lightning streaked the sky, stinging his eyes.

* * *

On board, Adam laid Oriyanna gently onto the floor of the bridge, wiping her wet and tangled hair from her eyes with shaky hands. Blood from the wound on her head pooled out around her.

"I'll check her in a second," Taulass said, closing the access door and rushing to get the Niribus into the air. "In under a minute, this whole place is going to explode!"

Adam registered the tugging sensation in his gut as the small interplanetary craft shot into the sky, cleared the clouds and entered Earth's orbit. Far below them, an insignificant bubble of fire lit up the darkened landscape and spread out across the desert much like a ripple in a pond. No one paid any attention, their focus on Adam who was still futilely clearing wet hair from Oriyanna's pallid face, his dripping wet fingers trembling.

Leaving the station, Taulass joined Adam and the others on the floor. He examined the wound on Oriyanna's head and placed his cheek close to her mouth. "She is still breathing," he said with a good deal of relief. "It's very shallow, though. Another blow to the head and he would have killed her. It's going to take her a few days to heal fully, but I'm confident she will make a full recovery. To be on the safe side, I am going to transport us back to Arkkadia," he said. "Our work here is done."

"I'm not leaving her," Adam announced, his voice a little lighter with relief, yet still wavering and shaky.

"Well, I'd suggest you get Oriyanna comfortable in the medical bay and get her dry. You will need to keep an eye on her for the next day or so. You can dress her wounds to help stem the blood flow, but they will begin to heal soon enough. I'll get us underway."

"Are we going home?" Lucie asked, her wide eyes on Sam.

"Yeah, I guess we are," he grinned. "In a manner of speaking, anyway. I don't think London is any place to raise a family now."

"You know!" she blurted, her eyes filling with tears. "How?"

"That's not important right now. I love you." Sam wrapped her in his arms and kissed her deeply as Taulass spun the craft around and activated the wormhole drive. In the blink of an eye, Earth was gone.

Epilogue Part 1

For three full days, Oriyanna remained unconscious. Her wounds healed gradually, but not at the normally speedy rate afforded by the Gift. Taulass wasn't surprised, nor was he worried. Adam refused to leave her side, and on the second day, after Taulass had checked her healing skull, he explained to Adam Oriyanna would likely need further treatment when they returned to Arkkadia. He suspected a large number of her tiny, nanobotic life preservers had been killed off due to the head injury. '*Thankfully she has maintained a large enough number to keep her alive,*' he'd said. '*It was a closer call than I first imagined.*'

On the third day she finally came around, and the only indication that anything had happened to her was a total loss of memory from the point when she'd escaped the room aboard Arkus 2, after slamming Asmodeous' face into the ship's computer screen.

On the fourth day, with Oriyanna out of the medical bay and fighting fit, Lucie had voiced her own concerns regarding what the anxiety and stress might have done to her unborn child. Oriyanna had rested a hand on Lucie's tummy, smiled and reassured both her and Sam that all was still well and the infant was fighting fit. She'd asked if Lucie wanted to know the sex of the child but both had refused. Oriyanna had smiled and promised to keep the news to herself. Still a tad on the sceptical side, Lucie had insisted on being checked in the ship's medical bay using some proper apparatus. Oriyanna obliged and placed a series of small wireless sensors on Lucie's abdomen, then using a holo-display she'd brought up an incredibly realistic 3D projection of the infant. '*I'd say you are about twelve weeks along*,' Oriyanna had told her, watching the image. That night, and for the first time in days, Lucie slept soundly.

Sam's shoulder had also needed attention. The wound, although clean, seemed reluctant to heal and kept scabbing over, then bleeding again. Taulass carried out a procedure which was close to stitching, only it used a fine laser beam to knit the torn skin together. '*If you want it*,' Taulass had suggested, '*they will reinstate the Gift when we get back*.'

Sam had refused, arguing that no man should watch his wife and child grow old while he remained frozen in time. For him, the return to mortality was a welcome one. Sam had never seen the gift as an amelioration of life in the way many would. Certainly, it had its benefits, but to him it had far greater drawbacks.

* * *

Adapting to life on Arkkadia wasn't as hard as Lucie had envisaged it would be during the seven-day trip. There was much about the planet and way of life which was so similar to Earth it was almost frightening, yet on the flipside some of it was vastly different. Lucie thought it was the way Earth should be, devoid of all wars, suffering and famine. There were no political or geographical boundaries, no individual countries to speak of, just districts and territories. There were no borders and anyone was free to go anywhere they liked. The Arkkadian council, which governed the entire planet and had done so for thousands of years, saw to it that any Arkkadian had the right to live and work where they wished. The planet was theirs – a shared asset and not a thing to divide into geographical boundaries and then squabbled over. It was a Utopian ideal, the likes of which Lucie suspected could never exist on Earth.

Following their arrival, Lucie's life had reached what she'd class as celebrity status on Earth. Like Earth, Arkkadia had media and entertainment and she, along with Sam and Adam, found themselves at the centre of attention. For Adam and Sam it was the second time they'd found themselves in the limelight. The media interest lasted a full three months before it began to subside, thus permitting her to resume a more normal life.

In the last few months before giving birth, when Lucie swelled like a balloon, she and Sam lived just outside planet's capital city, Unia. Lucie spent her days working in the educational system, teaching young Arkkadian children about Earth and the people of her home planet. The children were always fascinated by her, and her teaching times often overran due to the amount of questions which followed every lesson.

It was during one of these lessons when she went into labour, three weeks early. Five hours later, Sam and Lucie's son was born. They named him Xavier, after the Watcher who'd sacrificed himself in the bowels of the Great Pyramid, thus saving both planets.

Once again there was a bevy of media attention for Lucie and Sam to endure. The first Earth-Human child to be born on the planet was big news. It was around this time when Adam and Sam began their campaign, wanting the people of Earth to know the truth, and wanting the Arkkadian council to announce themselves. They believed it would help to unite Earth and bring an end to such an era of uncertainty. With the aid of Oriyanna, who was highly placed on the council, they gained an audience with the planet's governors and presented their case. The council members voted, and to Sam and Adam's disappointment their case was denied with a one hundred percent majority against going ahead. The matter was closed, for now. Thanks to their tenacity they'd managed to get the council to agree to reviewng the matter, once every ten Earth years. It was going to be a long road but as Adam had joked, *'I've got a bloody long time to live, and we'll get there in the end.'*

Epilogue Part 2

The council chambers in Unia were vast, and set on the banks of the Unas; the main river whose deep blue waters snaked the length of the Thurerlusa district, before finally meeting with the ocean. The main chamber room was an amphitheatre affair, a cavernous half circle of twenty tiers. Each tier had fifty seats, and in those seats sat the governors for each of the one thousand districts and territories which made up Arkkadia. In the very centre of this amphitheatre, halfway up the twenty tiers Elohim, the head of the council and leader of all Arkkadia sat. To his left and right were the senior council members, Oriyanna being one of them. She caught Adam's eye, her hair shimmering like golden honey in the deep afternoon sun which streamed in through the cathedral-like windows. Holding her gaze for a few long seconds, he was pleased when she offered him a reassuring smile from across the room.

Adam took a deep breath and took a moment to study the one thousand expectant faces who all watched him with deep scrutiny. He turned to Sam, who as always, joined him in the speakers' box, just as he had done on eight other occasions over the past eighty years. Sam's sandy blonde hair was a mixture of deep and light greys now; his eyes though, still glinted with a boyish charm and seemed to belong to a man a quarter of his age.

"Today's the day," Sam announced, his voice frail and thin. "I can feel it."

S T Boston

"You said that last time, and the time before that," Adam replied, not looking a day older than he had when the Gift had been bestowed on him. He looked at his friend for the briefest of moments and hoped that today was indeed going to be the day. In Earth years, Sam was one hundred and fourteen. The Gift, it seemed, during the two years he'd felt its effects, had left his body in peak condition. In conjunction with the unrivalled healthcare on Arkkadia it ensured Sam's longevity, but with nature left to run her course, even the fittest and healthiest bodies wither and eventually die. Adam knew that for Sam, this was his last chance. Sadly, there would be no prospect of him being by Adam's side in another ten years.

It had been five years since Lucie had passed on, and after such a long life together Adam had fully expected Sam to follow not long after, but he hadn't. It had been a tough time for everyone. Adam had begun to grasp just what the Gift meant, because Sam and Lucie's family were his family. He was a great, great uncle now, and Xavier, who had been born not long after their arrival on Arkkadia was an old man and in his autumn years. Adam was destined to remain frozen in time and watch generation after generation of his family come and go, like the passing of the seasons. Had it not been for Oriyanna and the love he held for her, which grew stronger year by year, he'd have gladly returned to mortality in an instant. They still had no children of their own; there was no real rush for them, and they had all the time in the world, so to speak. Adam wasn't sure he could cope with watching his own children grow old and die – it had been bad enough seeing it happen to Lucie and Sam's.

"We are here today to hear the case brought before us by Adam Fisher and Samuel Becker," began Elohim, his voice booming through the chamber. He stood in his booth, his deep brown hair flowing down from his shoulders in waves, highlighted by the royal blue cape he wore over his white trousers and long-sleeved top. Both garments were decorated with a pattern of golden glyphs running down the arms and around the neckline, much like the one they'd found Oriyanna wearing all those years ago. Like Oriyanna, he was thousands of years old, but looked to be a man in his mid-fifties. His face sported a full beard, but his hazel eyes sparkled with knowledge and were soft and kind. He addressed the council in Arkkadian, but the small earpieces which Sam and Adam wore translated the language instantly into English. Both had learned the native tongue over the years, but for matters such as this, still preferred the language of their home world. "This is the eighth such meeting of this council, as Adam Fisher and Samuel Becker make application for legislation to be passed which would see the Earth-Humans learn the truth behind their existence. We all know this has been the hope of the council for many thousands of years, but we need to consider how this will affect the planet as a whole. The main point being – are they ready? All previous applications have been rejected, and as always, once you have listened to the evidence presented by the applicants, the council will need a majority vote of eighty percent for the legislation to pass. I will now hand the audience over to the applicants." He glanced over at Adam and added, "Good luck."

"I'll let you do the talking," Sam whispered, his thin lips turning up a smile. "You always were better at this stuff. I'll just stand here and look pretty."

"Members of the council," Adam began, smothering a grin at Sam's comment. "We appear before you today to make the aforementioned application," as he spoke his voice emanated through the room in Arkkadian. "In truth, I do not have anything further to present than I did last time I addressed you, so I respectfully won't take up too much of your valuable time. You all know why you're here, and I have no doubt that you knew how you wanted to vote before you even set foot in the room, because this hearing is just the end of another ten years' worth of work toward our cause. I would, however, ask you to consider the following. Compared to the Arkkadian race we are still young, and with that, comes foolishness. Over the years, you've watched over us, seen us make no end of mistakes, and on more than one occasion fight wars which have killed millions. In that are we not so dissimilar from yourselves. While you've had no domestic conflicts on this planet in thousands and thousands of years, you understand the necessity of war. It is my hope that now, after the Sheolian conflict more than eighty Earth years ago, war will now truly be a part of your history. Sadly, without aid and guidance, it will take Earth many, many more years to reach this same point and millions will die as a result. Nonetheless, all those wars and conflicts we've fought have helped to shape humanity into what it is today – just as it has with you.

I have kept appraised of my home world over the past eighty years and while I personally haven't returned, I believe I'm in a position to say that we're not the same people we were in the days leading up to the Nazca incident. The planet is still free of nuclear weapons, it has been this way for the past seventy-five years after the non-launch ready stockpiles were mothballed. Work on the Hundred Year Starship program is nearing breakthrough, and your scientists estimate in a further thirty years, Earth-Humans will have a prototype ship using the same technologies you developed. I know for a fact that this planet is known to Earth, but only as a speck of light seen from the Kepler Space Telescope many years ago, when I was a young man. We are where you were, many thousands of years ago, looking to the stars and wondering if we're truly alone. I can guarantee you that when they do launch that prototype, this will be one of the very first places they send a probe, just like your ancestors did with Earth. Arkkadia is the embodiment of everything I believe the people of Earth can be, and with your direct help and guidance I believe they can reach this same destiny. Oriyanna once told me that you view the people of Earth as a parent would view a child; if this is the case don't you believe that it's every child's right to know its parent?"

"What are your views now, on how this will affect the planet's religious dependence?" Elohim asked.

"It had widely been accepted that when the human race discovers it is not alone in this vast universe, it will have massive implications for religion. I am, perhaps, not the best person to advise you on this matter as I've never held any of the religions on Earth as a belief. I do know, though, that religion is a two-pronged sword. It has an overwhelming power for good, but it has also been responsible for some of the worst atrocities the human race has seen. There is no question it will be the biggest event in human history, there is no doubt that it will shake the planet to its core. However, in our very being we are adaptable to change and it's my belief that in the end, this change will be for the better. Although I have lived on this planet for the majority of my life, at heart I'm still a child of Earth. As such, I believe that myself and Samuel are best placed to know how this revelation will affect our home world. Elohim, members of the council, it is my belief that we've been ready for many years, and the time is right. Never more so than now. Pass this legislation and help us be all that we can be."

"Do you have any further evidence to bring to the council's attention?" Elohim asked.

"No, sir, that's all."

"Very well." Elohim stood and addressed the room. "You have heard the statement as read by Adam Fisher, it is now your responsibility to vote and pass judgement."

One thing Adam did like was the speed and finesse with which the Arkkadian political system worked, there would be no lengthy discussions and adjournments, and the matter would be decided then and there. If unsuccessful there were no appeals; it would be another ten years before a further opportunity would come to pass.

With more than a little unease, Adam waited in the speakers' box with Sam as the vote was decided. After what seemed like an age, Elohim stood and addressed the room.

"As you may recall, last time the council met on this matter the legislation was denied by a vote of sixty percent no to forty percent yes." He paused and looked directly at Adam, his eyes sparkling. "There is no question that you have both slaved over this campaign relentlessly over many years and today's hearing is merely a brief part of the work you've done to convince the council. Adam, Sam, it would seem your hard work has finally paid off." He shifted his focus to address the room. "It is the finding of this council, by a majority of ninety percent to ten, that new legislation will be passed which will allow Earth-Humans to learn the truth about their origins."

"You did it!" Sam said, slapping Adam on the back.

"No, we – *we* did it," he corrected, still struggling to believe the result.

"Well done, both of you," Elohim said. "You have changed the course of our futures with this decision. I just hope it is the right one."

"I can assure you it is, sir," Adam beamed.

"Which now brings us to the matter of when and how this will be accomplished. As leader of this council, I decree that in one Earth year from this day, a mission will be launched to Earth conveying the news. In the ensuing period, we will discuss just how this information should be passed on. You will both be heavily involved in this preparation."

"We wouldn't have it any other way, sir," said Adam. "I would also like us both to be on that craft when it travels to Earth."

"Of course," Elohim replied.

Adam looked at his friend, and hoped Sam would be well enough in a year to make the trip. He wasn't certain his dearest friend would make it.

Epilogue Part 3

Xavier Becker emerged from the transportation hub and immediately cold, unforgiving rain hit his grey hair, plastering it to his face. The icy cold droplets ran down his brow and chased each other along the wrinkles in his skin, which had become increasingly prevalent over the past few years. He barely noticed the tiny electrical charges which ran over his skin, and why would he? The hub was the only way to travel on Arkkadia, a seemingly infinite number of tiny gateways which crisscrossed the planet allowing the user to travel instantaneously to any point on the globe. It was fast, but more importantly, it was completely carbon neutral and powered by the planet itself. It was a smaller and less power-hungry version of the Tabut, which his father and uncle had used to travel to Arkkadia many years earlier. His parents, as well as his uncle had told him stories as a boy, stories of Earth and the millions of cars and other fuel-hungry devices which were used by Earth-Humans to travel across their planet. Although technically a child of Earth, he'd never seen such things, and to him they seemed as odd and alien as this marvellous system would to any Earth-Human.

Without thinking he pulled the off-white collar of his coat up, hunching it further over his shoulders in a futile effort to stop the intruding rain from running down his neck and reaching his back. Without pausing, he made his way along the path toward Adam and Oriyanna's residence.

The structure, like many on Arkkadia appeared seamless, as if moulded in its entirety at the point of manufacture. The large windows were shiny and black, as if onyx had been fed into the mixture at the time of production. It meant one thing – neither Adam nor Oriyanna were awake yet, and why would they be? It was earlier in the day here than in Unia. Arkus, the planet's sun was still low in the sky, hidden behind the brooding grey skies. Behind the three-story property the land rolled down to a beach, and in the distance Xavier could see the closest of the Halethian Islands, the rest obscured by mist. A dreary and depressing dawn was on its way to creating a new day. For the briefest of moments, Xavier thought how fitting it was that a day, such as this day, was a reflection of his own sombre mood.

His shoes splashed across the water-logged path and he arrived at the door; like the windows it was as black as night. There was no time to worry about the earliness of the hour, and clearing his throat Xavier thumped hard on the door, his wet hand balled tightly into a fist. Time seemed to pass in slow motion as he waited, one foot tapping impatiently on the path, splashing up small droplets of water that beaded on his shoes. When he raised his hand to knock for a second time, the blackened glass in every window became clear, and on the other side of the door, completely dry and wrapped in a robe was his uncle. Adam's youthful face was still half asleep, his eyes squinting in the dim light to see who was calling at such an early hour. Seeing his nephew, his face paled, worry creasing his brow.

"Is it?" began Adam, pulling the robe tighter around his body as he opened the door and rain fell on his face.

"Yes," Xavier replied solemnly, "he's been asking for you; for both of you." Xavier stepped into the house and shook a little of the rain from his coat; the droplets pooling on the black tiled floor.

Adam turned and made his way toward the bedroom. "How much longer does he have?" he asked, , his voice already starting to waver.

"An hour, two at most. The nurse said it could be less; they just don't know. He's going downhill swiftly." Xavier raised his voice as Adam disappeared from view. "They've tried to treat him, but he's having none of it. He says it's time." A minute later his uncle reappeared dressed in pale slacks, pulling a thin blue jumper over his matted brown hair. He ran his hands over the material, immediately freeing it from any creases.

"Obviously, he's still being as stubborn as a mule."

"Always," Xavier replied, managing a half-cocked smile.

"Some things never change."

"Is the hub still open for the return trip?" came Oriyanna's voice as she paced through into the lobby, pawing at her long, sleep-tangled blonde hair in an inane effort to tidy it. She was dressed, but her black leggings and red tee-shirt looked as if they'd been thrown on in a hurry.

"Yes, we can go straight to the hospital, but we must leave now!" Xavier turned, pushed the door open and stepped back out into the cold, wet weather. Not bothering to grab a jacket, both Adam and Oriyanna followed suit, and the three huddled figures hurried down the path, reached the transportation hub and vanished.

* * *

Adam found Sam laid up in a partially-reclined bed. A single small, white square hung four feet above his frail body, monitoring everything from his pulse to his bowel movements. A small screen to the left of the bed displayed the readings in Arkkadian.

"This is... the... same hospital... they had... us in— right back when... we... first came through— the Tabut," Sam croaked, when Adam and Oriyanna reached his side.

"I know," Adam replied, taking hold of his friend's hand. It felt bony and cold, reminding Adam of a bird's claw. "Is there nothing they can do?"

Sam smiled, his lips no more than thin lines against his mottled flesh. "Probably, yes," he croaked. "This... isn't the NHS, you... know."

"Then let them help you," Adam pleaded. "We're so close now to going home, and I need you there."

"No," Sam said, his face creased with pain and his cold grip tightened on Adam's hand. "I'm tired. This... is... your thing, Adam. We both... knew I wouldn't make that trip, not alive... anyway. I... got to... see us succeed... that's enough." He broke into a harsh coughing fit, and when he got it under control he grinned. "Hey – those NASA guys – are... going to be... pissed when they... find out they're not... the... first to get a human... to an alien... planet. One... small step... and all that shit." Sam broke into another fit of hacking coughs which shook his frail body, and when it finally subsided he managed a half-cocked smile.

Adam smiled, too, but it was forced. "Joker 'til the end," he said, fighting back tears which seemed destined to fall no matter how hard he tried to quell them.

"I... fully intend... on being... on... that mission. Me and Lucie," he said, each word seeming harder for him to say than the last. "Take... us home, you know... where."

"Oxlease Meadows, where you proposed?" The tears were falling in earnest now, and when Adam looked across at Oriyanna he saw her blue eyes were swimming with them, too. Xavier was sitting on a chair at the opposite side of the bed, clutching his father's hand.

Sam nodded, his head moving slowly against the pillow. "That's the... place. Unless they've... built... a... council estate... on it since we... left." Sam tried to grin, but the side of his face drooped slightly. "We... made a... difference, didn't we?"

"Yeah," said Adam, his voice breaking. "I think we did. It was a hell of a ride, though, huh?"

Sam didn't offer a reply, merely managed to nod his head as if satisfied before falling asleep. Deep, rattling sounds echoed from his frail body.

"He is very close," Oriyanna said in a sad voice.

That was the last time Adam spoke to him, and he never regained consciousness. Much to everyone's amazement, Sam held on in that comatose sleep for the rest of the morning and most of the afternoon. None of them left his side. Occasionally, he would mutter something inaudible as if conversing with someone. Occasionally, he called Lucie's name with amazing clarity, sometimes Adam's, too, as old memories washed through his mind. Adam and Xavier held his hands the whole time, occasionally brushing a loose strand of grey hair away from his clammy forehead.

By early afternoon, the morning's rain had cleared and a breeze chased the clouds away, leaving behind a beautifully bright day. Sam died peacefully as the sun began to set behind the distant mountains, casting his hospital room in a golden, almost serene light.

Epilogue Part 4

The July morning was warm and pleasant as Adam and Oriyanna walked across the dew-covered grass toward a pair of tall oak trees, which stood alone on the fringe of the small forest at Oxlease Meadows, just on the outskirts of a very different looking London to the one Adam had left behind on a very wet and miserable September afternoon, a little over eighty-one years ago.

"It hasn't changed much," Adam announced, referring to the park. He watched a dog walker throwing a stick for an overweight chocolate Labrador, who chased it down eagerly, although quite slowly. In the distance, a whole new host of skyscrapers littered the London skyline, reaching into a clear blue sky, and all far taller than any he could remember. It reminded him more of New York, than the capital of England.

"This is the place then?" Oriyanna asked, when they stopped by one of the dark brown tree trunks.

"Yes, I'm certain. We used to climb these oaks as kids, then try to knock each other out of the branches by throwing acorns at one another." Adam smiled at the memory. "So long ago." He gazed at the distant London skyline for the briefest of moments before returning his attention to Oriyanna. "Let's put them to rest," he said wistfully.

Adam unscrewed the tops of the two small metallic urns he'd been carrying and passed one to Oriyanna, and together they scattered the ashes onto the grass at the base of the tree.

"Home," he said, hot tears welling up in his eyes. "It was a long journey, wasn't it?" Lucie and Sam's ashes mixed together on the light breeze and scattered, becoming one with the ground.

"Do you think they are with us now, watching?" Adam asked, looking at her questioningly.

"I don't know," she replied. "It's possible – yes. No matter how advanced you become, or how much science you study, the universe still holds on to its share of secrets." Oriyanna smiled and took hold of his hand, interlocking her fingers with his.

Adam nodded thoughtfully. "I guess so," he finally conceded.

"Today is the day then," Oriyanna said, purposely changing the subject. "One mass, simultaneous broadcast across every media platform on Earth."

"It's the safest way," Adam smiled. "Did you never see that movie where the aliens just hovered over the White House in a massive, city-sized spaceship?"

"No," Oriyanna said, sounding uncertain of the direction he was taking.

"Well, it didn't really work out well for anyone," Adam grinned. "This is by far the safest option. And it will also ensure no government can cover it up. The people have a right to know; this is for everyone."

"Do you ever wonder what happened to that book of yours?" she asked, as they strolled hand-in-hand across the park, looking no different to any other couple enjoying the clement Sunday morning air.

"Not really," Adam said dismissively. "I somehow doubt I've become a bestselling writer that in my absence."

"Well, you never know," she grinned. "This is going to be quite a lengthy mission, and we're going to be on Earth for quite some time. Maybe you should work on a sequel."

From the Author

Well, here we are again. This is certainly nowhere I envisaged either one of us being when I first began to write Book One! But nonetheless, here we are, at the end of Book Two!

I'd like to personally thank you for reading the Watchers books and I sincerely hope you enjoyed the ride. Unfortunately, this is where the story ends. I hope you like what happened to the characters at the end. It took me a little time to figure out just where their lives would go after the main story and I didn't really want to leave it to your imagination. What I do however leave to your imagination, is exactly how the human race will take the news that Adam and Oriyanna are about to deliver.

S.T Boston

The Silent Neighbours
ISBN: 978-4-86752-881-5

Published by
Next Chapter
1-60-20 Minami-Otsuka
170-0005 Toshima-Ku, Tokyo
+818035793528
11th August 2021